D1270552

# The Lost Journals

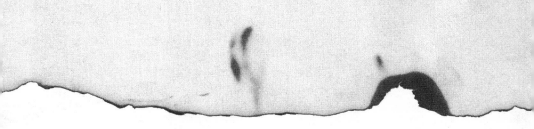

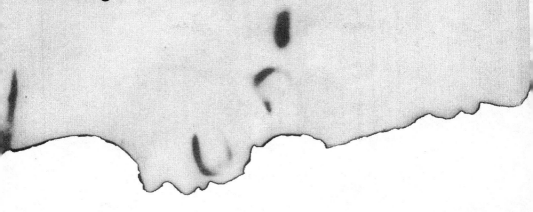

# of Sylvia Plath   A Novel

Kimberly Knutsen

SWITCHGRASS BOOKS   NIU PRESS   DEKALB

Published by Switchgrass Books,
an imprint of Northern Illinois University Press

Northern Illinois University Press, DeKalb 60115
© 2015 by Northern Illinois University Press
Printed in the United States of America
24 23 22 21 20 19 18 17 16 15    1 2 3 4 5

978-0-87580-725-6 (paper)
978-1-60909-184-2 (ebook)

Book and cover design by Shaun Allshouse

Library of Congress Cataloging-in-Publication Data
Knutsen, Kimberly.
The lost journals of Sylvia Plath / Kimberly Knutsen.
     pages       cm
ISBN 978-0-87580-725-6 (paperback)—ISBN 978-1-60909-184-2 (ebook)
1. College teachers—Fiction. 2. Domestic fiction. I. Title.
PS3611.N85L67 2015
813'.6—dc23
2015030904

# Contents

For Curt,

    Lily Rose,

        Elijah,

            and Henry

# Acknowledgments

Grateful thanks to everyone at Switchgrass Books for all their hard work and dedication, and for taking a chance on my book!

To everyone at Mindbuck Media for all their help and support.

To my amazing kids: Lily Rose, Elijah, Henry and Dasha.

To my literary muses: Beverly Cleary, your books saved my life! And Jackie Collins, wow, you have no idea how exciting your books were when I found them on my mom's shelf—you made me want to write!

To my wonderful teachers over the years, especially Mrs. Meyers at Cleveland High School, Cynthia McCoy at UNLV, Antonya Nelson and Robert Boswell at NMSU, Judith Grossman at Iowa, and Jaimy Gordon and Stuart Dybek at Western.

To my family for all their love and support: Mom and Dad, Krissy and Bryan, Clint and Lucy, Paula and Dustin, David, Lindsay and Jordan. And Arllis and Warren, Shelley and Nicole.

To Phillip Torres, amazing artist and friend.

To my friends along the way: the one and only Sally Keenan, storyteller extraordinaire! And Abby Hepburn and Carrie Potter in New Mexico, Lisa Anthony in Iowa City, Troy and Krista Daily in Michigan, and Chuck Kunert, the best friend and reader a person could ask for.

And to Curtis Dawkins, genius, soulmate, best friend.

"Love is like a child,
That longs for every thing that he can come by."
—Shakespeare, *Two Gentlemen of Verona*

# Prologue

## Katie

I wish I was small again, I wish I was a kid again, I wish I was me again, the me I was before everything happened.

When I was four, I wanted a canopy bed, pink and ruffled—a bed fit for a princess. One night after dinner, Mom and Dad and I left our apartment behind Grant's department store and walked up the street to the neighbors' house. It was a hot summer night, dark already, and it was just me, the way I liked it, my baby sister curled in my mother's womb, not quite ready to be born.

At the neighbors' house we watched *Cinderella*—the TV show, not the Disney movie—on their new color television set. I'd never seen color TV, and I sat spellbound in that strange rumpus room with the wall-to-wall carpeting. When Cinderella went to the ball, everything came alive, burst into color. I wanted to go there, to her world, immediately, where life was brighter than the stars, more colorful than tulips. I knew it was where my princess bed and I belonged.

There were two worlds when I was a kid. The Cinderella world, with its fancy light, is the one I miss. It lasted until I was eight. Then it disappeared.

In the Cinderella world, I was small, and everything was fun and candy, and I wasn't a body yet, I was everything, the whole world, humming along on my green Stingray like the cloud of bees at the camellia bushes, the lilacs wiggling in the wind, the raindrops dancing on the sidewalks.

Everything was alive—the hill of stinging red ants at the edge of the driveway; the old oak at the curb with its trunk full of knotty, groaning faces and its mossy green lap you could rest in; the creek at the duck park, a sunlit universe of minnows and crawdads and billowing clouds of sludge.

Everything was simple. 1 2 3. A B C. It's what I love about being a mom now. Things become simple again, distilled to their purest state. Before kids, life was too complicated. Now I can wake up in the morning and know I don't even have to leave the house. What a relief. All I have to do is fix meals—easy things like peanut butter and jelly—wash clothes, read the smallest, sweetest books. Sometimes I'm so touched by Clifford and Franklin and Blue I could cry. They offer kindness and understanding and the tiniest seed of knowledge, like the fact that sharing is good, and your mom and dad care, and it is safe to snuggle into bed at night and sleep because the moon that is your friend will watch over you.

Maybe I need to get a life.

But that world was real—it is real—and I miss it.

There was a second world. It was the texture of pumice. It was the taste of metal in the mouth. It was the stopped heart, the brain that could never catch its breath. This world eclipsed the Cinderella world, and it visits me still in the night, sliding along the edges of the room, slipping into my mouth to sit in my throat, acrid and black, its tendrils snaking down to hook, but good, my heart.

## Katie
1973

It was the last night of my life.

It started out innocently enough, but by the end, I had been *marked*.

I didn't know it right away, but I would. Like a diseased elm, I would soon be felled, my roots jerked from the earth, then fed bit by bit into the chipper.

Only I wasn't a diseased tree. I was a little girl.

The sky in Portland was the color of rose petals. It was 1973, and I was eight, and it was the first summer I had to wear a shirt. I could no longer go topless like the boys in the neighborhood, and I hated it. It was confusing. What was so shameful about a girl that she had to be covered when the boys on the block could do as they pleased, whipping off their tank tops in the heat of day, running free at night, the summer breeze cooling their sweaty skin?

It was my first hint that there was something wrong with being a girl, that we were dangerous, somehow, although I had no idea *how*. I didn't think about it much, just wore the same baggy cutoffs and faded swimming suit top every day, as close to naked as I could get. My ponytail was long and tangled and orange, and my feet were filthy. We were always grubby kids. Back then moms didn't care about baths or clean clothes—at least ours didn't. By summer's end, the soles of my feet were so tough I could have walked across hot coals without feeling a thing.

That night, my mom and baby sister and I walked to the Renaissance Fair at Reed College, blocks from our home. The fair was like a living thing, a filthy dragon, puffing smoke, trailing dirty streamers, and we sat on a blanket in the center of the hubbub—in the belly of the beast. It was exciting at first, the strange atmosphere of drums and trilling lutes, but after a while, it was hard to breathe.

January and I ate dinner—pita tacos and orange pop—as our mom, Iris, arranged the macramé necklaces she'd brought to sell. She'd worked hard on them, staying up late at night with Johnny Carson on the TV and a bowl of popcorn on the dining room table. All the little fire-clay faces, the suns and the moons, the goddesses and bears and stars, tinkled around her like charms.

"Don't play, eat," she warned my sister. Three-year-old January looked up, surprised. She was like winter, even in August, pale and insect-like with bright green eyes and a wick of white hair, like a Kewpie doll. She caught colds all the time, and was so skinny she couldn't take swimming lessons, even in summer. Now she ignored our mom, pouring more of her pop into the dirt and slapping it with the palms of her hands.

"Eat," Iris urged.

January stuck a muddy finger in her mouth, then popped it out, laughing at her own cleverness.

"No. Icky, dirty," Iris scolded, but with a smile. My mom was pretty, with her brown skin, her chipped front tooth and crooked smile, her smell of spices and sweat, her black hair that was warm to the touch. She reached up now to wind it into a bun. Her arms were thin, and I liked that I could see the dark stubble in her armpits—it was comforting.

Our mom had "found herself" that winter, flying back and forth to San Francisco to primal scream. I wasn't sure what that was, only that you screamed and felt better. One afternoon, back in Portland, she was reborn in a tub of warm water. "I was a breech baby," she said excitedly, newly born, her hair still damp from the tub. She threw her car keys on the table. "I specifically remember my foot getting stuck. And I was furious because I knew I didn't want to come here in the first place."

"Why didn't you want to come here?" I asked, hurt.

She laughed. "Why would I? Why would anyone?"

*Why would I? Why would anyone?*

That scared me. Where else would you be but in the world where you belonged?

Not long after that night, I would discover what it was like to disappear, to no longer *be* in the world, no matter how hard I tried to get back.

1973 was the summer we listened to Carole King, over and over, with the hippie babysitter across the street. "I Feel the Earth Move" was my favorite. January and I loved to sing and dance along. *I feel the earth move under my feet.* We got *down.* The babysitter had a beaded curtain on her closet, and we'd play with it, running the orange beads through our fingers while she lay on her bed and talked on the phone to her girlfriend in a fierce, excited voice.

1973 was the year our mom blossomed. Her cat glasses with the rhinestones were gone, replaced by green contact lenses. And her flip hairdo was gone—she'd grown her hair long and silky, just like Cher's. Sometimes, if she was feeling funky, she wore a flowing orange caftan, like a *nightgown* during the day.

Iris left our dad sitting alone in the kitchen with a bowl of cereal and his golf magazine nearly every night. She was directing the youth choir at the church, and they were doing a big show, something about love and Jesus. Our dad didn't seem to mind that she was gone all the time. He wasn't big into love or Jesus, only golf and the new Jacuzzi at the club.

What I mean to say is, there was so much life, so much possibility—but somehow I got left behind.

"Looking good, Sis," a young man, shirtless and pale, called out to our mom as he rattled past on an old bike, a plastic daisy stuck to its straw basket.

I made a face. The guy with the rainbow afro had been a student at Reed for as long as anyone could remember, sailing through the neighborhood on his bike, Jesus sandals flapping, skinny neck looking barely able to support his wild, wobbling head of hair. "That is one happy cat," our babysitter said whenever he happened to float by.

He was a weirdo, and 1973 was the summer our mother befriended weirdos.

Like Larry Johnson, the man who would destroy me.

Even now, writing this, I see only a shadow, faceless. He was our dad's golf buddy from the club, and as night spilled its blue ink across the sky, he appeared at our table.

The shadow appeared.

I force myself to look.

Back then, in the beginning, he was just a man from the neighborhood, and he was nice. He wore a brown leather jacket, and his black hair was swooped up like Elvis's. Maybe it was an odd look for a summer night, but to me it was neat. He had a baby face with big brown eyes, like the cute doctor on *Medical Center*, the one I loved.

"How are you, Iris?" he asked, soft-spoken and polite.

"I'm good." She set down her plastic cup of beer. "How are you? Played any golf lately?"

Larry smiled, bashful. "You know I'm no good. It's almost embarrassing how bad I am."

"You exaggerate, I'm sure."

He didn't. He *was* bad. We just didn't know yet.

Larry held up one of the necklaces, a sad-faced star, and nodded enthusiastically. "These are beautiful. Really classy. What do you call this?" He touched the tiny knots in the cord.

"Macramé. And I made the faces—"

"You could—oops, sorry, I cut you off—"

"Oh no." Mom blushed. "I was just saying that I made the faces out of clay—with a manicure stick."

"You could sell these in stores."

Mom told Larry that she *had* sold them in stores—well, in Perkins, the restaurant near the club.

"What?" He looked surprised. Extra surprised. "At the pancake place? What?"

Mom nodded, pleased.

"Amazing. Top rate. Dan must be impressed."

I laughed. My dad hardly cared about necklaces.

In my mind, Larry Johnson equaled candy. Earlier that summer, he'd brought us all-day suckers after playing golf with our dad—swirls of yellow and green as big as our heads. January had screamed until our mom let her sleep with hers, then woke up the next morning with it stuck in her hair.

Right off, I'd wanted Larry Johnson to like me. Candy dispensed, he'd sat at the dining room table with our dad, and that was when I noticed he looked like the doctor on *Medical Center*, so kind and fatherly. I'd heard my mom tell the hippie babysitter that he wasn't married and that he'd come from her hometown in eastern Oregon—a dirt hole in the high desert where she and her friends threw watermelons off the backs of trucks in the summers and ate only the hearts, where her family's first house later became part of a pig farm.

"He was in the service, he has short hair, and he likes country-western?" the babysitter said coolly, suede hot pants setting off her suntanned legs.

'I'm not positive about the army thing, but yes, he's very sweet," Mom said.

"Riiiight."

Now Mom and Larry chatted. No candy was produced, so I tuned out. It was almost time for fireworks, nearly dark, the sky prickly with stars. That summer I'd begun to notice that there were no colors at night. They disappeared, and if you really looked, you'd see that your bare legs were gray, your shorts black, and your sister's wick of hair, so bright and sparkling in the sunlight, was no color at all.

I didn't know it yet, but the light of the Cinderella world had gone.

I was sweating but cool too, my body like the night, velvety and black, alive with hot stars. I stared up at the sky, waiting for it to explode.

Mosquitoes, invisible in the dark, bit me, and I scratched my itchy ankles. The roar of the fair grew louder. I smelled burning flowers. Sparks showered from a bonfire, and the thunder of drums made my heart beat fast.

"Are you staying?" Mom asked Larry. "You're welcome to join us—there's plenty of room on the blanket."

I looked up. He seemed to relax at her invitation. His shoulders dropped almost imperceptibly, and from my position on the ground, he looked taller—taller and wider and blacker, like the silhouette of an enormous tree. As I stared, the moon shrunk to the size of a baby aspirin. The overeager golf buddy disappeared, and someone new—someone slick and stealthy—stepped inside his body.

He looked at me then, a strange, searching look, and I closed my eyes tightly, too shy to meet his gaze.

# Part One

## In the Vagina

"When I am pinned and wriggling on the wall . . ."
—T. S. Eliot, "The Love Song of J. Alfred Prufrock"

# One

**Wilson**
2002

In a crappy condo in Kalamazoo, Wilson and his family slept. Wilson's wife, Katie, had chosen the place—she'd lived there with her son before they met—and at first, he found it charming. It was nice the way the pitched rooftops rose black against the evening sky, the way the boxy brick buildings glowed orange in the afternoon sun. But lately, with the winter days bleak and gray, what the neat rows of fourplexes resembled most was a military base. It was called the Reserve, and each street was named for a bottle of wine. Wilson and his family lived on Merlot Court. This, though, he only presumed, as the street sign had been missing since he met Katie. They had a horrible time ordering in pizza.

"Maybe we live on Mogen David Street, or Night Train Lane," he said once, trying to be funny. And wasn't it funny? Only a couple of years earlier, before meeting Katie and promptly making two babies with her, he was a drunk. Now he lived, sober, in a wine cellar. Katie didn't like to talk about the drinking. She preferred to think of it as a momentary lapse rather than what he feared it was—his calling in life. Katie liked to talk about the condo. She hated the carpeting, wanted glass doors on the fireplace and new medicine cabinets in both bathrooms. "It's a rental for Christ's sake," he said, but she was adamant that they fix it up.

"It's important," she said. "Where you live means something, it's an echo of who you are on the inside."

"Then I'm a freaking eight-year-old girl." He sighed, closing his eyes to the ballerina-pink walls surrounding him. After the wedding in Las Vegas the previous summer (the three kids in tow), and before she let him move in, Katie made him paint. He sometimes wondered if she would've agreed to any of it—the marriage, the living together—if he hadn't. She was stubborn and self-sufficient. What did she need with a clown like him?

Maybe it was the ring. Would she have become his wife without the antique blue-diamond and platinum ring? Every time he saw it, blazing like a blue bumblebee on her pretty hand, he felt sick.

"You're supposed to spend six months' salary," she'd reminded him. "Don't forget, it's *forever*." Since his six-month "salary" as a graduate assistant at Midwestern came to a little under five hundred bucks, he'd bought the ring on credit. When his office mate, the imposing Dr. Gloria Gold, laughed meanly and told him that you traditionally spent only *two* months' salary, Wilson had felt duped. How would he ever pay it off? He couldn't even think of their collective student-loan debt of nearly ninety grand. And it wasn't like they were neurosurgeons. They were English majors, professional students with seven degrees between them—eight if you counted Katie's cosmetology "degree," which he didn't—who found it easier to start yet another program than to find a job.

Painting the marital home—permission secured from management—was a rite of passage, a way for him to make his presence known in the family, and a way for Katie to let go of her fierce single motherhood. When he'd finally finished, after her silent and thorough inspection—"Is that a smear on the ceiling? Is it supposed to be bumpy here?"—she'd announced that she loved it. "Soft and pink on the inside, spiny brick on the outside, and here we are, safe as baby pearls," she'd cried, hugging him hard.

"A baby pearl," he said, annoyed. "Just what I've always wanted to be." After weeks of backbreaking work, he realized he'd created a vagina, a great pink yawning vagina, in which to crouch humbly for the rest of his life. What had he done? Wasn't it enough to be the happy visiting dad, the "household imp of fun," as Katie called it, and leave the tough stuff to her? But even as he thought longingly of his former homes, a quiet lake-view apartment, and then a rented basement in Vicksburg with red velvet walls, a six-foot-tall stuffed bunny that often startled him, and a parade of shifty roommates, he knew it wasn't enough. The family he'd created—four-year-old Paul, baby Rose, and Katie's eight-year-old, Jake—deserved his full surrender.

Katie, not liking his sarcasm, had ignored him the rest of the night. And that was it: He was in. He was a family man, deputy to Katie's sheriff, father of three, and co-owner of the beloved and elderly dog, Lovely. Who could forget Lovely? He was never to forget Lovely when doling out treats or love. If he did, Katie wouldn't sleep with him for a week. Withholding sex was one of the few ways in which she was a typical female. In other ways, she was odd.

"In a fabulous way," she'd add. She talked to herself, wore colors that didn't match, and was far too sensitive about her living conditions. Everything had to be warm and cozy and sweet like a fucking Barbie doll dream house. As a kid she'd wanted to live in a bottle like the genie on *I Dream of Jeannie*, and as he saw it, her wish had come true. Their home was alive with oversized pillows and throws and rugs, all in wild dizzying colors—lemon yellow and fuchsia and her favorite battery-acid green—colors that made his heart beat fast and spots swim before his eyes.

In the bedroom, batik fabric rippled on the walls and swooped from the ceiling, and there were too many goddamn blankets on the bed. Their mattress on the floor wasn't a "nest" as Katie claimed. With the kids and the dog and the unbelievably heavy Korean blankets—remnants of Jake's hippie dad, no less—it was a kind of hell.

There, he'd said it. *Hell.* They warned you not to date in the first year of sobriety. He now understood that there was a reason for this, and that once again, he was *not* the exception to the rule. As terrifying as his life seemed, however, he slept peacefully. Flat on his back in his boxers, his hands folded on his stomach, he was sternly handsome, his body a perfect sculpture, inviting touch. Yet he liked to think of himself as untouchable, existing somehow apart from the ignorant culture that surrounded him in Kalamazoo, the Midwest, maybe the entire Western world. He never watched TV except for sports or *Cops*. He grumbled when Katie bought the kids Happy Meals, and he made fun of her when she read *People* magazine.

At thirty-three, he had a hard time believing in life. Even as a kid, he was the bad party guest, the jerk that refused to wear the pointed paper hat and sulked in the corner while the other kids, the *normal* ones, enjoyed a rousing game of pin-the-tail-on-the-donkey. He'd thought about counseling, but it went against his belief that all answers to life could be found in literature. Katie was a habitual counselee. She'd gone, off and on, for nearly half her life. She liked to chat and communicate and reveal every secret part of herself whereas he was the opposite. Half the time he didn't know who he was or what he was feeling. This made Katie furious.

When they first dated—those two magical weeks before he got her pregnant—she used to watch him sleep, sometimes nudging him awake to comment on his full pretty lips, his blond curls, his utter peacefulness. One night after they married, however, things changed. "I have no idea who you are," she said, poking him hard in the ribs and making him yelp. "Do you ever cry? Do you have nightmares? Do you even dream?" There was an edge to her voice, and he realized that, beneath her vague cheeriness, she felt the same as he did, that they'd made a terrible mistake and were trapped.

What had brought them to the king-sized mattress on the floor of the overpriced condo in Kalamazoo? He was a good Midwestern boy. She was a single mom from the West Coast, a free spirit, he'd thought, although he quickly discovered how wrong he was. Neither liked condoms, and one or both were incredibly fertile. They had two babies in less than two years, and that was it, their lives were set.

"You are not going to believe this," Katie said the day she discovered she was pregnant again, with Rose, their youngest. Her words had chilled him. He'd thought he was going to pass out, and could only stare as she squatted on the toilet, holding out the test stick with a nervous smile. It wasn't that he didn't love the kids. He did. It just seemed that, like in the John Lennon song, life had happened while he was busy making other plans.

"I'm perfectly human, the same as you," he'd assured her the night she jabbed him so rudely awake. He'd wrapped her in his arms and pulled the covers over her shoulders. Beyond being human, he didn't know. Sensitive genius that he was, his moods ranged from nervous to enraged and back again, with occasional uneasy stops at happiness. It was during these respites—when he touched baby Rose's funny pointed ears, or watched Paul crayon wildly on the awful pink walls—that he felt as if something inside, something quiet and good, was awake for the first time since he was a kid.

Katie slept beside him, curled around the baby, her bottom in her big, white maternity underwear pressed into his side. She looked lost, even in sleep. Her long red hair hung in her face, and her body in the unattractive underwear made him sad. It was pretty, curvy and pale and sexy, but she sometimes seemed slumped in the middle, as if she were very tired. Her arms and legs were long and thin and were always entwining things— babies and chair legs, themselves when she did yoga, his back when they used to have sex—but she hunched over her full breasts, as if no one had ever told her to stand up straight. This, too, made him sad.

Rose, seventeen months, slept in fuzzy pink socks and a diaper, her chubby thighs crossed, feet pressed into her mother's soft belly. She'd finished nursing, and Katie's nipple rested against her cheek like a discarded berry. Her lips continued to suck. She paused, grew still, sucked some more.

The two boys, like yin and yang, slept beside her, little Paul, pale and fragile and whiney, and Katie's Jake (who usually crept in from his room around dawn), dark and chubby and obnoxious. At the foot of the bed, on Wilson's feet, sprawled Lovely, one hundred and twenty pounds of solid yellow Lab mix, his legs in the air, his droopy face crumpled in a friendly snarl. As if a timer had gone off in his head, he flipped upright, scratched at his ear, and groaned loudly.

"I had a dream," Wilson said, half-awake. He shoved the dog off the bed with his foot and turned over, pulling Katie closer. He buried his face in her neck. She smelled warm and sleepy. "There were aliens. It was sunny out, but it got even brighter. They were floating in front of me."

"You were probably abducted as a kid," Katie whispered. "That would explain things."

"What do you mean?"

"You know, the way you feel so alienated all the time. Maybe, as a kid, you were actually, physically alien-*ated*, or made alien."

Wilson was silent. "What?" Even half-asleep, she could psychoanalyze him to within an inch of his life. "Sometimes," he said, "an alien is just an alien."

"I hear you. Were they in spaceships?"

"No. Just floating. They knew I saw them, but they didn't try to hide."

Katie was quiet. He thought she'd gone back to sleep. "You'd think they'd try to hide," she mumbled after a moment.

"Who?" He was confused. "Oh yeah. Aliens." He stretched the s into a hiss. "One would think."

"And your sister was there," he remembered, but Katie was asleep, breathing heavily in his arms.

Outside, under a clear green sky iced with stars, fresh snow glittered. It muted the Christmas lights into soft purple balls and muffled the drone of trucks on the interstate. Soon, the bastard with the snowplow would roar into the lane, blocking Wilson's car in the driveway with an enormous barrel of snow. Snow had softened the world, washed it clean. It drifted against the front door, dusted Katie's giant Halloween pumpkins—cheery and half-rotted on the porch—and hung like frosting from the eaves. Inside, in the warmest and pinkest and most inner chamber of the shell, Wilson lay awake, listening to the steady breathing of his family.

In the garage, in a dark and dusty corner, two mice, recently evicted from the neighboring condo by a frisky feline tenant, skittered behind a beat-up trunk, over a mesh bag of soccer balls, and began to busily chew their way into a bag of Lovely's dog food.

# Two

**Wilson**
1998

Wilson had fallen painfully in love on their first date. Before she asked him out, he'd always thought of Katie as simply a pain in the ass from his Shakespeare seminar. She always had an opinion, and she actually rolled her eyes when someone said something stupid. She liked to argue for argument's sake, and she held her single mother role over everyone, prefacing everything with, "As a mother . . ."

"As a mother," she'd say, "I can see that Hamlet never actualized through his Oedipal complex with Gertrude." Later she told Wilson that, months away from collecting her degree, she was so sick of school, she no longer cared about being diplomatic. "It's so much more fun when there's a jerk in the class anyway," she'd said, and he had to agree.

One spring evening, after a stultifying seminar on *King Lear*, during which the pretty but viciously cold professor burst into tears over her recently deceased father, then flipped into a cheery monologue about a limousine and a black leather miniskirt and a once famous, now dead actor, a story that Wilson had hoped would get sexual, Katie called him.

He picked up the phone, his mouth full of French fries from McDonald's, wondering who could be calling at 10:30 on a weeknight. Since moving to Kalamazoo and getting sober for the last time—he knew he didn't have another one in him; if he drank again, he'd drink until he died—he didn't talk to many people, spending most of his time at meetings or teaching or lying on his couch watching tennis on TV with the sound turned low. He lived carefully, as if he'd just emerged from a coma, and treated his tender body and soul gently.

"Hi. It's Katie," she said. Her voice was intimate, as if they were already lovers.

"How did you get this number?" He was surprised. He'd always thought she hated him. He was the main person she rolled her eyes at, and every time he spoke in class, which made him nervous enough, she was always the first to jump in, saying, "Well, not to disagree completely with Wilson, but . . ."

"How did I get your number?" Her voice was different than in class, softer and kinder. "I looked it up on KRISIS, on the university system. I have the password."

"You know that's secure information."

"I am aware. I also know that you only got a B in the Twain seminar—"

"Hold on—"

"And your GRE scores were, frankly, weak." She laughed.

He set down his Coke, nervous. Just who the hell was this girl? He had the strange sense that she'd appeared in his life with the specific purpose of fucking with his sobriety, and he had the urge to hang up before it was too late.

"Don't freak out," she said as if she'd read his mind. "I'm just kidding. I looked up your number in the phone book, how else would I get it?"

But he *had* only gotten a B in the Twain class, and his GRE scores *were* atrocious—he'd taken the test with the worst hangover of his life. When he told her so, she only snorted and said, "Grades. Test scores. How can you quantify a person's knowledge—true knowledge—of literature?"

*Well, easy*, he thought, but he didn't say it. After a few minutes of small talk, during which he quietly ate his Quarter Pounder, covering the mouthpiece of the phone when he chewed, she asked if he'd like to see a movie sometime. "It's so boring here," she said. "And I haven't really met anyone . . ." Her voice was wistful, and she sounded lonely. He could hear cartoons chattering in the background.

When he didn't answer because he didn't know what to say, she said briskly, "OK. I'll let you go. I know you're busy eating—"

He then spoke the words he'd come to rue a million times in the following years. "No," he said. "Wait. Don't go."

The next night, Wilson fell in love. It was a warm spring evening. The sky was blue, the sun golden, and the daffodils he'd planted as bulbs in pots on his deck had grown into little shivery green shoots. He sat among them in the director's chair he'd bought, dressed in his best jeans and a pale-yellow oxford shirt, and felt sick. He hadn't dated or slept with a woman in years. When he was drinking, he'd been too wasted to care, or too drunk to do much of anything. Then, after getting sober, he was too horrified by the thing called life that was there, unfiltered by drink, just there, in living color, screaming in his face twenty-four hours a day, to even think about women.

She was a single mother—what could that entail? Was there a violent ex-husband in the picture? Was her kid a brat? She'd definitely been around—that was intriguing. And there he was, Wilson A. Lavender, sober doctoral student, popular instructor of women's studies, sitting on his clean deck in a clean city, watching the sun burn golden behind the fir trees across the street. He was showered and fresh and ready for his date, but too nervous to smoke, and when he checked the bills in his wallet, his hands shook. At his feet were his daffodils that would soon bloom into perfectly fluted yellow cups. He had only to wait, to tend them faithfully, to have faith.

He sighed. How easy it would be to call the whole thing off, to go back inside and sink into the couch, watch *Cops* on TV, and order a pizza. But something told him that it was important that he go with this strange, sarcastic girl in the grubby overalls. Why, he had no idea.

He'd given her careful directions. *Park in the lot next to the office and buzz me at the front door, there at the north end of the building*, he'd said. He heard footsteps, and Katie appeared on the sidewalk below, as if his thoughts had conjured her. His first impression that spring evening of the girl who would change his life was that she was beautiful. He wondered why he hadn't seen it before.

She was wearing girl clothes instead of her usual baggy sweatpants or overalls. She trotted beneath him in chunky black boots and a short skirt, heading in the opposite direction of his building's front door. Her red hair, normally up in a messy ponytail, was long and loose, hanging nearly to her waist, gleaming in the dying light. She walked purposefully, a dreamy smile on her pale face.

"Hey," he said, but she didn't hear. He whistled and said it again, louder. "Hey. Katie."

She looked up, scanning the apartment decks until her eyes rested on him. "Is that you?" She squinted. "My eyes are bad. I'm going to the north end."

"No." He motioned her to the other end of the building. "You're going in the wrong direction. Go back where you came from. Go to the other north end."

Minutes later, she was at his door, as fresh as orange juice. "Here I am." She smiled, her lipstick bright, her narrow blue eyes bright, dressed in a sheer green camisole and a silky miniskirt in a psychedelic print that reminded him of the scarves his grandmother used to wear in the '70s. But this was not his grandmother, not this bright girl with the long legs and chunky ugly boots, this girl with such a pretty body he couldn't imagine why she hid it beneath sloppy clothes.

He liked how her skirt clung to her rounded hips, and he wondered if she was wearing panties beneath it. It was her legs, though, that got him. They were long and pale and sexy and turned him on, but they also made him sad in a way he couldn't quite understand. Wouldn't most girls with such winter-white legs wear tights or panty hose, or at least go to the suntanning booth? Her shins were bruised, and there was an enormous bloody scab on her left knee. She saw him looking at it.

"Rollerblading," she said darkly.

He reached out and touched the scab.

"Yow," she said. "Be careful. Don't poke it." She scowled, but he could tell she liked the attention. He wanted to protect her then, to buy her knee pads and panty hose, to touch gently all her bruises and sore spots. When she leaned into him and hugged him briefly, she smelled cool and sweet, like roses.

"I'm glad we're going to the movie," she said shyly. "I have, like, no friends in this hellhole."


After two weeks of rambunctious sex and dark declarations of love that only the neediest of people can make, Katie announced she was pregnant. It was Wilson's thirtieth birthday.

"You are not going to believe this," she began.

His first impulse was *not* to run. It was to surrender.

An image came to mind: a spaceship and a black hole, purple and churning. It was from a movie he'd seen as a kid, and when that ship was sucked into the black hole, Wilson wasn't scared like everyone else, he was enthralled. How badly he had wanted to be that spaceship. How comforting it would be to let go, your future, your eternal trajectory, decided for you. And now, here was his chance.

He dropped to one knee. "Will you marry me?" Katie was at the stove, stirring Kraft macaroni and cheese for her three-year-old son who, at midnight, apparently still had business to attend to.

"Ma-ca-ro-ni, ma-ca-ro-ni." The small boy with the chubby cheeks jumped on the couch in the living room, bare feet pounding the cushions, dark hair pushed back in sweaty spikes.

"Come and get it, monkey." Katie whapped the orange slop onto a plate and searched in the silverware drawer for a spoon. After a moment she gave up. "Guess what? You get the big spoon."

"Yay." The boy accepted his midnight snack and trotted back to the couch, mixing spoon held aloft like a spear.

Wilson stood up, feeling ridiculous. The kitchen smelled of fake cheese. The linoleum was hard, he was wearing shorts—he should have brought a knee pad. *Had she not heard him? How could she ignore the momentous occasion?*

"Yes." Katie didn't turn around. Her shoulders were thin in her flowered sundress. She stood like a dancer, bare feet turned out on the shiny floor.

Wilson's heart flipped. A feeling of heat spread through his chest. It was an odd sensation, neither pleasant nor unpleasant. She'd said *yes*.


Reality sank in. What had he done? He should be focused on his sobriety, not marrying some half-baked hippie he hardly knew. Maybe he didn't want to be in the black hole. But it was too late now. He grew frightened and clingy as Katie, for reasons known only to herself, became furious and mean. Within a week, the lovers were no longer on speaking terms.

As Wilson endured the final weeks of the Shakespeare seminar (they'd never gotten off the tragedies), he could feel her glowering at him from across the conference table, and was careful never to look her way. He once dared to make a comment about Hamlet, whom he secretly felt akin to, thinking on practically every page of the play: *That's me.*

"He's a tortured soul," he said, carefully choosing his words so she'd have nothing to ridicule. "The first 'modern man' if you will, and life—his life—is too intense for him to handle." He paused then added for good measure: "Not to mention his raging case of penis envy."

Just as he'd feared, Katie couldn't wait to attack, and since no one else in the class ever spoke up as no one else ever read the material, she had the floor.

"That 'first modern man' stuff is from the *Norton Anthology*," she said, "and I completely disagree. It doesn't mean anything. And as far as penis envy goes, a, he *has* a penis, and b, you can't analyze a character in Renaissance literature with Freudian constructs that came centuries later anyway. Hamlet isn't a tortured soul. He's a spoiled baby who wants everyone to believe he's this sensitive genius so he never has to act. So he never has to grow up and be a man."

Wilson looked at her, this beautiful girl he'd fallen so hard for who now hated him. It was the story of his life, he realized, starting at the beginning, with his unbearably sad mother. Everyone he loved left, as soon as he trusted that they wouldn't. And they not only left, they left hating him. *No. Wait. Don't go.* He'd been saying those words his entire life.

He'd had enough. Katie had just pointed out to the class his trick of passing off criticism from the *Norton Anthology* as his own. And *she* used Freudian nonsense to analyze character all the time—he'd copied her because he thought it sounded smart. Finally, he was not a baby. He was a man, and he was confused and hurt. Never again would he open his heart. This time, he rolled his eyes.

Katie glared back, her cheeks pink, breasts full in her tight T-shirt with the stupid Orange Crush logo. She looked as if she'd like to leap across the table and strangle him.

"Anyone else?" the professor asked dully. When her invitation was met by dead silence, she sighed. She'd been depressed since *King Lear* and no longer seemed to care if she engaged the students or not, often asking Wilson to set up and show movies of the plays rather than lead discussion. Last week they'd watched Mel Gibson in *Hamlet*, and everyone—psyched that they hadn't had to actually read anything—enthusiastically agreed that Mel was good, really good.

The professor eyed the class wearily. It looked as if she'd stopped washing her long blond hair, and Wilson felt a pang of empathy. She was so pretty, in her cold and brilliant way—what in her life could be hurting her so? Surely it wasn't this group of losers, slouched in various stages of indifference around the table.

"Katie and Wilson both have a point." The professor stood and crossed the room, pushing open the tall, narrow window, designed during the riotous '70s to prevent students from taking over the building. "Anyone else?" Spring air, smelling of baby grass and damp earth, blew into the stifling classroom. The train that ran from Chicago to Ontario rumbled along the edge of campus. It whistled once, and then again. Students shouted, a dog barked. Wilson looked down at his hands, pressed against the conference table. They were greenish in the fluorescent light, and he wondered if he was dying.

"Don't worry, I'm not going to jump," the professor said dryly, her back to the class. When she didn't turn around, and continued to stand at the window, staring out into the green spring night, the students quietly stood and filed from the classroom.

"Awesome," whispered the laziest of the bunch, a guy with red dreadlocks and dirty sandaled feet. The students moved down the hallway swiftly and silently so as not to break the professor's reverie, amazed at the good luck of getting to leave only fifteen minutes into class. Wilson looked for Katie, but caught just a glimpse of her orange T-shirt before she disappeared into the stairwell.

# Three

## Katie
1998

The garage seduction occurred on a hot bleached Indian summer after-noon. The temperatures were in the high 90s, but it was mercifully dry. If it had been humid, Katie would have killed herself. There was only so much misery a person could take. She had terrible hay fever, was hugely preg-nant, and she and Wilson hadn't spoken in months. She'd spent the morn-ing watching her son, Jake, scribble with sidewalk chalk on the driveway as she sat on the porch and drank Coke, sneezing and peeing and praying that the caffeine would calm her allergies.

Jake watched as she wiped her nose with a soggy paper towel.

"You need to quit sneezing, Mom," he said, his voice solemn. In his chubby hand he held out a perfect pink egg of sidewalk chalk. Katie heaved herself up and took it from him. Together they spent the next twenty min-utes drawing a driveway-sized likeness of Bob Marley, pink and purple and yellow dreadlocks flung out like tentacles.

She wrote the words *One Love* beneath the drawing with a shard of blue chalk. Sweat dripped down her back.

"What does that say?" Jake said.

"One love."

"What does that mean?"

She thought a moment. "I guess I don't know. What do you think it means?"

"That you need to watch out for the hot lava!" With that, he threw down his chalk and ran across Merlot Court, as fast as his chubby brown legs could carry him. "I'm visiting," he shouted when he got to the neigh-bor's porch.

"Wait," Katie called. *It's the cute guy's porch. No! I'm going to have to retrieve you, you little shit, and chat, and I feel like a hideous beast.* Ignor-ing his mother, Jake turned and pushed open the door, slamming it shut behind him. Although he was only three, Jake, like Lovely the dog, was a social butterfly. Everyone at the Reserve knew them.

"Your dog comes and has coffee with me every morning," the widower across the street with the lonely, drooping eyes once told her. "He's my best friend these days."

When the ladies on Katie's end of the court asked if she was Jakey's mom, their voices were reverent, as if the Dalai Lama himself had sprung from her womb. Jake liked to drop fistfuls of squashed dandelions on their welcome mats, knock on their doors, and run. Visiting, it seemed, would be his passion in life. It made Katie, social loser that she was, proud.

She finished her Coke, wiped her chalky hands on her shorts, and headed across the street. She knocked on the cute guy's forest-green door. An expensive gas grill stood in the corner. Cigarette butts littered the porch, and crushed beer cans hung like ornaments in the bushes. *Charming*, she thought. When no one answered, she let herself in.

Steven Carl James III dressed like a thug in sagging jeans and an oversized Detroit Red Wings jacket. At nineteen, he was mysteriously wealthy, and a single father to a rabbity girl, three years old like Jake. He sometimes swept up hair at his mother's salon, and he liked to drink. In between classes at the community college, he brewed big brown bottles of foul-smelling beer in his bedroom on Merlot Court. Despite all of the above, Katie liked him.

Still, she hesitated in the foyer. It was wrong to just walk into someone's home, but how else to retrieve her child? And wasn't a part of her excited? Steven was hot. She liked chatting with him as their kids played on the swings. Maybe today—yes, please—something good would happen, something sexy and dirty and fun.

His place was like hers but darker, with all of the mini-blinds drawn. The living room was filled with giant furniture, armoires and couches and love seats, as well as a strange glassed-in collection of evil clowns. He had the upgraded blond wood cabinets, but he didn't have the new Berber carpet, and she was glad to see that his beige rug was stained and worn—filthy really—just like hers.

Jake was lying on the floor with Abby, Steven's daughter, watching a Batman cartoon on a large-screen TV. An enormous Tupperware bowl of some sort of sugary cereal, crap Katie refused to buy, was open between them. They ignored her, stuffing handfuls of marshmallow bits into their mouths, hypnotized by the slick candy colors on the screen.

"Don't forget to knock next time. OK? Jakey?"

"I don't think he's listening," Steven said from the kitchen.

Katie jumped. "Shit. You scared me." She gestured at her son, then sneezed and wiped her nose on her paper towel. "Sorry. He just came in."

Steven shrugged. He calmly popped the top off a bottle of beer, as if it were perfectly normal to find the lady from across the street standing in his living room.

"It's hot," she said, feeling awkward.

"Yep."

She smiled, waiting for him to say something else, but he just nodded and drank his beer.

"Do you like bars?" he finally said, setting down the bottle.

"Bars?"

"Yeah. A bar. I just built one. In the garage."

"Oh." Katie didn't know what to say. "Really?" *How odd*, she thought. *How stupid and immature.* Steven ran his hands over his reddish crew cut. He looked like a delinquent in sagging shorts and a big Guinness T-shirt, but he had an air of class, too, as if he came from a good family. He was laid back. *Maybe too laid back for an early afternoon*, Katie thought, watching as he opened another beer.

"I guess I don't like bars," she said. "They give me panic attacks. But if you want to show me yours, I'd like to see." She knotted her sweaty hair into a neater ponytail. God, she was lonely. She'd gotten pregnant so quickly, so stupidly. What kind of loser was she? Not only was she disgusted with herself, she was alone and disgusted with herself, with no one, besides innocent Jake, to take it out on. Wilson was gone. There was no one to cry to or yell at or send to the mall for French fries, immediately, before she threw up.

The physical attraction between Katie and Wilson had flamed out the instant she found herself pregnant. Her first thought was, *My God, what have I done?*

Wilson had a dark side. She sensed it, and it made her uneasy. There was nothing she could put her finger on. Unlike her, he didn't yell or throw things. It was just a feeling, but it gnawed at her.

There was the incident with the coat. They'd gone sledding at the grade school, and Katie had worn his ski coat. As she ducked through a hole in the chain-link fence, the sleeve caught on a wire and tore. Wilson was angry. Surprisingly angry. "I'm sorry," she said. The tear was small, no more than an inch long. She would fix it. But he wasn't appeased. He glared, and the coldness in his eyes frightened her. As if she were nothing.

*A shadow, faceless.*

*The moon shrunk to the size of a baby aspirin.*

*You know I'm no good.*

In that moment, Katie wanted out. But she said nothing. On the way home, Wilson apologized. He made her laugh. They had make-up sex. She wondered if maybe *she* had overreacted. Within a week, she was pregnant, and then it was too late. She was trapped.

Katie never considered abortion. She loved babies. It was men—men like Wilson—who scared her. She turned cold, picking fights, hoping to drive him away. One night he sank to his knees and yelled that she was exactly like his insane mom, and God help him that he hadn't realized it earlier. As summer stretched into fall and her belly grew, they decided to pretend they'd never met. Or rather Katie decided, and Wilson had no choice but to go along.

*You're welcome to join us—there's plenty of room on the blanket.* Katie remembered that: her mother, inviting the demon in. No. Not on *her* blanket. She stared at the beige linoleum of Steven's kitchen floor. Cartoons chattered. Her heart beat fast and her cheeks grew hot. *No.* Steven reached out, brushing her hand with his fingertips. "Let's go, pretty mama." She shook her head, as if to rid herself of a dream, then followed him into the garage.


The room was stifling, thick with heat and dust and the faint smell of cat pee. It made her think of New Mexico, of the desert, and of Jake's dad, who had made her feel calm.

"You paint, right? I sometimes see you there in your garage. Maybe you could paint this." He gestured to a hulking black thing—the bar, she assumed. "Something wild. Jimi Hendrix maybe."

"I just drew Bob Marley on my driveway."

"I saw."

Katie was silent, waiting for the compliment.

"It's good," he said shyly. "I like the dreds."

"Thanks." She was pleased and told him that of course she'd paint his bar, knowing she was too lazy to ever do it.

He seemed to have a boundary problem. He was standing so close she could smell the beer on his breath, and she wondered how long he'd been drinking. Was he shy or just drunk? She was definitely excited. She hadn't been alone with a cute guy in months. Everything about him was big—his furniture, his clothes, his Tupperware. His big body radiated heat, and he smelled good, like hot cement and clean laundry. It was a comforting smell. Katie closed her eyes, breathing it in.

She was exhausted. Hating Wilson, and hating herself, had taken its toll, and as she stood in the garage on that hot summer afternoon, she vowed to stop. Let the whole world go insane. She gave up. So she was stuck for life with someone she couldn't stand, with someone who couldn't stand her—was it really so bad? The romance was done. It was time to move on. She looked at Steven, at his plush hair and round brown eyes. He was like a sexy teddy bear. Perfect. Despite the dust in the air, she'd stopped sneezing.

Steven showed her the shelves behind the bar, stocked with beer mugs and shot glasses, with clear and amber bottles of premium liquor and neat stacks of cocktail napkins. Katie picked one up. A naked lady with big breasts and black stockings fell into a martini glass. *Bottoms Up!* she cried.

"You're like a junior Hugh Hefner," Katie said.

"All right."

A galaxy of beer signs in blue and purple neon hummed on the walls, and in the corner sat an overstuffed couch with sparkling tangerine-colored cushions. A baseball bat leaned against the wall. Katie picked it up. "Is this for beating the crap out of unruly guests?" she said, whacking it into her palm.

"Things can get a little wild." Steven took the bat and tucked it behind the couch. He seemed embarrassed, and she felt bad for making fun of his stuff. When he set a shot glass on the bar, filling it to its gilded rim with Cuervo 1800, she felt worse. He knocked back the shot, chasing it with beer, then poured another.

"Oh God, don't drink it," she cried. She was going to be sick. She could smell the tequila, could imagine its planty taste in her mouth, its burn in her throat and stomach. *Don't think*, she willed, but it was too late. The heat and the smell of liquor were too much. She took a deep breath, dizzy. Her eyes and mouth watered, and her stomach clenched. She leaned over, hands on her knees, horrified that she was about to be sick.

"Oh, ugh." She gagged and spit, then gagged again. *Don't do it*, a voice in her head warned. She bit her cheek hard. After a moment, her stomach relaxed. She sighed and looked up. Steven was watching, amused. He rubbed his scruffy red goatee. She could just hear him telling his buddies about the lady across the street who came over and yakked, right on his floor.

"Could you get me some water?" she said weakly. "And crackers? And quit laughing?"

He returned with a bottle of water and half a roll of Ritz crackers. She sank into the couch, its cushions rising around her like dough. "Sorry for spitting on your floor," she said. "It was just . . . ugh. The tequila. And sometimes, at the end, the morning sickness comes back. At least it does for me."

"It's OK. I wasn't laughing, I promise."

"But you were laughing. I saw."

"But I wasn't. Abby's mom, when she was pregnant, she got sick in the Taco Bell drive-thru." He sat down, the couch so low-slung his knees came up to his chest. "And it looked just like—"

"Stop," Katie cried.

"Sorry." He grinned and shook his head. "Oh, man, it was funny. Of course she was pissed."

"I'm sure she was. I'm glad you find pregnant ladies so hilarious."

"No, I don't. Look at you in your T-shirt. You're pretty, like a pumpkin." He rested his hand on her belly.

*A pumpkin?* Katie made a face. She nibbled a cracker and sipped water, shifting into a more comfortable position.

"Did you know your dog stole my hot dog buns the other day?" Steven said. "Right off my porch. I was getting ready to grill."

"Oh my God. Yes. The buns. He did have a bag of buns. He was eating them on the side of the house. I thought he'd gotten them from the dumpster." Thinking of Lovely made her feel better. Warmth from Steven's hand radiated through her thin shirt. She closed her eyes, wishing she could stay there forever. The fat ball of couch held her nicely. All she wanted was sleep.

She opened one eye.

No, she wanted him. The kids could watch cartoons and eat sugary cereal, and she and Steven could—

"God, you're huge," he said.

"Thanks." Tears filled her eyes.

"Are you freaking out?"

"No. Don't panic. No." She sniffed and wiped her cheeks. "I'm just . . ." How to explain how good it felt to be noticed, and touched?

"I could tell you a thing or two about hair."

"What?" Katie looked at him, curious. Like styling tips? Like what kind of mousse to use? Who was this dude? Well, for one, he was nineteen, and she was far too old to be sitting beside him, alone in his garage, dirty sunlight swirling all over, so close she could smell the tequila on his breath.

"Hair. About hair."

"Like what?" Her exhaustion faded as he moved closer. The excitement returned, so intense she could barely breathe, and at the same time she thought, *I cannot believe I am sitting here with this punk, this drinker, so excited I can barely breathe.*

"Like it could kill a person," he said.

"Please."

"Seriously. It gets stuck in your skin and gets infected. The ladies at my mom's shop get it all the time—hair infections." He leaned over and kissed her then, slow kisses on her lips, her neck, behind her ear. He was practiced in the art of garage seduction—of course he was, he was barely out of high school. She knew she should push him away, but she didn't. She liked how he said the word *ladies*, his voice soft and respectful.

"And then you're dead." Steven lifted her tie-dyed T-shirt and placed his hand on her bare skin. It felt good, his hand heavy and soothing, but it also felt wrong, very wrong. Wilson, her estranged boyfriend, father of the child resting inside her, would freak. She politely pushed Steven's hand away and pulled down her shirt. He moved it up to her breast.

"Hair infections. Wow. The world . . . it's such . . . so . . . dangerous." She had trouble getting the words out. What was wrong with her? He slipped his hands down the back of her awful pink spandex maternity shorts. She didn't move. She closed her eyes, waiting to see what would happen next.

"And it rots. Have you ever smelled a big garbage can—"

"Stop." She giggled, pushed him away. She took a deep breath. That was it. He was an idiot, talking about rotting hair, of all things, in his garage bar, of all places. She was going home.

She willed her legs to move.

"A big garbage can full of rotting . . ." He leaned in again and kissed her deeply this time, his tongue warm in her mouth. His body enveloped her, making her feel small and pretty. She kissed him back.

Steven felt like home. He reminded her of the boys she'd hung out with as a teenager, hard-core partiers who lived to get high. It was the substances that made them seem safe. If they weren't fully present, how could they hurt her? Steven was easy. He was the kind of boy Katie knew what to do with.

She rested her hand on his crotch, then slowly unzipped his shorts.


The romance lasted one day. When Katie knocked on Steven's door the next afternoon, he looked stunned and sober, the hood of his sweatshirt pulled low over his face, Unabomber-style. "Lucy's here," he muttered, gazing past her shoulder at the trash can.

"What? Who's—"

"My *girlfriend*."

"Oh." Katie laughed. "The way you're peeking out the door, it's like I'm some kind of serial killer, about to force my way in."

Steven didn't smile. He looked frightened.

"Ohhh." It was halfway between a sigh and a moan. Katie turned and walked quickly back across the street. *Bastard*, she thought, surprised at the hurt and humiliation churning in her gut.

She called Wilson that night. "I'm sorry," she began.

Hours later the lovers reunited. "Maybe I was just hormonal," Katie mused. They lay in her bed, legs tangled beneath the sheets.

"Or scared." Wilson pushed her hair out of his face. "Don't think I'm not. Here we are, two sensitive souls with genius IQs—who knows what we're about to unleash on the world."

Katie smiled. "It's just . . ." She shook her head. How to explain the feeling that gnawed at her, the sense of two worlds, one pink and alive, the other pure desolation.

*Is this right?* she wondered, meaning *them*, Katie and Wilson. She pressed her ear to his chest and listened to his breathing, steady and distant, like ocean waves. She stared out the window at a star like a silver snail curled in the sky. Her next thought startled her: *I have no way of figuring this out.* Some part of her, some internal compass, was broken. Wilson could be her savior or he could be the end of her, and she would never know until goodness or disaster struck.

*So. Stay where you are. With the father of your child.*

Katie gave up. She was done fighting and second-guessing herself. All she wanted was peace.

The baby kicked her hard in the ribs, and she tried to grab its foot.

There was a price. There was always a price—she'd learned that as a child. In order to have peace, to have Wilson on her side and not against her, she would have to excise a part of herself. The fear, the rage, the *past*—there would be no room for it in this new life. Kick the broken doll with the broken doll heart into the back of the closet, forget the ugly thing ever belonged to you.

And wasn't that a relief?


Life with Wilson became routine, circular and safe. This was nothing like the monkey business with the immature hair sweeper across the street. This was an adult relationship with a real man, one who had his appetites in check. Wilson allowed himself one cup of coffee in the morning and one before his midnight AA meeting. He smoked four cigarettes a day, no more, no less. He was sober. He was alert. Wilson was a good family man.

One day in December, months after the reconciliation, Katie told him that Steven's daughter was named Abby, and that it was short for Absinthe. Their new baby lay between them on the bed. It was late afternoon, cold and sunny, and the walls were covered with rainbows from the crystal ball she had hung on the window latch.

The baby had a cold and they were watching him sleep. He was almost a month old, a wrinkly bald creature with enormous eyes. His body felt almost weightless when Katie lifted him to nurse, and he looked lost in his pale-yellow sleeper. She touched his flushed cheeks, his ears, large and dignified, like Wilson's. He was an exact replica, in miniature, of his father. "Paul," they said, a hundred times a day. He had finally arrived, his whole solemn and watchful self.

"Absinthe? Are you serious?" Wilson whispered, sneering gleefully. He pushed his blond hair behind his ears. His goatee was scruffy and he looked tired. "And it's actually *Absinthe*, on the birth certificate?"

"No. Steven's mom made him change it at the last minute."

"What about the baby's mom? The crack whore. Didn't she have a say?"

"She thought it was neat," Katie whispered. "And don't say that word. You know I hate that word. She's an *addict*—something you should understand."

"Whatever." Wilson rolled his eyes. He hated the word *neat* and anyone, besides Katie, who used it. "So the kid's Abby on paper," he said grandly, "but—and please excuse the pun—Absinthe in *spirit*."

"You idiot." She smiled, resting her hand on Paul's back, feeling the steady rhythm of his breath in her palm. She felt guilty holding up Steven and his love of anything to do with drinking for Wilson to ridicule. But how else to appease him? She had, after all, slept with Steven when she was pregnant with *Wilson's* child. She'd confessed one lazy afternoon shortly before Paul was born, in a fit of ill-advised honesty, and she'd regretted it ever since. If she'd just kept her mouth shut.

"Un-fucking-believable," Wilson said.

"I agree." She rolled over, away from him and the baby, tracing the stitching on the quilt with her finger, an intricate path of swirls and loops and flowers. She felt guilty but safe, too, in the quiet bedroom, as if, lying there with Wilson and the new baby, she was exactly where she belonged. She had made the right choice. With Paul's birth, goodness had arrived. "Besides. Who are you to talk? The love of your life was named Divinity."

"Hey now."

Katie closed her eyes, smiling. Divinity had trashed the heart of the budding genius when he was a freshman in high school, dumping him for a varsity football player, of all people. Any mention of her name was strictly off-limits.

# Four

**Katie**
2002

On a winter morning four years after the garage seduction, Katie sat in the pink velvet La-Z-Boy, a wedding present from Wilson, and tried to cry. "Fuck," she said aloud. At that moment, marriage seemed difficult, and worse than that, it seemed boring. Really fucking unbelievably boring, if you wanted the truth.

She needed something: Coffee. Steven. Coffee *with* Steven. Perfect.

Wilson was teaching and Jake was at school. Paul, a night owl like his mom, was still asleep in the bedroom, snuggled beneath Katie's favorite Korean blanket, the thick, fuzzy one the color of mangoes. The baby was nursing, settling down for her morning nap. The condo was quiet. It was mommy time.

If Katie drank or got high, she would do it now. Instead, she searched for the phone.

In the field behind the house, waves of snow sparkled, and dried sunflowers scratched at the window, a ray of sunlight turning them into silvery torches. The sky over the field and the woods and the curve of interstate was cornflower blue, and on the horizon, clouds as pale and pretty as carnations bloomed. Katie liked to think of the land outside the window as *hers*. Deer sometimes ventured into the field from the woods. "Horsies!" Paul would cry when he saw them, their soft brown heads rising above fuzzy green clumps of ragweed.

She switched the baby to the other side. Rose arched, then grabbed for the breast like a greedy mole. Katie closed her eyes and tried again to cry, to dissolve the ache in her chest, but it was warm in the living room and she just felt sleepy. Something smelled of coconut. She sniffed Rose's head, then the knee of her own sweatpants, but smelled only baby sweetness and, faintly, laundry soap.

She reached down the side of the chair, coming up with a handful of miniature Snickers wrappers but no phone. She wiped her sticky fingers on her pink bleach-spotted sweatpants, her uniform since successfully defending her dissertation the previous spring. It was then, when she was finally done, that she'd decided to never again teach, write, or even discuss in earnest a book. From that moment on, she vowed, her life would be simple. No more thinking. No more furious sessions of mental masturbation in overheated classrooms. She would live off her "Grandma Edith money"—money her dad's mother gave the grandchildren twice a year—and be a mom. It was fulfilling. It did not make her brain hurt. The first thing she did as a free person was hide her treatise on the "sacrificial child" in contemporary American literature (she'd focused on *Lolita*, Joyce Carol Oates' *Blonde*, and the scary work of A. M. Homes) in the back of her closet, under a pile of silky, flower-splashed underwear that had somehow grown too small. Then she planted sunflowers. She dug holes in the hard clay soil beneath the windows and carefully buried the striped seeds she'd bought at the supermarket. When the sunflowers sprouted, then grew enormous, their yellow-maned heads bowing by summer's end, she felt blessed.

Their wide-open faces were alive with prickly bumblebees and Japanese beetles when she married Wilson. Like the sunflowers, the marriage seemed right. She had felt lucky then, as if whatever she touched would flourish. And what could be simpler than the full-moon shape of a family—a mom, a dad, three kids, and a dog? Besides, as much as she hated to admit it, she couldn't do it on her own. It was easy to be a tough and hip single mom when you had just one child. But three? She wasn't a masochist. She was thirty-six years old. She was exhausted.

That morning, after getting Jake on the school bus and helping a furious Wilson dig out his car, after arguing with him about who would feed the dog, then giving his hood a smack when he refused, she'd come inside, kicked her snowy boots into the corner, and put on her most depressing '90s mix tape: ALICEMOTHERLOVEGARDEN. It wasn't that the songs were sad, it was that she'd listened to them over and over with Jake's dad, during a time in her life when she felt young and sexy and thin. Jake's dad had made her feel calm. And her hair had been thicker then, she was sure of it. Under the vast and friendly New Mexico sky, she was never tired.

Rose snored in her lap, her curls damp, her chubby cheeks flushed. Katie held her bare foot, touching the perfect pink toes. The heat clicked on and the humidifier hummed. What in the hell was that coconut smell? Had Wilson worn scent, some sort of essential oil? Had he found a girlfriend so soon? Katie let herself dream. He would run off with a dull undergraduate, someone with no sense of humor who was inferior to her in every way. She'd wear braces as an adult and be bad in bed. And Katie would be the wronged wife, brilliant and unforgettable, left alone to . . . to what? To not fight, to not put up with his moods, to never again have to *get along*.

She sighed and shifted the baby. She knew that without Wilson there'd be no Rose or Paul. Jake wouldn't have a dad. And during those first weeks after Paul was born, he'd really seemed like *the one*. He was kind and loyal and responsible. He was a genius, and he made her laugh every day. He had a big penis, and when he slowed down and made an effort, he was good in bed. Maybe, despite the fact that he drove her insane, he was still the one. She rubbed her eyes. The kids deserved a good dad—that was what it came down to—and parents who loved each other, who tried.

Ugh. She found the phone in the box of wipes and dialed Steven's number. No answer.

Dammit. The baby was asleep and it was *her* time, time to have fun, to break through the numbness she'd been feeling all winter. What was wrong with her? Was it the fact of Larry Johnson? No. That was done. After years of therapy, she was talked out. He was the past. Wilson and the kids were now. Even thinking the name, though, made her spine tense, and she blocked out an image of his face, seeing only a shapeless form in a brown leather jacket.

Katie bit the inside of her cheek. A Gregg Allman song came on. How on earth had Cher married the guy and *not* known he was an addict, as she'd claimed in *People* magazine? Katie had instinctively sensed Wilson's rough past. The hint of danger in his worn-looking eyes as he sat in class and babbled about Hamlet was what had turned her on in the first place.

What was it like to be Cher? Was it easier than being Katie Jane Lavender, wife of Wilson A. Lavender, mother of three? Was it worse? As a kid, she'd loved Sonny and Cher. She could remember a summer evening after watching their TV show when her mother had taken her and her little sister to the drive-in. They saw a movie about dolls that ate people. The dolls had sharp, pearly teeth and snapping jaws, and they followed a screaming woman up a flight of stairs to her room. They must have eaten her, but Katie couldn't remember that part, only the woman's terrified screams, and how they'd echoed in the steep, empty staircase.

"Why did you bring us to something like that?" she asked her mother, years later. She was sitting at the bar in her parents' kitchen nursing a baby—Jake, probably. "I was like six. I had nightmares," she half-joked. "It still creeps me out."

Iris laughed and denied that they'd ever gone.

"But we did," Katie said.

"Never. Why on earth would I take you girls to something like that?"

"I don't know. That's what I'm asking. It's not that big a deal; it's not like you took us to see *Deep Throat*. But we saw a movie about dolls that ate people. I know we did. I remember. Why would I make it up?"

"Jesus, Katie." Iris threw her dishcloth into the sink. She'd pulled her black hair into a messy ponytail, exposing ears that stuck out, just like Katie's. She looked tired. "Who cares? What if we did? You've got this computer file in your brain of all the ways you were wronged in the past, and I'm sick of it. Sometimes I think you make half the stuff up."

Katie glared.

"Poor, pitiful Katie," Iris added, squirting soap into the sink and turning on the water.

*I hate you*, Katie had thought. She remembered. Before the movie, they'd played at the playground in the corner of the lot. She swung, and January stuck her hands in the dirty sandpile. They wore PJs. Their feet were bare. Iris had laughed at something, and her voice had sounded far away and clear at the same time. They were *there*. Katie's mom was there, and her sister was there, and she was there, swinging under a dark blue sky, stars like silver bugs squirming all over the place.

"It was a happy memory"—that was what she'd wanted to say. It was thrilling being out in the dark, in pajamas, *swinging* of all things. She'd loved her mother with her long silky black hair just like Cher's, and she'd loved her sister, wallowing in the sand like a piglet.

Katie used to run her hands through Iris's hair, over and over, and then breathe in the smell from her palms. It was a wonderful smell, one of heavy cooking spices, of cumin and sweat and dirt, and something flowery, too, something like violets or lilacs, something comforting.

Sometimes she wished she could go back in time and stand once more in her mother's bedroom in Portland, staring out the round windows at the lilacs pressed against the glass, filling the room with their cool, grapey scent, their watery shadows falling on the scarred wooden floor. She missed her mom—maybe that was it. Or maybe she missed being a kid, small and new, like a flower.

The heat went off with a sigh, and for an instant her life in Kalamazoo seemed strange, like a dream, her real one caught in the past, in Portland, thirty years ago. She set Rose on the couch and covered her with a red chenille blanket. Iris was different now. She smelled different. The mother Katie had known as a kid was gone.

She dialed Steven again.

"I'm depressed," she said when he picked up. Katie and Steven had grown close over the years. He was one of her only friends in Kalamazoo—a flirtatious and difficult friend, but a friend nonetheless. "I'm such a bitch," she continued. "I don't know how anyone can stand me."

"You're right. I'm hanging up."

"Steven."

"You just need one of your four-dollar mochas." His voice was soft and husky and friendly. Hearing it, Katie felt better.

"I whacked the hood of Wilson's car when he wouldn't feed the dog, like some crazy lady in a trailer park."

"I'm sure he deserved it." Steven's voice was mild, no love lost between him and Wilson. "Were you wearing your glasses?"

"Yeah, why?"

"And the tight long underwear with the reindeer on them?"

"What if I was? What are you saying?" Katie laughed.

"I'm just saying that I'm sure you looked perfectly," he hesitated, "sane, as you beat your husband's car—"

"Stop," Katie said, not wanting him to stop at all.

They arranged to meet at her place, then go get coffee, and she hung up, feeling a thrill in her gut. She found her wallet and checked to see if Wilson had pilfered the twenty she'd put in the night before, but it was still there, as well as her debit card. She slipped Rose into her fleece bunting, careful not to wake her, relieved to be getting out of the house. Something good was on its way—she could feel it. Paul was awake in the bedroom, talking to a stuffed cat wrapped in a pillowcase.

"Key Lime Kitty got me, so I put him in jail," he said. Katie scooped up her son and tickled him, and he screamed happily, warm and sleepy in robot pajamas.

"I love Key Lime Kitty." She gave the pale green cat a kiss, then roared like a monster and threw it into the corner.

"I said he's in jail," Paul yelled, running to retrieve the fugitive cat.


"Want to go to the coffee place?" Katie said in the car, buckling car seats.

"Oh yes, I would love it." Paul's voice sounded enthusiastic and fake, a tone she was sure he'd gotten from listening to her talk on the phone. His blue eyes were bright, and his white-blond hair stuck out in back where he'd slept on it. He'd been bald the first two years of his life, and even now, his hair was still so thin. He was small, too, barely on the growth charts the pediatrician had showed her, and it worried Katie. She touched his hand, resting on the car seat. Everything seemed so fragile. It made her sad and happy and sick, all at once. How could a person go on? She took a deep breath, licked her palm, and smoothed his hair.

When Steven arrived, they pulled out of the Reserve, stalling just once on a heap of snow on Chablis Lane, a street the snowplow guy, for some reason, had declined to plow.

Inside the condo, Lovely climbed onto the forbidden territory of Katie's big pink chair. He sank down with a sigh, cast a baleful glance at his dog food bowl. Despite all the arguing and hood pounding, it was still empty.


Steven was in such a good mood that Katie wondered if he was hungover or still drunk from the night before. His beard had grown in red, and his dark brown eyes were shiny. Although unusually cheery, he didn't smell of alcohol. When Katie hugged him, she smelled only clean laundry and snow, and she was happy, driving in her little car with him in his red knit hat beside her, the radio playing, the cold bright day glittering all around.

They circled the lot of the coffee shop, looking for a parking space. Steven sang along to "Ice Cream Man"—a song Katie never needed to hear again in her life.

"I hate this song—" she began, whipping the car into a spot narrowed by a pile of snow.

"Shhhhhh."

"What?"

Steven took her hand from the steering wheel. He pulled off her black mitten, a mischievous look in his eyes, then bent to kiss her fingers, sucking briefly on each one. He turned her hand over and licked the inside of her wrist.

Katie shivered. *What the hell?* "Coming from anyone else, that would be repulsive," she said, trying to sound stern. But inside she had melted. Inside, she'd been weakened by the feel of his hot breath on her palm, his mouth wet and warm on her skin. That was the thing: She admired her husband, Wilson, with all her heart. When she was near Steven, she had the primal urge to lick.

"All flavors and push-ups, too." Steven pulled off his hat and moved his mouth to her neck, his hair bristly against her cheek. "All my flavors are guaranteed to satisfy."

"Stop." Katie didn't move. She let him kiss her neck, his tongue lingering behind her ear. *But the babies—shit!* She shoved Steven away, then pulled him down where no one could see and kissed him until she was out of breath. He was insane and immature, and if her children weren't in the car, she would fuck him right there in the farthest corner of the parking lot, her dirty windshield smeared with sunlight, a mountain of filthy snow towering overhead.

• • •

The air in the shop was a warm net of coffee beans and vanilla. Paul and Rose gnawed happily on a giant cinnamon roll as Katie sipped her latte and Steven drank a Coke.

"We're getting married." Steven sucked up the rest of his soda, then rattled the ice in his cup. He grinned proudly.

"What?" Katie set down her drink, horrified.

"I asked her to marry me and she said yes. Lucy. Me and Lucy—we're getting married."

He continued talking but Katie no longer heard. *You're getting married and you just mauled my hand in the parking lot?*

When Steven was done babbling, he folded his hands behind his head and leaned back, legs spread wide. He looked at Katie as if he expected her to cheer.

"Hooray." That was what she should have said. "Good for you." But instead, her eyes filled with tears, and she forced herself to close her mouth. "People who are engaged shouldn't lick other people." Her voice was tight, cheeks hot, and she was instantly sorry when she saw the look of disappointment in his eyes.

After the coffee date, Katie once more kicked her snowy boots into the corner, reminded herself to feed the dog, then left the kids in the living room in front of *Blue's Clues*, a plateful of M&M's between them. Did that make her a bad mother? Probably.

*Tough*, she thought, tossing the bag onto the kitchen counter, candy scattering everywhere. She needed to shower alone, without Rose howling at her feet because she wanted to be held, her head thrown back like a coyote. She needed to be alone, to think. She needed to wash her hair with both hands, without a slippery baby squirming in her arm.

Steven was getting married.

She stripped off her sweats and threw them into the corner. The movie star lights around the mirror glowed. The bathroom was warm and smelled of grape soap. She could hear the guy that lived behind them banging around in his bathroom. His toilet gurgled, there was a final crash, and then quiet once again.

Wilson had laughed when she asked him to find pink light bulbs for the mirror, but after Rose's birth, the usual stark white light had been too depressing.

"I'm ready for my close up, Mr. DeMille," he teased as he screwed in the pink bulbs.

"Fuck you. I'm fat," she'd replied, in no mood to play, especially with someone whose jeans didn't fit over her hips.

A year and a half after Rose's birth, she could still barely look at herself, even with the kind lighting. After carrying three babies, her stomach looked deflated, as if something the size of a winter-fat woodchuck had lived in it, scratching out a nice warm pod, before suddenly abandoning its nest, leaving it to rot in the sun, to shrivel in the long dry winter. *Abandoned*—that was how she felt. Or maybe *finished* was the word. Everything good was behind her—finding a mate, having children—while Steven was just beginning.

She shook out her hair and pulled off her earrings, dropping them into a chipped blue bowl full of tangled jewelry. She was being ridiculous, she knew—it wasn't like she was eighty. She forced herself to think of something happy, but the best she could come up with was what she'd make for dinner. Maybe an oven stew, or lentils. Her coffee high was fading. Steven was getting married. And she was bored and obsessed with her body and had put less care into choosing a husband than she had choosing Lovely years earlier.

No, that wasn't true. One spring morning eleven years ago, as she was sitting bored and unemployed in her parents' backyard in Portland, staring at the dripping rosebushes, a friendly man in John Lennon glasses leaned over the fence that divided the yards, beckoning to her. When she walked over, he thrust a fat, yellow puppy into her arms.

"Hello," she said, stroking the wriggling bundle, its fur silky against her cheek.

"You're meant for each other." The man leaned on the fence, smiling indulgently, as if he were observing a newly married couple. "Look at the little dude. He loves you." He gave the puppy a friendly pat, whispered something that sounded like "sayonara," and went back to watering his lawn.

"You mean he's mine?" Katie called.

"He's yours. Take him home. Enjoy."

*Wow*, she'd thought. The puppy chewed the ends of her ponytail, its sharp claws digging into her breast. Its belly was fat, its little wick wet, as it had just peed—not on her, she hoped—and when it licked and gnawed at her chin, its puppy breath was milky.

She took the little dude home, as directed, and named him Lovely because he was such a sweet package of difficult, naughty love. He grew enormous, three times the size of the mother she'd seen loping in good-natured circles around the man's yard. He destroyed her furniture, shit in the house, barfed in her car, roamed the neighborhood for hours at a time, and even opened her refrigerator to devour the contents within, for years before finally calming down.

He ate her brand-new Birkenstocks. She came home one evening and knew instantly. Only one of her cream sandals sat on the chair where she'd left them. And when Lovely loped up, chewing on something, she pried his jaws apart, found a scrap of cream leather and a buckle with the word BIRK on it, and screamed before bursting into tears.

The point was: She hadn't wanted a dog. And when she asked Wilson to a movie one spring night years later, when she was feeling hopeful or bored or whatever it was she'd been feeling, she hadn't wanted a husband. Or maybe she had, but only in a dreamy, stupid, and naïve way, and that didn't count.

She'd never been able to say no. If something that seemed good came her way, like a puppy, or a cute needy guy, how could she? When there was so much bad out there, shouldn't you just grab all the good you could get, even if you didn't really want or need it in the first place?

Maybe she needed to rethink her philosophy.

She forced herself to look in the mirror, to smile. "I'm so happy for you," she said brightly. "So happy." It was OK. Her face was still nice: narrow blue eyes, ears that stuck out, pretty white teeth. It was the face she was used to—it was Katie. Her long red hair was OK, although it was thinner than it used to be, and it definitely needed a wash. She inched her vision down to her breasts and took a deep breath.

*You've been nursing for four years straight*, she sternly reminded herself. Rose wrestled with the breasts like a wildcat, pinching the nipples, biting, pulling them this way and that. Her latest trick was to stand in Katie's lap, clutch the breast in both hands, and hang as she nursed.

There they were. *No stretch marks*, she pointed out. They were pale and laced with blue veins, and she cupped them in her hands, lifting them. She let go. *Large, pendulous, sagging*, hissed the voice, no longer nice. Her eyes filled with tears. She pinched the fat on her stomach and turned the shower on hot. After a moment, steam had fogged the mirror, and she had disappeared.

# Five

## Wilson

Huddled in his dingy office in the women's studies department, eating a Polish sausage from the student union, Wilson thought of how nice it would be to have sex with Katie that night. Not *fuck*—he'd never been comfortable with the word. It made him think of some sort of gymnastic feat he wasn't quite up to. And certainly not *make love*, a phrase that implied an enormous emotional commitment, complete with talking and shared secrets and tears and promises, as well as cuddling afterward. Making love sounded even more exhausting than fucking. What he wanted was to have sex with his wife, to *do it*—nothing solemn, nothing fancy—just sex. And then they could part friends. She could take a bath, and he could stand alone on the porch in his boots and shorts, smoking in the frigid night.

In fact, there in the grimy office would be better. They would have to hurry—that was definitely a plus. Katie could sit on the cluttered desk he shared with the other part-time instructors, and he could spread her long legs, burying his face between them. But only for a second because they had to hurry. *Sorry*, he'd whisper in his sexiest voice. *We just don't have time for you, but I promise, later . . .* And then he'd slide it in, no condom (thank God for the vasectomy), only hurrying, blessed hurrying.

He would have to go about things carefully. There was a certain protocol to getting Katie into bed—be nice, don't piss her off, catch her off guard—and he would have to follow it to the letter. He gulped his Coke, then crumpled his greasy napkin and heaved it in the direction of the overflowing trash can. There would be no room for a misstep. From the moment he plowed his car into the driveway, over the mountain of snow left by the bastard of a snowplow driver, he must proceed with the utmost caution.

He flipped open his notebook, filled with notes for his dissertation, and scribbled the word *wife*. After a moment, he added a question mark. He gazed up at the tattered poster of Elizabeth Cady Stanton and Susan B. Anthony on the pee-colored wall. Imagine being married to one of those two. As obnoxious as Katie was, at least she was pretty. Old Elizabeth, with her white dollop of hair and overflowing skirts, looked like a fat and pampered Persian cat—the kind that bit your hand when you petted it. Susan B., sleeker and darker, reminded him of a battle-scarred alley cat, one you'd find skittering out from beneath your car on a cold fall morning, sporting one chewed ear and half a stumpy tail. She, too, looked dangerous.

"Ladies." He nodded at the founding mothers and shoved a pile of purple Take Back the Night flyers to the edge of the desk. He'd forgotten to distribute them to his students that morning. It had been a particularly trying class, and he still hadn't recovered. He'd meant to work on his dissertation all afternoon, but the creative burst he'd felt earlier had been beaten out of him by the students.

Lately, he spent most of his time in his office *not* working on his dissertation. It was relaxing as long as he avoided any thought of the future. Thankfully the overheated office, crammed with towering stacks of student journals, half-eaten lunches, and endless Styrofoam cups half-filled with cold coffee, was deserted, the usual pack of whining students and harried instructors that could make it a most unpleasant place to be, absent. They were so marginalized in women's studies they had just one office for six people.

Not that he gave a shit. It wasn't like he was an actual women's studies scholar. He was an English major, but when he'd come to Midwestern, the English department had been less than enthusiastic about him and had not offered him an assistantship, pawning him off on women's studies instead. Not that he cared. He was the most popular instructor in the department. His class on media and gender—in which he examined in graphic detail racy music videos and pornographic films (it was not for the faint of heart)—was always full.

The students loved him. *Wilson is a genius (and cute)*, they wrote on their evaluations. *Wilson changed my life. I broke up with my boyfriend, quit my job, and now I eat whatever the fuck I want.* And his favorite, by a lone, enlightened football player: *Wilson has balls. Rock on dude.*

He loved to be loved. And it felt good helping young girls see that they were much more than the two-dimensional paper cutouts the media would have them believe they were. Of course, his intro class was a pain in the ass, but what intro class wasn't?

Besides making him feel loved, teaching women's studies was giving him lots of ideas for his dissertation, a creative piece titled *The Lost Journals of Sylvia Plath*. In it, he planned on rewriting, in the voice of Ms. Plath, the last two journals leading up to her suicide, the ones Ted Hughes had destroyed and "lost." Wilson would not just be helping a depressed freshman dealing with the "freshman fifteen" find her voice, he would be giving voice to one of the greatest poets of his time.

"This idea of yours—it's idiotic," his advisor had barked when Wilson presented his abstract.

"Why don't you just do something normal?" Katie had said with a sigh. "Print out all your short stories and call it a dissertation. You could be done with this nonsense in a month."

His biggest critic was the imposing Dr. Gold, the only PhD (besides the director) in women's studies. She'd somehow gotten wind of his topic and had been horrified, shutting the door of the tiny office to interrogate him during one long scary lunch hour.

"I know you creative writers are 'artsy,'" she'd said, making quotation marks with her fingers and arching her brows. "But you do realize you're co-opting the voice of the greatest poet of our time." She knocked back a handful of M&M's from the fat glass jar on her desk. "You, a white male, who knows nothing about women. And to do this after Plath's voice has already been so thoroughly co-opted by Ted Hughes—the man I, and many, hold personally responsible for her death." She narrowed her Cleopatra eyes. "How dare you?" she breathed, taking a lacquered chopstick from her desk and stabbing it into her bun.

"Oh, I dare," he'd said, as inside, he withered beneath her glare.

"Then you are doomed to fail. And you'll bring down upon yourself the wrath of all feminist women."

"So be it," he said bravely, thinking it was highly unlikely that any feminist women, or any women at all for that matter, besides his committee members, would ever read the thing. And he'd already thought of all the reasons he shouldn't rewrite the journals—of course he had, he was always his own fiercest critic. But the more resistance he got, from himself and others, the more determined he was to make it work. Why not? It wasn't nuclear physics, it was writing—*creative* writing. Maybe he didn't know anything about women. But couldn't he learn, through his writing?

In the end, he'd decided to do what any good writer did—he would follow his muse. He, Wilson A. Lavender, would *rock on*.

He picked up his chewed copy of *The Collected Poems of Sylvia Plath*—it had literally been chewed, courtesy of Lovely—and turned to his favorite poem, the one about dying as an art form, a calling. Now *that* he could relate to. It sounded a lot like drinking yourself to death, something he'd worked hard on for most of his life. When he thought about it, there were a lot of similarities between Wilson A. Lavender and Sylvia Plath. They were both tortured geniuses, for one. *Genius*, he wrote. *Explore later.*

He scribbled the lines from "Lady Lazarus" and continued freewriting. *Please let's have sex tonight, Katie. Please let's be quiet. Let's watch TV, no fighting, no screaming kids, no one banging on the bathroom door.* He paused and sucked at his watery Coke, then wrote: *Mr. Lavender is such an evolved male he has no problem begging his wife for sex. He lets her have all the power she needs . . . he can handle it . . . he is truly a man . . . he can handle it, he can handle it . . . he can even handle the fact that she fucked the teenage JERK across the street when she was pregnant with his, MINE . . . MY BABY . . . fuck, fuck, fuck.* He filled the rest of the page with *fucks*, sighed, and turned to the poem he'd copied last week. *The dead woman, the smile . . .* He abruptly shut the notebook. "Edge" made him think of his depressed mother, something to be avoided at all costs.

The fact that Katie still hung out with the guy—that was what got to him. He looked around the desktop for candy, coming up with an old Bit-O-Honey that he tossed in the trash. The jar of M&M's sat temptingly on Dr. Gold's desk, but he was too afraid of her to help himself.

The office was empty because Dr. Gold and Alice Cherry, who normally held office hours at the time, were feuding. Young, hippie Alice, whose trademark fur hat looked to Wilson like a small snarling animal ready to leap at his face, had brought her hyperactive child to the office last Friday, and the kid had spilled hot chocolate all over the older and angrier and less attractive Dr. Gold's books, who was already disgusted that she had to share the office with a bunch of graduate student morons. A bitter, back-handed round of sniping had ensued, and today both women had elected to hold office hours elsewhere, to punish the other with her absence.

Was Katie punishing him? Why wouldn't she sleep with him? She would have plenty of excuses tonight. "I actually do have a headache," she might say. Or, "I feel fat." Sometimes she'd just look at him and groan, "Oh . . . ugh . . . no." How was that supposed to make a guy feel?

She'd be exhausted or emotional—too emotional to be touched. "You don't even have to move," he might cajole. "Just let me do all the work." But that never worked; it only made her angry. Her favorite excuse of late was "I just can't be intimate with someone I've been fighting with since the day we met."


On the windowsill of the women's studies office, Dr. Gold's potted gera-niums grew thick and fleshy, their blossoms prim balls of pink and white confetti. Wilson looked up from his notebook, surprised. He'd been scrib-bling the details of his and Katie's "courtship" for nearly an hour. He leaned back in his chair, satisfied. Writing about the hellish past always put him in a festive mood, as if he'd just graduated from high school and knew that, no matter what, he'd never have to go back there again. Things were infinitely better than they'd been when Katie was pregnant with Paul, when in his deepest despair, he'd seriously considered drinking and instead phoned his dad, who gave him the generic advice to "be a man," then asked how his car was running.

As the birth of his son neared, he and Katie slowly came back together. Paul was born, and then Rose appeared, surprisingly, as if a fat, smiling cherub had one day fallen out of the sky and into their home. Katie agreed to marry him. And if he still sometimes felt as if he'd been jumped into a gang he'd never had any intention of joining, he also knew Katie was his best friend. He couldn't imagine life without her.

Or maybe he could, but who would care for the kids?

He slipped his notebook into his backpack. Forget the dissertation—he had seduction on his mind. He'd go home and once inside the pink shell, proceed with caution. He'd make a nice dinner (Katie's gluey vegetarian dishes were stunningly bad) and let her take her bath while he got the kids into bed, being extra patient during the last hour before bedtime when they all went apeshit.

He'd read Jake a chapter from *The Wonderful Flight to the Mushroom Planet*, settle Paul in the big bed with his picture books and lullaby CD, and rock Rose to sleep in the baby sling. He smiled thinking of his little girl, the way she peered from the sling like an alien. She was subdued as soon as he curled her into it. At first the thing was embarrassing—it was so effeminate—but after several horrifying babysitting episodes during which Rose screamed so hysterically and for so long he joked that they'd have to take her to the psych ward, he grew to love it. He liked the feel of her warm weight against his chest. Her face was a small moon, pink and luminous, and he'd curl around her on the couch, the soft whisper of her breath soothing him, his heartbeat her lullaby.

But enough sappiness. The kids would be dispatched with the precision of a military maneuver. Swiftly, firmly: He would take no prisoners. Then, the *pièce de résistance*. He dug in his wallet looking for cash. He'd buy a large dog biscuit on the way home, and after the kids were in bed, he'd present it to Lovely with a flourish, looking like such a giddy dog lover Katie couldn't help but want to sleep with him.

It wasn't that he didn't care for Lovely. It was just that Katie pushed the damn dog on him so insistently. "All you have to do is love him," she'd say. "Just ignore it when he spreads coffee grounds from the trash all over the living room floor. They're *your* coffee grounds, you know you're supposed to take them to the outside garbage, and besides, he's old, he doesn't know what he's doing. Do you want someone judging you when you're old and senile and mowing the sidewalk in your underpants?"

Katie's "encouragement" gave him the perverse urge to push back, to be gruff with Lovely and withhold his steak scraps, to nudge him off the bed, and pet him only perfunctorily. But tonight, Katie and Lovely would both be pleased.

He dug in his pocket, finding seven cents. How much did a dog biscuit cost? He figured he needed at least a dollar—he wanted to buy a deluxe Lovely-worthy biscuit, guaranteed to get him laid. A search of his other pocket produced a toy lipstick and a baby sock, gifts from Rose, but no money. Katie had his debit card—she always had his debit card—and he'd misplaced his checkbook a week ago. "Fuck," he whispered. He didn't want to stop at the bank and figure out how to withdraw money without a bank card or a check. Money matters made him nervous. He wanted to go home and set his plan in motion. Not a single misstep. The biscuit, Lovely, the *pièce de résistance*.

He looked around for change. There were two desks in the office. Dr. Gold had her own, and the rest of the instructors shared the small one with no drawers. In Dr. Gold territory—airspace strictly forbidden, which was why the Alice Cherry/hot chocolate incident had been so serious—next to the jar of M&M's and stuck between a bag of Fritos and a half-empty bottle of Snapple, was a crumpled dollar bill. It was nearly buried in clutter, for despite her quick wit and scathing intelligence, Dr. Gold was a slob. She never would have noticed the hot chocolate Alice Cherry's son spilled on her books if another instructor hadn't narked.

Wilson turned his back on the stern gazes of Elizabeth Cady Stanton and Susan B. Anthony, reached out and pocketed the bill. Feeling brave, he grabbed a handful of M&M's and flung them into his mouth. When he turned to go, Dr. Gold was standing in the doorway watching him. He jumped, nearly choking on the candy.

Gloria Gold, PhD, was an immaculately groomed woman with a sleek black bun, red lips, and dramatic eyeliner. She was also a "woman of size," outweighing Wilson by at least a hundred pounds. Today, she wore a necklace of what looked like enormous yellowed teeth—*man teeth*, Wilson thought—and in her bun she'd stuck a jeweled cat comb. As he stared, the cat's ruby eyes caught the light and blinked.

"Wow, what is that, a cheetah?" he asked, pretending he hadn't just taken money from her desk.

Dr. Gold ignored him. "I've learned something about you," she said, scooting around him—no easy thing in the tiny office—and dumping a slippery stack of student collages onto a chair in the corner. "You not only steal the voice of great poets, you steal cash, too." She sank into her swivel chair, the only good chair in the office. "And it's a tiger. Cheetahs have completely different spots."

A collage slid to the ground, and Wilson inspected it, too embarrassed to look up. On a hot pink background, a student had glued a bright areola of female body parts cut from magazine ads—breasts, legs, and juicy open-mouthed smiles. In the middle was a spidery blob of metallic gold ink. He bent closer and saw that the blob was actually a word: FEEL. He wasn't sure he got it, but it was depressing, in a way, all the happy parts with no center to hold them. And it was just abstract enough—which he always wrongly equated with depth—to earn a good grade from him.

"Dr. Gold." He didn't know what to say. He turned and held out the dollar bill.

"Gloria," she said, looking as if she were enjoying watching him squirm.

"Gloria. Dr. Gold. I'm sorry." He forced himself to sound confident. Honesty always made people happy—he'd charm her, make her laugh. "I needed a dollar because I wanted to sleep with my wife." As soon as the words were out of his mouth, he took a step back, horrified. What was wrong with him? Had he no sense at all? He tried to smile but could only manage a grimace, like a frightened dog.

"She certainly sells herself cheap." Dr. Gold waved away the bill, an amused look on her face, and turned to a stack of papers on her desk.

Wilson sighed, relieved. Dr. Gold didn't give a shit about him or anything he might do in the office—of course she didn't, why would she? He slipped the bill into his pocket, his plan back on track. "I heard about your books," he said, pausing at the door. "That's so messed up."

"Oh yes." Dr. Gold set down her pencil, her eyes lighting up. "Alice Cherry." She lingered on her colleague's name, her voice dripping with sarcasm. Despite her size, Dr. Gold was pretty in an intense way. She frightened Wilson, and was much too smart for his comfort, but she had a face like a china doll (albeit a manic one) and small, graceful hands.

"Your poor books," he said again. What was he doing riling her up? He never got involved in office politics. But he felt as if he owed her something, and if there was one thing Gloria Gold liked, it was gossip.

"I know," she said. "Alice Cherry's beast did two hundred dollars damage. Some books, like my signed copy of *Cunt*, are irreplaceable. If you're going to bring your monster into the office, control him. That's all I ask." Childless by choice, Dr. Gold opened the bag of Fritos on her desk, the smell of corn chips filling the room.

"Alice had him in the library the other day, and it was like she'd unleashed a wild chimpanzee. The kid was screaming, pounding on the computer keyboards, flinging scratch paper everywhere." As Wilson spoke, part of him stood back, observing his cattiness. What was he doing? Had Alice Cherry, with her leaping fur hat, gotten under his skin? She *was* pretty. And she *did* soundly ignore him whenever their paths crossed. "Alice Cherry is just so . . . so . . ." He paused, searching for the right word. "So completely without boundaries." He looked away, disgusted with himself.

"That's it exactly." Dr. Gold opened the bottle of Snapple and sniffed it. "And as you know, cute doesn't work when you're forty. At some point in her life Ms. Alice Cherry is going to have to develop a personality. Those perky little tits will sag and that ass will spread, you mark my words."

"Well . . ." Wilson picked up his backpack, unable to continue his descent into bitchiness. "I have no more words." He turned and walked out the door, Dr. Gold's musical laugh chiming after him.

As he hurried down the long, murky hallway, the tall windows at the end glowing a dull yellow, he thought of Alice Cherry's "perky little tits." She never wore a bra, he'd noticed. Maybe he should have pointed that out to Dr. Gold. He clutched his biscuit money in his fist, so sick of school, and of himself, and so happy to be going home, he felt like weeping.

# Six

### Katie

After her shower, Katie wound her wet hair into two knots on either side of her head. She found clean maternity underwear on the floor of her closet, a tie-dyed T-shirt she hadn't worn in a few days, and of course, her pink, bleach-spotted sweatpants. She knew she'd have to go without them soon, if only to wash them, but not yet—they were warm and comforting, and she needed them. And since she couldn't stand anything tight, anything touching her waist, that ruled out all of her other clothes. One optimistic afternoon last fall, she'd gone to the mall and bought two pairs of the new low-rider jeans, but soon realized that every time she bent over, she exposed half her ass, not a good thing for a mom. She immediately reverted to her sweats.

The women in Katie's family were not known for their fashion sense. Iris still wore the same faded orange Wheaties sweatshirt she'd worn in the '70s, and when January was small, she'd dressed herself in whatever clothes she found on the bedroom floor: ragged green dungarees with torn knees, a summer dress trimmed with rickrack, various Underoos bottoms and tops, an unraveling yarn sweater, and on top of everything, her precious bunny jacket, yellowed and balding. She'd spent her entire kindergarten year looking like a bundle of rags. Iris and January laughed about it now, but it bothered Katie. She'd found January's school picture in her parents' garage a couple of years ago, and was saddened by how scruffy her sister looked. She was always careful to dress her kids nicely.

"Try," she told herself, looking in the bathroom mirror, the movie star bulbs making her skin glow pink. "Hooray that Steven's getting married. He'll be married. I'm married. Everybody's happy." In Rose's bottom drawer, beneath a tangle of baby tights, she found the silk carnation clips she'd bought at the Saturday market in Portland the summer before. She fastened them in her hair, a purple blossom in each knot, and put on lipstick before going into the living room to tear Rose and Paul away from the TV for lunch.

The kids picked at their sandwiches, full up on M&M's. They were so close in age and size they looked like twins, Paul a bit thinner, his sister more robust. Rose rubbed her peanut-buttery hands in her hair before dumping her water onto the table, climbing down from her chair, and wandering into the bedroom. Paul opened his sandwich and wiped jelly on the wall.

"Wonderful," Katie cried. "So creative."

After washing their screaming faces, she put Rose down for a nap, set up Paul with Tinkertoys, and threw herself into the daily whirlwind of dishes and laundry, sweeping, dusting, and vacuuming up endless amounts of dog hair, as well as cleaning pee off the floor around the toilets, courtesy of Jake's freestyling friends. Was it OK to tell neighborhood kids they couldn't use her bathroom? She wiped hand and nose prints from the windows and pulled a hunk of yesterday's frozen pizza out from beneath the couch cushions.

"Did you put this here?" she asked Paul. He nodded, brandishing a Tinkertoy weapon.

Katie was always surprised at how much she loved her children, their sweet animal joy, their ferocious shouts and tiny hands. She could remember as a kid loving her dog in the same tender way. Cinnamon was an itchy, stinky mutt that she'd coax into her bed at night until his snuffling and chewing and smell overwhelmed her and she had to shove him out with her foot. But that love had been careless, and came and went, unlike her love for her kids, which seemed as if it would never fade.

Jake, her firstborn, was a beautiful baby, fat and dark-skinned, his hair standing up like a handful of black feathers, his eyes like shards of sparkling green glass. His dad, Anthony, who'd long since disappeared into a world of drum circles and Rainbow Gatherings, used to put Jake in the backpack and ride with him on his bike along the sandy flats of the Rio Grande, the river black, Lovely racing behind, ears flapping happily, the whole sky a glorious mess of pinks and purples and reds. Katie loved that she and Jake and even Lovely carried this desert world inside—the crumbling adobe houses, the pink sand and enormous skies, the witch's cemetery in Old Mesilla and the Organ Mountains so naked and jagged and ugly—a world so different from western Michigan with its long, gray, endless, depressing winters.

Paul was a Michigander, she guessed, and the opposite of Jake, pale and small. With his huge blue eyes, neat features, and corn floss hair, he was ethereal. Katie suspected he'd be too smart for his own good, like his father. He could already "read" several books and write his alphabet letters. He knew his left from his right, and laughed in an ironic, knowing way (just like his dad) when Katie did things like call the *vacuum* the *stroller* (a common symptom of sleep deprivation). He was sensitive and didn't like crowds. Everything was too loud.

"Vigorous and friendly," Rose's pediatrician wrote when describing her. She was Katie's treasure, so pretty and delicate, her little girl after two boys. She ran like a girl, her hands flapping in the air, and waved like a tiny beauty queen. She adored her dad and flirted shamelessly, howling with joy every time he once again walked in the front door, even if he'd only stepped outside to smoke.

At 4:00, Jake arrived home, and chaos reigned in the tiny condo. Rose woke from her nap and stood in the bedroom, banging on the closed door, waiting for someone to rescue her. In the living room, Paul pulled fluff from the ripped couch cushion until Katie caught him, told him to pick it up, and he refused. The washing machine chugged, the dishwasher roared. A female "doctor" on the radio made snide comments to her callers until Katie switched it off, unable to take another second. She liberated Rose from the bedroom, put on a George Harrison CD, and gave everyone orders to dance. They happily complied.

Whirling into the kitchen to "My Sweet Lord," Rose laughing in her arms, she set the baby on the counter with a handful of Cheerios and went to work peeling a blood orange. The afternoon was turning out well, everything flowing nicely. All she had to do, she realized, was focus on her life, on her kids and Wilson, and let Steven go. How could she care that he was marrying when she had so many blessings of her own?

Some days were miserable. Maybe that was why she liked flirting with Steven. Nothing had happened since before Paul was born, meaning no intercourse, but there was always that edge, and it felt good. It was like chocolate, a harmless addiction, and it helped her get through the difficult days, the days when nobody got along, nobody minded: Jake teased, Paul screamed, and Rose wouldn't let Katie put her down for a second. On those days, she was in tears by the time Wilson arrived home, and if she'd lost her temper and yelled, which of course she had, she felt guilty, too, knowing she was a horrible mother and the kids would all end up drug addicts by the time they were twenty.

"Maybe you'll end up a drug addict," Wilson would say, a gleam in his eye. "Doesn't that sound nice?"

"Mom, you have to feed the dog," Jake said. "He's starving, can't you see?" Katie put the orange peel with its purple-spotted insides on the bar and arranged her Jesus and Mary votives around it. She looked at the dog. Lovely stood in the kitchen, head bent, staring into his empty bowl.

"He's either starving or senile." She lifted Rose off the counter, shooed her into the living room, and grabbed the bag of dog food from the garage. "Poor doggy, poor neglected guy." Lovely ignored her, his nose in his bowl, every muscle in his body tensed, alert for incoming food.

Katie's first thought was, *Why is the dog food moving?*

Then she screamed. "Oh Jesus, oh fuck." As the dog food poured from the bag, mice—two, maybe ten—flew along with it, clearing Lovely's head, landing on the edge of the bowl, and skittering beneath the refrigerator.

"Fuck. Oh, kids. Oh, fuck. Mice," she yelled. She couldn't control herself—she'd had a rodent phobia for years, ever since her gerbils ate each other when she was nine—and before she knew what she was doing, she was up on the kitchen counter, hollering, just like a fat lady in a cartoon.

The kids stared. Jake giggled, Paul looked shocked, and Rose squealed, lifting her arms so that she, too, could be part of the fun.

"Go get Steven," she ordered. Who else was going to help? Wilson would laugh if she asked him to come home for mice. Jake scrambled into his boots and out the front door. Lovely, unfazed, wolfed down his food. Katie couldn't quit replaying the horrible event in her mind—*Why is the dog food moving?* The flying dark bodies. The awful skittering. Gathering up her courage, she leapt from the counter, scooped up the kids, shoved her feet into her own boots, and ran outside.

They'd have to move. She couldn't stay there. Mice—what was next? Rats? They'd get a hotel room, and tomorrow Wilson could pack their things while she found them another place to live.

Steven appeared on his porch, holding a dustpan and broom, Jake at his heels, waving an enormous yellow flashlight.

"Oh my God, get them out," she called. "Don't kill them. Just catch them and take them out to the field, only don't bring them near me." She'd never be able to go back in. Her safe pink home of a moment earlier was gone. Who knew how many mice there were, or when they'd appear next. Would they scamper over her as she slept? Crawl into her mouth? There was no end to the things they might do. Life as she knew it was over. She'd find one in the box of Cheerios, a soft hot pulsing body brushing against her finger. They'd nibble her toes at night. Bite a hole in her carotid artery as she slept. Hadn't that happened to Gloria Steinem as a kid? Wasn't it in her book? No, they were rats, Katie remembered, and a new wave of revulsion shook her body.

"Katie, you're insane," Steven said, jogging across the street. "They're just mice."

"Yeah, Mom. Calm down." Jake swung his flashlight officiously, his green eyes bright. "You're scaring the kids."

Paul and Rose hung from her arms, their turtlenecks pulled up over their bellies, their faces flushed and excited. They hardly looked scared. The sky hung low and gray, and the world seemed dismal, a black and white mess of dirty snow and sticklike trees.

"I have a phobia," Katie said, trying not to shout. "It's on record. I was in the small-rodent-phobia study at the university. The professor said I was the worst case he'd ever seen."

"The small-rodent-phobia study." Steven laughed, imitating her sputtering tone. "Only you would be in a small-rodent-phobia study." He looked sleepy and sexy in his scuffed brown corduroy slippers and plaid flannel pajama pants. Katie noticed his baseball jersey was on inside out and backward.

"It was fun," she said, remembering how she'd sat in the tiny office in the psychology department, electrodes stuck to her chest, the professor, a skinny man with white fluffy hair, reading mouse-related words off flash cards in a solemn tone.

"I'm going to bring in a real mouse now, Katie," he'd said, carefully searching her eyes for her reaction.

"Yikes," she'd said with a smile. The whole process was like a seduction, all the talk—*small, gray, darting, squeaking*—mere foreplay leading up to the main event, the presentation of the rodent. She'd felt more special than she had in years, like a goddess, awaiting a sacrificial offering.

"Wait in my house," Steven ordered, and Katie felt a thrill at his firm tone. *I let you go with love*, she affirmed silently. But he was so rumpled and calm, she had the urge to set down the kids and make out with him right there in the snow. She turned to go, chanting in her mind, *I let you go, I let you go*, a wiggling, sock-footed child under each arm.

"Hey, Katie?"

"What? Did you want to ridicule me more for my participation in important scientific studies?"

"Well, what exactly was the purpose of the study?"

"To see if some people truly freak out at the sight or even the mere mention of mice. Like me."

"But didn't we already know that?" Steven moved closer and touched the flowers in her hair. "These are cute," he said softly. "You look like a Polynesian princess."

Katie leaned into him, and when he moved closer, she let her lips touch his neck. He rested his hands briefly on her hips, his breath warm against her cheek. "I hate you, you're leaving me," she teased, feeling better.


Steven's fiancée curled like a cat on his enormous blue velvet couch, wearing jogging shorts and a tight T-shirt, her pale face glowing, as if she'd just had great sex. Katie thought of Steven's backward jersey and languid mood and realized she probably had. The kids wriggled free from her arms, and she sank into the green corduroy love seat, embarrassed. Why hadn't he told her Lucy was here?

"Mice," she said, nodding in the direction of her house.

Lucy snorted and set down her can of Coke. "I don't know what Steven's going to do about any mice." The house was warm, warmer than Katie's place, and the shades were tightly drawn. Cartoons moved silently on the TV. Steven's home brewery bubbled in the bedroom, and the condo was filled with the yeasty smell of hops.

"What do you mean?" It was odd being in Steven's murky, gurgling home with just Lucy there. She felt disoriented, as if she were trying to find her bearings underwater. Lucy belonged, she didn't—she was just the neighbor lady from across the street, washed up into the middle of their quiet afternoon.

"He can't do anything unless his mom's holding his hand." Lucy blew a strand of hair from her eyes. Everything about her was subtle: her arms, her breasts, her curved hips and shapely legs. Her features were regular, her eyes round and blue, her blunt-cut hair a clean ash blond. Even her personality was plain, or maybe devoid of emotion was more like it. Katie had never seen her act nervous or awkward like most other human beings. It was disconcerting, and made her feel enormous and hysterical. "He's a total mama's boy." Lucy shook her head, smiling affectionately.

*I bet you won't think it's so cute five years from now,* Katie thought, smiling back.

"His mom wants him to go to beauty school," Lucy continued. "So he can work with her at the salon. Is that the gayest thing you've heard or what?"

"Not all male hairdressers are gay," Katie pointed out. "And Steven seems to be pretty straight."

"Well, *yeah.* But I'm not going to be married to a male hairdresser." Lucy pouted prettily, and Katie had the urge to slap her. They'd only met a few times, but Lucy irritated her. She was perfect, and perfectly confident—an annoying combination.

"I don't think you need to worry," Katie said. "The only thing Steven is interested in when it comes to hair is the way it rots."

"What? Gross. Hair doesn't rot. It's dead."

"Really? I thought . . ." Katie was confused. "Anyway. Lucy, you have it good. They say you can tell how a guy will treat you by how he feels about his mom. And Steven adores his mother, so—"

"I don't give a shit about his mom." Lucy dismissed Katie's theory with a wave of her hand. Her engagement ring caught a stray beam of light, flinging a spray of rainbows across the wall. "It's Steven. He's a big baby. Maybe I'm making a huge mistake. He can't even sleep unless he has some part of me in his mouth." She stretched out her legs. Her toes were long, like a velociraptor's.

"What do you mean?" Katie was nervous, unsure why Lucy was confiding in her. Was it some sort of trap? "You mean like your fingers?"

"No." Lucy coyly smoothed the silver chain around her ankle.

"Your toes?"

"No."

Katie looked at her, expectant.

Lucy smiled back, adorable.

"My T-shirt," she finally said, sitting up to demonstrate. "He needs my sleeve, or the tail of my shirt—the one I'm wearing to bed—in his mouth in order to fall asleep. For security."

"Wow. That is babyish." Katie smiled, relieved. There was more to Steven than she knew.

"No. It's infantile is what it is." Lucy raised her eyebrow in a faux-intellectual way—a twenty-three-year-old college girl convinced she knew everything.

Rose and Paul, finished with pulling all of Steven's cigar and girly magazines off the coffee table, turned and ran into Abby's room to inspect her toys, sending Abby into a meltdown. "Get them out of here," she screamed, throwing what sounded like books against her bedroom door. Lucy rolled her eyes, ignoring her soon-to-be stepdaughter. She looked at Katie and mouthed the words *Fucking. Brat.*

*I like you better already,* Katie thought, drawing her legs up onto the love seat. She'd often thought the same about Steven's poor daughter. "You know, I have the opposite problem," she said, "with my husband. Wilson hates his mom, so sometimes I think that, because I'm a mom, he takes it out on me. Like I trigger things . . . or something."

"Wow. Weird." Lucy lifted her T-shirt and inspected her stomach, flicking the small silver hoop in her belly button. Katie watched, waiting for her to speak, but Lucy had obviously decided not to pursue the topic. "Hey." Lucy perked up, pulling down her T-shirt. "Why doesn't Steven like Wilson?"

"I think they like each other fine."

"No they don't. Steven calls him 'that skinny bastard.' He's always saying what a jerk your husband is."

"I don't know. I just . . . Lucy . . . I think they like each other fine." Katie tried to make her voice firm. Wouldn't most people think it rude to tell someone their husband was an ass? She inspected her hands. They were definitely aging, the skin wrinkled and sun-worn. If she and Lucy were apples, Lucy would be hanging ripe on the tree, while Katie lay in the grass below, rotting. *You are not eighty years old*, she told herself fiercely. *Be confident, for God's sake.*

"If you don't want to tell me . . ." Lucy got up and walked into the kitchen, throwing a bag of popcorn into the microwave. "Ever since I got engaged, I've been starving," she called happily.

"That's excellent. It's good to be hungry." Katie sighed. Where the hell was Steven? She was tense and hungry, too—sick actually, as she hadn't had anything to eat since her latte and a few handfuls of M&M's that morning.

"I don't like these kids bugging me," Abby warned loudly from the bedroom. Lucy ignored her, busy with her popcorn. She poured it into a bowl and stuffed a handful in her mouth, then turned and made claw-hands at Abby's bedroom door.

*Poor Abby*, Katie thought, *your future looks bleak*. She watched Lucy eat like a hungry horse. It was her plainness that made her pretty. Her skin was like pale, luminous wax, accentuating the clear blue of her eyes, the subtle blond of her hair. Even her engagement ring was understated, a small sparkling solitaire on a narrow band that set off her small hands.

"Congratulations," Katie said, looking down at her own ring, the diamonds cold and blue in their art-deco setting. "I'm so happy for you—" A blast of icy air filled the room, and Steven and Jake stomped in the front door.

"We know there were mice," Steven began.

"Of course you do. Katie told you." Lucy opened another can of Coke. Soda fizzed onto her hand, and she flung it into the sink. "Did you think she was making it up?"

"No. I'm just saying, when we were in the kitchen, Jake—"

"I saw them, Mom." Jake jumped up and down, holding his crotch. "They were behind the refrigerator, and when Steven kicked it, they ran across the floor, just like little rats. I could see their little legs and their little feet and their little pointy noses, and they ran into that hole underneath the cabinets, which means they're probably going to live there forever."

"I am going to barf." Katie's depression returned with a vengeance. She asked her son if he had to pee, but he shook his head. She turned to Steven. "So you didn't catch them and take them out to the field?"

"It's not that easy," he said. "It's not like they're going to march right up and surrender."

"Mice don't surrender, Mom."

Lucy laughed, back on the couch, her feet tucked beneath a big blue cushion. "They're just mice, Katie. They're a lot more afraid of you than you are of them."

"Thanks, Lucy. But somehow I don't think that's possible."

"We're infested, Mom, Steven said—"

"Jakey. Go see what Abby's up to." Steven set down his dustpan and rested his hand on Katie's shoulder. "You're not infested," he said, grinning sheepishly. "I was just trying to rile him up. You've got two mice, and you'll probably never see them again." He idly played with her flowers. "Or else, if you want, I can set some traps."

"No. So I can hear them dying horrible deaths in the middle of the night? No thanks." She rested her hand on his, looking up at his calm, brown eyes. He was so sexy. Maybe it would be OK, like he said. Maybe the mice had already found their way outside and were off in their own micey world as she spoke, never to return. "Hey, you kicked my refrigerator," she said softly.

"Sorry." His voice was husky. "I was getting into it."

"You talk like you're lovers." Lucy stretched out long on the couch, her pale body floating against the blue velvet.

"Oh no." Katie shook her head, embarrassed. She moved away from Steven, turning her attention to *Scooby-Doo* on the TV.

"I don't think so," Steven said, annoyed. "It's called being friends, Lucy."

Lucy laughed. "I'm kidding." She wiggled her long toes. "Don't get excited."

Home again, Katie stood in the middle of the kitchen, her heart racing, wishing the solemn professor with the fluffy white hair were standing beside her, observing her with his dispassionate, yet oddly comforting, gaze. She forced herself to stand still as she spoke to the mice. "I'm not going to kill you or poison you or even trap you," she said. "As long as you promise to never, ever, ever show yourselves again. Eat all the dog food you want, I don't care, just don't let me see you or hear you again." She turned up the heat, walked into her room, and flopped on the bed, the kids jumping merrily all around her, everyone waiting for Daddy to come home.

### Katie
1973

I know nothing. That's my new mantra. I think I'll just let go and drift awhile, like Benjamin in *The Graduate*.

I caught on fire once, when I was eight, the night of the Renaissance Fair. We sat on the hill behind Reed, me and my mom and January, watching fireworks explode over the river like fiery flowers. The sky filled with pink and gold and blue droplets of light, starburst dahlias and fat expanding camellias. The air on the ground was thick with yellow smoke. Bottle rockets hissed, Chinese spinning lotuses screamed. A fury of firecrackers filled my ears, leaving them hollow and ringing.

His name was Larry Johnson.

"You're welcome to join us," Iris said. "There's plenty of room on the blanket."

January liked him. As soon as he sat down that night, so big and awkward in his leather hide, like a cow come to tea, she crawled onto his lap. I leaned against our mother on the old orange beach blanket, sleepy and happy, sand from the beach gritty beneath my bare thighs. A radio was playing, scratchy in the dark. "Come down off your throne and leave your body alone."

I wanted him to like me, but I was too shy to talk, and I looked down, making my fingers into pinchers, the way I did when I was nervous. Sipping my orange soda, fireworks dancing overhead, I sneaked a look. He was jiggling January on his knee. She laughed, happy. What was wrong with me that he didn't want to sit me on his lap and jiggle me? It was because I was grubby and grouchy, I knew. I never minded my mom. I was naughty because it was fun. My ears stuck out like a chimpanzee's.

He looked like the doctor on *Medical Center*. After watching my favorite TV show, I sometimes dreamed about sitting on the cute doctor's lap and hugging him. I daydreamed about Elton John, too, so exciting with his pig shave and glittery platform shoes. I'd sit in the old green rocker, my dad's puffy black headphones clasping my ears, and listen to *Goodbye Yellow Brick Road* for hours.

"She might get scared," I warned Larry Johnson. I casually held my hands over my sticky-out ears. It was a lie—January loved fireworks and sat in a happy trance, staring up at the sky, squealing happily.

"And what about you, Katie. Katydid. Do you ever get scared?" His voice was merry. I blushed and looked down, inspecting my toes.

What an odd question to ask a child. And what did I tell him? Maybe I said never. That would have been the truth. I only remember a hot feeling washing over me, as if a firework had sunk into my body and was exploding somewhere deep inside. I remember smiling brown eyes, filled with the attention I craved. He'd laughed then, his teeth big and white.

I thought of my dad, home watching TV. He never asked me questions. He left me alone. When I was small, I used to go with him to mail his letters at the post office in Sellwood, but that stopped. "Go with your dad," my mother urged. "You're going to hurt Daddy's feelings if you don't." I didn't, and he lost interest.

The fireworks were almost over, the sky filled with liquid color, expanding, exploding, trickling away. My mom put her arm around me. I moved away, turning to Larry Johnson.

"If my sister's bugging you, I can take her," I said. But January was nearly asleep by then, her nose chapped, her fists curled into her chest the way they did when she was tired.

Along with her macramé necklaces, our mother had brought sand candles to sell, setting them on a crate beside her table. She'd lighted a few before the fireworks began, and their flames stretched long in the night, throwing our shadows across the blanket. Larry Johnson's was enormous, shaggy. To be rescued by someone larger and warmer than yourself—that was my fantasy. I hugged my knees to my chest. Someone like a dad, someone who thought you were neat.

We'd made the sand candles at the beach, collecting coffee cans of cold wet sand at Haystack Rock. The rock was thick with flowery anemones, their purple fleshy bodies closing up tight if you dared touch their wet centers. We watched as our mom poured hot wax into the sand, a few amber drops of vanilla oil added to make it smell nice. The wax was dark green, dark orange, dark yellow—deep, rich colors. We balanced the wicks in the middle of the candles with Popsicle sticks. Later, we dug the candles out, soft and warm and fragrant—interesting sand creatures with little sand feet.

"You're on fire." Larry Johnson nodded at me. He said it casually, the same way he'd say, "You're a little girl," or "You weigh sixty-five pounds."

I smiled, thinking he was joking. Then I smelled it. Burning hair is the worst smell, acrid and dead. My long orange ponytail, dry from my days spent floating in the Sellwood pool, practicing to be a mermaid, had dipped into one of the sand candles when I moved. It was on fire.

"Mom," I cried, panicked. I jumped up, and Larry Johnson clapped out the flame between his hands. Charred chunks of hair fell to the blanket.

"Oh my God, Katie." Iris laughed. "What the hell were you doing?"

"I wasn't doing anything. I was sitting." My cheeks were hot and I was shaking. January lay on the blanket where Larry had set her, asleep. She could sleep through anything. Her toes gleamed like tiny stones in the candlelight.

Now, looking back, I see that I'd been touched. That night, my life shifted, closed and turned inward, as smoothly as the sea anemones on Haystack

Rock. The girl I was—Katie, age 8, daughter of Iris and Dan, 775-0277, 7531 SE 31st—left. I had the sensation of something rising from my chest, fluttering away into the night. My stomach was nervous, my legs weak.

Larry Johnson leaned in close, speaking softly so Iris couldn't hear. He smelled of cologne, and beneath that something earthy, the way I imagined a large, hot animal would smell. He wore a gold ring, a lion's head. I'd never seen a man with a fancy ring. My dad smelled clean, like limes. He wore only the thinnest wedding band. I shivered.

"I know you, Katie," Larry Johnson said. "I know you . . ."

# Seven

## Wilson

"Mice," Katie moaned when Wilson found her in the bedroom after work, the funky electronic version of "I'm a Little Teapot" blaring from the boom box. The kids were finger-painting in the kitchen, fighting and laughing and screaming and crying. The carpet was littered with orange goldfish crackers, and Paul had something sticky and red—Jell-O maybe—in his hair.

The condo was uncomfortably warm, but Katie was lying on the bed wrapped in one of her quilts. It was the fancy one made of velvet and bright lightning bolts of silk, the one only she was allowed to touch. Her sister had sent it from New Mexico a couple of years ago, a Christmas present, wrapped in baby shower paper, that arrived in July.

Katie's eyes were puffy and red. She wore flowers in her hair, and he wondered nervously what it could mean. Had he forgotten a special occasion, some secret obscure anniversary, like the first time they went grocery shopping together? He wouldn't say anything, just to be safe. The purple petals fluttered in the breeze from the heating vent. She stared disconsolately at the pink wall that was covered, he noticed, with grubby little footprints. "Oh my God," she cried. "I've still got the heebie-jeebies."

"Heebie-jeebies." He smiled. "I like that you say things like heebie-jeebies." A memory of his mother flickered in his mind. When he was six, she found a mouse in the silverware drawer and went ballistic, sobbing and cursing, forks flying everywhere. It was near Halloween, and she fell into such a deep depression, she was unable to drive him to the five-and-dime for a costume. He went trick-or-treating that year in his everyday clothes, one of his grandmother's scarves tied around his head. Whenever anyone asked, he said he was a kid with cancer. He'd thought it funny at the time, but now, looking back, it seemed disturbed.

"We'll set traps," he said. "The mice are history. Don't worry for a second." He was nervous and wasn't sure why. He was home—what was more natural, more comforting, than that? Most guys waited for this moment all day long. But he only felt a jolt of terror as soon as he opened the front door.

Remembering the deluxe dog biscuit he'd bought on the way home—basted with meat juice for extra eating pleasure—he pulled it from his pocket with a flourish. "Look what I have—" he began. Before he could get the words out, Lovely rounded the corner, leapt into the air, and snatched the biscuit from his hand, swallowing it in a single gulp.

"What was that?" Katie sat up, wiping her nose, alert for the first time that evening. "I hope it wasn't people food. He's itchy. He's been scratching all day. And the vet says—"

"I know what the vet says. I've paid hundreds of dollars to hear what the vet says. It wasn't people food."

"Because he's itchy. He's an itchy dog, Wilson."

"I am aware."

"And he's scooting again."

"He's scooting? God, that is so disgusting."

Katie gave him an accusing look. A boisterous version of "Happy Birthday" bounced off the walls, and loud clapping and stomping came from the kitchen. "He's not scooting for the fun of it. Obviously he needs to." She paused, tears filling her eyes. "And I just feel sick. Horrified. Don't set any traps. I'm not going to lie here and listen to mice dying horrible deaths in the middle of the night. That I could not take."

Wilson knelt down and hugged her, pulling her soft body into his. Fucking mice. Fucking dog. Nothing was easy. His life sometimes felt impossible, as if it required the energy of six men just to keep an even keel. Katie's hair smelled clean, like grape bubblegum, and he nestled his nose into her neck. "I'm sorry I wasn't nice about the scooting," he whispered. She lay limp in his arms, her silence dramatic.

In the kitchen, Paul screamed and Jake giggled. Something large, the size of a jet engine by the sound of it, crashed to the floor. "Oopsies," Jake called, his voice cheerful.

"The Wheels on the Bus" came on. Wilson thought he might scream himself. Who made this horrible, happy music? Could he track them down and strangle them, a high-strung parent acting in self-defense?

He had the urge to fall to the floor, curl into a fetal tuck, and never move again. He wasn't cut out to be a member of a family. He'd failed the first time—his sisters still treated him like the drunken surly bastard he was—and he was failing again. It was the noise, the chaos—he couldn't take it. He'd been home five minutes and was already on the verge of a massive panic attack. Maybe he could go to the ER and get a prescription for Vicodin or Xanax. "They're just too loud," he'd sob before collapsing in a weeping heap. "And they move . . . so fast." If he refused to get up, they might drag him to the psych ward and shoot him full of Thorazine. He sighed. It sounded wonderful.

Rose wandered into the bedroom, singing softly, her hands dancing in the air. She wandered rather than walked, exactly like her mother. Her shirt was off, and her round belly was a bright mess of pink and purple and yellow finger paint.

"Walk with me." Katie wrapped her arms around his neck and pulled him close, whispering in his ear. "Let's go for a good long walk. It'll be fun. I promise."

Out of the corner of his eye, he spotted Rose. She was running, giggling, about to throw her paint-smeared self against his white dress shirt. He tried to lurch away, but Katie held on tight, preventing him from moving. "I'm not letting go until you say yes," she said, laughing. She reached out her long legs, wrapping them around his waist and locking him in. "Kids, come look," she yelled gaily. "Daddy's trapped."

"If you live in the Midwest, you don't walk a dog at night in the dead of winter," Wilson said to Katie. After tending to his ruined shirt and cleaning up the potted plant the kids had hurled off the kitchen counter, he had spent dinnertime outside, smoking and decompressing. He could now watch calmly as his wife rummaged in the coat closet, her bottom in the air. Her sorrow about the mice had disappeared once she'd trapped him, and after releasing him, she'd leapt from the bed in a burst of energy, fixing dinner and cleaning up in record time.

He didn't want to walk, he wanted to put the kids to bed, eat leftover macaroni and cheese, and have sex. But he seemed to have no say in the matter. Katie threw his gloves at his feet. "It's a West Coast thing, walking at night," he said, trying reason, "where it's mild and there's no chance of dying from the elements."

"Elements," she scoffed, tossing him his hat. It was damp and smelled of old snow. "I don't believe a word you're saying. Everybody walks. You're just lazy and making excuses. You never walk."

"I do. I use my feet every single day. I ambulate constantly." He touched her ass, squeezing it, bending his knees to press his dick against her. She sighed and moved away.

"What I'm saying is you don't *walk*. It's a spiritual thing. There's a difference." She shut the closet door, briskly zipped her coat, and clapped her hands once. "I'm ready." She gave him a challenging look.

"I bought Lovely a biscuit," he said, not moving.

"You what?" Katie handed him his coat, impatient.

"A biscuit. A dog biscuit. A fancy one, with meat juice."

"Well, give it to him. Why are you telling me?" She laughed, pushing him out the door.

They left the kids with the neighbor girls, plunking them down in front of the Cartoon Network with juice boxes and a bag of animal crackers. *The Powerpuff Girls*, squeaky heroines with superpowers and big pansy-like eyes, zipped and sputtered on the screen. The children were freshly bathed, wearing matching stretchy yellow pajamas, and they looked adorable, like gymnasts.

"Have fun, get along, be nice," Katie said, kissing them good-bye. The neighbor girl waved from a haze of incense at the dining room table, not looking up from her phone call. Her long frosted hair hung in her face, and her bare feet rested on a snoring and slobbering English bulldog the size of a large medicine ball. The other neighbor girl was in the shower, the radio blasting rap music. Their names were Megan and Mandy, and Wilson had no idea who was who. Not that it mattered. They had cable TV and the kids liked them—what more could you ask for? He spread a beach towel over the small space in Katie's backseat that wasn't taken up by car seats and invited Lovely to jump on in.

"You're sure they're not going to get high around the kids?" he asked as they drove out of the Reserve, past identical snow-heaped homes, the lamps in the yards glowing like oversized fireflies. Colored lights sparkled in the pine trees, and a few chimneys puffed smoke into the night. The neighbor girls were young and pretty and liked to party—he'd often smelled marijuana smoke last fall, drifting from their open windows. They drove a white convertible and were from Texas, which made him nervous for some reason (although not so nervous he felt the need to retrieve his children). "They're not going to blow pot smoke into the kids' ears or anything, are they?"

"What? You're crazy." Katie laughed.

"You know, like jerky guys in high school. This one guy, a total loser—I think he was my best friend—used to blow smoke into his cat's ear to get it high. It was the happiest cat, huge and white, and it used to just melt on top of the TV set, purring blissfully. Did you ever know anyone like that?"

"Anyone who purred blissfully?"

"Yeah."

"No. I mean yes. You make me purr." She winked, making him laugh. "And the girls are nice. Don't worry. Don't be paranoid."

"I loved watching that cat. Spiderman. Isn't that a good name for a cat? It never moved. I can't remember the guy's name at all." The roads were slick, and he stopped at an intersection, lightly tapping the brakes. The traffic light rocked in the wind, staining the snow beneath it pink. "It made me feel so peaceful. Sometimes its paw would dangle down over the screen. We used to watch *The Richard Simmons Show* after school, for some stupid reason. And the cat would wave its tail, back and forth, slowly, like it was underwater. 'Blow it out,' Richard Simmons would say. It was great. We should get a cat."

"No. So it can pee everywhere? No. Not in a million years." Katie smiled, touching his arm. "Where is all this cat love coming from? It's not like you. Are you having an affair with some cat girl or something?"

"A cat girl?"

"Yeah. Like an icky old cat lady, with a million stinky cats and a million cans of stinky cat food all over the place, only younger."

"Hmmm. Now that you mention it." He rubbed his chin and grinned, lowering his eyebrows in a wicked scowl. It was his Stephen King look, and it always cracked her up.

She laughed, delighted. "You look exactly like him."

"Well, Tabby . . ." He hacked, pretending to cough up a hair ball.

Ozzy Osbourne's "Crazy Train" came on the radio. He turned it up loud and lit a cigarette, feeling good, free, like he was back in the eighth grade again, hanging out in his good buddy Victor's bedroom, listening to *Blizzard of Ozz*. He was so stupid then with his big puffy hair and braces, so inno-cent. Mad Max and Conan the Barbarian were his heroes, and everything bad was still to come—the drinking and drugs, the hangovers, the wrecked cars and long nights spent in the county lockup.

He pulled into the gravel parking lot of the old Boy Scout camp with its acres of trails, reached over and rested his hand on Katie's thigh. "Rockin'," he said, banging his head a little.

She giggled. "I remember January going to this concert when she was about ten, and freaking out because Ozzy hung a midget. I think she thought it was real." She hugged Wilson. "Isn't music great? All the happy things."

A grown man hanging a midget in front of thousands of screaming losers waving lighters didn't sound particularly happy, but he hugged her anyway. Her cheeks were cold, and he kissed her once on the lips. She giggled, pushed him away, then kissed him back. It was a momentous occasion. They were alone and free, the kids were off in cartoon heaven, and they were both in a good mood at the same time. He slammed the car door, shrugged his shoulders a bit, and jogged in place, warming up.

• • •

The woods were deep and dark, and he had no idea where he was or where he was going. Enormous black pines crowded the narrow path, hulking and sweeping and rattling like bones. A wan moon hung listlessly overhead, stars like teeth scattered in its wake.

Being lost was a familiar feeling, one he'd had his entire life. When he taught Joyce Carol Oates' "Where Are You Going, Where Have You Been?" to his intro class, he always wanted to say about the alienated teenage protagonist, "Oh, and by the way, class: That's me. Connie is me. I am Connie. Could you tell?"

His intro class hated him because, unlike his media and gender class, he didn't show them dirty movies. His every remark, even the most benign, such as "take out your journals," was met with smirks and giggles and a wild rolling of eyes. It made him depressed and defiant, and he'd taken to eating big messy breakfast burritos in class, or sitting at his desk and staring silently until they squirmed in their seats. It was an unpleasant situation for all, made worse by the 7:30 a.m. meeting time.

Still, he could relate to Connie. He knew that the definition of a narcissist was seeing one's self in everything—at least that was what Katie-the-psychologist said—but so be it. Pretty teenage Connie, who lives a wispy, barely there existence and hates her mother, was Wilson A. Lavender in a nutshell. Connie has a perfect—and perfectly annoying—sister. Wilson had two. The only difference he could see was that, unlike Connie, he was pretty sure he wouldn't end up raped and murdered, as is hinted in the story, by a serial killer with tin cans in his boots.

He watched his wife walk. It was a new Katie, one much different from her usual lazy, sulky self. She moved purposefully, swinging her arms and jutting her hips for maximum aerobic impact. She looked determined and confident, as if she knew exactly where they were going. But he'd known her long enough not to trust appearances.

He looked closer. She wasn't really walking at all—she was trotting. Yes, it was true: He was married to a girl whose idea of fun was trotting through the woods on what had to be the coldest night of the year. That said something about a person. But what? That they were crazy? Ebullient? He wasn't sure, but either way it was annoying.

He tried to trot, too, to give his stride some lift and good cheer, to see how it felt to be Katie, who regularly threatened to form a skipping group like the one she'd read about in *People* magazine, but he immediately stumbled on a tree root and fell, smashing his knee on the ice.

As he tended to his throbbing lower leg, teeth gritted, eyes watering, he remembered that the antagonist in the Oates story was a demon lover, one who, as he told his students (who couldn't have cared less), "marks his intended before consuming them." Hadn't Katie chosen, or marked him, the night of the first phone call?

"I'm so bored," she'd said. Of course she was bored—she hadn't yet found her next victim. And she'd known so much about him: his bad GRE scores, his poor performance in the Twain class, even the fact that he was eating a cheeseburger as they spoke.

The pain in his knee spread upward toward his groin. He began to limp, hoping Katie would notice and take pity on him. She didn't and he stopped. He remembered that the victim of a demon lover must always invite the demon lover in. It wasn't enough that the demon lover choose his intended. Like a picky mother-in-law, it must be made to feel welcome.

"No. Wait. Don't go," Wilson had said, the night of the phone call. Remembering this, he walked faster, excited. Just as young Connie opens her front door to the guy with the cans in his boots, so did Wilson open his door to Katie, who waited patiently on the other side, banged-up and bewitching in her short skirt and ugly shoes, a white-legged, bleeding creature, ready to devour.

It was all becoming perfectly clear. He felt energized, and realized he was practically skipping himself. He bounded up to his wife and smiled. She smiled back, a quizzical look in her eyes. His theory, when he took the time to think it through, had turned out to be correct. Once again, genius prevailed. The question now was: Would he, like Connie, be destroyed by his insatiable need for love?

They walked and walked, and just when he thought Katie had had enough, they walked some more. At this rate, he wouldn't need to walk again for another year. On his only other hike with her, they'd battled their way through a field of neck-high ragweed, trying to get to the blackberries she'd promised were on the other side. "It's an adventure," she shouted. An adventure that ended with Wilson shoving a swamp-soaked Lovely up a muddy slope, the elderly dog scrabbling wildly, flinging sludge in his face.

Wilson felt nervous again and wished he didn't. It was his main problem, he thought, that he couldn't relax and enjoy normal everyday activities like all other people on the planet. He tried, but it seemed to be physically impossible, like trying to think squirrel thoughts when you were clearly a human being.

The snow beneath his feet was frozen solid, and the air felt breakable, like glass. It was far too cold to be out strolling—what on earth had he been thinking? Lovely ran ahead, leaping like a wild dingo. Katie clucked at him to "keep up the pace." She had no idea where they were going—of course she didn't—and they would soon be hopelessly lost.

As he grew colder, his face numb and stiff, his entire body tensed against the wind, his good mood sputtered and went out. He hated walks. Now he remembered why. They were pointless and boring and uncomfortable to the point of being excruciating. His hopes of wooing Katie, or pleasing her, or whatever it was he was doing, vanished. He was exhausted and his knee was killing him. The tensions of the day—the teaching, the weird interlude with Dr. Gold, the biscuit anxiety, the horniness—had finally gotten to him.

And he would never write his dissertation. As he walked, another truth became clear. All he'd done was dink around and read poems and write stupid notes in his stupid notebook, mostly about the fact that Katie had slept with the jerk across the street. Now that would make an interesting topic: *Why My Wife Hates Me* by Wilson A. Lavender, cuckold. He'd make himself a Hamlet-esque character. The goon across the street could be Claudius, and at the end, Wilson would beat his ass in a boxing match.

He smiled, enjoying the image. But that was his problem: He'd much rather imagine his work than actually sit down and do it. He didn't want to write the damn dissertation. An entire book? He didn't even like to get off the couch to find the channel changer. And who cared about the faux musings of a crazy woman in the months before her suicide? Where had he gotten such a lame idea, and why hadn't anyone stopped him from pursuing it?

He walked grimly, mired in doom.

His mother had been disturbed, à la Ms. Plath, often threatening not to kill herself but to move to California. That, of course, was the key to his dissertation. But since he avoided all contact with and thoughts of his mother, he had a problem.

He would quit his program, immediately, first thing Monday morning.

A blast of frigid wind pushed against his back. He sank deeper into his ski coat, stomping his feet. Up ahead, Lovely barked once, a high happy yip, and disappeared around a bend. Katie mumbled something and laughed. He was surrounded by happy creatures—was there anything more depressing? "I can't believe I'm doing this," he grumbled, trying to wiggle his numb toes.

"Just have fun." Katie took his hand. "You were having fun two minutes ago. God, you're a moody motherfucker."

"Thanks. I try. And I am having fun. I'm just finding it hard to breathe in the subzero temperatures." He pulled his hat down over his ears and walked dutifully, careful not to slip on the ice. He was about to feign a seizure, to make her laugh and to jerk himself out of his bad mood, when two deer crashed across the path in front of them. In a flash of doglike fur, flaring nostrils, and liquidy eyes, they were gone.

"Wow." Katie grabbed his hand and shook it. "I told you this was going to be good." She was shouting, her eyes bright.

"Did you see how big they were?" he shouted back, excited in spite of himself.

"Yeah. I was right here. I wish they'd jumped right over us. What do you think Lovely thought?" As if on cue, Lovely raced up, panting and grinning at his feet.

"Oh my God, he rolled in something," Katie cried. "Do you smell it? Oh yuck, stupid dog."

"Lovely, come here." He bent closer to the dog's back and inhaled tentatively. The stench of rotting carcass nearly knocked him out.

"Yuck. Stinky, naughty dog," Katie scolded. Lovely fell to the snow, wallowed furiously as if to reenact the crime, and galloped off. "So what do you think he thought? About the deer." Katie smiled, her annoyance with her noxious pet gone. Of course it was—she wasn't the one who'd be up all night bathing the stupid beast.

"Lovely thought nothing. Lovely is an idiot. Not a single thought runs through that dog's brain except the desire for food and the urge to scoot."

"You're so mean. Say something nice. What did he really think?"

"I have no idea. Who cares what he thought, Katie, leave me alone." He slowed his pace, lagging behind, wishing he could turn and run back to the car.

"They were so beautiful, so serene. So much better than us." Katie sniffed, and even with her back to him, he could tell she was crying. He sighed. It was never easy. It was never just a walk. But then he felt bad. What kind of husband was he, annoyed with his crying wife when she looked so pretty, so hopeful, in her brightly knit hat with the earflaps and pom-pom on top.

"What is it?" he said, trying to keep the dread from his voice.

"I just . . . I wish I had a tribe."

"A what?"

She bent over, sobbing into her hands. "I'm sorry," she said, ignoring his question. "I've had a shitty day. I'm about to start my period, and I'm fat and bloated and hideous. I don't know how you can even look at me." She wiped her eyes, her hands small in her leopard-spotted mittens, and mumbled something he couldn't quite make out.

"What?" He patted her thick jacket. He had no idea what was going on.

"I said, the world is going to hell in a handbasket," she shouted, shaking him off. "And I'm sick of it."

He laughed. Finally someone who shared his worldview. "So am I," he said, grabbing her and pulling her close. "So is everyone."

After a steady decline, the forest ended and the trail opened into the bottom of a ravine, a huge shell of mud and ice cracked open to the night sky. It was as if they'd walked out of the woods and into some prehistoric world. Wilson tensed his shoulders against the clutch of an unseen raptor. The steps gouged into the mud slopes were big enough for a giant's foot. The stars seemed far away, the moon as small as a pebble.

He looked at his watch, but it had stopped at 7:00 p.m., about the time the walk began. That was ominous. They'd been walking a good forty minutes, he figured. His legs were burning and his shoulders ached. He was a skinny guy—surely Katie hadn't forgotten. He couldn't last long in cold weather. He had no reserves.

Katie climbed the steps briskly, pumping her arms, the pom-pom on her hat bobbing. He tried to keep up, but she moved so quickly. His breath came in ragged gasps, and he could feel his heart pounding in his ears.

"Come on, lazy." Katie grabbed his hand and pulled him up the last step. Her cheeks were pink, and her tears about the deer or her PMS or whatever it was were gone.

"You're out of shape." She laughed, always gleeful at his shortcomings. "Wilson, you've got to quit smoking."

"Yes," he said, which was what he always said. It wasn't a promise to quit, it was simply a confirmation that yes he should. They stood at the edge of a vast meadow. The earth was soft and rolling, as if large beasts slept beneath its crust. Something rustled in the brush, darting away when he turned to look. Were there bobcats in Michigan? He wasn't sure, but he hoped not. It was late, way past his bedtime—he couldn't take much more excitement.

"I can't believe we saw deer," Katie said. "I love it. Let's go all the way to the lake and look at the swans in the moonlight." She ran ahead, skipping every few steps, her arms swinging.

He'd never understand her. Her bad moods swept in like a cloud of bats, scared the shit out of him, and just as quickly flitted away. He rarely cried. He tried but couldn't. It sometimes worried him, his lack of grief. He seemed to live his life in a permanent state of shock. Katie cried easily and furiously and always felt great afterward, stretching and shouting,

"I'm alive," like a great fallen monster rising from the rubble, its powers restored. He envied her.

They stood at the edge of a frozen bog, looking for swans. Did swans live in Michigan in winter? Again, he had no idea. It was becoming obvious he knew nothing about the natural world, but he also didn't care. Like a lab rat, he'd be perfectly content to live the rest of his natural life indoors. Snow-tipped cattails rustled in the wind. The water was frozen and cloudy. There were no swans in sight.

"I just want to live in nature and be through with the whole fucking business," Katie said, hugging her chest and hopping up and down. "Just me and my tribe."

"What kind of tribe?" He wondered where she got the energy for hopping. She must lounge all day, saving up her vigor for when he got home, depleted.

"With people who are like me. Who know me and understand me. Where I feel like I'm part of a larger community rather than just some lone mom stuck in the house, making myself crazy because I never talk to any grown-ups."

He shook his head, smiling. He loved it when he knew more about a subject than she did. "Believe me, you don't want to be in a tribe. I grew up in a small town, I know. You wouldn't like half the people, and half the people would hate you. You'd only want to get away. You'd hate it. Everyone would be judging you, watching your every move, talking about your business. I promise, you do not want to be in a tribe."

"I do," she said stubbornly.

"You don't. Hillbillies live in tribes. Does that sound like fun?"

"Yes." She sighed, kicking the snow. "I don't know. I don't care. I'm just sick of everything. All I think about is food and being skinny. It's boring. It's like, is that who I am at the core? This stupid girl who only cares about being cute and skinny and pleasing? It's boring. I'm sick of it. I'm sick of myself."

"But you're always happy," he pointed out. "You love life."

"It's just an act," she said dramatically. "I've been acting my entire life."

Somehow he couldn't feel sorry for her. If she had the energy even to *act* happy, then in his book, she was way ahead of the game. "I'll be in your tribe. As long as I can be chief."

"You are chief." She smiled. "And I guess I miss my mom. I wish we lived closer. And I wish that January were around."

"That would be a disaster."

"No."

"Yes. Your mom lives in fantasyland. She acts like what happened to you never happened. And January's a mess. Why would you want to be around that? She didn't even come to the wedding."

"You don't understand. She was depressed and freaking out when we got married. You can't fly like that."

"El Paso to Las Vegas takes twenty minutes. She couldn't pull herself together that long?" He was annoyed. Katie was always longing for other people, which in his immature mind automatically discounted him. If he wasn't her entire universe, then he was nothing. It was a simple mathematical equation, as any alcoholic would confirm.

"You don't get it." Katie's voice was cold. "It was a stupid Las Vegas wedding. It took seven minutes, the music sucked, and we fought the entire weekend. And look at your family. Look at you. You're all a bunch of repressed judgmental assholes. Look at you—you're a mess. You tried to drink yourself to death, and you're saying your family's better than mine?"

He sighed. The walk had devolved into the "whose family is worse" argument. Of course it had. He was never to criticize Katie's family. She could make fun of his all she wanted, but hers was strictly off-limits. That his day would end fighting his difficult wife next to a frozen, swan-less bog, on a walk he never wanted to go on in the first place, sounded just about right. The cattails rattled like matchsticks. He was dying for a cigarette, but, patting his pockets, he realized he'd left them in the car. "It's not a contest," he said. "Whose family is the most dysfunctional—"

"No. But if it were, your family would win."

"Please." He would not get sucked in. He would be rational and calm. "Like people on the West Coast aren't judgmental. You guys are the most judgmental of all. All you hippies are so hypocritical. If it's not your way, then it's wrong. You don't give the other side a chance."

"Because we're right. Because it's right to live and let live."

"Then why do you hate my family? How 'live and let live' is that?"

"I don't hate them. I like them. But when you tell me things about them, I think they're judgmental. You're the one that says so. You're the one that feeds me the information."

Of course it was his fault. "But when you say they're judgmental," he said in his best lawyerly voice, "aren't you, yourself, being judgmental—maybe even more judgmental than them?"

"Wilson. Your dad spanked you with a belt. He pulled down your pants." Katie's face was pale and furious. "That makes me sick. And they're never getting near our kids. If anyone ever tried to—"

"Oh, for God's sake. No one is going to spank our kids. Why did I even tell you that? Why do I tell you anything? You always want me to talk and reveal and disclose, and then you use it against me the first chance you get."

"Whatever." She walked away, her long pink legs bright against the snow. The wind groaned. Ice crunched beneath her boots.

"Why are we fighting?" he called.

"Why are you fighting?"

"Because I'm a selfish bastard. And I'm about to die of hypothermia. But the truth is, your mom and your sister don't care, they don't care about you, so can we please just go home?"

She stopped and looked at him, her face drawn. "OK, fine," she said calmly. She stared at him a bit longer, then turned and ran into the woods. "And guess what?" she shouted. "You don't get to be in my tribe."

"I don't want to be in your tribe. I'm just saying I *am* your tribe. Whether you like it or not."

"And you ruined another walk." She was screaming, but her voice was already small and far away.

"Where's the dog?" He looked around. Everything was still, the snow and the ice, the soft-tipped cattails, the black trees floating on the horizon. Lovely was nowhere to be seen, and Wilson was sure he hadn't followed Katie. Come to think of it, he hadn't seen the dog since the deer crossed their path, miles back. "Where's the dog?" he shouted into the silence. The night was so clear he could see the man in the moon, scowling down upon him.

# Eight

## Katie

Wilson was giving her the silent treatment with the force and persistence of a high school girl. Katie sighed, squirming deeper beneath the covers. Everything else was perfect. The bedroom was peaceful. Silvery fingers of moonlight trembled on the walls, and the tie-dyed pillowcases she'd made, with their wobbly circles of pale Easter egg colors, were soothing. Even the children and dog slept soundly, the little ones beside her on the bed, Jake on the floor in his sleeping bag, Lovely, freshly washed and fluffy, at his feet.

But Wilson was angry, and she couldn't even fall asleep to escape—she was too hopped up from their walk. She curled her knees to her chest, stretching her stiff upper back. The clean sheets she'd put on that morning felt delicious against her bare legs, and the thought crossed her mind that if *he* weren't there, seething beside her, she'd be in a great mood.

She wondered if Steven was still awake. His blinds had been open when they returned from the walk, and she'd seen him at his dining room table, studying. He was dyslexic and spent long hours bent over his books, a small table lamp making a pool of light in the otherwise darkened condo. Katie found his diligence touching. He was taking Chinese but refused to speak a word of it in her presence. This she found cute.

What if she called him? Or slipped out of bed and ran barefoot through the snow to his door. "Wilson hates me . . ." she'd begin, stepping into his circle of light.

She leaned over her husband, who closed his eyes at the sight of her, found her headphones on the floor beside the bed, and slipped them on. The rock station was playing "Let It Be"—much more pleasant than his cold silence. Her crime: She'd left him in the middle of nowhere. He hadn't known where he was, and although he'd never say so, he was scared. When she thought of it that way, it seemed like a horrible thing to do to a person.

She plumped her pillows, scooted Rose and Paul over, and tried to relax. She caught a glimpse of the eye bag one of Wilson's sisters had given her, pulled it out from beneath Rose, and placed its silken weight over her eyes, inhaling lavender. It was supposed to be soothing, but lavender made her think of brittle old aunts and Emily Dickinson. It made her feel shriveled and sad, and she flung it across the room where it hit the wall, bursting in a shower of seeds.

"Oops," she said.

Wilson looked at her as if she'd suddenly sat up and shot someone.

The seeds had sounded like rain falling. They reminded her of Portland, of lying in bed as a kid, January asleep beside her, the rush of rain filling their bare room. The branches of the lilac trees would tap at the windows as shadowy raindrops slid down the scarred walls and the train that skirted the neighborhood thundered, shrieked, and fell silent in the night. The memory was vivid, and it made her sad, as if she'd lost something there in that damp room, something she couldn't name.

"Let It Be" faded into "Something," and she turned it up. A wave of loneliness swept through her. Lying in her condo, a mother now, there was no sound of rain falling to soothe her to sleep. There was only the steady moan of cars on the interstate and a strange clanking sound coming from the kitchen. It was like a spoon hitting a pot at random intervals, and she was sure it was the mice, going berserk in their new, crumb-filled home. She pictured them darting over the stove, wriggling their way into bags of sugar and flour like sperm into eggs, and shuddered.

She would not think of them. Only good thoughts were allowed in her bed, and if they decided to skitter up her legs in the middle of the night, at least she had Wilson. He was brave. He would lift them by their tails like fat, furry cherries and transport them outside, the man in charge of household rodents.

She'd inform him of his new duty as soon as he was speaking to her again. "And I'm not a bad person," she'd say. "You just bring out the worst in me."

"Believe me, it's not hard to do," he might answer, and then they'd laugh and everything would be OK.

She needed a friend, that was the problem, someone to laugh with and share secrets with, to reassure her that there were other people on the planet far more disturbed than she. Wilson was too busy with his Sylvia Plath project to talk much, and Steven was more likely to wear pink tights and tap-dance on his porch than discuss anything deep. A gay guy would be perfect, a real drama queen, someone who could do her hair, ridicule her clothes, and share her love of Bob Fosse musicals and the literary works of Jacqueline Susann.

She knew she was difficult, but what woman liked to see mice fly across her kitchen, or for her husband to tell her that her own family didn't care, as Wilson had on the walk. Even if it was true, it wasn't nice. She looked at him, at his full lips, his blond hair silvery in the moonlight. His hawk-like nose made her think of an Indian chief, of someone noble. *My chief*, she thought, remembering the fight. He didn't look mean, lying beside her with his eyes closed, he looked kind, like her friend, and she wanted absolution, immediately, so she could sleep.

"I think I hear mice," she ventured, pulling off her headphones.

"You do hear mice. They're in your kitchen, running around as we speak." Wilson's voice was flat, and he didn't move or open his eyes.

"That's so mean."

He didn't answer.

Katie sighed. She slipped her headphones back on. It was going to be a long night.

Maybe she'd be easier to get along with if she had something to do, a project. What did other moms do? She could rock preemies at the hospital. She could counsel crack addicts. Or, more realistically, she could start painting again. When she set up her watercolors and easel, everything felt right, and a voice in her head would say, "So that was what was wrong—you weren't painting." The women in her goddess group—a self-help group she'd attended that fall—said that creating art made a woman "juicy." But she could only paint when she felt thin, which she didn't, so . . .

Could one be thin and juicy at the same time? She'd have to ask.

She'd never felt juicy in her life. No, she had, with Jake's dad. In New Mexico, surrounded by sky and dust and the dried snake of the Rio Grande, she'd felt alive, as bright and fleshy as a cactus flower. And there was the time, all those summers ago, in Steven's garage bar, when she was hugely pregnant and had reclined on his sparkling tangerine couch like a tie-dyed goddess, her cheeks flushed, her damp hair pulled back, her entire being bursting with life. When he'd told her stories of hair and its dangers, and instructed her on how to home-brew the perfect honey stout, and then kissed her as if she were the most desirable, dirty-footed pregnant woman ever to grace his lair.

Everything then was like fruit: juice dripping, full to bursting, seed-filled, alive. Not to be disgusting. It was also fun, and sweet. It made her happy.

Lately, she felt as if she were turning into her grandma Edith, the grandmother who sent the checks that allowed her to stay home with her children. Grandma Edith led a busy, bossy and, as far as Katie knew, celibate existence, which was fine, she guessed, if you were ninety-one and had had your fill of sex and romance and all the nonsense that went with it.

Katie was still hungry. She sometimes imagined her soul mate. Who was he? Was he looking for her? Did he live in Europe? Did he make a lot of money? Maybe it was Wilson and she just didn't know. But in her mind, her perfect match was someone much more active than her lazy husband. She thought of her soul mate as someone with whom she'd practice tantric yoga, swim with the dolphins, bike the Appalachian Trail, eat vegan. He was tall and bearded and smiling, a happy, hippie cross between a cruise director and a sexual god. Like Jim Morrison, maybe, but with a positive attitude.

Was she trying to force Wilson to be her soul mate? Was that why she harassed him, made him do things he hated? He liked to nap and he liked to smoke and that was it, and she should be smart enough by now to simply leave him alone. He was never going to walk and enjoy it. He'd rather be eaten by a dolphin than frolic with one.

The walk had been a bust. Wilson had gotten frozen and grouchy and they'd fought about nothing, and then she'd had to sit in the car for a half hour with the stinky dog, waiting for him to quit pouting and find his way back. When he did, slamming his palm on the driver's side window and scaring the shit out of her, he was furious. He drove them home in silence, sliding on purpose on the icy roads, not laughing or even smiling no matter how many funny things she thought to say.

He'd never go again. For that matter, she'd never ask him to go again.

She turned over, bumping him with her hip, hoping he'd laugh. But he only said what sounded like "big ass" and moved to the far edge of the bed. She smiled, shocked. Surely she'd heard wrong—he'd never say such a thing. He loved her body, and was always complimenting it and pawing at it. Maybe he'd found someone else, someone very small. She remembered the strange coconut smell in the living room that morning. In her experience, a sudden positive grooming shift was a sure sign of cheating.

If he had dared call her a fat ass, she hoped he fell off the bed.

"You don't *like* anyone, do you?" she said, not expecting an answer.

"Are you wearing a new cologne?" she tried. "Something coconut-y? Or waxing your hair?"

Wilson snorted, pulled a pillow over his head.

Was she too heavy? She had no idea. One day she felt OK, the next like a lumbering beast. She ran her hands over her stomach, sucking it in, pinching the flesh.

"All mothers have pouches in which their babies have lived," a know-it-all goddess in her group had said at their last meeting. They were standing in the sacred circle, talking about their bodies. "It's a magical thing," the woman gushed, "an animal thing. Earthy and ancient, this flesh should be celebrated, not dieted away." Then she turned to the goddess beside her and kissed her wetly on the cheek.

"Oh God please don't let there be kissing," Katie had prayed, her entire body stiffening.

"Pass it on!" the pouched goddess had crowed as Katie stood, panicked, in the sacred circle, in the cold basement of the YMCA, surrounded by thirteen intense, fragile, kissing strangers.

"No physical affection," she'd wanted to cry out, but could only grimace tensely and forget how to breathe. The other women had no problem; they were laughing, having fun. A few were weeping, smiles shining through their tears.

Katie hated every second of it. She didn't want to be touched by anyone but her kids, her dog, Steven, and maybe Wilson, if she was in the mood.

And she hadn't bought the pouch business. She'd looked at the offending goddess, at her bravely exposed belly and starry deluded eyes, and thought to herself, *Babies don't do that, Twinkies do*. She never went back.

She would start an exercise program first thing in the morning. Getting up at five a.m. and running daily would be perfect. She'd be fit and friendly, like a good dog, and everyone would love her. Steven would love her. He'd renounce Lucy, and they could have wild sex every afternoon in his fragrant, bubbling bedroom. But first she'd have to find a babysitter, which, as every mother knew, was next to impossible, so . . .

The trick to running was the getting up at dawn. She glanced at the clock. It was almost midnight. If she fell asleep instantly, she'd get five hours of sleep, about half of what she needed. It wouldn't be pretty. She'd be thin, maybe, but she'd also be sleep-deprived and manic, a scary mom on the fast track to a nervous breakdown.

If she and Wilson could only get along, life would be so much easier. After the walk—after he'd washed Lovely, cleaned his ears, fluffed him with the hair dryer, brushed his few intact teeth, and threw his collar in the wash—Katie had begged his forgiveness. When he didn't answer, she pointed out that all he'd had to do was follow. And Lovely was fine. He'd never been lost in the first place. He had excellent homing devices and had met up with her halfway to the car, having instinctively known, the way a child does, that the fighting had begun and the fun was over.

Thinking about it, she was now much more angry than contrite. Wilson still wasn't sleeping. He lay beside her in a kind of furious limbo, and she had the urge to pinch him and ask him to sleep on the couch. How could she rest beside his toxic mood? It was debilitating. He knew you weren't supposed to go to bed angry. It was rule number one, they'd learned, at the first of the few therapy sessions they'd attended before deciding that the counselor was a money-hungry troll more interested in selling them six hundred dollar magnetic sheets than helping them get along.

The therapy—or the gleeful revelation of each other's weaknesses—had enraged both of them. This seemed to bother the counselor's delicate sensibilities. She addressed her comments to the wall behind the love seat on which they sat, a scared look on her pug face, and always seemed relieved when the session was over and she could watch them stomp grimly up her basement steps, their check clutched in her fist.

Katie tried to breathe slowly, to block Wilson from her consciousness. How long was he going to punish her? All he'd had to do was follow. He was acting like she'd left him there to die. For God's sake, he was only a half mile from the main road in the first place. And he was the one with the supposed perfect sense of direction.

Unlike him, she was fine; she was over it. Her anger had lasted about five minutes, and then she'd let it go. She hadn't even minded waiting. She'd listened to the first side of *Dark Side of the Moon*, the heat blasting, her cold fingers and toes slowly tingling back to life as Lovely panted happily in the backseat.

She'd always liked waiting in cars. When she was little, it was a special treat to drive with her dad to the 7-Eleven for a gallon of milk, or to the post office to mail his paperwork. She'd wait in the dark, January tumbling from the backseat to the front and back again, the lights on the dashboard glowing, the heater blowing its hot breath on her bare feet, feeling wonderfully cocooned, as if she were exactly where she belonged.

She shouldn't have quit going. Maybe then her dad wouldn't have lost interest and they'd be close now. If she hadn't strayed from his protective shadow, maybe Larry Johnson would never have noticed her.

"I know you, Katie . . ."

But he hadn't, not one bit. He hadn't known that she liked to read Beverly Cleary books, or that she had a dollhouse made from a wooden wine crate in which her Spanish señorita doll from Disneyland lived. He hadn't known that she liked to rock in the battered green La-Z-Boy, listening to music. He hadn't known that the *Goodbye Yellow Brick Road* album made her feel achy and happy at the same time, or that she once dreamed of Elton John on a flying unicorn, handsome in his pig shave and Captain Fantastic glasses, landing on a downtown rooftop, its orange bricks glowing, come to carry her away.

"I know you . . ."

"No you don't," she said aloud, curling into a tighter ball. Her legs ached, and her chest hurt as if something big and unfriendly sat on it. She touched Rose's plump cheek, her fat bright lips. She was perfect. When did things change? She and Wilson certainly weren't perfect; they were a mess. And like them, the children would grow up, collecting worries and scars and unpleasant personality quirks along the way. It was awful to imagine. They could turn into chubby, mean, pro-life, anti-choice, Rush Limbaugh–loving idiots, and there wasn't a thing she or Wilson could do.

When you thought about it, the whole business of life was horrifying. But maybe that was the point, to quit thinking and just *be*—blind, faith-filled. It made her furious.

She listened to the last line of *Abbey Road*. She wanted to tell Wilson how much she loved it. Or maybe she wanted to quote it to him as a kind of warning. Either way, she resisted. Better to leave him alone, let his anger burn itself out. She shouldn't have left him. But how the hell was she to know he'd panic? He was so strong, so in control—it was what she loved about him.

She pointed her toes and flexed them, staring up at the ceiling. The fabric she'd tacked up billowed lazily. It was midnight blue and covered with plant-green fish, hundreds of skeletal fish, all of them glowing slightly and pointing in the same direction, as if each knew exactly where it was going.

She could feel herself relaxing, drifting off. Her bedroom always made her happy. Everything was nice: the fish on the ceiling, the soft walls and clean carpet (it was the only room in the condo where the carpet wasn't trashed), the framed finger paintings, the pictures of her gorgeous babies, gilded now with moonlight. On the wall opposite the bed, she'd hung one of her watercolors—the first she could honestly say made her proud. Against a swirling yellow and pink background, a faceless woman held an overflowing basket of blackberries, the berries leaping from her arms, abundant, alive. It was how Katie felt when she watched her kids sleep, as if she'd been gifted with more than she could possibly hold.

"Why doesn't she have a face?" Wilson had asked when she showed it to him.

"Because she's *every woman*," she'd said just to mess with him. "It's about fertility, the eternal life force, and also the way the primal mother in us *bears* life in so many more ways than just the literal."

"Sounds painful," he said with a smirk. "Your goddess ladies will go apeshit." Wilson loved it when he had something to ridicule. Katie knew this and was always happy to throw him a bone.

"Do you think you'll ever talk to me again?" she said now, trying to sound kind.

Silence.

"Are you traumatized for life because you were too stubborn to follow me back to the car?"

Dead silence.

Fuck it, then. Let him be miserable. She had happier thoughts to think. There was Steven, for one. He was getting married. She couldn't believe it. He was much too young. What on earth was he thinking?

Why hadn't he thought of her?

Steven was simple. He had few moods and they all seemed pleasant. He was easy. It took no effort to be with him. Sure, he wasn't a genius like Wilson. And he was young and liked beer and boxing and all sorts of things she had no interest in. But like Jake's dad in New Mexico, he made her feel calm and, if you wanted the truth, safe. He wasn't going to change, suddenly fly into a rage or fall into a black depression. She even liked his mother, who cut her hair and always complimented her on her natural strawberry color, even gave her free conditioner—the good stuff.

"I wish you'd talk to me. I'm sorry, I'm sorry, I'm so fucking sorry," she said, not sounding sorry at all. "Wilson, please."

Silence.

With Wilson, what came to mind was the Pink Floyd song about the "loonies" and the "path." That was how it felt sometimes, their marriage, as if they were two lunatics out on a walk, each one constantly fighting to be first, and neither of them getting anywhere. Being married to Wilson was the opposite of easy, which wasn't necessarily a bad thing. It was fun sometimes, and it was definitely real, whatever that was. She could depend on him, and they had a great time with the kids. But it was also difficult and awful and boring. His past wasn't bright. He didn't come from a nice family. And he had a million issues to work on that were all rooted in the two big ones—control and intimacy—that she struggled with daily.

Being with Wilson was like being married to her own self, a fate she wouldn't wish on anyone. He was a mirror that forced her to look at her dark side, and vice versa, which was a good thing, maybe, but no one in their right mind would call it fun.

With Steven, she saw . . . nothing. It was nice, like watching TV.

"Of course it's nice," she could hear her mother say. "You've always liked the drunken losers. They're easy to control. You can run right over them. But with Wilson"—at this point, Iris always chuckled —"you've met your match."

Iris was Wilson's biggest fan, and it annoyed Katie. Her mother liked him better than she did her own daughter, and always took his side whenever Katie dared to complain. "All he does is sleep," she might say, and Iris would come back with thirty reasons why this was so. "Of course he needs to nap," she'd say with a sigh, as if Katie were stupid. "You exhaust people. You always have."

*I hate you*, Katie thought. She rolled over and lifted Wilson's T-shirt, touching his bare stomach, the hard muscles beneath silky skin, the line of hair that ran from his belly button down into his shorts.

"You know there are perks to being married," she said, pulling her hair from its ponytail and letting it brush against his bare skin, the way she knew he liked. "It's not all fighting and misery. Shouldn't we take advantage of the good stuff?" She looked up, hopeful.

He grunted and rolled away.

She was going to scream, any minute now. God, he was a punishing bastard. She exhausted people? Well, so did he, and she would phone her mother and tell her so, first thing Monday morning, as soon as she met with the divorce lawyer. *Steven was nice. Steven was kind.* Her thoughts of him took on a desperate edge the way they often did when she was angry with Wilson. She thought of his hand touching hers, the way his body enveloped her when they hugged, his plush crew cut, his sexy kisses. She wanted to cry out to God, or whatever idiot was in charge, to get her out of the mess she'd made of her life. She was sorry she had the relationship skills of a bad dog, but hadn't she been punished enough?

Steven had licked her wrist that morning, in the car, after they'd circled the lot of the coffee shop, looking for a parking space. She shivered, remembering.

"I'm sorry. I truly am, Wilson. I know I'm a bitch. I know I'm awful. Please don't be mad anymore. It makes life . . ." she paused dramatically to get her point across, ". . . horrible. Just horrible." Tears sprang to her eyes, surprising her. But it was true. She was tired of fighting; she couldn't do it much longer.

She'd once found a card with a picture of a man and a woman struggling to escape from the grip of a giant blue hand. "Me and you, stuck in the great blue fist of fate," she'd written before placing it in the book she'd bought Wilson for Father's Day (*Revolutionary Road* by Richard Yates, which he'd loved). They'd laughed then, but sometimes it wasn't so funny.

"I am aware that it sucks," Wilson said, softening at the sight of her tears, as she knew he would. "You're angry at me 90 percent of the time."

"Thank God you're speaking." Katie wiped her eyes.

"It doesn't mean I'm not still mad." He sighed, pinching the bridge of his nose and squeezing his eyes shut as if he were in terrible pain.

"Please." A fresh wave of tears flooded Katie's cheeks.

Wilson didn't answer.

"All flavors and push-ups, too," Steven had whispered. "All my flavors are guaranteed to satisfy." *He had turned her arm over and licked her wrist.* Remembering that precise, ridiculous moment made Katie ache inside.

"Did I tell you?" she said now, turning to Wilson. "Steven is getting married." She made her voice light, as if she'd only thought of their neighbor that second.

"Who'd marry that clown?" Wilson's voice was gleeful as he flipped his half of the blankets off, dumping them on her. His anger was gone, and Katie quickly whispered a prayer of thanks to the god of bad relationships.

"Lucy. You know, the blonde. The pretty one." She moved closer, resting her head on his chest.

"Oh yeah. With the belly button." Katie could feel his voice rumble in his chest, and it excited her. "How old is she?"

"Twenty, I think. What do you mean 'the belly button'?"

"She's always wearing those short tops. Her belly button is pierced." Wilson smoothed Katie's hair. "As for your little teenage boyfriend, I give the marriage six months. Max."

"Let's be happy for them." Katie suppressed a smile, pleased that Wilson had called Steven her boyfriend. "How long do you give us?"

"Oh, we'll be trapped in this hell for eternity."

She giggled. "Why didn't you just follow me to the car? We'd circled around and were almost back to where we'd started. You were so close. Wilson, you weren't lost at all."

He pushed his hair behind his ears. "I didn't follow you because the damn dog was gone. I knew I had to find him. If anything happened, if he'd starved to death or froze, or tried to walk home and got hit by a car, or got eaten by raccoons, it would somehow turn out to be my fault, and I'd never hear the end of it." He paused. "I was going to be the hero. I was going to save your dog."

Katie laughed. "That's so funny because he was safe in the car the whole time." She sat back, resting her head on her hand. "And you weren't really trying to save him; you were trying to save yourself."

"Thanks for pointing that out. The fact is you left me. You left me in the wilderness to die. How could you?"

"Wilson. Silly." Katie patted his chest. "You were never in any danger."

He sighed dramatically.

She decided to change the subject before he got mad all over again. "Have you ever known anyone who, when you ask how they are, they're like, 'Oh, wonderful. I'm really, really, *really* good. I am just great. I am amazingly happy'?"

"No one who isn't certifiable. Why? Who's like that?"

"Lucy, Steven's fiancée. And it always makes you feel so inadequate because, of course, you're not that orgasmically blissful—who is? So she wins. She always wins." Katie was quiet. "It's really hostile." She paused, careful not to sound jealous. "I guess I just don't like the girl at all. I think Steven's making a big mistake."

"I guess I don't give a shit."

"Well, you should." Katie laughed and kissed his neck. Who cared about Steven and his stupid girlfriend? She was married, she had a life, she was wanted, right here in her own bed. She touched Wilson's throat, smoothed his wild blond curls. Rose had his hair. Her curls were tight and platinum blond, giving her the look of a happy little clown. Katie rolled over and touched her daughter's soft head, wrapped a curl around her finger.

"She's going to hate you for this hair when she's a teenager," she said, looking back at Wilson.

"Oh, I know." He leaned across Katie and placed his hand on Rose's head. "It's the Lavender hair. My sister used to stand in front of the mirror with the curling iron for hours before school, sobbing and yelling, my mom screaming, my dad making ridiculous threats. Up to then, I'd never known hair could be so . . . scary."

"Oh, it's scary all right. It's a very scary thing." Katie made her voice dark, thinking of the time she'd become so enraged she threw her curling iron into the toilet where it had hissed meanly as she sobbed, feeling like the ugly ugly ugly girl she knew she was. She was thirteen then, but really, how much had changed? And what about Rose? How would she get through the horrible years between seventh grade and senior year? She wouldn't attend school, Katie decided; it was the only solution.

"She'll be beautiful," Wilson said.

The future was what made Katie determined to make things work. She and Wilson held it in their hands, an entire world, together. *The Lavenders. The Lavender kids.* How lonely it would be to walk into it alone, to divvy it up into half weeks and months in summer, to never see how things turned out.

Lovely jumped onto the bed and stretched out on top of Katie, his paws on her shoulders, his weight forcing the breath out of her. It was one of his favorite places to be. She rubbed his head as he grinned, showing his pink tongue, his broken teeth that looked like Indian corn. "He's so soft. He feels so nice. You did a good job."

"Hmmm."

"Ugh. I can't breathe. Lovely, get off."

The dog didn't move.

Wilson laughed, watching Katie struggle. "He loves like you. 'Let me pin you down and suffocate you.' Big mean Katie love. It's a scary thing, isn't it?"

Katie succeeded in shoving the dog off the bed. He trotted out the bedroom door to the kitchen where they could him hear lapping water, chomping dog food. "Do you really think that?" She sat up, smiling. "Is it . . . am I . . . that awful?"

Wilson was thoughtful. "I don't know," he said. "Maybe." He sighed, sinking back against the pillows, his arms limp. "I can't talk anymore. I'm exhausted. Can we please just go have sex? Quietly? Please? No more talking?"

"I don't know." Katie hesitated, pulling the covers up to her chin. "We're getting along so well. You know how sex always makes us fight."

## Katie
1973

If I'm good, I won't die. If I'm good, he won't get me. If I'm good, it will never have happened at all. I still think that way—I still *live* that way—only there's no longer any bad guy around, is there? To be good for?

Maybe it was all a bad dream, and I was safe in bed the whole time, half-awake, the nightmare lingering in shreds, like a dirty rag. I watched shadows of raindrops slide down the walls. Lilacs scratched at the window. The wind hummed loudly. And there was the train, circling the neighborhood, around and around like a toy on a track.

Beside me, January slept, a curled ghost in her long white nightgown. I could feel her heat, hear her breath. She never moved when she slept. She lay motionless, and when she stayed in her own bed, her thin pink blanket and flower-spotted sheet were as neat in the morning as when she'd crawled beneath them the night before.

When we were grown, she once told me that she never dreamed. By then, I knew she was full of shit 99 percent of the time, but I believed her. There was something eerie about the way she slept, as if, once unconscious, she crawled out of her body and went somewhere else, somewhere fun judging by her good mood when she woke up.

One night when I was eight, I stayed up past midnight, waiting for my parents to come home from a party. I'd never been up so late. It felt as if the world had shifted, become one I hadn't seen before, where everything was cold and still and dark, fog like tumbleweeds rolling down the deserted street. I loved that things kept going, and for such a long time, after I crawled into bed like a good girl at eight p.m.

I had a new telescope, a small one. As my mom paid the babysitter, chatting about Transcendental Meditation and Jim Croce, and my dad, who'd had too much beer, staggered off to bed, I grabbed it and sneaked out to the front porch. I focused on the moon. I saw nothing at first, just sky—cold wet night sky that I could smell and taste—and then there it was: fat and full, and I couldn't believe how bright, how alive its face was. It was pitted and scarred, but glowing an intense whitish-yellow, so different from the sun.

I fell in love with the moon that night. It became my friend as I stood, barefoot in my dad's long undershirt, on the rickety porch of our old Victorian, paint peeling off the railings, the old oak at the curb a wobbly blot of ink against the sky, and my mom inside, sparkling, the way she got after a late night out.

When I took away the telescope, the moon was as small as a pearl, caught in the seaweed of our tree. I could hold it in my cupped palm.

On weekend mornings, our dad golfed. I knew that the tennis court or the golf course was where he came alive, became his true self, the one he saved up, hidden away, when he was with us. I'd picture him strolling across the green grass, happy under a happy face sun, his clubs snug in their bag, in their soft knit hats with the little pom-poms, and the dimpled balls, safe as eggs in the pocket of his checkered pants.

He golfed with his buddies—Ray Lee, Chip, and Ken Yi. Larry Johnson sometimes. They were a club. They called each other on the phone, speaking urgently in what sounded like code. "Give Yi a call, we'll play the back nine at Rose City at three." They wore similar clothes, fancy and frightening, and they sealed their closeness over plastic cups of cold, foamy beer at the clubhouse.

There are all sorts of secret clubs when you're a kid. When I was nine, I had a make-out club in my garage. My best friend Kelly and I lured cute boys up into a fort we'd built in the rafters. The boys were fourth graders like us, but undersized and silly, and we'd make them play Spin the Bottle, or Truth or Dare, until they freaked, leapt from the rafters, and raced down the driveway and out into the street, needing to be boys again. To burp and armpit fart freely, without crazy girls like us *liking* them. I didn't blame them. There *was* something dangerous about girls, I'd discovered, and it was our love: big and bad and bossy. We could bewitch, shape-shift, became other creatures entirely, powerful beings within which our scared little girl selves could disappear.

In the eighth grade, we had a club whose sole purpose was to hate. Every few weeks, we'd hate one girl, one of our "friends." "I hate her," we'd hiss, narrowing our purple-lined eyes. We'd ostracize the girl, send her cruel notes, laugh in her face, ridicule her hair that didn't feather right, her fat Lip Smacker–smeared lips, her big butt. When we got bored, we'd turn our attentions to another girl. Sometimes that girl was you—surprise, surprise—and that truly sucked.

I used to watch the old Mickey Mouse Club. I envied those kids. They could tap-dance and sing, and they all rooted for each other. Who rooted for me? I had no idea. But I knew you could root for yourself. I wanted to take tap lessons and learn how to be cute, how to be a star, beloved, with golden curls and a clean pink dress, my bobby socks drooping just so, like Cheryl, pretty, perfect, dimpled Cheryl.

When I was eight, my mother went back to work. She'd primal screamed and found herself that winter, and in the fall, when the Indian summer sun turned the world fat and orange and honeyed, she took herself back to work. She'd taught first grade when I was small, but quit when January was born. Now she was a music teacher. Our back bedroom where the battered old piano stood was full of jingle bells on sticks and piles of rattling, clattering tambourines that we'd bang furiously, three at a time, until she yelled at us to quit.

I became a latchkey kid. A latchkey kid without a key because our front door was always unlocked. If it wasn't, it was easy to jimmy the lock with a credit card, or in my case, a library card that I kept in my Partridge Family lunch box for just such a purpose. January went to the babysitter around the block. I was supposed to, but I didn't and nobody seemed to notice, so every day after school, I walked home, scuffing through piles of dead leaves with their sweet dirt smell, let myself in, turned on the TV in the TV room, got the cookie jar from the kitchen, and made myself comfortable.

Sometimes there were no cookies. Then I had an apple. I knew it was important to have a snack after school. I'd watch all the shows: *The Flintstones, The Brady Bunch, Match Game '73, The Courtship of Eddie's Father, Gilligan's Island*. I'd watch the shows, and when they were over, around five or six, my mother would come home, January in tow. The front door would bang open and she would yell for me, January shouting something about the babysitter's cocker spaniel biting her (she teased it relentlessly), and it was like life had paused for a time and was now ready to begin again.

Sometimes they were late. Or my dad got home and left again, having forgotten to pick up January. Sometimes, Larry Johnson visited. I didn't tell anyone. It was a club, a secret club of two: a grouchy little girl with tangled orange hair and a grown man, held together by a thin membrane of silence. In our club, the meetings were quiet, the members voiceless. Nothing happened, and if you read the minutes, you'd find page after page of blank paper. It began that fall, after he watched the fireworks with us at the Renaissance Fair, the night my hair caught on fire.

"I know you, Katie . . ."

On a cloudy Friday afternoon, he knocked on the front door of our house, wearing the brown leather jacket. At first I was pleased. I'd been sitting at the dining room table looking at the leaves I'd collected on the way home from school, feeling bored. They were newly dead, pale green alien hands, mottled with fuchsia, purple veined.

"My dad's not here," I said, leaning against the doorjamb, holding my leaves. "He's golfing," I added, although I vaguely remembered you were never supposed to tell anyone where your mom and dad were when they weren't home. But wasn't that just on the phone? I wasn't sure.

"Ah, Dan's golfing . . ." Larry Johnson just stood there, his black hair gleaming. He took up the whole doorway. How did he get his hair so shiny? And the jacket—I noticed cracks at the elbows, a tear that had been mended on the side leaving a darker scar. The gold lion's head grinned on his ring finger. I could smell his perfume and beneath it the animal smell. For a moment, the feeling I'd had the night of the fair rushed through me. It was as if everything were shifting, as if I were standing on wet sand and the world beneath me was being sucked away. But then it disappeared, and I stood there, holding my leaves, confused. "But I came to see you."

"Me?" I smiled even though I tried not to. "Why?"

"Well, I've had a hankering for ice cream all day. Do you like ice cream?"

"Yeah."

"So let's go." He grinned as if he'd just come up with a brilliant idea.

I hesitated, but only for a second. I knew I shouldn't leave—I wasn't supposed to be home in the first place—but what was more important than ice cream? Nothing. I opened the door wide, letting him in, then pounded up the thirteen steps to my bedroom, counting each in turn, the dark green carpet threadbare beneath my stocking feet, and grabbed my tennis shoes. I looked at January's bed, the pink blanket tick smooth, and at my own rumpled bed, the fluttery spread in a heap at the foot, the bare bones of the canopy curving like a rib cage. Who was getting ice cream? Me. I dropped my leaves on the floor. Not January, small and cute, but me, obnoxious Katie. Why? Because I was special.

Larry Johnson's car looked like it belonged in the dump surrounded by old refrigerators, a raccoon nesting in its backseat, weeds growing from its wheel wells. It was battered and brown, an old Chevy Impala, and it rumbled and shook when he tried to start it.

"Goddamn son of a bitch," he muttered, gritting his teeth. I tried not to smile. It was the same curse my dad uttered when he was really mad, which, as far as I knew, had been exactly twice: once when he was putting together our candy-striped swing set and accidentally drove a screwdriver into the web of his hand, and once when a dog chased us on a bike ride, sank its teeth into his calf, and wouldn't let go.

The seats of the car were shiny and brown and cracked, like Larry's jacket. The engine caught, and he turned to me, sitting beside him in the front seat, and smiled, his white teeth shining. Next to his bulk, I felt small and pretty. I pulled my ponytail over my shoulder and smoothed it, picked out the bits of dry leaf that had somehow gotten into it. Larry draped his arm over the seat and neatly backed the car out of our steep driveway, the hum of the engine rising in a mosquito scream.

The inside of the car smelled like bananas and dirt. It wasn't an unpleasant smell. It was just different. We drove out of the neighborhood, past the babysitter's house, its shutters newly painted a watery violet. A tricycle sat alone in the postage stamp yard. January was nowhere to be seen. At the corner of 28th and Bybee, I spotted the guy with the rainbow-colored Afro. He was perched on his bike, pale and bug-like, arguing good-naturedly with the paperboy. His hair was almost all blue. The straw basket and the daisy were gone. Larry Johnson noticed me staring.

"Fucking hippie," he muttered. He coasted to a stop at the stop sign, then pulled out with a roar into the traffic on Bybee Boulevard. The car backfired once, chugged, and backfired again. I felt like I was on a carnival ride. We drove past the golf course, its grass unnaturally bright beneath the overcast sky. I wondered if my dad was out there. "Are you going to date a hippie when you grow up?" Larry asked.

"Nahhh." I blushed. I was never going to date anyone. I didn't even like boys, at least not the boys at school. I liked the doctor on *Medical Center*. And I really liked Fonzie on *Happy Days*. I was in love with Fonzie and watched the show religiously, every Tuesday night at 8:00, after gymnastics practice. Fonzie slicked back his hair, like Larry Johnson. He wore a leather jacket, too, only his was black.

"Good," Larry said. "Hippies are anti-American, no-good peaceniks. Do you know what a peacenik is?"

"No."

Larry pulled the car around a bus and back into our lane, narrowly missing oncoming traffic. I grabbed the armrest. There were no seat belts in the car, and every time he jerked the wheel, which he seemed to do a lot, I slid on the slippery seat.

"A peacenik," he said, his voice soft and friendly, "is someone who would have us all speaking Chinese by now, or Russian. Would you like that?"

I shook my head.

"The peacenik," he continued, "would have us all dying of radiation poisoning, right now, as we speak." He spoke calmly, as if none of what he was saying bothered him much.

At the same time, he seemed happy—much happier than he'd ever been drinking beer at our dining room table with my dad. In our dining room with the high round windows, lilacs spilling their watery shadows all over the table, he never said much. He certainly never cursed. I had no idea what he was talking about, but I was happy, too. The day was gray and cool, the sky mottled like cantaloupe rind, and I was sitting in a car with someone, a grown-up, who was talking to me.

We pulled into the parking lot of the Dairy Queen in Westmoreland. The blacktop was cracked and weedy. A cyclone fence ran along the back of the lot, torn in places, the shiny dark leaves of the rhododendron bushes poking through. A ponytailed mother with three grubby toddlers stood at the walk-up window, trying to keep an eye on the children, scampering like monkeys over the picnic tables, and order at the same time. A car full of laughing teenage boys sailed through the drive-thru without stopping.

"Do you know what radiation poisoning does to a person?" Larry asked. We sat at a battered picnic table, gouged with names and hearts and F-words, waiting our turn. I barely had time to shake my head when he interrupted. "Let me tell you. It makes your hair fall out. Your teeth fall out. You're spitting blood, your bones are crumbling—you literally rot from the inside out." His voice was quiet and singsong, like he was reciting a lullaby. "Or, if you're lucky, you're at ground zero when the A-bomb hits. Do you know what ground zero is?"

"No." Obviously, I knew nothing. But the things he described sounded like something that happened in cartoons, not in the real world. I wondered why he'd make them up. Was he a liar, one of those liars that couldn't help it? There was a kid like that at school, and he was always getting sent to the principal's office for saying things like his dad was in the CIA, or he'd gotten run over by a car the previous summer. "But it's true," he'd sob as the teacher stood over him, stone-faced, pointing to the door of the classroom.

The lady with the ponytail gathered up her kids, wiggling with anticipation, and walked past us, balancing four twist cones in her hands. Larry Johnson gave her a polite nod before continuing.

"Ground zero," he practically whispered, "is where you disappear, turn to dust. In a flash, you're nothing more than a shadow on the sidewalk."

He leaned forward, looking at me carefully, as if to gauge my reaction. I made my eyes big and excited to show I appreciated his story, although I didn't believe a word of it. He nodded approvingly. *Chinese, the peacenik, a shadow on the sidewalk . . .* As we walked to the window to order, my head spinning, I realized I was having fun. I liked being noticed. Plus, ice cream.

"I guess I'll have a banana split," I said, scuffing my worn Buster Browns. I made my voice nonchalant as if that was what I always got, although I knew my mother would never buy me something so fancy.

"Hold on there." Larry jingled the change in his plastic change purse and smiled at the girl taking our order. His change purse was red and opened like a mouth when he squeezed it. "How about a dip cone, those are good."

"Well, maybe just a Peanut Buster Parfait." I played it cool, pretending I didn't understand.

"Hey, you're breaking the bank." He looked again at the girl in the window, slouched and bored, and laughed. "Just get a cone. You're a little girl. There's no way you can eat all that. It'll rot your teeth. How about a Dilly Bar? Those are good. You can get chocolate, cherry . . ."

"Butterscotch," the girl added, her freckled, ratlike face coming alive.

"Yum, butterscotch," Larry said.

"OK." I shrugged. "Can I get a Coke, too?"

After we got my Dilly Bar and Coke, we sat in his car. He was quiet, and it felt awkward just sitting there staring at the white sky, at the grocery store across the street with its loopy red letters where my mother sometimes bought éclairs.

"Were you in the war?" I said. I knew about the war. There were pictures of soldiers on the evening news when I was younger, and I remembered the words "cease-fire," repeated over and over, like a mantra. I'd thought it was something like a bonfire, like the fat sparking ball of fire the weirdos at the Renaissance Fair danced around. I knew my mother was against the war. And I knew because she'd told me that my dad had gone to college, gotten married, and then had me, so he wouldn't be drafted.

"No. I was never in 'Nam." Larry shook his head and looked out the window. "I was 4-F. Do you know what that means?"

"4-F?"

"Yeah."

"No. Is it like a club?" I ventured. "Like 4-H?"

He laughed. "No. 4-F means you can't fight. Do you know why?"

"Why?"

"Because you're damaged. There's something wrong with you. You're defective with a capital *D* and Uncle Sam doesn't want anything to do with you." He smiled as he spoke.

"Oh." Larry Johnson didn't look defective. I wondered what was wrong with him. Was there something missing? He had both his hands, both his feet. He sipped his coffee, tapping his foot on the floor. He wore shiny black boots that stopped at his ankles, and I noticed that his feet were small, much smaller than my dad's. I thought of the Bionic Man on TV. Was Larry like that? Did he have fake parts? I was too shy to ask. Instead, I asked why he hadn't gotten ice cream when he'd been hankering for it all day.

"Because I'm fat, Katie." He patted his stomach inside his jacket and looked at me again in that intense way, as if to see if *I* thought he was fat. "I'm a fat man." He sighed. "Do you know any fat guys?"

I shook my head. I felt shy, and I set my Coke on the floor of the car and rubbed my palm on my plaid pants. I ate my Dilly Bar carefully so I wouldn't drip. "My dad's skinny."

We were quiet after that, the bleached sky pressing against the car windows, the smell of bananas and dirt no longer strange. When I finished my ice cream, Larry tossed my stick out the window and started the car.


"There's this guinea pig at school," I said. Larry drove slowly through the leafy tunnels of my neighborhood, taking the long way around, past the ivy-covered store where I bought Doritos and orange pop after school, past my school itself, its worn brick building and cement playground deserted. I didn't mind taking the long way. I didn't want the trip to end. "I always want to take it home for the weekend, because we can take it home for the weekend . . ." I hesitated.

"Yeah?"

"And when the teacher asks who wants to take it home—the guinea pig—I'm always too scared to raise my hand." I said the last part all in a rush, ashamed. "I hate that," I added, staring at my hands, making my fingers into pinchers.

Larry laughed, not like he thought I was stupid, but like he liked me, like he thought I was neat.

"Fuck the guinea pig," he said in his happy voice.

I laughed, delighted.

"I'm serious. What do you need with that particular guinea pig? There are millions of guinea pigs in the world. Millions. I spotted six in my back-yard just the other day."

# Nine

## Wilson

"Mice can't climb," Wilson, the expert on mouse behavior, stated firmly.

"Because if one darts out and touches me, I'll die," Katie said. "So promise."

"I promise," he lied.

After quick, friendly sex in the living room, they stood in the kitchen eating ice cream. Rather, Wilson stood. Katie sat on the white-speckled counter, refusing to let her feet touch the ground. She swung her long legs, eating ice cream with a serving spoon. The soles of her feet were pink.

"We have three spoons in this house," Wilson said. "Why is that?"

Katie shrugged. She wore panties and his David Letterman T-shirt—the one he'd bought after sitting in the audience and watching Dave tape the show live—and she looked pretty, he thought, with her shiny hair falling across her shoulders, her narrow eyes a hot, happy blue. The shirt was tight on her; she was going to stretch it out. He almost said something but didn't. She was happy. They were happy. Her hair was the color of red licorice in a dark movie theater. He remembered a night, years ago, when they were first dating, and she'd sat in the same spot, giggling as he squirted honey from a honey bear onto her bare thighs.

"We always had lots of spoons," he said. "Most families do. My mom polished them."

"So go live with your mom."

"I will. When I'm ready to drink myself to death." He leaned against the sink. The clock on the microwave read 1:07. It was late. *He* was late. He was off schedule for the next day, and it hadn't even begun. Earlier, lying in bed after the walk, not talking, he'd decided to give the whole dissertation thing one last chance. He'd get up at five a.m., drive to his office, and work. He'd found a book on Kali, the destroying mother goddess, and he'd look through it, find some good images, some interesting parallels. *Sylvia Plath, the lost journals, women, mothers, death, art . . .* Thinking of it now, however, it seemed like far too difficult a subject to tackle first thing in the morning. But didn't he want to finish, wrap things up? Of course he did.

Images of dead babies, a snake and saggy boobies, flashed in his mind.

No, he didn't. He really didn't want to do a thing. But it was settled. He picked up a cup off the counter, sniffing it before filling it with water from the tap. He would rise at dawn, diligent scholar that he was, and write. Or maybe he'd stay up all night, get an even earlier start. He'd be like Hemingway or Faulkner—one of those guys who lived hard, wrote hard, and drank themselves to death. He wouldn't drink, of course. Despite the fact that more and more lately, he'd felt the urge for something—a Xanax, maybe, or just the tiniest slug of scotch. One beer, a syringe full of Demerol . . .

He must quit thinking, immediately. He would stay up all night and work, sober. And in the next few months, he'd finish the dissertation, defend it, find a job, and make everyone call him doctor. *Wilson A. Lavender, PhD. Dr. Lavender. Professor Lavender. Oh hello, this is my husband, Wilson—the doctor.*

There was only one problem: It didn't sound like fun. It sounded like work—unbearable, soul-consuming work. He set down his bowl, nauseated. "Katie." He didn't try to hide his desperation. "I think I hate my life."

"No you don't." She stretched out her leg and touched his thigh with her foot. "It's the middle of the night. You know you're not supposed to think about your life late at night."

"I know." He was silent, watching as she picked chocolate almonds from her bowl and set them in a row on the counter. Of course she was right. You didn't think at night, not without at least a quart of vodka on board. Screw it. The dissertation would get done; awful things always did. If the pompous asses in the English department at Midwestern could finish, he, Wilson, of the clear mind, sharp wit, and boundless mental capacities, surely could.

Did he have to write the entire thing now, in his head? Of course not. He could put it away, somewhere deep inside, and take it out tomorrow, when he was ready. Or, better yet, he would take tomorrow off and rest up, get a fresh start on Sunday, or maybe even Monday. He *was* exhausted—didn't he deserve two days of recovery after his long night spent "socializing" with his wife? He did. Genius must be pampered; it was not to be squandered. He would follow his own good advice and take the weekend off.

With the dissertation put in its place, filed away neatly in his mental in-box, he felt light, almost giddy. Relief flooded his heart; his soul sang. Like a bad girl in a B movie, one who has just renounced a life of pills, booze, and one-night stands, he felt as if he could live again, and he turned to his pretty wife with whom he'd just had friendly sex on the dog hair–covered carpet in front of the gas fireplace that neither of them could get to work, and kissed her pale cheek.

He looked at her small creamy hands, her milky legs and cheerful eyes. She sometimes reminded him of a nurse: She could be so calm and focused when she wasn't busy freaking out. She removed the troublesome nuts from her bowl as delicately as a surgeon. *My nurse*, he thought, feeling, for a second, infinitely lucky.

"There's all this crap going on at school," he said, moving closer, holding a hank of her hair. "This girl, Alice Cherry . . ." He paused, purposely not thinking of his colleague's round breasts and tight red sweaters, her big black eyes, as indifferent as flowers. "She brought her kid in, and he spilled hot chocolate all over Dr. Gold's books. You know, the big lady?"

"You like her." It was a statement rather than a question. Katie lifted her legs, put her feet on his chest, and gently pushed him away.

"What? Who?" He felt caught, guilty, and he hadn't done a thing.

"That Alice girl. Alice Cherry." Katie rolled her eyes. "What kind of name is that? What is she, a stripper?"

"No. And I hardly like her. She's obnoxious."

"Obnoxious girls are your thing." Katie coolly swept the almonds into her palm and tossed them into the sink. "And no one brings up a person, out of the blue, unless they like them."

"You were talking about your high school buddy not five minutes ago."

"That doesn't count. Steven doesn't count." Katie shook her head, never one to hold back when she could argue instead. "He's getting married. It's valid news, Wilson. Factual."

"Whatever."

"And he's twenty-three and I have no friends, so if you want me to stay in the house, all day every day, alone and lonely with the mice, I will—" Her voice rose, finding the hysterical edge that made him want to curl into a ball and hide.

"OK. Will you shut up?" He dropped his spoon into his bowl. "I have something funny to tell you."

"Really?" Katie grinned, flipping her hair back, its grapey scent wafting across the kitchen. "Hooray. Tell me."

"First, please don't push me with your feet. Ever again. It makes me feel weird."

"That's so funny. I'm sorry." She laughed, not looking sorry at all. "I was just getting you away from me. Why does it make you feel weird? Did somebody push you with their feet when you were a kid?"

"I don't know. It just bugs me. It's like you're a monkey or something. A mean monkey." He hadn't realized how much it annoyed him until he spoke.

Katie looked down at her hands, abashed. "Sorry. Note taken." Her voice was small.

"OK." He sipped his water, waiting for her to speak. She didn't. He cleared his throat. "Now I feel bad. I didn't mean you were . . . *mean*. It's just . . . nobody likes feet on them." He made his voice soft. "Should I tell you my story?"

"Yes." She looked up, sad.

"Are you going to be in a good mood again?"

"Yes, sir. I will be a happy monkey, sir. Whatever you say, sir."

She could be such a bitch. He would ignore her and tell his story anyway. "I was teaching today," he said, warming up, the terrifying thrill of a truly bad teaching experience making his heart beat fast. "And you know how I hate it whenever someone starts talking about . . . vaginas." He lowered his voice.

"Right. You hate it when things veer into 'coochie territory.'" Katie smiled, over her funk.

"Yes. And that's stupid. It's a women's studies class, about women and their sexuality, and there's an entire classroom of women, sitting there, women with . . . vaginas." He lowered his voice again, unable to help himself.

"A roomful of vaginas—"

"Stop." He frowned at Katie and shook his head, mock disapproving, making her laugh. "So anyway, they . . . vaginas . . . are bound to come up once in a while. And it's the context, I think. I mean if I'm deconstructing a film, or an advertisement or something, it's OK. But when it's personal, real women discussing their actual vaginas—"

"It's harder to handle."

"Correct. So all of a sudden, we're talking about feminine hygiene products. About how ridiculous they are, you know, making your, as you would call it, you-know-whatee, smell like cherry air freshener—"

"I like the way you say you-know-whatee."

Wilson frowned and shook his head, making Katie laugh again. "We're talking about how they can cause infections, how douching is bad, how it messes up the bacteria in your body. It's getting graphic and I'm becoming more and more nervous, and you know that feeling you get when you're teaching and you're so overstimulated it's like you're out of your body?"

"Yeah. That's why I'll never teach again. But wait," Katie pulled her legs up onto the counter and settled in, cross-legged. "How do you know all this stuff, about bacteria and douching? You're telling them all this?"

"Well, both. They're telling me, but I know things, too, from what you've told me. You're always saying how bad douching is, right?"

"Yeah. But you're not a doctor, Wilson." Katie lifted her eyebrows, skeptical. "I'm just making sure you know what you're talking about, that you're not feeding them false information. It's a sensitive area."

"Don't worry about it. Just listen. So then I say something awful. So horrible. So embarrassing. I can't even think about it now without wanting to die."

"What?"

"I can't say. It's awful. It just flew out of my mouth."

"Wilson. Tell me." Katie giggled. "What did you say?"

"And this is the class that hates me anyway."

"Your intro class, I know. They don't get to see the dirty movies. Come on."

"I was getting into it because for once they were talking and they never talk, and I said that you don't need feminine hygiene products. The female body cleans itself." Wilson hesitated, a fresh wave of humiliation burning his ears. He took a deep breath. "Then I said it, it came from nowhere, I said, 'So unless you're storing sandwiches up there, you're OK.'"

Katie laughed, horrified. "Oh my God. Yuck. Why did you say that?"

"I know. I don't know. I said it, and everyone stared at me with the most disgusted looks on their faces. This one girl in the front row—the one who's already complained to the department head because I made the mistake of saying I thought abortion was a necessary evil—just sneered. They were all silent, and everyone looked ready to fly out of their chairs, as soon as class was out, and go report me to the dean."

"But what did you mean? It doesn't make sense. Sandwiches? You're insane."

Wilson chuckled nervously. "OK. Remember when you told me about your friend Samantha's husband and how he was going out with that girl and she had that terrible smell . . . down there . . . and she finally went to the doctor and she had a tampon up there that had been there for like a month?"

"A birth control sponge. But so?"

"Well, I thought about that. And how that girl would need to douche."

"I guess. But where did you get sandwiches? God, Wilson, that's so gross." Katie was gleeful. She loved his social blunders, as long as they didn't directly involve her.

"I don't know. Maybe I was hungry. I just meant, the human body is clean. You don't need to take drastic action unless you have stuff up there rotting. I don't know where I got sandwiches. I should have said tampon, or birth control sponge, I know. I shouldn't have said anything."

"You were hungry." Katie shook her head, amazed at his idiocy. She sighed. "*Students*. I hate students."

Wilson didn't answer.

"Are they going to fire you?"

"One can only hope." He hung his head. "Katie, help me, I'm such a fool."

"I know." She touched his hair, pulled it back from his face. "You're crazy. You're disturbed. You should never be allowed to teach again. I think I'll write a letter to the dean first thing tomorrow morning."

"Thanks." He smiled. "Remember when I put honey on you? You were sitting right there." He rested his head between her legs. She was warm and smelled musky, the full flesh of her thighs faintly marbled with blue veins.

"Yeah, yeah." She pushed him away the way one would an overfriendly dog. "But I'm thinking about the mice now. Wilson, you have to feed Lovely from now on. Every day. I mean it. I'll never pour anything again."

That night, in the crappy condo in Kalamazoo, Wilson and Katie, the kids and the dog, slept. Katie dreamed of spring, of tulips in pastel colors, nestled like waxen candies in grassy green beds. She dreamed of daffodils, their peachy cups and limp skirts, and of cherry blossoms, baby pale and fragrant, drifting in piles on the sidewalks, floating in the air like confetti.

Wilson dreamed someone shot him in the neck.

# Part Two

## The Rock Star

"she always had the feeling that it was very, very dangerous to live even one day."

—Virginia Woolf, *Mrs. Dalloway*

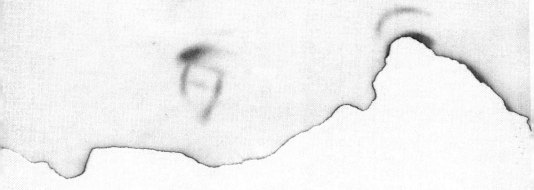

# Ten

**January**
2002

In a tiny town in the middle of the sandy nowhere where New Mexico, Texas, and Mexico sift together, January dreamed of the Rock Star. January who was born in August, "but you were so pale, so small, so contained," her mother gushed, "it was like you were far away, off in a vast, snowy wilderness, or on your own frozen sea, afloat on an ice floe, and you were content there, you didn't need a thing—certainly not from us."

January who didn't need a thing.

In her dream, the Rock Star looked just as he had in 1984: long hair striped blond and blonder, a few streaks of black and hot pink thrown in. Tall and skinny, he wore tight jeans and January's pink Marilyn Monroe T-shirt, shredded to within an inch of its life, exposing his pale stomach, the line of hair that ran from his belly button down. His nails were painted black, the polish chipped, and his eyes were sexy and tired, smudged with liquid liner. He smelled of Aqua Net, January was fifteen, and the whole world was a slick, purple puddle of love.

In her dream, the Rock Star had just begun therapy. January asked if he talked about her during his sessions. She asked the questions everybody asked: "What did you say? What did the therapist say? About me? Me? Me me me?"

"I *did* talk about you." The Rock Star jangled. He wore chains on his wrists and around his neck, a purple-studded leather wristband, a collar with metallic pink spikes. He took a drag off his cigarette. "Old man cigarettes," January had cried the night she met him by the pool at the Tropicana motel. She'd sat on the pinball machine in the lobby, wrapped her legs around him, and let him kiss her, this tall skinny guy with the New York accent and ratted hair.

With a kiss, she was his. They partied together, lounged together, slept the days away together, a stuffed dog settled between their naked bodies, her fingers in his mouth, his legs between hers, their long hair entwined. Alone they were nothing (well, *she* was), but together they were one: Stevie and Jan, ragged halves of the same rockin' whole.

In her dream, January couldn't hold his attention. He kept looking away. She kept having to reel him in, to make things the way they used to be, when everything was LOVE and she could breathe; when the sky was purple, the air smelled like swimming pools, and the moon bobbed over the Pacific Ocean like a happy, golden whale.

"What did you say?" January held her breath. She needed him to come back. He'd left. He'd taken his things: his neon-spattered drum kit, his earrings—bright, liquidy teardrops—his bubblegum-pink biker jacket, the stuffed dog they slept with. They'd given the dog a name, but she could no longer remember what it was.

"About me?" Her voice was pitiful. "What did you say?"

The Rock Star shrugged. "I said you were OK."

January could see by the flatness in his eyes that he no longer cared, that he'd already moved on . . . to the next girl . . . and the next . . . and on down the line. *Did she get it yet?* He smelled of dead grass, of smoke and sky and everything that disappears. He stood and walked away, trailing the blackened shards of January's heart. Sparks shot off his body. She started to cry.

*I was way more than OK.* When she woke, she was surprised to find that her pillow was dry. She was thirty-three years old. He'd been gone for fifteen years, and still she dreamed of him. How loserly was that? Someone should do a case study.

She got out of bed, stumbled to the bathroom, and looked in the mirror. She had no idea who she was. The house was silent, as if she lived in deep space. It was dawn, the sky in the window over the tub an eerie green. The room smelled of dust and limeade soap. She brushed her teeth and got back in bed. She was a girl with clean teeth. The dog jumped up beside her, and she petted its spotted belly, nicely, so it would stay.

# Eleven

Pete lavished fruit on January. It wasn't like he worked around it, he just had it. Watermelon was his specialty. He'd knock one open on the cement stoop out back and stand there in the mess, holding out a luscious, dripping heart for her to try.

"Here you go, baby," he'd say, his hair hanging in dark curtains around his face, juice dripping down his wrist. "No need to bother with the rest."

He brought her strawberries, and she smashed the leftovers and froze them. He brought her raspberries, limes, and lemons.

Pete had followed her home one evening from the gas station. He had a bunch of purple grapes in a paper bag. They got to talking. He liked Metallica, Mother Love Bone, and the Cure. He used to roller-skate at a rink in El Paso. January asked did he ever rollerblade? He explained in detail why roller skates were better. She ate her Popsicle and listened. As she walked down the sidewalk, she squished the spiked, brown mulberry balls beneath her feet. When they reached her house, she offered him a glass of water.

January and Pete ate grapes. They sat on her front step in the lavender dusk, their feet in the dirt, and talked. It had rained earlier, and the air was sweet with the smell of sage. Looking back, January could see the grapes were an omen. They were from Juárez, and she forgot to wash them. They made her palms itchy and red.

"Shit." She shook her hands. She felt tense and itchy inside. The knot of her halter top dug into the back of her neck.

"What is it?" Pete set his glass in the cracked flowerpot at his feet.

"I don't know. Something weird. Some kind of attack."

"What kind of attack?" Pete didn't look alarmed. He looked amused, but not in a bad way. His expression was motherly, his eyes big and kind, hair tucked behind his ears.

"An attack, I don't know. My hands are burning. I feel weird and hyper inside."

Pete laughed, like they were having fun. Or maybe he was just nervous.

January glared. The shadows on the porch deepened. Her paranoid self wondered if she'd been poisoned, if her new friend was trying to kill her. *Jan, use your smart part*, scolded the reasonable voice in her head. The reasonable voice belonged to Geordy, the counselor at Lutheran Family Services that her mother sent her to at age fourteen. Her crime: She hated school. Geordy was short, almost as short as she was. He had bouncy clown curls. His soft, frayed dungarees were the color of sand. *Jan, use your smart part*, he'd whine. January was to use the "smart part" of her brain. That would make her quit skipping school. She didn't understand. Maybe she had no "smart part." Maybe that was why she didn't understand. Geordy was always trying to *wheedle* her—into what, she didn't know. Their sessions were confusing. *When life gets you down, have a glass of wine*, he would say. He had a thing about "government cheese." *Finish school or you'll be eating government cheese for the rest of your life.* January would look at him with his bare feet and smug smirk and think, "What the *fuck* are you talking about?"

On her porch, Pete kissed her, abruptly. She wasn't expecting it. He pushed her against the wall of the house, the stucco rough against her bare shoulders, his hands on her cheeks, oil-stained, smelling of gasoline. Maybe he thought his kiss would cure her. Maybe it did. Almost immediately, the burning in her hands subsided. The heat of his mouth took over. She quit feeling mean inside. She kissed him back. Night fell. The dogs down the street began to bark.


January liked Pete. She liked him a lot, for a time. A week after they met, he climbed up onto her roof and got her cable TV for free. Then he settled in.

For the longest, hottest month of August, he'd climb back onto the roof, soak the straw pads of the swamp cooler with cold water from the hose, grab a jelly jar of Kool-Aid, slump in her broken-down blue chair, and watch TV. He usually watched The Learning Channel. He loved the reality shows—the baby show and the dating show and the wedding show.

Sometimes he'd cry. January would see tears well in his eyes. At first it was touching—he was so sensitive. Then it was annoying. "The prettiest little miracle," he'd say when a mother gave birth. After a failed blind date: "Oh man, they were perfect for each other!" As if any of it mattered.

January would try to act interested, but she hated TV, and she really didn't like Pete anymore. He was sexy and sweet and she liked to sleep with him, but he was also depressed. Really depressed. His sorrow was like a big, black, stinky cape he dragged around behind him. It was something you instinctively wanted out of your house. It sucked the life from a room. Not that she was Miss Sunshine and Light. Still.

And Pete was fine—there was nothing to be sad about. His eyes were the shiny black of Tootsie Pops. His hair was long and wavy; it hung nearly to his waist. But he drooped. Everything drooped: his eyes, his goatee, the seat of his worn-out jeans. Even his heart drooped. It made her mad. She wanted to bark, "Get it together, man." He had everything, his body smooth and tan, his hands, soft and kind.

They would have sex, or not, and then he'd watch his shows, through fall and on into winter. The fruit trickled off. January thought he'd bring her carrots, yams and pumpkins and squash, but he didn't. By December, she was going crazy. She wanted this boring man with his boring shows to get bored of her and go. She'd crouch at the end of the couch like a prisoner, ready to flee, barely breathing, feeling like she was going to shoot through the roof. But then what? Where would she rocket off to? And who would she fly there with? She'd watch Pete with his sexy lips and limpid eyes. Her body was satisfied, but her mind could not rest. "Why *not* Pete? Why *can't* I love Pete?" The question became her mantra. If she used her "smart part," he seemed OK. But inside, her soul cried, "No, are you crazy? No."

And then she was depressed, too.


One prickly December afternoon, January said, "If you love all this love, why don't you go out and get some? Find someone to marry. Have some babies. Or take a girl on a date—a fancy one, up at the steak house, with wine."

"That's not nice." He sounded hurt.

"I want you to be happy."

Pete set down his jelly jar on the upended crate she used as a table. He cleared his throat but didn't say anything. Thunder exploded in the distance. It started to pour, raindrops clattering onto the roof like someone had hit the jackpot. The back door blew open. Over the low coyote fence, January saw thunderheads gathered on the horizon. Pearl whined. January got up to shut the door. When she returned, the dog had stolen her spot on the love seat. January shoved her over. Pearl gnawed on the bones of her wrist in a friendly way. The air smelled electric.

A commercial came on. Pete muted the set. "Look at me, Jan. I'm forty years old, I work at the Conoco, and I still live with my mother. Would you want a guy like me?" He wore a faded Blue Öyster Cult T-shirt and jeans hacked off at the knee. He didn't look at January; he was busy examining the blister on his hand. A couple of days earlier, he'd scalded himself with hot tea. He was worried about infection. "The hand is a direct line to the heart," he'd said. "You get an infection in the heart and that's it: Adios, fucker." He'd smiled then, like he was excited. Pete worried about his heart, but in a breathless, anticipatory way. Sometimes it went nuts. Maybe it knew he was waiting and wanted to give him a show. He'd press January's hand to his chest so she could feel it, beating hard and fast, through the flannel of his shirt. "*Would* you want a guy like me?" His voice was soft. He didn't turn around.

January hesitated. "If I wanted all that, then yes."

"What do you mean 'if I wanted all that'?"

"You know—*that*: kids, a dog, a husband. Then yes, I would want . . ." Her voice faltered. Wind groaned in the chimney. The room had grown dark. She couldn't make herself say *you*. "That," she finished lamely. She felt guilty and confused.

"See?" Pete twisted around in his chair, a triumphant look on his face. He'd pulled his hair back in a black stretchy headband, and he looked interesting, like an artist. "Even a girl like you doesn't want a guy like me."

"What do you mean 'a girl like you'?"

"You know. Weird . . ." Pete trailed off.

January sighed, annoyed. She didn't need to hear more. She knew what he meant. She was no prize. She wasn't the prom queen. The color faded from the room. January didn't turn on the light. She closed her eyes, listened to the thunder. Lightning flashed behind her eyelids.


It was evening, green fingers of sunlight slicing through the clouds. Pete switched the TV to a basketball game. He hadn't moved from the blue chair. It was a puffy, overstuffed chair. It seemed to have grown around him. With each day he sank deeper into it. Pete was no longer welcome on the love seat with January. Pearl had gotten into the habit of wriggling between them when they sat together and shoving him off with her legs.

January thought of going for a walk, but her body didn't want to move. She was bored. She'd already brushed the dog and painted her toenails neon yellow. The smell of polish remover hung in the air. Water dripped from the gutters. Why hadn't she removed Pete from her chair months ago? Why did she continue to sit and watch and suffer?

It was all about *the waiting*. Waiting was her default reaction to life. She was a master waiter; she could outwait anyone. And she knew that if she waited long enough, Pete would, eventually, go. She was weak. Or lazy. She didn't like having to *say* things to people. A commercial came on. Wild boys rollerbladed and chugged soda. She thought of something. "Do you think you'll ever roller-skate again?"

Pete perked up. "Oh, man. I was cool, I was a badass. You know the movie *Xanadu*. Olivia Newton-John was in it? Everyone was on skates?"

He turned to her, his voice dramatic. "Jan, I could have been in that movie."

"I know. You've told me a million times. But how were you cool? How were you a badass? Why *weren't* you in the movie?"

"I wasn't in the movie because I live in Luna, silly." Pete smiled. "But I *could* have been in it—that's how good I was." He paused. "In my last year of competition, for my solo, I had the most awesome costume. It was a white suit, like Travolta's in *Saturday Night Fever*, only fitted, all one piece, *soaked* in rhinestones, it must've weighed twenty pounds—"

"Like Elvis," January marveled.

"No. Better." Pete was silent, lost in the past. "When I skated, the music blaring, light shooting off the suit, the girls in my skate club screaming, it was like I was a superstar. I *was* a superstar." He bent his head and sniffed at his blister. "Nothing will ever be that good."

"Maybe you're still a superstar. Maybe you need to skate again."

"Please." Pete looked at her like she was an idiot. "For you to say that shows how little you know about the skating world."

"But—"

"A skater is washed up by the time he's—"

"But you can't just stop." A feeling of desperation crept into January's gut. She didn't know why. What did she care if Pete skated or not? "You can't stop," she repeated.

"Actually, you can." Pete's face was smug. It was the same look he gave the dog when it ate his fast-food wrappers and barfed them up an hour later. It made January want to scream.

"You enjoy giving up. You take pleasure in not trying."

"How many forty-year-olds do you see skating around in disco suits, Jan?" Pete picked up the remote, no longer entranced by the past. "Things end. Deal with it."

"Things don't end. They only end if you want them to end."

"And that makes sense, how?"

January didn't answer. She had no idea what she was talking about. Pete stared at the set. She watched him watch TV. He leaned forward. He'd pulled off his headband, and his hair fell across his cheek. His injured hand rested on his knee. *Bastard*, she thought meanly. *You hate life. You want to punish it.*

As if he'd heard, Pete reached blindly for her hand. "Are we going to fight, or are we going to watch TV?"

Before she could think, January had stood and grabbed the remote off the arm of the chair. Her heart pounded. The tips of her ears were hot. "You need to . . . watch TV . . . elsewhere."

"What?" Pete looked up, confused.

On the love seat, Pearl groaned in her sleep.

January turned off the set. "You need to watch TV somewhere else. I'm not watching it anymore. I'm sick of . . . fucking . . . TV."

"Are you telling me to go?" Pete's eyes were wide.

She hesitated. "I guess I am."

"Why?"

She shrugged. Tears filled her eyes. "I feel like I'm going to die."

"I don't understand. I thought we were having fun."

January didn't answer. *How could he have thought this was fun?* She forced herself to hold Pete's gaze. She searched his eyes. Beneath the confusion she saw anger, and beneath that a bottomless well of sorrow. It all seemed too much to bear. She pried the cover off the remote, whacked the batteries into her palm, then dropped the whole thing to the floor.

Neither of them spoke.

"Whatever." Pete stood and pulled on his navy gas station jacket. "Psycho," he added for good measure. He didn't say it meanly; he sounded awed. After finishing his Kool-Aid, he set his jar on the crate and left, shutting the front door behind him. He didn't slam it. He wasn't that kind of guy.

January got up and wandered into the kitchen. Pete had left his address book on the counter. She'd always wondered about it. He carried it with him everywhere. She grabbed it, fell over the back of the couch, and slumped into the soft, corduroy cushions. Pete's orange T-shirt hung nearly to her knees. It smelled of him, earthy and warm, like a garden. For a moment she missed him. She glanced at the blank screen of the TV. Guilt and relief churned in her gut.

The sound of church bells wafted through the open back door. They seemed hollow and far away. Pearl trotted into the yard to bark at the neighbor's Great Dane. January yelled at her to stop. Silence. Seconds later, she began again. The Great Dane, Cesare, never barked back. January laid her palm on Pete's book. She wondered where the Great Dane—not just Cesare but any Great Dane—fell on the canine intelligence scale.

The address book was nice. It had a leather cover and a heavy gold pen tucked into the penholder. She opened it, inhaling its musty, papery smell. Every page was blank. And the dates were wrong. It was for the year 1990, and here it was the new millennium. There wasn't a word scrawled in it, not even Pete's name. It was as if all his sorrow lived inside the book, and when January opened it, it filled the room, crashing over her like a wave. She took a breath. Tears blurred her vision. What a horrible person she was, lying on the couch, flipping through the blank book of Pete's life. Who was she to judge—to *mess with*—someone else's sadness? Hadn't she given up on life years ago, the day the Rock Star disappeared? Wasn't it her sorry, sucking depression, and not Pete's, that scared her?

She carried the book to the porch and left it by the cracked flowerpot. Sand spilled onto the walk. The sky was lilac, the horizon a band of dark purple. Maybe he'd come back for it.

A few days later, the TV fuzzed static when she turned it on.


## 1987

January's house, half-buried in all that sand, was a gift from the Rock Star, a fabulous parting gift, like on *Let's Make a Deal*, the game show she watched as a child at the babysitter's, curled in the flying saucer chair, the big kids off at school. And she was the clown, the housewife dressed as a rag doll, with no grocery receipts in her handbag to turn over to Monty Hall for cold, hard cash. There was nothing behind curtain number three. She'd lost and she was to leave, immediately. She was to take her house and go and never return—the game was over. This was the end. It wasn't the beginning, and she wasn't cute and new, sitting on the pinball machine in the lobby of the Tropicana motel, her legs wrapped around him, the Rock Star, the one that would make her life WILD. It was the end. She'd tilted— *did she get it yet?* GAME OVER in bright, flashing bulbs.

"He wants you to be settled," Dale, the band manager, said. It was afternoon in West Hollywood, and he was breathing at her over the phone. The Santa Ana winds blew hot, the palms outside the dirty window rattling their death rattle, dying, always dying, except they never did, just gasped and shook, hanging on for days at a time. The sky was white hot, and it was impossible to breathe; it stuck in January's lungs as she sat alone on the filthy carpet in the empty place that was once theirs.

"Where will you go?" Dale was businesslike, his breezy tone jerking her back to the present. It was shocking when the phone rang, when Dale spoke, when cars on the street whispered past, when the Tower Records on Sunset burned yellow in the night. How could life go on when, for January, the world had ended the night Stevie Flame disappeared? They grilled chicken breasts by the pool and ate grapes. After dinner he left to distribute flyers at the Hollywood Rose show at Madame Wong's West. *He never returned.* The long night turned into days turned into a week turned into the end: a perfect autumn afternoon, ocean-swept, cars sizzling in the sun, Dale knocking at the door with two roadies to clear out Stevie's stuff.

Dale let her know the Rock Star's thoughts on the matter. January should consider leaving LA. What did the City of Angels hold for her?

"It's like this," the Rock Star said when she finally got him on the phone. The band was about to rehearse. She heard someone tuning a guitar. "Wait," he said, "did you know that we were at A&M this afternoon and ran into Herb Alpert, the *A* in A&M?"

"Yuck. I hate his songs. Did you know that one of his songs was on *General Hospital* when Luke raped Laura?"

"Luke didn't rape Laura. They were in love."

"Too bad you're wrong. They kept playing the song, over and over, an awful song, that horrible instrumental shit . . ."

Stevie laughed. "Jan, there was no song." His voice was soothing.

She wiped tears from her eyes. "I don't care about Herb Alpert. Fuck Herb Alpert."

"Baby. You should care. And you're wrong. There was no song." He covered the phone, shouted at one of his bandmates. "Anyway, I had the stuffed dog. Remember we'd tied him to the kit for the show at the Palace? Herb saw the dog. He said, 'I like your dog.' Cool, huh?"

"Did you tell him to fuck himself?"

"You're miserable." Stevie sounded impressed.

January blew her nose. She didn't care if he heard. "It was our dog. Give it back."

"No, hon. I'm keeping the dog." A lighter clicked. Stevie exhaled. "I have *custage*. Funny, huh? *Custage*. It's a cross between *custody* and *hostage* . . ."

January didn't answer. How could he joke when the whole party was going to go on without her? Did he have any idea how it felt?

"It's like this." The Rock Star grew serious. "We're about to hit it big. BIG—the biggest of the big time. We've got the huge advance—unheard of—the album is out, the tour is about to start. And you . . . you're extra. You have no business in LA, I mean, what do you even do? It makes me uncomfortable, like I'm responsible for you. It's like if, all of a sudden, *I* moved to Portland, and you were there—you were the only one I knew—and I had no business there, I was just hanging out, totally dependent on you. How would it make you feel?"

"I would love it," January whispered, but it was the wrong answer, it made him mad and she was to go, quickly, get out of LA and leave him alone. He had business to attend to. It was hard work becoming a STAR. Portland, he explained, was her place. LA was his. People needed to be in their own place, the place where they belonged.

Now, as a grown-up, January was struck by his egomania. Like you can make someone leave an entire city just because they're bugging you. Back then, though, she believed in him. She believed in what he said, he knew about everything—black holes, strange glam bands like the New York Dolls and Hanoi Rocks. He'd even been to the place where they make Hershey bars. And she was young and hadn't yet learned to think for herself. If he said she should go, she'd go. So when Dale called, the manager who looked like one of her dad's friends with his suits and pointy shoes, but snorted coke and was gross like the roadies, she sobbed into the phone, "New Mexico," because there was no way she would return to Portland and be boring.

Dale found her a house in a tiny town on the border. Luna, New Mexico. *Crazytown* the locals called it. January flew out, wondering why he hadn't chosen a nicer place, like Santa Fe or Taos. It never occurred to her that she should be the one to choose. If someone bought you a house, wasn't it rude to be picky?

When she arrived in Luna, she was stunned and called Dale immediately. "This is not the New Mexico I was talking about." He groaned but she ignored him, not caring anymore what he thought. She'd turned hard and unkind on the flight from LA. It felt good. "I wanted the orange rocks, the Indian stuff, the cliffs, the cactuses with arms. All there is here is dirt. Brown dirt and no pretty rocks, nothing orange, no pretty cactuses. I hate it. Even the names of the places are icky: Furr's, Luby's. Would you eat at a place called Luby's? Or shop at a grocery store called Furr's? It's all sexual, it's disgusting."

"Jan," he said in the hip drone everyone automatically tuned out. "They're just names. That's all. Only names. They don't mean a thing."

"What about the murders? I get here and a bunch of people were just shot at the bowling alley. They lined them all up at the end of the lanes and shot them. Gangland style. What about that?"

"It's not true. Who told you this?"

"It was in the paper."

Dale sighed. "You know not to read the papers. They're full of lies—you know that. Did you ever wonder how many shootings there are in LA in a day? Execution-style?"

"No."

"Hundreds." Dale sneezed violently. "Listen," he gasped. "He wanted to get you a place so you could settle. There's a university. He thinks it would be good. Or beauty school—have you considered that? You like hair, right?"

"No. Yuck. And what about—"

Dale cut her off. "I know he still cares." His voice was firm, no longer slippery. "Even if he can't show it."

"Really?"

"Yes." Dale was lying. He always seemed to be lying, even when he told the truth. So maybe he was telling the truth. Maybe Stevie *did* still care.

"For sure?" January didn't want to hang up. Dale-who-she-hated was being nice to her. *One good thing*, she prayed. One good thing, about *him*, and life would be bearable. "Absolutely. Just the other day . . . SHIT." Dale was overcome by another fit of sneezing. "I'm dying here," he wheezed. "Need my pill . . ." The line went dead. January never spoke to him again. *Just the other day . . .* Just the other day, *what?* Dale was lying, she knew, it was his vital skill, it was what he was paid to do, but she made up endings to the lie anyway. *Just the other day he told me to get you back, no matter what. Hunt you down, tie you up, stuff you in the trunk, and bring you home. He loves you so much he wants to crawl up inside, all the way up inside. He loves you so much he wants to shrink you down and wear you in a locket. Just the other day . . . That's how much . . .*

She found a job in a Laundromat. She paid taxes. During her first month in the Land of Enchantment, she walked to the plaza in the old part of town, bought a *ristra*—a garland bursting with healthy red chiles—and carried it home, draped across her shoulders like a stole. She hung it by the front door, and every time she went in or out, she touched it for luck. There was a Bible verse in a pamphlet at work: "The Lord shall preserve thy going out and thy coming in from this time forth, and even for evermore." *Evermore*—she liked the word. She would for *evermore* love Stevie Flame.

# Twelve

She'd never had a lot of energy. It was January's basic, underlying problem. She was lazy, or more specifically, weak. Or maybe she wasn't. But it was easier to live as if she were. Was that weird? She didn't know. It didn't make her bad. Some people found it charming.

It was winter, weeks after the breakup with Pete, and she was walking to the mall with the dog, blue sunshine shining all over the place, the Organ Mountains—corrugated and brown—holding the desert city in their arms. The cross over the old adobe church behind her house glowed white in the morning sky. She felt as if she could walk forever.

She took the shortcut, following the dog down into the sandy arroyo and through the tunnel beneath the freeway. Tumbleweeds clamored against the entrance. Inside, the walls were webbed with graffiti. It smelled wet. Broken beer bottles crunched beneath her feet.

The tunnel reminded her of when she was a child. There was another tunnel—a large cement pipe, the height and wingspan of a kindergartner—that carried a creek beneath busy Bybee Boulevard. She and her sister used to shoot through the pipe on their backs, starting in the shady water behind the fire station and landing with a foamy splash in the sunny pond on the other side. It was like a ride in a water park before there was such a thing. It was like the Olympics.

In the pipe there was danger: the icy, swift water, the rush, the merciless dumping into the sun-swirled waters of the pond. There was fear: the idea of rats, the darkness, the rhythmic thumping of cars overhead, the dank underground smell. January would hold onto the cement lip of the pipe and lie back, ears clogging with cold water, long hair streaming behind her as she surrendered, let go, into the dark and out the other end, emerging scraped and bruised, but despite the pain—*because* of it—it was the best thing she'd done. It was life distilled, everything perfect condensed into one sunny, shivering moment, her cutoffs soaked and heavy and hanging off her butt, her teeth chattering, her sunburned arms wrapped around her body as she stood on the cement ledge of the creek—cars whizzing past on the boulevard, water pouring like Niagara Falls—and thought, *Wow, look what I just did.*

"You did *what*?" her mother said. The alarm on her face made the shooting of the pipe even better.

January realized then, at age six, that there was life—everyday and boring—and then there was *fun*, which was something entirely different. Fun, you created. You thought it through. You took the time to add just the right elements—danger, fear, a certain darkness—and then you let go, surrendered to the rush. Of course, as a skinny kid, she didn't yet know about sex, drugs, or rock 'n' roll. But her heart did. It was waiting, beating black and wild.

Pearl barked from the mouth of the tunnel, jolting her back to reality. The dog's spotted coat was dusty. She switched her hips and grinned her pink dog grin, too excited to stand in one place. An empty wine bottle tilted drunkenly in the dirt near January's foot. She emerged into daylight, raced up the hill, and looked back at the church behind her house. Her heart pounded. She could see only the cross now, blue in the white sky. It made her think of the word *grace*.

She was pregnant. She'd taken the test that morning. She could feel things quickening, life pouring back into the broken and empty tunnel she'd become.

She turned away from the church, taking the back way to the university. The dust on the road was pinkish and blown into neat waves. A dead bunny lay in the scrub. There were always dead bunnies—she hated it. And roadrunners, just like in the cartoon. She couldn't believe it the first time she saw one zipping down the road at warp speed.

It was early on a Saturday morning. The parking lots of the university were nearly empty. The naked trees looked breakable in the clear, jelly light. The lawns were vast and rolling, the grass dead, the color of wheat. She passed married-student housing: squat cement blocks that reminded her of the dog pound.

There was the matter of Pete. Pete, the fruit guy, was the father. The dog pound made her think of him. Sometimes she felt ashamed of the way she'd acted. Pete was a nice guy. He was nice to her. But the truth was: She hated him. He wasn't the Rock Star. He was never going to make her life WILD. He was normal, and if that was true, it meant that she, too, was nothing.

Like everything, it all boiled down to self-hatred.

*So why are you having his baby?* January ignored the voice in her head. Couldn't a person just *be*? Go where the day took her, without analyzing every little thing? Fuck the "smart part." She'd finally ended it with Pete. How easy it felt to *never* invite him back. To let go, surrender to the rush alone.

As she walked, a brilliant idea came to her. She was pregnant—who was the best mother she knew? Katie, her sister in Michigan. January would winter there, take mothering lessons from a pro, and when it was time to give birth, she'd fly home and have the baby in her room. With a midwife, of course. Or out in the yard under a full desert moon, the rabbit curled in its womb a sign of fertility and luck.

Or maybe not, because what about the drugs?

She ran across the rolling lawns of the university. Her lungs burned and her body felt weightless. "Let's be free," she yelled at the dog. "Free of Peeeeete." Pearl raced ahead, back legs tucking up like a jackrabbit's. The morning air was alive, soaked with creosote and sage, and January ran to catch up, over the last stretch of dead grass before the campus ended and town began. All that freedom, all that space.

The mall was a mirage—rose-colored, shimmering behind traffic fumes—that moved farther away the closer January got. An hour later she was there, exhausted. She hadn't known it would take so long to walk—it was a short drive—and now she was too tired to shop, too tired to head home. Her feet were blistered, her legs shook. The dog was happy. Pearl could walk for days. Even in her sleep she ran, paws twitching as she chased bunnies in her dreams.

After tying Pearl to the bike rack, January entered the cavernous building. The first store she saw as her eyes adjusted to the dim light was the travel agency, a crayon sailboat and happy face sun scrawled on its sign. Perfect. It was destiny. As she stood at the counter buying a ticket to Michigan with the last of her savings, she could feel the fatigue in her legs drain away. Her Midwestern journey had begun. Joy shot through her. The agent handed her the ticket. She would depart from El Paso that night.

In the center of the mall she found Anthony—Katie's Anthony, father of her son Jake. He sat glumly at his incense kiosk. He wore an ornate vest, velvet-patched, shot through with metallic purple thread, and was drinking a giant cherry-lime from Sonic. Surrounded by candles and glittery backpacks, he looked like a prince, like he should be sitting in a tent in some Middle Eastern country, sucking on a hookah. At the same time, he looked like a scared kid. He plucked a cherry from his soda and ate it, then fished out a lime and sucked on that.

"Hey, January." He smiled shyly, revealing the gap between his front teeth. Anthony was charming. January knew she shouldn't like him, but she did. He was polite, always calling her January and never Jan in his soft West Texas accent. His crew cut was plush and black, his skin tan. He wore black-framed glasses—*birth control glasses* he said they called them in the army—that added a touch of endearing awkwardness to his good looks.

"Guess where I'm going." She sat on a brick bench, an explosion of jungle plants behind her.

"Where?"

"To Michigan. I'm going to spend the winter with Katie. I'm pregnant . . ." January stopped when she saw the hurt in his eyes.

"You're going to see her?"

She shrugged, feeling guilty for bringing up the subject of her sister. Although Anthony was the one that cheated, Katie had broken his heart. "Don't be jealous."

Anthony didn't answer. He tossed a handful of lime rind and cherry stems into the trash can at his feet. Besides Katie, Anthony had an ex-wife named Bobbi. They had two children, only Bobbi recently told him that the younger—a boy—might not be his. She might have lied when she was pregnant to get him away from Katie. Anthony was dark: black hair, brown skin. The boy was as fluttery and pale as a moth.

Anthony had always lived several lives at once. He doled himself out—a bit here, a bit there—like a cat with owners all over town. He moved like a cat, too, gracefully, with a low center of gravity. He once told January of the night a mountain lion strolled in front of his car. He was driving in the mountains near Taos. It was a winding road, he was going about twenty-five, when suddenly, out of the darkness, a cat stepped into the road. It crept across, its muscles rippling, moving so slowly it was as if time had stopped, as if Anthony had slipped into another dimension.

"It's a sign," January had said. "The mountain lion was telling you something. By moving so slowly, it was letting you get a good look at who you truly are. Deep down, Anthony, you're a cat—"

"A cat." He'd looked doubtful.

She nodded.

"How?"

She thought a moment. "You prowl. You don't stay in one place long. The harder a girl tries to hold on, the faster you turn to smoke and slip away."

He'd smiled then, satisfied with the image.

Anthony was in the first Gulf War. After Katie kicked him out, she and January had found an army pamphlet in the garage. It covered everything from the correct way to write a check to how to sneak up on a person and kill them with your bare hands. "Ooh, that's Anthony," Katie said. He screwed up the day to day things, like paying bills or returning movies to the video store, but when it came to the bigger mysteries of life, he was naturally covert. Eleven years ago, he returned from the war, young and confused, a married man at age nineteen, father of a baby girl.

Anthony proceeded to spin his web. Within a year he had his pregnant wife and little girl in a trailer on one side of town. On the other side of town he had Katie in her duplex, pregnant as well. There was Poppy the cat there, Lovely the dog here. Scrappy Bobbi, neurotic Katie. No wonder Anthony turned to drugs. Sometimes January would see him drive by her house. It was always the same time—four a.m.—which happened to be when Pearl liked to go outside and pee. She never mentioned the sightings to her sister. She just thought Anthony worked odd hours. Now she knew that what she saw, cruising past in the cool dawn hours, heading toward the gleam of green light on the horizon, was a man between lives. It must have been his best place, in his car alone, Alice in Chains blaring, the earth cracked and vast, the sky above nothing but space.

Neither of the expectant mothers knew about the other. It didn't last. One morning, Katie received an anonymous phone call from a woman who sounded like a telephone operator. In a sympathetic voice, she informed Katie of everything: Anthony was married, not divorced as he'd told her, and his wife was five months pregnant. It was like talking to an angel, Katie said. She wasn't surprised. She had sensed things. Her recurring dream was of a skinny blond girl, underwater, trying to tell her something. Katie used to tell January how Anthony would go for a Popsicle at the gas station and be gone for hours. "And he always brushes his teeth and gels his hair first," she said, never quite getting it.

On the other hand, it was a shock. Now, you couldn't tell the smallest white lie without her going nuts. "Do you know what it feels like to be betrayed?" she'd shout, eyes shiny with tears, and you'd have to hear the whole story again, sift through all the clues that never added up until the phone call.

Eventually, Katie took the baby Jake and left, moved to Iowa, which is what she did when she didn't like a person anymore. She left.

Last spring, Anthony became a father again, to another little boy. That brought his progeny to four: three boys and the original girl. The mother, Anthony's new owner, was an attorney who did hair wraps on the side. She had a bungalow near the university. Anthony said she was bossy but beautiful and didn't mind if he stayed home and painted. January had never met her. She wondered if she knew about the others.

"How's Jake?" Anthony took off his glasses and cleaned them on his white T-shirt. Squinting at her, he looked goofy and lost.

"He looks just like you." Anthony didn't contact Jake often, but nobody judged him. Everyone was just glad Jake had Wilson. Wilson the reformed drunk. He went to thirty meetings a week and knew how everyone on the planet, including January, should act. So that was good . . . for Jake.

"I'm getting a package together. For his birthday."

Anthony was always getting a package together. Jake's birthday was last July, but January didn't say anything. The air near the kiosk was sweet and spicy, so much nicer than the plastic mall air. Lined up on a shelf were the bright clay incense holders Anthony made. Some were shaped like small hands and feet, others like femur bones. On one shelf were seven yellow laughing dogs, their eyes and ears outlined with seed beads, their bodies curled like shrimp. January held one. It was heavy and round, pleasing in her palm. "It's Lovely."

"Yeah." Anthony smiled. He poked a stick of incense into the eye of one of the dogs and lit it. "I miss that dog."

January complained that her feet hurt, that she didn't want to walk home. Anthony glanced down. "You don't walk to the mall in flip-flops," he said, arranging a row of hot pink skull candles. "You don't walk to the mall, period."

She looked at him.

"Dumbass," he added.

She watched Anthony work. He had a talent for beauty. She could see him in his own perfume shop, creating scents in glass beakers, surrounded by rose petals and essential oils. The mall was deserted as usual. It was very small. There was no food court. After a while, Anthony went to buy gummi worms at the shop with the dream catchers. He brought January a Coke. "I fucked up. I drove her away," he said, slumping on his stool.

January didn't answer.

"She was so into me. She was so hot. I didn't know what I had . . ."

They sat quietly.

"You're like a cactus," January said, hoping to make him feel better.

"Shut the fuck up." He paused. "I thought I was a cat."

"No. A cactus. A big one, with arms."

"A saguaro?"

"Yeah. With all your kids, Anthony, you're a saguaro. You've got the desert mice living down here, birds up there, bunnies burrowing inside, flowers, snakes. You're an entire ecosystem. It's lucky."

"Not." Anthony dangled a bright worm over his open mouth, chewed sadly. He had so many children he was paralyzed, didn't know what to do, how to pay for or father any of them. He avoided Bobbi and her kids, didn't call Jake. Maybe with the new baby it would be different. At least they lived in the same house. January wondered what it would be like to have all that fat baby goodness and be too scared to enjoy it.

"Who's the father?" Anthony nodded at her stomach. He crumpled his empty bag, hooked his black sandals on the rung of the stool.

"I don't know," she lied.

"It's the dude that looks like the guy in Soundgarden." He pushed his glasses back on his nose. "What's his name? The guy that works at the gas station."

"Pete." Guilt squirmed in. She touched the ticket in her back pocket.

"Pete's the father."

January hesitated. "You think he looks like the guy in Soundgarden?" She was intrigued. "Which one? The singer? He's in another band now."

"Yeah. He looks just like the guy. Chris Cornell. Back when his hair was long. Before he got it cut. 'Outshined.' Temple of the Dog. He's a good-looking dude. Pete. Not the usual sociopath you go for."

January felt a rush of gratitude. They talked a while longer. "Well, there's Oreos at home, so . . ."

Anthony opened a small bottle of patchouli oil. "Right on." He dabbed a drop of oil onto his finger, wiped it on his neck.

After persuading him to drive her to the airport in El Paso that night, January finished her Coke and set out for home, slowly this time. The noon sun was mellow, the buildings of the university peachy and cracked, hollow now, empty of students. She was in a good mood, thinking of Pete. Maybe he wasn't depressed; maybe he was just *tortured*. She drifted past the clock tower, the new library glassy and insect-like, crouched in the dirt. Pete. Chris Cornell. "Outshined." *Feeling California, looking Minnesota.* "Jesus Christ Pose." *I'm gonna . . .* And then they were at the Ag buildings—the stink hit her first—and all the cows were outside, mooing up at the cow-blue sky, their great cow mouths open wide, as if they'd like to swallow it whole.


## 1987

"PID," the doctor shouted, hot hospital lights haloing his head. "I knew it the minute you walked in, hunched over, clutching your belly, sobbing for painkillers."

"What did you know?" January was curled on the gurney in the ER of the tiny town in New Mexico, wanting to kill him for being so loud.

"That you had PID—pelvic inflammatory disease." His jacket glowed with a greenish intensity that made her head spin. "You were doing the PID shuffle. That's what we call it around here, you know, hunched over, shuffling."

"You said that."

"And you're pretty green."

"Thanks."

"Don't worry. We'll fix you up." The doctor was cheerful. *Dr. Lopez*, the stitching on his jacket said. He wore beautiful blue suede shoes. She'd noticed them right away. His dark hair was pulled back in a ponytail, and he wasn't as old, or as loud, as she'd first thought. His voice was kind.

"We're trained to see surfaces." Dr. Lopez took her blood pressure, pumping up her skinny arm for what seemed like forever. "You know: fat, thin, short, tall. Ugly like me. Pretty like you." He winked. "Do you know what we really are?"

January thought about shaking her head.

"Tubes. Wiggly tubes of water and light. How amazing is that?"

She stared up at him. What was he talking about? She was dying. She didn't want to die, but she was. She even knew why she was dying. It was the hatred. She'd been in Luna a year, and she hated it, hated her life, hated herself. The hatred had grown inside of her, heavy and hopeless, weighing her down, until it exploded in a black mess, a mass of fiery tendrils ripping through her gut. Earlier in the night she'd woken in unbearable pain. She couldn't sit up, couldn't lie down, could only crouch around the *thing*, the hatred, and pray. Sweating and shaking, she called a taxi, waiting on the front porch with her head between her knees until it arrived.

"Everything touches us. Everything goes deep." The doctor's voice was soothing. Fluids dripped through a tube into her hand. Someone had brought her a heated blanket, bundling her like a baby.

"Yes," she said, or maybe she only thought it. He'd given her a shot by then, and the pain was gone. It was floating around the room, no longer interested in her. "He did. He touched me. It's in my bones and it hurts." She started to cry, tears making puddles of the bright lights. "On the TV. In magazines." She meant him, the Rock Star, for his band *had* hit it big, bigger than big, and he was everywhere. It was as if her own private nightmare had leapt from her mind and grown enormous, taking over the world. What could be worse than losing him, and at the same time, seeing him everywhere she looked?

"Many people think TV is the anti-Christ."

"What?"

Dr. Lopez ducked between her raised knees. Her bare feet rested in stirrups, in soft lamb's wool. The gurney was a cloud and she was floating, her naked body bathed in white light. The doctor stood with a grunt. He held something silver and gleaming. "Everything that touches you leaves its mark." He stepped out of the spotlight. "Everything."

"Is that a pop can?" There was the crushed can in the lot, the dumpster, the fat roadie, the gravel, up her nose, in her mouth. *Did she get it yet?* Hollyweird. Lalaland. Califuckinfornia. Like a song and then it ended. The room smelled of cold water and ammonia. She wanted to ask him for another shot, just one more shot to knock her out completely, but she couldn't think of the right words. She never knew what to say. "You never say anything, I mean, who are you?" the Rock Star cried. He was frustrated. He was no longer enchanted—by her, by her silence. "What do you think? What do you feel? It's like you're not here, like you're not real. Even when I kiss you, all I taste is gum. I want to taste you, January, not gum." He threw a heavy glass ashtray across the room. It stuck in the wall. A cloud of ash bloomed and disappeared. She took out her gum, tears streaming down her cheeks. She stuck it on the bed, crawled toward him.

"It's like this," he said, sitting at the end of her bed, only it wasn't a bed, it was a gurney, and it wasn't him—it was never him—it was the doctor with the pretty blue shoes. Dr. Lopez. "You are a woman. And women are like butterflies. The butterfly, you see, has a sort of magic dust on its wings. That's how it flies. And if you touch it, the oil on your hands pulls off the magic dust, just a bit, but over time, it adds up. Eventually the butterfly is left with no magic dust. Virtually wingless, it is unable to fly, and all it can do is die."

"That's so sad."

"Yes, it is. It's very sad." Dr. Lopez rested his hand on her belly, looked into her eyes.

"And . . . I'm a butterfly?"

"Yes, you are."

"And no one . . . no one will . . ." She took a deep breath, wiped her eyes. "Touch my wings . . ."

"Correct." The doctor smiled, the corners of his eyes crinkling. "No one will steal your dust, touch your wings. Unless, of course, you let them."

"OK."

"Excellent." The doctor scrawled something on a prescription pad. He handed her a piece of paper. The lights dimmed. He was gone. The curtains around the bed shivered in his wake.

# Thirteen

Anthony's van was a psychedelic love machine. On it were naked women with suns radiating out from behind their heads, naked women with full moons nestled in their bellies, coyotes, peace signs, and a languid polar bear, its fur tinted pink, yellow fish leaping from its paws. The van was Anthony's masterpiece. He'd finished painting it a week earlier.

"It's Katie." He rested his palm on a red-haired woman hugging a giant purple-spotted toadstool.

"Nice." January started to make a smart remark about the toadstool/penis but thought better of it. Anthony was too sensitive. She told him her sister's waist wasn't that small. "You flatter her."

"I remember." He spanned the waist of an invisible woman with his hands. "Will you tell her that I miss her? And that she's a bitch for . . ." He dropped his arms, kicked the tire of the van.

It was cool in El Paso but sunny. They were early for the flight. After letting the dog pee in a patch of white gravel, they waited in the van. Anthony lit a joint. January stuck her bare feet out the window. Sunlight bounced off the glass walls of the terminal. Behind it, planes dropped and rose like bugs. She caught a glimpse of herself in the side mirror. She looked skinny and a bit rough, makeup smeared beneath her eyes, hair that maybe she should have washed. The pregnant glow had not arrived. Beside her, Anthony was feline and fabulous in his salmon-and-chocolate-striped shirt.

"You don't leave a house alone." Anthony pinched the cherry off the joint without offering her any. He stared at the ashtray, neatly pulled a thread from his cuff.

"Why not?" January watched her lips move in the side mirror.

"Pipes freeze. Squatters will move in."

"You're a squatter. Don't break in. You'll do something bad, I know."

Anthony laughed. "I'll clean. I'll water your plants."

"I have no plants." *No plants*, she mouthed at her reflection.

"OK. I'll get you some." Anthony ran his hands over his shaved head, settled back in his seat. Sunlight winked off his glasses.

January was contemplating his well-rounded skull when he leaned into the back and pulled something from his knapsack. "Give this to Jake, OK?" He placed a small wooden box in her hands. On the lid was a picture of an Indian chief in a feathered headdress, the words LAS VEGAS painted beneath it in swooping red letters.

"Funny." She touched the chief's face, his rosy cheeks and long hair. "He looks like a white guy. Like Charlton Heston."

"Yeah. It's old, from the fifties. It was my dad's."

January rattled the box. "What's in it?"

Anthony lifted the lid and handed her a set of dog tags. *Anthony Julio Chavez. A bunch of numbers. Catholic. O Positive.*

"It's creepy that they put your religion on there." She fingered the metal tabs.

"For last rites. What's creepy is that if you die, they nail the tag to your big toe."

They sat in silence, sunlight puddling in their laps. January liked army lore. It seemed to be an honest world—no illusions of civility. Anthony had stories. A truck drove over a land mine and blew up in front of him. The guys in his unit cut the head off a wild dog and put it in a pizza box.

"You had pizza over there?" she'd asked at the time.

He ignored her. "Fucking ignorant hillbillies. They were the ones you had to watch out for." The enemy was a bunch of ragged, starving guys surrendering by the hundreds. *Gas masks, MREs, underground bunkers . . . tiny white pills in the event of nerve gas . . . night-vision goggles that flipped night on its back, revealed its underbelly, twitching and green.* Anthony had insect repellent that practically burned the hair off your arms when you put it on.

She closed her eyes. Anthony's scent of oranges and cloves and skunky pot washed over her. "Get this," he began. Last weekend he'd taken peyote, driven out of town, and buried himself in the sand. "The stars—you would not believe: huge and icy, hanging in the black sky, so close I felt I could touch them. Everything was raw. The moon was a pale, carved mask, and me—I was just a bunch of bones, lying in the dirt." He took off his glasses and wiped his eyes. "I *was* the planet—water, oxygen, minerals. There was no line between me and the rest of the universe. The line, January, is a lie." He looked tense, as if his newfound knowledge hadn't brought the expected release.

"The line." She stared at her hands, at the fanned bones, the dirty chewed nails. *I am the planet.* The thought made her head float. She vowed to do strange and awesome things like Anthony.

It was time to go. After she checked the dog, Anthony hugged her. January didn't want to let go. His shirt was silky against her cheek. Life had changed overnight.

"Don't be an idiot," he warned. She watched as he shuffled out of the terminal. The sun had dropped. It hung over the mountains, a pinwheel of pink light. Which life would he slip into now? Would he crash at Bobbi's trailer? Break into January's crumbling old adobe and clean? She looked down at his box, his vital statistics. The dog tags were warm in her hand. She lifted the lid and dropped them in. Glued to the bottom of the box was a photograph. In it Anthony was shirtless, looking up at the camera, a tough expression on his face. His glasses were off, and he was holding two flaming devil sticks. It was night. His tattoos were smeared and black, and those, along with the fiery torches, gave him the look of a tribal warrior. YOUR DAD!!! he'd scrawled on the picture, an arrow pointing to his unsmiling face.

Night fell, the plane rose. January leaned her forehead against the windowpane. The moon hung low over El Paso, riding the rolling hills. The stars were tiny spurs, and all the fast-food places shone like fool's gold.

The first time she flew, she was fifteen. She'd wanted to live in Hollywood and dance in music videos. Her mother said that if she got her GED, she was free to "explore." Iris was big on freedom. "Free to Be . . . You and Me" was the girls' theme song. Katie and January never had a bedtime. January didn't wash a dish or eat a vegetable until she was twenty-five. On a rainy summer afternoon, she sat on a plane in Portland, wearing her best sundress and denim jacket with the "Eddie" patch—Iron Maiden's ghoulish mascot. *Prepare cabin for takeoff.* Tears filled her eyes. No one had stopped her from leaving.

"She's miserable," Iris had told anyone who would listen, pointing at January, hunched and glowering at her side. "Some kids aren't cut out for school. Strange little birds like this one need to be set free." On the plane, January inked the word FUCK on her knuckles, hating her mother because she was scared. The plane roared to life, rushing faster and faster down the runway, knocking her back in her seat. She couldn't believe the force roaring through her. It seemed wrong, obscene. She landed in LA, stayed with Katie in her studio apartment near UCLA until she was kicked out for general slovenliness. January met Stevie Flame and was sucked into the tornado of his life, where she whirled and whirled and whirled until she was spat out like a stunned cow, hundreds of miles down the road. In Luna, New Mexico, to be exact. She was eighteen.

She was thirty-three. Stevie Flame was nothing but a handful of glitter, stuck in the crack of her heart.

The plane landed. The first thing January noticed about the Midwest was the cold. It was an unearthly, bone-rattling cold and she was not yet outside—she was in the tunnel that connected the plane to the terminal. It was as if they'd landed on another planet, one on the far, unfriendly edge of the universe. *Socks.* Why hadn't she worn socks? She never wore socks, but she could tell she'd entered sock country. *Big fat wool socks*, she thought, clenching her numb toes.

January dug Pete's faded yellow sweatshirt from her backpack and pulled it on, then made her way to the baggage claim. The dog panted in its crate, quietly terrified. She searched for a rental car desk. The ticket to Chicago was half the price of one to Kalamazoo. She'd drive the rest of the way.

After reserving a car, January wrestled Pearl into her sweater and took her outside to pee. The dog found a patch of dirt and peed for ten minutes straight. It was so cold her pee turned to steam. It was so cold January's nostrils stuck together every time she breathed in. *If I were naked I'd die*, she thought, suddenly getting why people in the Midwest—meaning Wilson, the only Midwesterner she knew—didn't fuck around.

A black-haired woman with the eyes of an alien slouched near the coffee cart, her chubby baby stuffed into a Snugli. The baby batted at the woman's cup. She moved it out of reach, then kissed the baby on the nose.

They looked happy. For a moment, January let herself imagine the future, when everything had turned out fine. She was home in Luna with her baby, wandering the yard, showing her all the pretty things: the fountains of ornamental grass; the pomegranates that turned the dog's mouth hot pink when she chewed them; the crabgrass, sharp and yellow and full of deadly goat heads.

Beyond the yard were the pecan orchards. The trees stood knee-deep in water when they flooded the orchards in spring. At night things bloomed, doubled, one world falling into the next. There were the real trees and the water trees. Black silhouettes. Ghostly branches shimmering in water. And everything—the earth and the sky—was littered with stars.

In her vision, January walked along the irrigation canals, through the nighttime orchard. She told the baby the names of things. The baby grabbed at the sky with tiny, star-shaped hands.

"How do you like being a mom?" January moved closer to the woman, dumping cream into her own coffee.

"It's a nightmare." The woman's voice was cheerful.

"I'm expecting," January added shyly.

"What's your name?"

"January, Jan."

"Well, January, Jan. Expect that life as you know it will soon end."

January didn't know what to say.

"Forever." The woman smiled.

Her name was Sophie. She was forty-two—older than January first thought—and had given birth to her daughter in her living room, in a plastic swimming pool. She was in labor for twenty-two hours. Water leaked into the apartment below and she was almost evicted, but it was worth it. She warned January that no matter what, she should not have her baby in a hospital.

"Why?" The coffee was bitter and sweet on January's tongue. The dog barked in its crate behind her.

"They won't give you the placenta." Sophie smirked. "It goes to pathology, like it's something dangerous, which I guess, to 'the man,' it is."

"You mean the afterbirth?" January vaguely remembered her babysitter's cat eating a bloody hunk of something after having kittens. "Why would you want it?"

"You eat it." Sophie acted like it was the most natural thing in the world. "You slice it up and cook it in a stroganoff. Or you can freeze-dry it and stir it into shakes. It's exactly what the woman needs, nutrient-wise, after giving birth. It just seems weird because we've gotten so far away from the natural world." She sighed, resting her cheek on the baby's head. "Sometimes I think we're so co-opted, we're barely alive."

"I've felt like that." January set down her cup, excited. "Barely alive. Like I'm . . . defective or something . . ."

Sophie gave her an encouraging nod.

"And I'm tired . . . all the time . . ." January trailed off, embarrassed.

"Of course you are. Society sucks the life out of women like you. And you're not defective. Obviously. You're charming." Sophie ducked her head shyly, wiped her hands, and tossed the napkin in the trash. The baby moved with her in a dance, dipping backward when she leaned over, jiggling when she brushed off her hands. "The fact that you feel defective shows how sick our world is."

"Right. Why should I feel wrong? Is that what you're saying? That maybe I'm not the problem?"

"Exactly."

Sophie pulled up her shirt and offered the baby a fat, banana-shaped breast. January stood beside them, watching quietly. Sophie's large eyes were tilted and wide-set. Her dark bangs were cut suicide-short, and she wore black eyeglasses with rhinestones in the corners. She was small, and dressed in some sort of Chinese communist pajama outfit of pale, creamy linen. On her feet were black canvas slippers. Her look was liberated—her loose pajamas made for dancing, her slipper-clad feet built for speed.

In the rental car lot, in a pool of orange light, Sophie pulled out a lighter and a small soapstone pipe. "Want some?"

January looked into the backseat. The traumatized Pearl was jammed into the corner, eyes big and black and glassy. Baby Wisteria stared at her, amused. Drool dripped down her chin. She shoved her fist into her mouth and gnawed. "No."

It had turned out that Sophie and the baby were headed east, too. When Sophie suggested they share a rental car, January had agreed, relieved. She rarely drove in Luna. She was known for getting lost.

Sophie packed the pipe, lit it, and inhaled. A seed sparked and popped. "You sure?"

"Yeah. I'm pregnant. I don't want a baby with two heads . . ." January edged down her window, inhaling the cold, watery air.

"Look at Wisteria. Do you see two heads on that girl?" Sophie's laughter turned into deep barking coughs.

"Hah." January's voice was flat. It wasn't that funny.

Sophie sucked on the pipe, talked while holding her breath, laughed about nothing. Stoned people were boring. "It's a weed, an herb," she gasped. "It's nothing but good. They've done studies in Jamaica, and all the little Rasta babies, they're way fatter and happier than the rest."

"I can imagine." January pictured the Rasta babies, chubby coffee-colored tots in crocheted caps, giggling in their cradles. "You go ahead," she said, feeling pure, telling herself *this is what it's like to be a mom*. You let the whole fucking party go on without you, and you don't mind, not one bit. You like it even, because you know you're right and everyone else is wrong.

January considered the stranger driving her rental car. Sophie drove like a bat out of hell. She looked like a bat, too—or maybe Batgirl—her leathery black coat hanging in loose folds from raised arms, her glasses masklike in the shadows. Grinning like a superhero, she sped up to a toll booth, barely slowed, threw a handful of change into the basket, and raced onto the expressway. January had never seen a toll booth. It was a whole new world.

The heater in the car was broken. Cold air blew onto her frozen feet. She jammed her hands under her thighs, but it wasn't enough. After much coaxing, Pearl crept into the front seat, wary eyes on Sophie. January warmed her hands on the dog's belly. Pearl smelled like home, like dust and grass and sun. She buried her nose in her fur, inhaling deeply.

"We're running away," Sophie said merrily, shoving a tape from her purse into the console. Chris Isaak's moody guitar filled the car. She turned it up.

"Who? You and I?" January look at her, nervous. Had she been kidnapped? *Now, Jan,* warned her smart part.

"No. Yes." Sophie laughed. "*I'm* running away. With Wisteria, of course."

January asked why, but Sophie was lost in the music. Chris Isaak moaned. January prayed they wouldn't have to listen to the whole unhappy album. "It's so black, so spare," Sophie murmured, swaying to the beat. They zoomed up on an SUV and sat on its tail until it moved into the slow lane. When the road cleared, Sophie told January how she and Wisteria had come to be in Chicago. The day before, Ray—Sophie's partner and Wisteria's father—went off to Buddhist camp to learn the way of the peaceful warrior. For no particular reason, other than it "felt right," Sophie moved all of Ray's belongings into a storage unit. Then she ditched his car in a cornfield and threw the keys into the Iowa River. She took the baby and left. "The peaceful warrior is going to shit," she chuckled now.

"Why would you do that?" January's new friend seemed different, more psycho. The connection they'd had at the coffee cart was gone.

"Why wouldn't I?" Sophie's voice was sharp.

"It sounds like a lot of work, for one."

Sophie shrugged. A song by Rose Red, Stevie Flame's band, came on. "Ugh." Sophie ejected the tape and flipped it out the window. "Rose Red sucks." She glanced into the rearview mirror, pleased with herself.

January didn't say anything. The song was the "power" ballad "Apple of My Eye." She remembered when Stevie wrote it. It was a rainy afternoon. They were lounging in bed. He made up the words, haltingly, tapping out the rhythm on her bare back. January used to beg him to practice his beats on her back. It made her feel *perfect.*

"I love to make you cry," it began. Animal, the singer, used his wobbly, sensitive voice, accompanied by a lone acoustic guitar. "Can't help but wonder why . . ." After the quiet opening came the funky bridge: "You rock me girl, your legs so sweet, you kick my ass, it's you I eat . . ." Which devolved into screaming guitars, ripping drums, and Animal's anguished, ungodly howl: "And I'm bleeeeeeeeeding." There was a dramatic pause, a few clicks of the drumsticks, and the entire sequence—slow, fast, insane burst of emotion, silence—began again.

An image of the first album cover flashed in her mind. On it crouched a naked, fanged groupie, her jet hair ENORMOUS, blood dripping sexily down her chin. She held out a bloody, bitten apple. Scrawled above her cowering body were the words TAKE A BITE.

An awful, sulfuric smell filled the car. Sophie nodded at an ugly mess of factories in the distance. Orange flames leapt atop what looked like enormous candles. Smokestacks belched clouds of yellowish smoke into the night. "Ugh. Are we in hell?" January pulled her sweatshirt over her nose, trying not to breathe.

"Gary, Indiana," Sophie noted. "Birthplace of the Jackson 5, murder capital of America."


January couldn't get out of the car. Sophie had talked about Ray and only Ray for two hours and forty-seven minutes. January knew about his comic book collection, his selfishness when it came to sharing his car or French fries, the actual skeleton in his closet, and his hemorrhoids. She knew more about Ray than she ever had about Pete. By Sophie's reckoning, it took fourteen hours to make Ray's world disappear. It was the idea of hiding a life, losing it in a cornfield, throwing it into a river that disturbed January—it was such a violent act.

Sophie sat calmly in the driver's seat, her winglike coat wrapped around her body. In the back, Wisteria and the dog slept. The car seemed to expand and contract with their breaths. It was early morning but still dark. The stars had blurred on the horizon.

There were no hills, no edges to this Kalamazoo world, nothing to hold a person in. The snow was pretty, blanketing the ground, piled atop buildings and parked cars, heaped in a mountain in the corner of the lot. It was dusky blue, gold beneath the streetlights. The mountain was gouged with purple shadows. It was as if they'd arrived someplace magical, like Tibet, rather than at the airport in Kalamazoo.

You could smell the snow, clean and watery and inviting.

The plan was to return the rental car. Katie would come for January, and Sophie would find a place in town to rest and "reassess her journey."

But January couldn't move. She'd give anything to be back in bed in Luna, the dog drowsing at her side. She'd "acted on impulse," as counselor Geordy would say, and now she was paying the price. She had cold feet, literally and figuratively. She thought of clocks, of the one in Geordy's office, to be exact. The second hand was a spaceship. As he droned on and on, January would watch it glide around the blank blue face of the earth. It never stopped, only spun, not quite of the planet, but not quite separate from it either.

Had Geordy wanted her to fail, all those years ago? He'd certainly enjoyed it when she confessed to sleeping away another school day at a friend's, when she told him she'd skipped first period so often, she'd forgotten where the classroom was. You failed and then you paid. That's how it worked in Geordy's world. He liked to quote Jim Morrison: "No one here gets out alive."

Plus Katie hated her, a fact she'd failed to consider. January had skipped her sister's wedding in Las Vegas last summer. It was too hot to fly. She had tickets to the B.B. King concert. Katie was furious. She had Wilson call and scold January—in a bored voice; what did he care if she showed?—while Katie listened on the extension, butting in every once in a while to yell. January hadn't spoken to either of them since.

Sophie whacked her cigarette box into her palm. "I'm exhausted. All the packing. My shoulders are killing me. I think I pinched a nerve." She looked wide awake, ET eyes bright, gloved hands resting on the wheel in a perfect position of 10 and 2. She grabbed her lighter, gave it a vigorous shake.

"Where will you go?" January asked, stalling for time.

"We'll find a shelter." Sophie cracked the window, blew out a stream of smoke.

"Like a homeless shelter?"

"No. A woman's shelter. A shelter for abused women."

"Did Ray hit you?" Sophie, with her quiet mania, would be the last woman January would beat, were she a wife beater.

Sophie looked at her, amused. "Ray didn't have a death wish."

It didn't seem to be a joke. *You are a weirdo*, January thought, touching the fogged glass.

"I was *victimized*," Sophie added. "Abuse takes many forms. It was an intolerable emotional atmosphere." She exhaled. The edges of her face blurred. She told January again of how Ray refused to lend her his car— she'd once had to ride her bike, *in the snow*, to get weed. She'd begged for the keys. He'd refused, called her a bad mother. Wisteria had cried and cried. "I was ready to stick my head in the oven," Sophie said now. "It was Ray or me. One of us had to go."

January stared at her feet. Desperation crept in. A gust of wind blew by, shoving the small car. She hated this feeling. It was too familiar, sucking the life from everything. *It's only a feeling. Feelings can't hurt you*, Geordy would say. But that was a lie. They're the most powerful force on earth. They'll crush you into the couch and never let you up. They'll back you into a corner, knock you to your knees. Without them life would be so . . . fucking . . . easy.

The day before Katie's wedding, January was at work at the Laundromat, flipping through magazines. There was a picture of a woman who'd died of heatstroke in the desert, trying to cross the border. Her body had lain for months in the blistering sun. It became mummified, lips drawn back from white teeth, brown skin clinging tightly to bones. Her arms were raised, fingers curled into claws, as if she were reaching for something, there in the indifferent sky.

As she swept lint from traps, January couldn't shake the image. How could a person disappear? Sink into hot sand and never get up, the sun that had once woken you, that had warmed the top of your head as you played outside as a child, turning you to dust?

She threw away the magazine, called her mother, and told her she wouldn't be at the wedding. "Hmmm," Iris said. She didn't need to say more. Her "hmmm" held enough disdain for a dozen lazy daughters.

That night when January's shift ended, she went to the B.B. King show—good old B.B., heartbroken and cheerful—and felt better. But now Sophie's story had brought it all back: the uneasy feeling she had that summer day, a day so hot everything smelled metallic and dry like the inside of a clothes dryer. The sun beat against the glass walls of the laundry, and when you went outside, it was painful to open your eyes. There was the image of the ruined, reaching hands, haunting her as she worked, as she stood alone at the show, surrounded by smoke and cheap beer and blues—blues as if the earth itself had cracked open and were pouring out its secret sorrow.

"*Intolerable emotional atmosphere*," she mused. "What does that even mean?"

"You're not getting it." Sophie sighed loudly—January was too dumb for words. She reached into the backseat, grabbed January's bag, and dropped it into her lap. "January, Jan." Her voice softened. "You're a beautiful girl, and you're going to have a beautiful baby. And thanks for listening to all my shit." She made a wry face, and for a brief moment January liked her again. Sophie rested her hand on January's. "Go on. Go call your sister. I'll meet you around back."

January pulled her hand away. "You're hot. Do you feel OK?"

Sophie smiled, looked mysterious. "I'm burning up."

Unable to take another second, January shouldered her pack and stepped out into the cold. Her lungs filled with icy air; salt crunched beneath her feet. She was about to grab her purse off the seat when Sophie pulled the door shut. There was a pained expression on her face, as if she were about to cry, or burst into hysterical laughter. January stepped back, confused. Sophie pulled away from the curb, tires flinging up fountains of dirty slush. "Wait," January yelled, but Sophie didn't stop. She looped around the parking lot, slowed at a stoplight, then sped onto the main road. January watched her go. Within seconds, the rental car, along with Sophie, Wisteria, and Pearl, was gone.

# Part Three

## Shelter

"Do I dare

Disturb the universe?"

—T. S. Eliot, "The Love Song of J. Alfred Prufrock"

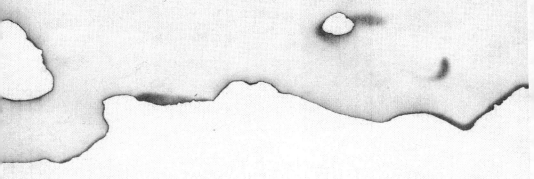

# Fourteen

## Wilson

The phone rang early Saturday morning, jolting Wilson from a sound sleep. He'd been dreaming of airplanes falling from the sky, sticky purple flowers, and a gaping hole in the side of his neck. It was a little after seven but still dark, the condo silent, filled with the stillness of sleep. He quickly did an inventory, but they were all here, all his people—the little ones and Katie asleep beside him, Jake snoring at the foot of the bed in his Scooby-Doo sleeping bag, Lovely sprawled out on the bathroom floor, on the cool linoleum, having become too hot for comfort in the Lavender family "nest." Speaking of heat, how high had Katie set it? He was sweating, his heart racing. And still the phone rang, the lonely trill that occurs only in the darkest hours before dawn.

He sat up, climbed over Katie, and lurched into the living room, sure it was someone calling about his mother. She was gone, he knew it. She'd finally done it, finally killed herself, the years of depression come leaping back to the present, despite her recent success with the Paxil that made her so damn serene he wanted to strangle her. It was as if none of it had happened. The past was not just suppressed, it was erased, with one tiny pink pill, and they were all supposed to go on being the perfect family they'd always pretended they were. But what about him? What about the kid he'd been, setting fire to rugs, knowing nothing he did could make her care?

Now she was happy. Now she loved her grandkids, and it infuriated him to see the mother love he'd so desperately craved skip a generation, landing on his kids in a shower of gifts and photo sessions and hugs. But the roosters had come home to roost. His mother was dead—for wasn't it suicide, and not her moving to California, that was his secret fear all along?—and he was alone, and that was the way it would be. He picked up the phone, resigned to his fate. "Yes?" he said, trying to work up the energy to cry.

"Oh my God." A woman, not his mother, was on the line, crying, babbling something about a dog. Wilson took a deep breath, relieved. Whatever it was, it was not about his dead mother, thank God. That and the dissertation would send him over the edge. He steadied the phone, his hands shaking.

"I think you have the wrong number." He was about to hang up, already back in bed in his mind, curled around his wife's lush body. Wind cracked in the chimney. The Christmas lights glowed purple through the slats of the mini-blinds. Something made him hesitate. The woman was still crying, but softly now, and she sounded so pitiful. "Wait," he said, rubbing his eyes. "Are you OK? Do you need help?" Maybe it was a tragedy. Maybe she'd been beaten by a boyfriend, and he could rescue her, take her to the shelter, have a great story to tell his students Monday morning.

"She took my dog," the woman said, before dissolving into sobs. *She,* she'd said. Was it an abusive lesbian relationship? He'd heard about those, butch women who looked like men and acted like men and beat the crap out of their partners, just like men. He adjusted his boxer shorts, wide awake, excited to be of service. He wondered if she was pretty.

"Where are you? How can I help? Are you safe?" He looked around the desk for a pen and a piece of paper, settling for a yellow crayon and a blank page torn from one of Katie's self-help books.

"Of course I'm safe." The woman's voice was strong, coming through loud and clear. She sounded familiar . . . spoiled, strident. His heart stopped. "I'm at the airport," she continued, as if it were something he should have known. "This crazy lady stole my dog, and I need Katie, now, so we can go find her, so we can hunt her down before she does something bad."

He hesitated. *Hang up,* a voice in his head told him. *Hang up now.* But he knew it wouldn't work. She'd find them. She'd hunt them down, pound on their door, and tell Katie what he'd done. "January?" he said, praying he was wrong, knowing he was not.

"Yeah?"

"Is it you?"

"Yeah."

"Are you here, here in Kalamazoo?"

"Yes." She sniffed loudly. January. Of course it was January, who else would call in the middle of the night, scaring him half to death? January, of course. And she was here in Kalamazoo, at the airport, although unlike most people, she'd failed to let them know she'd be visiting. In fact, they hadn't heard from her since she'd skipped their wedding last summer. January. He sighed.

"Is Katie up?" she said, her voice officious. "I need her now. I'm freaking out. Please." Of course Katie was up. It was before dawn on a Saturday, why wouldn't she be? She was in the garage, tap-dancing. He'd go and get her.

"She's here," he said, hesitant. "But she's sleeping. I'm not going to wake her. The kids will get up and it'll be a nightmare. I'll come for you. Stay where you are. I'm on my way." Why hadn't he hung up, gone back to bed, let her handle her disaster like a big girl? He slipped on his jeans and found his car keys on the bathroom floor. Outside, the morning air smelled of pine and wet earth. Snow-pink clouds, like wispy goddesses, danced on the horizon, announcing to the world the arrival of the little sister.

January sat like a queen in the big shoeshine chair just inside the terminal, deep in conversation with the shoeshine guy himself, a short indignant-looking fellow in a jolly red sweater vest. He was the first to spot Wilson as he hurried through the electric doors. "You the brother-in-law?" he said, eyeing him suspiciously. His face was like dark, crumpled leather. He reminded Wilson of an old blues musician.

"Yes I am." Wilson turned to his sister-in-law, making his voice sympathetic. "Hey, Jan, what's going on?"

"So you're the brother-in-law." The shoeshine guy sat down on his platform with a grunt. January slumped deeper into her seat, eyes narrowed, arms limp, as if it would take too much energy to speak, let alone get off the throne and follow him to the car. Wilson and January clashed. There was no kind way to put it.

Last Christmas in Portland, at Katie's mother's Christmas Eve party for her church choir—a party at which he'd somehow found himself against his will—January had gotten drunk on eggnog, called him an ass, and thrown a piece of fudge at him, for no reason other than the fact that she had no boundaries, no impulse control, and everyone was supposed to go along like, hey, no problem, it's January, what do you expect?

He'd been sitting at the Christmas table, laden with cold cuts and mini slices of rye bread, cookies and a crystal punch bowl brimming with eggnog, avoiding the drunken Portland choir members, choir members he didn't know and had no wish to know, especially the lecherous head of the McPheeney clan, a father of six who kept trying to engage him in conversation about Iris's collection of naked lady oil paintings. "Does that look like pubic hair to you?" he'd said before Wilson made his escape.

He'd just finished constructing a salami sandwich when January plopped down across from him, resting her chin on her hand. She watched him eat but said nothing. Wilson was glad and ignored her. After a while, though, she sighed and began to regale him with her theory of time, how it was an artificial construct, man-made, and she'd follow her own personal clock, as she always had, thank you very much.

"The human biological clock is actually twenty-five hours, Wilson," she'd said, starting in on a plate of swirled butter cookies. "Did you know that? No wonder we're all so cranky."

This after she'd made the entire family wait in Katie's dad's freezing minivan earlier in the evening, ready for church, Iris's choral music trilling on the car stereo as they waited, waited, waited for January to quit dinking around in the bathroom and get her ass in the car, which she did, twenty minutes later, reeking of weed and giggling like a teenager, a fact everyone in her family ignored.

"All righty," Katie's dad said, his voice cheerful as he backed the minivan out of the driveway. "Everybody ready?" He'd turned around then, his arm draped across the passenger seat, and grinned at Wilson as if to say, *I've got it figured out. Just keep your mouth shut and drive.*

They'd arrived at church late and had to sneak in, all eight of them—dancing candy-cane-chomping kids included—down the long aisle, everybody staring, and into the front row because Iris, who'd been choir director for thirty years and was church royalty, always sat in the front row. The minister, a gentle, long-haired guy who looked as if he'd stepped from a 1970s production of *Jesus Christ Superstar*, paused in his opening remarks. "And a very merry Christmas to Iris and her family," he'd said with a laugh, as the entire congregation joined in, roaring jovially, because apparently Iris and her family were always late to Christmas Eve services and it was something of an inside joke—a joke that Wilson did not find funny.

"Do you believe in friends?" he said later that night at the Christmas party as January ate and drank and blathered on about time. "Because if you keep pulling stunts like the one you did tonight, making all of us wait so you can get high, you're not going to have any."

January stared. "Don't be an ass," she said, laughing. Then, just like that, she threw a piece of fudge at him. It glanced off his shoulder and landed on the floor where it was quickly devoured by Iris's overweight beagle. At the same moment, Katie walked into the dining room. "Did you feed Stan?" she asked, giving him an accusing look.

Now, almost a year later, January seemed exactly the same, a skinny princess with funky blond hair and artsy purple suede clogs, reclining languidly, waiting for the world to kiss her feet. Wilson bent to pick up her backpack, a fringed hippie affair that was surprisingly heavy. The fact was: She was upset. And whatever had happened in the past, he would be the bigger party and let it go. Who cared if she thought he was an ass, or that she'd assaulted him with a large chunk of Christmas confection, getting him in trouble with his wife and hurting his feelings at the same time? She was his sister-in-law. She was family, and no matter how much the thought made him grit his teeth, he would rise to the occasion and help.

"You want him carrying that?" The shoeshine guy nodded at the pack.

*Take it*, Wilson thought, smiling, dangling it from his hand. *Take her while you're at it.*

"Whatever." January's voice was disconsolate. She climbed slowly down from the chair, taking the shoeshine guy's outstretched hand in her own. He wore fingerless gloves, and his movements were graceful, as if he were leading her in a pas de deux.

"Hold on." January turned to confer privately with him. Wilson watched, tapping his foot, feeling left out. She glanced over her shoulder once or twice, and the shoeshine guy looked at him and shook his head as if Wilson were the cause of whatever had January so upset. *Freaking out*, as she would say, not in New Mexico, where she belonged, but in the middle of his life, on a Saturday morning, on one of his only days off.

"Bye," she said, shaking the guy's hand.

His face collapsed into a smile. "You're going to find it. Don't you worry. Get out there and bring that dog home." January nodded gravely, then turned and followed Wilson outside.

He adjusted her backpack on his shoulder. "Do you have a coat?"

She shook her head. She wore glittery jeans and a tiny T-shirt, the fancy purple shoes and no socks. Her bare ankles were red from the cold. "Put that on." He nodded at the sweatshirt tied around her waist. She did as she was told but still looked pitiful, big ears sticking out of her scraggly hair, skinny shoulders hunched against the wind. Reluctantly, Wilson took off his down coat. "Here," he said, already starting to shiver.

"Oh no, I can't," January protested as she pulled it on, zipped it to her chin. She sniffed the collar, made a face. "Wilson, are you still smoking?"

Was there anything more comforting than the orange-and-brown décor of a Denny's, a Grand Slam breakfast steaming on the table in front of you? Wilson thought not, and was glad January had agreed to stop and eat, to take the time to make a game plan regarding the retrieval of her dog. He was starving. Rescuing pampered princesses was hard work, he thought, as he speared a bite of sausage and continued his interrogation. "So you did not get on your flight to Kalamazoo, is that correct?"

"Correct, yes. I did not. I never had one. I was always going to drive." January wrapped a sausage link in a pancake and picked it up, eating it like a taco. She'd been much more animated since he told her he didn't think it would be a problem finding the dog. The woman had probably made a mistake and wanted to return the beast as much as January wanted it back. All they had to do was connect. She was at the shelter? They'd drive there and get Pearl, case closed. The fact that January was too lazy to file a police report about her stolen purse only made his life easier.

"Instead, you accepted a ride with some woman you didn't know, someone who turned out to be nuts?" Wilson sipped his orange juice, enjoying the warm restaurant, the hot food, the smells of coffee and bacon and pancakes. As a kid, he'd sometimes gone to eat at the Denny's in Effingham with his grandpa Jack, his favorite grandpa, as he had the same skinny legs and knobby knees as Wilson did, but never cared, and wore shorts whenever he pleased.

"Yes. No. Wilson, I didn't know she was weird until we were halfway here. What was I supposed to do? Get out of the car in the middle of nowhere?"

"No." He stirred sugar into his coffee. "You did the right thing, you had no choice. But you might want to rethink your habit of getting into cars with complete strangers."

"But she was nice." January was like her sister in that she never conceded a point. It was so obnoxious it was charming. Her hair stood up in happy peaks, and her green eyes, narrow like Katie's, were bright. "She knew about all sorts of things," she continued. "Stuff I'm interested in: having babies, the placenta, feeling like you're not a part of the world, like you're some sort of alien, and the thing is, it's not your fault, it's the world's fault . . ." January trailed off. "Anyway, that's what she said."

Wilson was silent. *It's not your fault, it's the world's fault.* He felt that way often, but according to the program, that was wrong, it was only stinkin' thinkin' and would lead you back to just one place: the bottle. "Wait," he said, sitting up. "The placenta? Why on earth would you be interested in *placentas* of all things?"

"Oh yeah, I'm pregnant," January mumbled, intrigued by her hash browns.

"Really?" Wilson smiled. Katie was going to freak. And what would Iris have to say? January certainly wouldn't be the perfect little sister anymore. She'd have to relinquish her crown, give back her banner. He couldn't wait to get home and tell his wife, aka *the problem child*. (He and Katie were both the black sheep of their families, Katie because she told the truth no matter how much it pissed off her mother, Wilson because he'd chosen to drink and take drugs and set fires.) "Who's the father?" he said, wondering if she knew. "Is he in a band? Have we seen him on MTV?"

"Whatever."

"No really. Who was that guy? Stevie Flame? Rose Red, right? God, they were lame."

January stared.

Wilson laughed nervously. "Don't you think?" He repeated a few of the song titles, trying to get her to smile. "'Walk Like a Rocker,' 'Good Time Groupies,' 'I Think about You All the Time'?"

January didn't smile.

"Hair bands . . ." Wilson trailed off, looked out the window. "I bet it was exciting, though, meeting all those—"

"I'm not talking about . . . this kind of stuff . . . with you," she interrupted, her cheeks pink.

She was embarrassed, Wilson realized, and he felt bad. He stared down at his plate, at the soggy pancakes, the ketchup-tinged hash browns. She was right. He was an ass, making fun of her just because she'd once dated a guy with giant hair. What was wrong with him? He returned to his eggs, hoping she wouldn't report his faux pas to his wife. They finished their meal in silence.

"I feel like I just had breakfast with Elvis," he said as they walked to the cash register. He nodded at her glittery pants, burning brightly in a patch of sunlight.

January laughed. "I love that. They are like Elvis pants. I beaded them myself. Maybe I'll do a matching shirt." When she smiled, her face lit up, and she no longer looked bored and spoiled. She looked eager, her eyes nearly disappearing, her overbite pronounced and endearing. She was tall and pretty in a dramatic rock 'n' roll sort of way. He could see why rock stars had wanted to fuck her. Maybe the visit would be OK, he thought, as he handed the cashier a twenty. As long as she was up and out and on a plane back home no later than the first of the year. He looked at her, busy fiddling with a machine that dispensed Skittles for a quarter. She turned the knob. Bright candies poured out over her hands and onto the floor. "Wilson," she cried. "I hit the jackpot."

He nodded and smiled. She had twenty days.


How to find a shelter for victims of domestic violence? Surely the address wasn't in the phone book. Wilson knew all about safe houses, secret entrances, unmarked buildings, videotaped parking lots. There was a hotline they could try. 1800HELPME1—was that it? He was sure it was. He'd distributed the flyers every semester and had always been struck by how stupid, how victimizing the letters of the phone number were. HELPME: a dying woman's cry, a weak woman's lament. How about something *empowering*, he remembered thinking, like 1800KICKASS, or 1800DIEJERK? Something that would make the ladies feel strong, like they had a chance. And what did the 1 mean? He never figured it out. In any case, he'd call the hotline, find out where they were, and pick up the damn dog. Which was just what they needed, he thought, as he watched Katie and January get reacquainted in the living room, screeching and hugging and screeching some more—a sister-in-law and another dog, all crowding into the tiny condo.

"No, no, I'm not mad. Not at all," he heard Katie say in her loud, excited voice as he crouched in the kitchen, searching the bottom cupboard for the phone book.

"I just, I knew it wasn't a big love match, I mean, you guys already had a bunch of kids, and—"

Katie shushed her sister. They giggled.

"Thanks," he called, his feelings hurt. He hated the way women relayed every intimate detail of your relationship to any female around: their sisters and girlfriends, their mother, their hairdresser. Katie, to his horror, had on several occasions chosen to include *his* sisters and *his* mother in her circle of trust. "Your son has just been neutered," she announced to his mother over the phone last summer as he lay on the couch post-vasectomy, burning with embarrassment despite the bag of ice in his shorts. It seemed that once a guy was in a relationship, he became transparent, like one of those clear plastic men in which all systems—circulatory, lymphatic, nervous, digestive—were visible. Nothing was sacred; all was revealed. At least that was his experience. And for him, it had been a "big love match"—it still was, and it hurt to know she'd said otherwise. He sat back on the kitchen floor, noticing three Hot Wheels and a Super Ball that had rolled beneath the stove. "Where the hell's the phone book?"

"By the washing machine," Katie called. "On the floor, next to the wall."

"Of course," he mumbled. "I should have known."

When he looked up DOMESTIC VIOLENCE in the yellow pages, he was pleased to see that his photographic memory had, once again, served him correctly. The number was, indeed, 1800HELPME1. He moved to the desk in the dining room and dialed confidently, smiling at January and Katie, who watched, quiet now, from the couch in the living room. The kids were still asleep. The silence was perfect.

"Hey. This is Suzanne. What's going on?" the woman who picked up the phone said. Her voice was annoyingly comfortable, as if she and Wilson were already best friends.

"Hey, Suzanne," he said, trying to match her laid-back tone. "This is Wilson Lavender, doctoral candidate at Midwestern. I teach women's studies there?"

"Yes?" Had her voice chilled? He wasn't sure, but her *yes* seemed distinctly less intimate than her greeting.

"Yes. Well. My sister-in-law is here visiting from New Mexico." He looked up, giving January a smile and a thumbs-up. "And the thing is, a woman has accidentally taken her dog. A woman who was headed, this very morning, to your shelter."

"I'm sorry, I can't help you." Suzanne's voice was definitely ice cold.

"You don't really need to help me," he continued. "If you could just let me know where you're located, we'll drive on down and pick up the dog." He hesitated. "If it's all right with you."

"No. No, it's not all right. We don't give out our location over the phone."

"Oh. I understand. But like I said, I work with women. I can assure you I'm not some perpetrator looking to—"

"Excuse me?"

Shit! Why had he said that? He took a deep breath, forcing himself to sound calm, friendly, unthreatening—which was exactly what he was, for God's sake. "I'm sorry. What I mean is, I teach women's studies at Midwestern. I just want to get the dog. But to get the dog, I need to know where you are."

"I'm going to have to ask you to hang up," Suzanne said. "Now. Right now."

"Suzanne, please." He tried to keep the desperation from his voice. January and Katie stared at him from the couch. Katie mouthed at him to hurry up. If he failed in this, they'd turn on him, he knew it, the vibes were already in the air, and it would be his worst Christmas on record (worse, even, than the time he'd totaled his Dodge Stealth, flying across a dark midnight highway, drunk off his ass, and ending up in jail, where his dad had let him stay until the New Year, barking, "You've already fucked up Christmas," when Wilson protested). "I know you give out your address. How else would abused women . . . victims, I mean . . . find you?"

"I'm going to have to ask you to hang up," she said again, her voice firm. He laughed—totally inappropriately, he knew, but he'd never heard such a thing. What kind of person asks you to hang up, and then stays on the line like a watchdog until you do? It took nerve.

"I'm not going to hang up," he said, trying to sound threatening yet harmless, a difficult tone to achieve.

"What are you doing?" Katie jumped up from the couch. "Don't piss them off. Find out where they are." January buried her head in her hands. She looked to be working up an emotional bomb, ready to detonate, any minute now, in his living room. *Fuck*, he thought, staring at the water-stained ceiling. He could hear Suzanne, breathing vigilantly on her end of the line.

"This is ridiculous." Katie, always mellow until she exploded, stomped over to the desk and grabbed the phone from his hand. "Hi," she said, turning her back to him. "My husband just beat the shit out of me and I need shelter, so if you could tell me where you're located—" She listened a moment, then threw the phone across the room. "She hung up on me."

"Of course she did." Wilson kept his tone neutral. "You're a rage-aholic. You need anger management." He climbed off the desk and sank to the soft carpet, wishing he could nap right there.

"I think that's a guy thing?" Katie laughed, but nobody joined her.

In the living room, January began to cry. Katie turned on him, as he knew she would. "Happy now?" she mouthed, rushing to her sister. She gave the phone a kick on her way.

Wilson moved deeper beneath the desk and curled on his side, resting his head on his arm, on the doggie-smelling carpet, lost in thought. Why had Suzanne hung up on his wife, when with him, it had seemed as if she were ready to sit on the line all day until he did as he was told? It was a mystery, an episode with deeper meaning, he was sure, something to do with the differences between the sexes, but he couldn't put his finger on it. Were women more threatened by other women than they were by men— was that it? Were men the true victims in Western society, subjugated and silenced by the emotional tyranny of their female counterparts? He had the urge to call Suzanne back, to find out exactly what she'd meant by her actions, to find out the politics behind her person, but he knew he'd be in big trouble if he dared go near the phone.


They placated her. *Monday morning*, they promised, patting her thin back, bringing her cups of chicken noodle soup, making her coffee with lots of real cream, the organic kind that doesn't turn you into an enormous cow-sized American, as it isn't pumped full of bovine growth hormone and steroids and antibiotics and who knew what else. *Yes, he would go to the store and get the right cream, yes he would find the right gummi worms, the kind that were super sour and had that salty stuff on the outside, and yes yes yes—he absolutely* knew *that everything would be OK. First thing Monday morning,* he promised. He'd go to work and talk to Dr. Gold, the imposing and imperious Dr. Gold, a woman of size who did not mess around, and she—he knew—would lead him quickly to the shelter where she would demand that the dog be released into her custody. *Immediately,* she would say, narrowing her Cleopatra eyes. And then they would sue the crap out of the personable Suzanne, holding her liable for emotional distress, for inflicting intentional emotional distress on Wilson and the members of his family. But mostly on Wilson for it was he who had been the most disturbed by the long, bleak weekend of whining and sorrow.

January stayed on the purple velvet couch, bundled in several fleece blankets, drinking coffee and staring at the fireplace that nobody knew how to work.

On Saturday night, she melted tangerine-scented candles all over his TV set.

On Sunday, she slept. All day. The kids poked at her and giggled and ran away squealing, and still January slept.

Now, Monday morning, the day that everything was to be fixed—the dog found, January appeased, his life set to rights—Wilson had a problem. The problem was that Dr. Gold was nowhere to be seen.

He slumped at his desk in the shabby office, waiting for her to show. It was the week before finals. There would soon be exams and portfolios to grade, and then final grades to mark and turn in to the registrar by the end-of-semester deadline. None of it fazed him. His daunting final exam was already copied and sitting in a pile on his desk, ready to be unleashed on unwitting and unprepared students. He'd long ago perfected the technique of spending no more than four minutes on any student paper—he used an egg timer to keep himself on track. For Wilson, finals week was a breeze. The real news was that just moments earlier, as he waited for Dr. Gold, he'd scrawled the first line of his dissertation in his notebook. He was on his way. And once begun, the dissertation would pour from him, he knew, wrapping itself up in a matter of weeks.

He examined his first line, proudly, like a father touching the tiny toe of a new baby. *Felt like singing today,* he'd written, for he wanted to start out on a happy note, to better contrast with the darkness sure to seep in soon enough. *Felt like singing today.* He loved it; it was perfect. Graceful, alive, tinged with just the right amount of hope. *Felt like singing today.* He reread the sentence, this time adding an exclamation point. Excellent, he thought, rubbing his hands together. Now what? He stared at the page. He had no idea.

*By noon today.* Katie's dark words echoed in his mind. *By noon today, we need that dog.*

*Or what?* he thought, feeling tired. Someone had stuck one of Dr. Gold's geraniums on the graduate assistants' desk, and he leaned forward, breathing in its spicy smell. He was thinking of Dorothy in *The Wizard of Oz*, of the way she'd simply fallen into the field of poppies and slept, and of what a beautiful experience that would be, when Dr. Gold burst into the office. He was so relieved to see her, he shouted out a greeting, forgetting that they were merely colleagues, and except for the times when she energetically quizzed him on his suspect feminist motives, cordial but indifferent colleagues at best.

Dr. Gold was in a foul mood. She ignored him, shaking her head, her sleek black hair, knotted in two low pigtails, unmoving. "These people have no idea what they'll be missing when I'm gone," she announced, her voice ominous. Gloria Gold was always on the verge of quitting. He couldn't blame her. Although she was a PhD, she wasn't a full professor, and so was stuck in adjunct hell, teaching four classes a semester for a token paycheck and no benefits. Wilson scooted his chair closer to his desk in order to let her pass, then looked back, scooted it in a bit more, and smiled. She moved past him, a strange look on her face. At her desk, she rudely swept away a stack of papers and plopped down the salad she'd been carrying, as well as a can of Diet Coke and a small cup of what looked like oil-and-vinegar dressing.

*Great,* Wilson thought as Dr. Gold flipped open the lid of the salad and began to eat, stabbing morosely at chunks of iceberg lettuce and anemic tomato. On the one day it was imperative that he talk to her she was not only in a rotten mood, but she'd begun a diet as well. The last time she'd dieted, she'd gotten two graduate assistants fired. Several students had complained that when approached, she was sarcastic and hostile. She brought strange soup from home, soup that filled the office with the smell of boiled cabbage.

He doodled in his notebook, keeping an eye on her, waiting for a chance to speak. She was doing something strange with the dressing, dipping her fork into the cup before spearing the lettuce, repeating the fork-dipping process with each bite. What did it mean? Why not just pour the dressing on the salad? Dr. Gold ignored him, staring at the wall as she ate, at the posters she'd hung of ballets attended in years past. She set down her plastic fork and looked over at him. "I was one, once, you know," she said, nodding at a poster of a man and a woman clad in the barest lavender wisps. Their thin, impossibly long-limbed bodies were so entwined they appeared to be one.

"A dancer?" Wilson was surprised. He noticed her annoyed look and quickly revised his reaction. "Really?" he said, turning his chair to face her. "That's fascinating."

"Yeah. I was a ballerina. I studied under Balanchine at SAB." She gave him a wry look. "Hard to believe, huh? With these jumbo thighs."

"No, not at all." Wilson sat back, resolute in his decision to say nothing more. Weight was the trickiest territory of all when it came to women, a fact he'd learned long ago, growing up with two pear-shaped sisters. "I can see it, I really can."

Actually, he could. There was a certain grace in the way Dr. Gold lifted her chin, in the way she sat, or more precisely, perched, on the edge of her chair. Her feet, clad in thick pink tights and loafers with gold tassels, were neatly turned out, and she'd flung a necklace of enamel rosebuds around her neck in a way he thought very diva-esque. Her eyeliner was dramatic, her swoops of emotion, airy. And wasn't she downright regal in the way she threw her weight around the office, stared down sassy students, gave specific and stringent orders via telephone to the campus lunch delivery service? His colleague, Dr. Gloria Gold, was a star, a swan, a goddamn sugarplum fairy—no wonder she hated it here in this dreary office, hanging out with the graceless likes of him and the other cloddish TAs.

He felt cheered then. Things weren't hopeless. If Dr. Gold had a fearless dancing sprite inside her, then all was not as it appeared, and good could be found in even the bleakest of places. Together, he and Dr. Gold could work as a team and excavate from the frozen winter city the missing dog that was ruining his life. Maybe they'd end up friends. Wilson and his sugarplum fairy—two geniuses prodding each other on to greater and greater intellectual heights. Dr. Gold returned to her salad. Wilson flipped the page of his notebook, his energy renewed. *Felt like singing today!* he wrote once again. The first line of *The Lost Journals of Sylvia Plath* by Wilson A. Lavender, PhD. He was starting out on a happy note. Things would degenerate quickly enough.

"Did you try 1800HELPME1?" Dr. Gold asked, dumping her loot from the vending machines—a Hershey bar with almonds, a can of real Coke, two bags of sour cream–and–onion potato chips—on her desk.

"Oh yes." Wilson leaned back in his chair. "I finally figured out what the 1 stands for: Give me a call because I *wanna* waste your time."

"Funny," Dr. Gold said, not laughing. "You need to talk to Alice Cherry." She grimaced. "Yeah. I know. But she did her undergrad internship at the shelter."

Which was how Wilson found himself in his car not a half hour later, Dr. Gold in the passenger seat, Alice Cherry in back, directing him to the shelter. *Leading me to shelter*, he thought, trying to stay calm. For Alice Cherry, trapped in his car, was wearing the same cologne that Divinity—the deadly Divinity of his high school days—had worn. Love's Baby Soft, and it was all coming back in a rush of powdery pink scent: the way she'd squirted it in her hair after they had sex to hide the smell, fluffing her fat blond curls, creating, he'd thought, not the air of purity she was going for but an invisible halo of lust. And the way she'd once sprayed it on his dick—she hadn't wanted to, but he'd whined until she did, annoyed—and it had burned like hell, he hadn't expected *that*, but he also hadn't cared because to him the soft droplets of cologne were Divinity, bottled: pure liquid intoxication.

He was fourteen when it began, a virgin who'd only seen naked (female-wise) his sisters and his mother, and once, accidentally and horribly, on a camping trip, through an open tent flap, his grandmother, leaning forward to catch her slack breasts in her bra. Thankfully, he'd blocked that image from his mind by the time Divinity decided it might be fun to let him watch her take a shower. Her parents were at work. They skipped 7th period Personal Finance, and as he stood in her fluffy pink bathroom, watching as she soaped with a fluffy pink cloth her fat bottom, her thin rib cage, and small pink-tipped breasts, he was so overcome with emotion, with fear and lust and joy, he'd had to retire to the fluffy pink toilet seat, sink his head between his knees, and breathe.

There was a rug on her bathroom floor, fluffy, pink, shaped like a foot-print. He'd examined it as his vision cleared, its big toe, then as the gray faded away, its other toes, right down to the smallest, a perfect circle of pink fluff. Unable to speak, terrified of the feelings lurching in his chest, knowing Divinity was about to exit the shower, he'd risen from the toilet, stammered something about having to vacuum his bedroom, and run all the way home.

The next day, Divinity invited him to skip 3rd period English and drink Mickey's Malt Liquor with her in her garage. The day after, she announced they were going together. Three months of bliss ensued.

Then she broke up with him.

It was a snowy afternoon and they were sitting beneath the desk in her father's den, sharing a clove cigarette (he thought cloves were for poseurs; she thought they were sophisticated). "I think you're getting weird," she said, never one to mince words. "You're starting to like me too much, and it's making me hate you." She straddled his lap, leaning in close, staring into his eyes, the look on her face pained and dramatic. "Do you know what I mean? Have you ever felt that way?"

"Like I hate myself? Yes. All the time." He'd pushed her off him and crawled out from beneath the desk, slamming his head on a drawer. He walked home, the brim of his baseball cap pulled low to hide his tears.

That afternoon was the last time he could remember crying.

He became obsessed with footprints. To him, they were emblematic of the entire mess, of Divinity, of his greatest loss. When he saw them—on his Hang Ten T-shirts and swimming trunks (of which he suddenly had too many), on the stupid God poster his grandmother had given him with its picture of a single set of footprints marching down a beach—he felt sick. Divinity had walked all over him; she'd walked away. Never in his short, unhappy life had he been picked up, smiled at, flirted with, given sloppy blow jobs to, and then dropped, in favor of a senior football player (he soon discovered), a guy who despite his huge, anvil-shaped head and girlish lisp was superior to him in every way.

It wasn't the end, precisely, that had destroyed Wilson—it was the shock of it. He hadn't seen it coming; he hadn't had time to prepare. Ironically, his superb early training in rejection at home had *not* equipped him to deal with the reality of being dumped, and so he'd chosen to spend the rest of his life, post-Divinity, drunk. Which had worked, for a time.

"Get off campus heading downtown," Alice Cherry ordered. Despite her aroma, she could not have been more unlike the Divinity of Wilson's youth. Divinity was blond, effervescent—bubbly like the 7 Up she liked to chug straight from the bottle, standing naked in front of her refrigerator door. Alice Cherry, on the other hand, was dark: her mood, her low voice, her black pansy eyes, her bottle-red hair that leapt from her head in an ominous, blood-tinged Afro. Her snarling fur hat sat beside her on the seat, keeping watch.

Wilson drove carefully, avoiding the students that tended to leap out in front of cars. As Dr. Gold and Alice trotted out their various credentials in the friendly way women had, fangs barely concealed, Wilson wondered how many students a year were run over on college campuses. Lots, he bet, as he slowed near the entrance to the rec center. Students dressed in workout clothes, in bright winter gloves, hats, and scarves, ambled past, inches from his front bumper. When all was clear, he started forward then stopped abruptly, a stray girl in striped tights having jogged in front of the car, ponytail bobbing.

The day had definitely taken a strange turn. His dissertation was officially begun, he'd discovered the inner fairy in Dr. Gold, and here in his car was Alice Cherry, bringing back the past like a slap to the face, making him remember, in full Technicolor glory and shame, his first and most complete failure with the opposite sex. No, it was his second, he decided, shifting gears. The first was his relationship with his mother, for hadn't she, too, lost interest early on?

He turned onto Stadium Drive, gladly leaving the bustle of campus behind. He felt excited, like a kid ditching school, the afternoon a blank, blue sky stretching out before him.

"Don't speed," Dr. Gold warned. "This street is crawling with cops."

Something about Dr. Gold using the word *cops* made him chuckle.

"He always thinks something's funny, this one does." Dr. Gold jerked her head at him, opening her can of Coke.

"Some people believe that when a person laughs inappropriately, what they really want to do is cry," Alice Cherry said, without a hint of irony.

"I can't cry," Wilson said. "I'm physiologically incapable, I think."

"No, you're just gender hypnotized."

"What?"

"Gender hypnotized." Alice pulled lip balm from her pocket and spread it on her lips, replacing the lid with a pop. "Stuck in your gender role, believing all the hype, you know . . . gender hypnotized." She leaned forward between the seats. A wave of eau-de-Divinity washed over him. Love's Baby Soft *and* cherry ChapStick—his head was starting to spin. "I coined the phrase. I'm exploring the idea in my next paper."

"Aaahhh." Wilson forced himself back to the present. *Gender hypnotized*—one of the more ridiculous things he'd heard. He remembered how David Letterman used to say "I'm hyp-mo-tized" on his show, and had to bite his cheek to keep from laughing aloud again. Maybe Alice was right. Maybe he *was* losing it and would soon dissolve into an ocean of sorrow. *But then they give you drugs*, he reminded himself. *A nervous breakdown means drugs—the good ones—so how bad could it be?*

"I said, how's the dissertation coming?" Dr. Gold made a knocking motion at his head, smirking at Alice over her shoulder. Wilson stifled the urge to open the passenger door and shove his hefty colleague from the car.

"Good. Great. I think that once I get into it—"

Dr. Gold interrupted and proceeded to explain his entire project, down to the smallest detail, to Alice, as Wilson cringed in his seat, horrified at how ridiculous it sounded.

"Aaahhhh," Alice said when Dr. Gold finished. Wilson wondered if she was making fun, but her tone was as flat as before. *Lack of affect.* He'd read about that in the DSM-III-R, a tome he'd perused regularly while waiting for his psychiatrist to appear during his failed stint in rehab, a spectacular failure for which he still owed eight grand. In line with her *marked* lack of affect, Alice didn't smile. When interested in something, as she seemed to have been when talking about her theory, she got a strange glower on her face, as if someone were pinching her as she spoke. "Have you read *The Silent Woman*?" she said, frowning at her hands. "The Janet Malcolm book?"

"Yes. I have." At least he thought he had. At the very least it was on his desk, in a pile with the rest of his special dissertation books.

"'I loved it. I saw her grave when I was in England. You know, Plath's. I was so hard-core back then. Shaved head, armpit hair down to here . . .'" Wilson glanced in the rearview mirror. The look on Alice's face was positively ferocious. "All the piercings," she continued, "female lovers only . . ."

Wilson tensed, excited. *You like her.* Katie's voice echoed in his mind. *Obnoxious girls are your thing.* He stopped at a light and slipped on his sunglasses, willing Alice to stop, and at the same time, urging her to continue, to give him all the dirty details. The snow piled at the curb was gray and filthy, and the sky, equally gray and filthy, seemed to be sitting on top of the car. The light turned green. He rolled down his window and accelerated, letting the cold air blow across his face.

"I made a rubbing," Alice was saying. "I could show you sometime. The *Hughes* is missing. People keep chipping it off—"

"Alice. Tell Wilson about your project," Dr. Gold interrupted. She stripped the wrapper off a Hershey bar and broke it into three pieces, handing the two smallest to Wilson and Alice. Wilson ate his portion quickly, embarrassed, feeling like a preschooler sharing a snack with his chums.

"OK, here I go." Alice's voice was grim. "You know how strippers are everywhere nowadays?"

"Yeah," he joked. "You can't walk across campus without stumbling across two or three."

"Exactly," Alice said, straight-faced. "They are everywhere: on Howard Stern, on TV, in movies, in music videos. Wherever you look, it's strippers, strippers, strippers."

"Entertainers of the lowest order," Dr. Gold broke in. "As opposed to the geisha who has held a venerated role in Japanese society for thousands of years."

Wilson and Alice ignored her.

*Get to the dirty part,* the voice in Wilson's sub-brain urged, for he knew that there must be a dirty part. There was something about Alice, as with Divinity so long ago—a slightly rank, slightly sweet aura—that screamed the words *naughty girl.*

"So, I'm infiltrating the Mermaid Lair," Alice continued. "I've been hired as an exotic dancer starting this week, and my plan is to work awhile and then write about my experience, a huge exposé that the *Gazette* or maybe even the *Trib* will run." She paused. "I'll incorporate my theory of gender hypnosis, of course." She fell silent, the look on her face either smug or fearful, it was hard to tell. She was definitely an odd girl. An odd girl in a red-furred sweater that showcased to perfection the most luscious braless breasts Wilson had ever seen.

"I think it's funny that you're going around talking about your big exposé," he said. "Are you undercover or not?"

"Yes, I am. I'm only telling *you*. You don't strike me as the kind of guy that hangs out at strip clubs."

Wilson didn't know whether to be pleased or offended.

"She's *un-covered*." Dr. Gold sighed, annoyed. "It really is the lowest form of entertainment, if you could even call it that, which I can't. Why not just stay home and masturbate? It's the same thing. The artistry is nowhere to be seen."

"As opposed to ballet," Alice said. "I know you were a dancer, Gloria, so I know what you're getting at."

*Uh-oh. I smell a catfight.* Wilson sat up straighter, ears pricked.

"Yes," Dr. Gold said. "And having been a ballerina, Alice, I know what it's like to be a real dancer—"

"Since when is starving yourself into some consumptive creature, some dying swan, simply to amuse the patriarchy, real?" Alice spoke in a bored voice, as if they'd had the same argument many times before. "At least strippers are clear about what they're doing. They're selling the illusion of sex for money, without hiding behind some delusional scrim of 'art.' And why shouldn't they profit from their own sexuality? In our society they're going to be objectified no matter what. At least this way, they're in charge."

"You sound like Madonna," Dr. Gold said. "And I think your gender politics are warped at best."

"You start this weekend," Wilson said. "Is it a topless club or totally nude?"

"Stop," Alice cried. Wilson and Dr. Gold looked at her, alarmed.

A hint of a smile flitted across her face. "We're here." She nodded at a run-down house the color of mustard, on a block of identical run-down houses, in the part of downtown Kalamazoo known as the "student ghetto." As they walked up the drive, rap music booming from some hidden source, Wilson noticed a small camera mounted high on the wall of the adjacent house, its ketchup-colored paint peeling. The camera was small and unobtrusive, something one would never notice unless it had been pointed out, and it seemed to be aimed directly at him: Wilson A. Lavender, married man, married man with sex on his mind, sex with someone other than his wife.

The girl could only be described as *minky*. She sported a shaved head, suspicious eyes, and pronounced eyeteeth, revealed when she grimaced in delight at finding Wilson A. Lavender on her doorstep. Her presence, too, was aggressive, vicious even, Wilson thought, her fight-or-flight system on high alert, her entire being prepared for attack. The hallway behind her was murky, and exuded the smell of creamed corn, a smell Wilson always associated with old people.

"Suzanne?" he said, feeling sick. "Suzanne *Greevy*?"

"Yeah. Hey, Dr. Lavender." Suzanne, *the* Suzanne of the Saturday morning phone standoff, spoke in the same mellow tone as before, as if she and Wilson had once been lovers and were still on intimate terms.

"Not yet. Not a doctor yet." Wilson tried to smile, his heart sinking. "Soon though, very soon."

"Do you two know each other?" Dr. Gold raised her eyebrow, a look of interest on her face. Alice Cherry stood behind her, swaying slightly, seemingly bored out of her mind. Despite her internship at the shelter, she obviously didn't know Suzanne from Eve.

Wilson, unfortunately, did.

"We do know each other," he said, making his voice bright. "Suzanne here was in my intro class."

Nobody said anything.

"But your hair's different," he continued, taking in Suzanne's strange mottled stubble. The words *scrappy, feral, rodent-like* ran through his mind, and he had the urge to retreat to the car, to let Dr. Gold handle it from here. He'd had enough of his afternoon outing and wished to be home now, napping in the Lavender-family nest, a nest in which he found great comfort during the day, when it was emptied of all small humans and animals.

"My hair *is* different." Suzanne ran long, possum-like hands over her head. "When I knew you, I could practically sit on it." She paused, gearing up for her big revelation. "And I *was* in your class. Two years ago. In fact, you flunked me." She turned to Dr. Gold and Alice, the color in her cheeks heightening. "He flunked me. I had to go to summer school in order to graduate, and my job plans for the fall were totally ruined. I ended up working at the Dairy Queen back home, I lost my scholarship to grad school, and now I'm thousands of dollars in debt because I had to pay my rent with my credit cards. It was a nightmare, the worst year of my life, for sure."

"Gosh. I don't remember that," Wilson lied. "Really? Did you fail? From what I remember, you were a very bright student." Of course she'd failed. Suzanne Greevy had been one of the most obnoxious students on record. She argued constantly, which would have been fine had she actually read the texts in question. She ate, drank, and even answered her cell phone during class, glaring at the other students if they dared shush her. Her biggest crime, however (besides skipping the final), was her 8–10 page research paper, a treatise she'd titled *Why Men Suck: A HerStory of My Own Personal Dating Life*, which, again, would have been great (if irritating), had it not been typed in sixteen-point font with three-inch margins and triple-spaced lines.

"And then my hair fell out," Suzanne was saying as Alice Cherry nodded sympathetically. Wilson cleared his throat, annoyed. Surely he wasn't responsible for this girl's hair falling out. She hadn't shown up for the final, what was he to do?

"I mean, I'm a woman." Suzanne hitched up jeans that looked about to fall off her boyish hips. "How on earth does a woman fail women's studies, you know? I am one."

*That's open to debate*, Wilson thought as the traitor, Alice Cherry, murmured in agreement. Dr. Gold tapped her nails on her patent-leather handbag, sighing impatiently.

"I guess even a woman needs to show up for the final exam," Wilson said, trying to lighten the mood.

Suzanne glared, not amused.

"Listen," Dr. Gold said, getting down to business. "I'd love to debate your grade for another half hour, but we're here because we're missing a dog."

"Yeah, I know." Suzanne's voice was sullen. "He called. And as I told him," she pointed accusingly at Wilson, "I can't give out information about my residents. I can't. It's my job to shelter, not endanger." She turned to Alice. "We had a lady here once with a cat, see, and the husband came and took the cat back home with him, and it was a total disaster. The cat was the woman's transitional object, you know like how a baby graduates from the breast to a blankie or a pacifier? Well, this cat was the woman's *pacifier*, and when it was gone, she lost all will to get out of her abusive relationship, and was soon right back home in the arms of her perp."

Wilson stared, dumbfounded. "And that has *what* to do with our situation?"

"We're not an animal shelter." Suzanne laughed. "I can't help you."

"It's a white dog." Wilson plowed ahead. "A white dog with black spots. A Dalmatian, like in the movie. Could you tell me, please, Suzanne, if you have a Dalmatian in residence, a Dalmatian resident named Pearl?"

"I cannot. No."

Wilson stared.

Suzanne stared back. Her thin lips curled into a smirk.

Wilson started to speak. Suzanne raised her eyebrow, and he thought better of it. He turned and slunk back to the car. Dr. Gold followed, shaking her head. Alice lingered a moment, then ran to catch up. "I shouldn't have flunked her," he said, tripping over a chunk of ice.

"This isn't because you failed me," Suzanne, possessor of preternatural hearing, called. "Oh my God. That would be so petty. That is so not who I am."

Wilson ignored her.

In the car, everyone spoke at once.

"The little shit," said Dr. Gold.

"I've never met that girl, ever," Alice Cherry said. "She definitely wasn't there when I was—"

"She actually talked on her cell phone during class." Wilson started the car and pulled away from the curb, the back tires fishtailing on the icy road.

"Then you had to fail her," Dr. Gold said. "That should be automatic grounds for failure. That and loading up your books before the professor is done lecturing—a big fat F, no exceptions."

"And acting like I'm responsible for her hair falling out, for crying out loud—"

"—a very unattractive young woman. Unpleasant inside and out."

"Feral."

"I asked," Alice said. "When you guys were walking back to the car, I asked if the woman I'd worked for, Betsy, was there, but she said no—"

"What's that?" Dr. Gold looked at Wilson, smiling expectantly.

"What?"

"The word you just said."

"Feral?"

"Ha." Dr. Gold laughed, delighted. "Feral. That's it, exactly. I love it. *Feral*: the perfect word for our new friend."

Later, after dropping Alice and Dr. Gold at the office, Wilson sat in his car, in the parking lot outside the library, delaying until the last second his trip home. The sun had dropped below the horizon, and the moon rocked mournfully in the blue twilight, a single gold star shining in its lap. He thought of nursery rhymes, of singing the kids to sleep. *Slumberjacks.* Paul had been obsessed with *slumberjacks* lately, a cross between lumberjacks and the sandman, as far as Wilson could make out. The library tower rose pale against the evening sky, the clock in its belly reading 5:17. He felt like crying, but that was no surprise—dusk had always made him want to cry. It was the in-between-ness of the time, the feeling that the earth had paused to sit and breathe, just a bit, before continuing on into night.

"You can't flunk people," he imagined Katie saying, her blue eyes sparkling. "You just can't. You never know when it's going to come back to bite you in the ass." A feeling of relief washed over him. It was good to be stuck, wasn't it? Stuck in the pink-walled shell? Stuck in a good way, meaning firmly ensconced in a place where you belonged, a place that could hold you, perfectly. He started the car, ready to go. As he backed up, something dark on the backseat caught his eye. Alice Cherry had forgotten her hat. He reached for it, thinking of what an unbalanced soul she seemed to be. Gender hypnosis, indeed. Holding the hat to his face, he inhaled its musty smell, brushed the silky fur against his cheek. When he felt thoroughly like a pervert, he set it in his lap and continued home, stroking the fur as he drove.

# Fifteen

## Katie

Animal shelters were called and visited, rescue societies were alerted, but Pearl, the fleet and elusive Pearl, was gone.

"She had the prettiest toenails, black pink black pink, alternating like that, and the paw pads, too, black pink black pink. Her pink toenails were so pretty, like little shells." January sat at the kitchen table, bundled in several pastel fleece blankets, like a gigantic Easter egg, eating handfuls of cinnamon Life cereal from the box. It was a Friday morning, and the temperatures had hovered around zero all week. Frost feathered the windows. Outside, snow sparked like static electricity. Other than their trip to the pound, January had yet to leave the house, choosing instead to lounge and talk on the phone long-distance, rarely changing from her big begonia-covered pajamas.

"Shells," Katie murmured. She finished loading the dishwasher as Rose bounced in the backpack on her back (the only place she wanted to be; the only place she'd stop screaming), rubbing her yogurt-y hands in her hair.

"Sometimes I'd wake up at night and Pearl would be awake, looking down at me, and I'd have the strangest sense that she was this complete being, just like me, this alien soul stuck in a dog's limited consciousness—"

"Paul, do not unroll the entire roll of toilet paper," Katie broke in. "I don't care if you're a Power Ranger. Power Rangers stay in the bathroom. Go in there and clean it up. Now."

"She'd leap into the air and grab your sandwich from your hand, swallowing it whole before your mind could register what had happened—remember that, Katie?"

Katie nodded as she raided the change jar for lunch money for Jake. "Two minutes," she barked, practically throwing his backpack at him, hurrying him out the door to catch the bus.

"She really liked Lovely." January held out her cup, smiling hopefully until Katie refilled it with coffee. "Remember when he dug the cave for her under my back porch? You could stand up in it, it was so deep." She spoke to Lovely, who lay on the floor at her feet, eyes closed, stretched out on his side. "Lovely. You were such a gentleman, digging Pearl a cave to shelter her from the heat."

Lovely didn't move. Katie nudged him with her toe, making sure he was still alive. "Jan," she said, trying to clean yogurt off her glasses with her T-shirt. "I think we need to move on—"

"I know. I know. She was just so pretty: Clorox white, plush black spots. She liked to go, you know, just walk and walk and walk. Ooh." January grimaced, covering her nose with her pajama top as Katie tied up the trash bag containing Rose's dirty diaper. When Katie returned from taking out the trash, January continued her lament. "She could go forever. And now she's gone."

Katie sighed. The weeping was about to begin.

"She was wearing her sweater."

*No, not the sweater!* Katie cursed inwardly as she dug in the freezer for something to thaw for dinner. The fucking sweater. Talk of the sweater always precipitated more weeping, and she could not take the dog sorrow another second. She couldn't. She loved her little sister, but this was not fun. There were the kids to deal with and the house to clean and the laundry to tend to and now this—this ridiculous event that was taking too much of an emotional toll on everyone. If she ever got her hands on that woman . . .

She slapped a pound of ground turkey on the counter, willing herself to calm down. It was too much. She needed help, not another baby in the house to worry about, to feed and comfort and clean up after. And where was her husband? Napping, of course. Or at the office, as he was now, working on his dissertation, *which better be good* she thought as she grimly wiped the counters, for all the time he was spending away from home.

"I knitted her the sweater." January's voice was hesitant, as if she sensed her sister's mood.

"Please don't talk about the sweater. Really. I'm going to scream."

"But I worked on it for so long. I wanted to make one for myself just like hers, so we could wear them together, but I never did. And then she got chubby and was outgrowing it—"

"No more. This has got to stop. The dog's gone—"

"Can I just tell you one more thing? Please. It makes me feel better, talking about her. Please?" January widened her eyes, clasped her hands in prayer.

Katie crossed her arms. "Make it quick," she said grudgingly. "And don't start crying again. Or I'm not going to listen, I swear."

"OK. I used to bring her to work at the Laundromat. I'd buy her Lorna Doone cookies from the vending machine, and it always made me feel so safe having her there with me in the middle of the night."

Good. They'd moved on to a different subject. That was good. Talk of laundry usually perked January up. It pulled her from her tailspin—Katie had no idea why. Laundry, it seemed, made her sister happy. Not that she'd actually do a load. She just liked to talk about it, especially lint.

Outside, the snowplow roared up the street, depositing more snow in the mountain of snow at the end of Merlot Court. When it backed away, Katie looked over at Steven's place. His porch light was still on from the night before. His blinds were drawn, and his car sat in the driveway, puffy with snow. Lucy's truck was nowhere to be seen. Which meant he was alone. Alone doing what? Katie wondered. She imagined him in bed, wearing just his shorts, his big body warm with sleep. And she could slip beneath the covers, slip into the comfort of his arms, slip her hand inside his shorts, leave it all behind—the dishes the vacuuming the laundry the *demands*.

"You wouldn't believe how many people do their laundry in the middle of the night, three a.m., four a.m.," January said, much cheerier. "And then they just leave it, take off. Sometimes they come back, sometimes they don't. And the lint, all the pretty lint. I wanted to make a sweater out of lint—lint and Pearl's hair that I was constantly vacuuming up."

Katie groaned. Here it came.

"There was so much of it, and when I go home it'll still be there, but she won't."

More tears. Copious tears. Torrents of sobs that seemed to have no end.

Katie Jane Lavender, PhD, wife of Wilson, mother of three, owner of the elderly Lovely, and now keeper of the traumatized and pregnant January, sighed. Paul wandered out of the bathroom, wearing his Batman underpants, wads of wet toilet paper stuck to his little arms and chest. For some reason, the sight of her older brother, gleeful and decorated, infuriated Rose, and she started to wail, tearing at Katie's hair in her effort to climb out of the backpack.

The day had just begun.

## Katie
1973

It was always there, that fat white melon of a moon. Sometimes it was a thin slice of rind. Sometimes it was a blank face, staring at me through my bedroom window.

Last summer, our garden was so pretty. Chains of morning glories dangling their heart-shaped leaves like charms, opening to the sun, closing against the poisonous light of the moon, and all the dahlias lurching over the compost pile, twisting, bowing, as if they couldn't get enough of its rich perfume. Baby cantaloupes nestled in a bed of vines, and the vines of the morning glories twisted together, entwining themselves into big, green knotted hearts. As if to say: Love Lives Here—Enter at Your Own Risk.

One year, the squash went wild, wrapping itself around the pine tree, dangling its fruit like bumpy orange Christmas bulbs. We've had baby pumpkins, giant pumpkins, and the perfect zinnias—fat yellow globes tinged with fuchsia—exploding in the middle of the leafy green explosion that was the garden.

My favorites, though, were the morning glories, glorious, pale with pink crosses, pink with purple crosses, purple with fuchsia crosses, pale with purple crosses, scattered all up and down the vines like medicine tablets, remedies for not enough love, translucent, marked with the sign of everlasting life.

Last fall, I hiked the old Boy Scout trails with the dog, in the afternoons when Wilson was home from work, the sunlight falling in a dusty golden slant. Dragonflies were everywhere. Red dragonflies, lucky red dragonflies, everywhere you looked, sitting on the path, flitting away when we came near, their liquidy red bodies a drip of neon ink, and their wings translucent, lucky.

I saw a small dead shrew with walrus whiskers, woolly bear caterpillars, bumblebees the size of gumdrops, a boiled sun, hidden behind a shroud of gauzy sky.


By the time I turned nine, the world no longer felt right. It rained every day. In summer the sky was white. Nothing was pretty. Nothing fit.

I looked like a chimpanzee. My clothes itched. My plaid pants—pants I was thrilled to have because one afternoon I saw Cindy Brady on *The Brady Bunch* in the same pants (pink and turquoise and yellow plaid)—were wrong. They were *skintight*, according to my new best friend, Kelly, and it was wrong, the *skintightness* of my pants, and it made me ashamed and I quit wearing them.

That summer, Kelly gave me two 45s for my ninth birthday: The Captain and Tennille's "Love Will Keep Us Together" and Elton John's "Someone Saved My Life Tonight." It was the perfect gift. Even now, when I hear "Love Will Keep Us Together," I think of Kelly. We were the best of friends for the longest time, growing apart during the catty high school years, but finding each other again in our twenties. Over the past few years, we've lost touch again—she's in Portland, I'm here—and I miss her. No one was smarter or funnier. No one made me laugh as much. Until Wilson came along.

The other 45, the Elton John song, was perfect for a nine-year-old, so deep, so dark and fascinating. Was he really singing about cereal? Was I wrong? Surely not. And the lines about freedom and butterflies . . . Another world existed in that song, a place where things were gorgeous and horrible in equal parts, and I wanted to find it. After Kelly gave me my gift, we spent the day at the Enchanted Forest in Salem, an old-fashioned amusement park with no rides. Instead there was the giant slide that shot out of The Old Woman Who Lived in a Shoe's shoe, the giant slide in the Wild West section of the park, one you rode on an itchy burlap sack, and the Indian caves: a mess of underground tunnels and dead ends that were so narrow you had to move through them in a squat. (I took my kids to the Enchanted Forest a few years ago and had a panic attack in those caves.)

At the end of our day, Kelly and I got Cold Duck Ice ice-cream cones on the way home, and they were so disgusting we let them melt all over the backseat. Instead of yelling at us, my mother laughed. Grubbiness never bothered Iris. She flipped her hair over her shoulder, wiped her suntanned face, shiny with sweat. "So now you're nine," she said, smiling, looking at me like I was the neatest kid ever.

"Duh," I said, but nice.

I was eight when life became dark, hard to navigate, with too many dead ends, too many switchbacks. I couldn't get my bearings.

Larry Johnson eclipsed that year, a shadow hovering over me. I'm walking home from school, a third grader. It's raining. I haven't met Kelly yet, and I have no one to play with. Do I go to the babysitter around the block like my mother told me? Or do I go home, eat, and watch TV, bask in the soothing blue light of the set, watch rain trickle down the windowpanes, watch all the happy people on my shows? It wasn't much of a dilemma. Home and TV, of course. I was a latchkey kid. The babysitter was an *option*, Mom said. "With power comes great responsibility," she warned before giving me my key.

In the fall, I'd discovered Cindy Brady wearing my pants. A few months later, she showed up in a shirt I owned. I couldn't believe it. Sitting in the shabby TV room, in the in-between world, the time between school and my mother's return when everything stopped, it seemed as if life—my life—had begun to fold into the life on the TV. The lines were blurring. If Cindy Brady had my pants, and then my shirt, it wasn't an entirely made-up world, right? And if that was true, then couldn't I have what she had: pretty colors, a certain brightness in the air, a family that encircled her, that never left her alone?

It was a knit shirt, short-sleeved, coral-colored, with a matching floral collar and cuffs. *She was never alone. Family surrounded her.* Even if they were angry, there they were. I hated it; I thought she was annoying. At the same time, I couldn't quit watching. It was my drug, my comfort, watching her, the stupid little baby, lisping and looking cute, in the midst of all that fun.

After a while, a pattern began to emerge. I saw that people were rarely alone on any of the shows. Not on *The Flintstones*, not on *Bewitched*. Even on *Gilligan's Island*, trapped as they were on a desert isle, they had each other.

It didn't make me sad. It was just something I started to notice.

I made up my own shows at night lying in bed, January asleep beside me or in her own bed across the room, the moon glaring, the curtains limp and shivering in the breeze from the open window.

In my favorite story, I'm walking home from school, thrilled, because dangling from my hand is the guinea pig's cage, dark and tarnished, and in it is the guinea pig himself, mousy-smelling, squealing like a piglet, ready for a weekend of fun. I burst through the front door, shouting, "I got it. I raised my hand when Miss Moss asked who wanted to take the guinea pig home, and she picked me. Here he is."

My mother, who is at the dining room table working on her découpage, gluing pictures of angels on round, beveled pieces of wood, is happy, and proud that I've finally worked up the courage to raise my hand. "Hooray," she says, admiring the stinky beast. January can't keep her hands off, she is beside herself, hopping in place, asking a million questions, and finally I have to tell her to back off, to *not touch*, because I am the boss of the guinea pig for the weekend, me and only me; I am the one who will feed it and fill its little drip bottle with water, clean its smelly cage and give it fresh newspaper to shred, me and only me; I'll play with it, let it scamper all over my bare stomach with its sticky-sharp claws, bury my nose in its rough, oaty-smelling fur, maybe even let it sleep with me, only me, the boss of the guinea pig because I was the one who raised my hand.

Of course, in reality, I never worked up the courage. And midway through the school year, I realized that Larry Johnson was wrong. There weren't a million guinea pigs in the world, there was only one, the one scrabbling in its cage by the sink in the back of Miss Moss's third-grade classroom, and I wanted it.

How can you not feel pretty in a shirt with angel wings? A few weeks after the trip to the Dairy Queen with Larry Johnson, I strolled home from school, swinging my Partridge Family lunch box, feeling pretty. I was wearing a new shirt with a shirred elastic bodice and floaty pink sleeves. My teacher, Miss Moss, who I secretly wished would adopt me because she was young and pretty and kind with her yellow beehive and black horn-rimmed glasses, had called my sleeves *angel wings*.

"You look just like a little angel, Katie," she'd said, smiling, showing her teeth, teeth I found fascinating because they were crooked and yellow, just like the guinea pig's teeth. After Miss Moss complimented me, for the rest of reading and all through lunch—when there was a milk-drinking contest and Linda B. drank nine cartons and threw up in the garbage can—I felt pretty.

Walking home down Rex Street, making sure to walk *around* the love pole and not *under* it, proving I was *not* a girl in love, I felt pretty. Floating free fluttering me—pretty, because Miss Moss had said so. I breathed deeply the clean air, moving farther and farther away from the stifling smells of chalk and books and overheated kids.

A car rumbled down the block behind me. I felt it at first, its vibrations rolling through my body, before I turned around to look. Idling near the curb was a brown, trashy-looking sedan, exhaust billowing from its tailpipe, and I knew right away that it was Larry Johnson come looking for me. My heart leapt. He honked the horn—three happy beeps even though I was standing right there—then rolled down the window and told me to hop on in.

I thought of birthday parties. He made it sound like a birthday party was going on, right that very second. Hats and streamers, cupcakes with fancy sprinkles. Hooray. Hey! Hop on in. This time I didn't hesitate. Pretty me, and here was my new secret friend, ready to take me for ice cream. I was lucky, I knew, much luckier than my little sister, trapped at the babysitter's, bouncing listlessly on the mini-tramp in the basement where the kids had to stay.

Larry Johnson looked the same as he had weeks earlier, only brighter. His hair was brilliant, his teeth sparkling. He wore a strange shirt, thick and silky and covered with flowers, which made me want to laugh. It was pink, it had a big floppy collar, and it seemed much too fancy for a guy like him. When he bent to fiddle with the radio, I caught a whiff of perfume coming from his hair. Beneath the perfume was the animal smell. Today, I'd say that Larry Johnson needed a bath—maybe his smell was nothing other than good old-fashioned BO—but back then, it seemed like more. It was as if he were so big, so kind and powerful, that he didn't smell like normal men, men like my dad, clean in his clean white tennis shoes, slipping out our front door like a ghost.

"Does the lady want a Coke?" The radio hissed static and Larry flipped it off. His fingers were fat. Black hair grew on the backs of his hands. It was repulsive in an exciting way, as if he were the Wolf Man, come straight from the Midnight Monster Movie looking for me, the pretty girl. And being the pretty girl, it was my job to let him capture me, to let him drag me to the ends of the earth as he searched for truth and justice and everlasting love.

I shrugged. "I have to be home by four," I lied. "I'm going shopping with my mom."

"Oh you are, are you?"

I shrugged again.

"Shopping. With Mommy." Larry spoke in a high, girlish voice, making me giggle. He slipped the car into gear and roared away from the curb. I fell back against the slippery seat, and when he turned a hard right, I slid across the seat, bumping into his side. The lion's head on his ring grinned.

I stared up at the giant bull on the Herfy's sign, big wads of cloud rolling behind it, thinking up ways to wangle French fries *and* a drink from my new after-school friend.

The bull had a ring through its nose, and I wondered why. I thought of putting a ring through January's nose and leading her around with a rope. Herfy's was a grubby hamburger drive-thru way up on Woodstock. My mother had a story about Herfy's. When she was in college, she and a friend went on a blind date with the two rudest boys in the Pacific Northwest. They took my mom and her friend to Herfy's, and when it was time to order, one of the boys said, "Two Herfy Burgers for two *hefty* gals," and then both boys laughed uproariously. My mother and her friend were mortified and never spoke to the boys again.

"But you're so pretty," I said when she told me the story, knowing that if fat was bad, then hefty was infinitely worse. I didn't want her to feel bad. I wanted her to be happy so she'd stay. *I didn't want to come here in the first place.* Wasn't that what she'd said the afternoon she returned from primal screaming, her hair still damp from the birthing tank? But I needn't have worried. Iris just laughed and made a face, and then she made me go try on her wedding dress, and when I did and it was too tight, she was happy so I was happy, too.

I thought of telling Larry the story, but I didn't. How could I? It was more of a feeling, a feeling of happiness, than anything real. Instead I asked if I could get fries with my 7 Up because I'd forgotten my lunch at home that morning. It was a lie—my lunch box sat on the floor at my feet—but I didn't care. I felt reckless, mysterious. I was a girl with a secret life, just like Harriet the Spy. What did other kids do after school? Who cared? They certainly didn't drive around the city, getting treats. Larry asked how much fries were, and the guy on the speaker replied in a spitting hiss of static. Larry thought a minute, and then he said that yes, I could get fries with my drink but that both had to be small.

I sat back, satisfied. I felt comfortable in Larry's car, safe. Surrounded by cracked brown vinyl in a shell of rusted steel, with Larry himself beside me, as big and soothing as the bull on the sign, I was happy.

Larry squeezed open his change purse, jingled the change inside.

"I'm wondering if you've ever known a person that lived in a hotel," Larry said, flipping his empty Styrofoam coffee cup out the window and pulling out of the parking lot. He said it like we were playing 20 Questions.

"We stay in hotels all the time, every time we go to Bend." I crumpled my French fry bag and stuck it in my pants pocket. Unlike Larry, I was not a litterbug.

"Not stay in a hotel. Live in a hotel. Full-time."

"Oh no." I stared, waiting for him to start telling one of his lies. My stomach shivered with anticipation. I remembered his talk of bombs, of ground zero, and the bad Chinese. It was crazy talk, I knew, but it was also fun and exciting.

"*I* live in a hotel," Larry said, his voice proud. "It's the perfect setup for a man like me. You pay by the week, come and go as you please, and when you're not there, you don't pay. Can't get a better deal than that. I don't know why more people don't do it."

"Where do you go?"

"Aahh." Larry grinned, the corners of his eyes crinkling. "It's a secret." He paused. "Do you want to see it?" His voice sounded strange, as if he were trying not to shout.

"I guess." I shrugged, feeling sure he was pulling my leg. But I was also thinking that if he really did live in a hotel, maybe he had candy. I knew that people usually had candy in their homes and that they usually gave you some when you visited, as a token of goodwill. Even my grandma Edith, who didn't like me and January and called us *rambunctious* and *spoiled rotten* whenever we visited, usually gave us one, and only one, piece of butterscotch to keep us quiet.

We drove through my neighborhood, past Reed College Place, rolling down the big hill beside the college. Black storm clouds were piled up on the horizon, and the pine trees, even blacker, poked at the furious sky. We drove past all the pretty houses: the weepy blue cottage, the soft lilac one, the white colonial with the navy shutters that was my favorite. We passed Linda B.'s house and I wondered if she'd told her mother that she'd thrown up at school that day, and if so, what her mother had done.

We zipped out of the neighborhood, meandered along the golf course, then turned right at 17th, following the bus route toward downtown. When I saw how far we were going, a part of me grew nervous. I pinched my fingers together, watching as the streets became more and more unfamiliar. Looking at the warehouses, the movie theater with the marquee that read XXX Deep Throat XXX, I told myself that it was OK, that everything was fine. Sure, I was a bit too far from home, but it really didn't matter, did it? Because who would ever know? Inside, though, I knew it was wrong. I'd been told to go to the babysitter's after school. I had definitely *not* been told that it was OK to go to Herfy's and then to a hotel with Larry Johnson, my dad's golfing buddy. At least not without asking first.

"I'm going to bring home the guinea pig this weekend," I said. "Tomorrow's Friday, the day you raise your hand."

"Listen, that guinea pig doesn't know how lucky it is." Larry smiled and made a fast left on a yellow light, narrowly escaping a speeding VW van.

My heart raced with fear and joy. He'd remembered! Plus we'd just about been killed.

Not a minute later, we turned into a parking lot and drove to the back of it, coming to an abrupt stop in front of a dented tan dumpster.

"Out we go." Larry opened his door, hoisting himself out with a groan.

"Here?" I sat in my seat, unmoving. "You really do live in a hotel?"

"What?" Larry grabbed at his heart as if it hurt, his fancy cuffs flopping back on his wrists. "Do you mean to say you didn't believe me?" As I climbed out of the car, he shook his head in mock disapproval. "Katie," he chided. "You've got to learn to trust your elders."

I followed him down a narrow pathway of broken cement slabs, overgrown shrubs scratching at us as we walked. We passed an empty swimming pool, its white paint peeling, its rust-stained bottom filled with wet brown leaves. I looked up and saw the sign for the hotel, invisible from where we'd parked. It was a pretty sign—a rose made of neon, spark-red, blooming and shrinking in the gray afternoon. It was a happy sign, and it calmed me, made me excited to see where Larry lived. Finally, at the back of a cluster of shabby white buildings, opposite of where we'd parked, we came to his room.

Number 15 smelled of smoke and wet carpet. It stunk like the fort I'd once made on the side of our house with rotting plywood and a blue tarp, the floor a slushy mess of leaves and moldy bricks. One Saturday morning, messing around in my fort, I'd actually heard a broadcast of *The Flintstones* on my transistor radio. I couldn't believe it, and for the next several Saturday mornings I returned to the fort, sitting in the rain, tuning my radio, trying in vain to find *The Flintstones* just one more time.

I remember thinking: *Maybe I dreamed it.* I'd once found a dead deer hanging from a rafter in the garage we shared with the neighbors. I thought I'd made it up until my mother told me to stay out of the garage that day *no matter what.*

"Look." Larry came up behind me and gently tugged my ponytail until my head tilted back. I looked where he pointed, at the ceiling peaked like frosting, full of a million glittery sparkles, alive in the dim light of the room.

"Pretty fucking fancy, huh?"

"Yeah. Neat." I grinned, happy that he felt free to use the F-word around me. It was as if he thought I was cool, too. "I wanted to paint my bedroom walls purple once, but my mom said no. Maybe she'd let me get sparkles."

"I wouldn't count on that." Larry opened a small refrigerator in the corner of the room and pulled out a can of beer. "Fancy ceilings are a hotel type of thing. They're not for the layperson, if you know what I mean."

I didn't, but I nodded anyway.

He offered to give me a tour of the room, which I thought was funny because it was just one room, and a cramped one at that. He showed me the refrigerator, which contained nothing but beer, and which I'd just seen, and then he showed me his prized painting: Elvis Presley on a black velvet background.

"My Velvis," he said, frowning like a genius. "A Velvis is what you call a velvet Elvis," he added, looking at me sharply to see if I got it.

"Oh." I gazed up at Elvis who smiled down at me, benevolent as a god. I took in his hair, slick and black, and his rhinestone shirt with its big collar and giant winged cuffs. "Are you trying to look like him?" I said, although I'd already figured out that he was. Larry just stood there, nodding and grinning like a cat with a cricket in its mouth.

"You bet. No one greater than the King."

On the scarred coffee table sat a big pink vinyl case that made me laugh because it looked exactly like a Barbie suitcase. What on earth was Larry Johnson doing with a Barbie suitcase?

As if he'd read my mind, Larry plopped down on the low couch and pulled the case toward him. "Take a gander at this," he said, swigging his beer. He kicked off his boots and swung his legs up on the couch, wiggling his small feet.

I sat gingerly on the edge. The couch was an ugly blood-red plaid and itched my bottom through my pants. As Larry slowly lifted the lid and slid the case around on the table, I held my breath, figuring by the way he was acting that it contained either precious jewels or a million dollars. Eagerly I looked inside, and found not diamonds or rubies or rubber-banded wads of hundred dollar bills, but row upon row of lipsticks and eyeliners and tubes of face lotion, each nestled into a pink plastic groove.

"Makeup? Why do you have makeup?" I couldn't believe it. What man had makeup? What did it mean? Iris had said that Larry was a bachelor, which I knew meant he wasn't married, so it couldn't belong to his wife. And I didn't think he had a girlfriend. I didn't think that real ladies—grown-up ladies with hairdos and high heels—would like him. Sure, I liked him, but I was just a kid. When I thought of dating, I thought of the bachelors on *The Dating Game*, and Larry didn't seem nearly as clean as them, plus hadn't the hippie babysitter across the street turned up her nose when my mother described him?

Larry laughed. "I sell it, door-to-door. Lookie here." He selected a tube, expertly twirled off the lid, and squirted a dollop of pink lotion onto the back of my hand. "Smell."

I did as I was told. The lotion smelled icky. It was powdery but with an oily, animallike under scent, kind of like Larry himself. I had the urge to wipe it off on the couch, but I stopped myself, knowing it would be rude. "Ooh," I said, squirming on the bristly plaid cushion. I looked doubtfully at the blob of pink, unsure what to do next.

Larry hooted. "You look like a bird just crapped on you." He grabbed my hand, rubbing in the lotion as he spoke. "Listen, this is great stuff—really phenomenal. It contains real mink oil, that's the kicker. It'll make you look ten years younger after just a few weeks of regular use."

"Then I wouldn't exist." I pulled my hand away, sitting on it so he couldn't squirt anything else on it.

Larry looked at me blankly.

"I'm only eight," I said. "If I were ten years younger, I wouldn't even be here yet."

"Ah. That's funny," he said, not laughing, the color in his cheeks deepening. "Come on, I'll show you where I sleep."

# Sixteen

## Katie

"She's pregnant," Katie said when her mother picked up the phone in her office later that morning with a breezy, "This is Iris." Iris was principal of a high school now, a workaholic who preferred to spend her vacation time getting her office in order rather than at home with Katie's dad, officially retired from his sales job, and Stan, the overweight and aged beagle, also officially retired.

Dan, Katie's dad, played golf, or watched golf on TV. Sometimes he read about golf in magazines. Stan slept. And Iris was as busy as ever: directing her choir, tending to her orchids, playing long trilling opuses on the piano that sent Dan and Stan straight up to the bedroom to watch TV, the door firmly shut behind them. She also loved, absolutely loved, the fact that her girls were on their own now, and (theoretically) no longer came to her with their dramas. Because by the time they were out of high school *she had had enough, she couldn't take it anymore, and she no longer wanted to be anyone's mother, especially her ungrateful and out-of-control daughters'*.

This, like many other things, made Katie angry. "Pay attention," she wanted to say. "It's just life and we're just people and things happen. We're not drug addicts, we're not freaks, we're just girls, trying to figure things out." She didn't say anything, though, just continued to call her mother whenever anything bad happened, especially if that something bad had happened to January and not her.

"Did you hear me," she said. "Your daughter's pregnant."

"I heard you." Iris's voice was grim.

"Well?"

"I know."

"And?"

"At least it's not you."

"What's that supposed to mean?" Katie could feel the anger rising. Her mother had always acted like she was the bad one simply because, of the two girls, she had the louder voice. It was physiological, and totally unfair. She could remember sitting in the TV room as a kid, a victim of January's silent teasing. Her sister's methodology was evil and precise. She'd begin by touching Katie's knee with one finger—a light touch, as soft as a breath—and when Katie slapped her hand away she'd do it again, the look on her face meditative, almost rapturous. Then she'd do it again, and again and again.

If this didn't send Katie into a frenzy, January had many other ways. Sometimes, she'd wait until Katie was engrossed in one of her shows, then sit as close to her as she could without actually touching her, and breathe. She'd simply breathe, in and out, in and out, but a little louder than normal, a little deeper, with a little more oomph to the exhale than was required. Sometimes she'd vary her breathing pattern, holding her breath then quickly executing six or seven breaths using a syncopated rhythm—out in out in out in out in out in out in out in out—that was sure to drive Katie insane.

"I'm going to kill you," she'd scream, descending on her sister with a flurry of slaps. Or she'd throw the cookie jar across the room. Or kick the door so hard it rocked on its hinges. Iris would appear, Katie would be sent to her room, and throughout it all, January would sit limply on the couch, the look on her face blissful yet pitying, a small smile that only Katie could see twitching at the corners of her lips. She never said a word.

*But I'm not bad*, Katie thought now. *And I'm not the one who's pregnant without being married, ha ha—at least not this time.*

"You're old," Iris was saying. "Too old to be having any more babies. You're almost forty. I had you when I was barely twenty-one."

"Movie stars have babies when they're like fifty, all the time." Katie had no intention of having any more kids, but she didn't like her mother telling her that she couldn't. "And someone's stolen her dog."

"You're kidding." For the first time Iris sounded genuinely interested. "Who would steal Pearl? She nips."

"I know."

"That's sad." There was a pause. "How's Wilson?"

"Fine."

"And the kids?"

"Fine. Rose is really chubby. She weighs almost as much as Paul."

"You're kidding."

"No." No more mention was made of January's condition. Iris gave Katie the number to their time-share in Hawaii where she and Dan would be over the holidays and told her to call if Pearl happened to show.

Katie hung up, depressed. The call had felt flat and sad, and she was tired of . . . of what? Of the feeling that once, long ago, her relationship with her mother had been rich and nourishing, and now it was broken, the life drained from it. When she was twenty-five, she'd told Iris about Larry Johnson, and had left her parents' house that evening feeling nothing but glad that she hadn't done so as a kid. Because she wouldn't have been able to handle it, the look of hatred on her mother's face, hatred—and this was the most awful part—directed at her and not him.

Her childhood fear had come true. *If I tell, Mom will hate me.* Without her mother, she would die. It was a life-or-death decision. Her silence was sealed when Larry Johnson said, "If you tell, I'll kill you. And your mom and dad." To tell would make it real—and this, too, would destroy her. Silence did *not* equal death. It was the only way to survive.

*What do you want from me?* Iris had said, her face a mask of misery and fear. *It's like you want something from me, and I'm telling you now that I have nothing more to give. Do you hear me? Nothing.*

Later that night, Katie's father had called her at home—she'd just finished bathing the puppy, Lovely—and told her to quit bothering her mother with her problems as it upset her. *Quit fussing*, he'd said, and those were his first and final words on the subject of Larry Johnson.

*The life drained away.*

Now Katie understood that there were perfectly good people, maybe an entire generation of perfectly good people, who did not accept ugliness. Period. It was met with disgust, swept away, and those that fussed needed to *get over it*. How dare you track ugliness into this house?

It was bullshit, Katie knew, but that was how it was.

Now when she and her mother spoke, the words were inconsequential, the truth behind them a strange beast that no one seemed to notice but Katie. To her mother the beast was invisible. Now when Katie was upset, she went to Wilson—which was as it should be, she knew. *Everything falls away.* Maybe that was the problem—she wasn't good at growing up.

"Happy?" She turned to January, sitting by her side on the carpet, still in her pajamas, a creamy pink blanket wrapped around her shoulders.

January nodded, pulled the blanket tighter. Her ankles stuck out of her too-short pants. If Katie squinted, the begonias looked like placentas, ripe and reddish-pink, blossoming all over her sister's skinny legs. For a moment, her heart filled with happiness. Another baby was on its way. And who was it, this little girl—for she was sure it was a girl—soon to plop herself into her crazy sister's life?

"She knows you're pregnant." Katie leaned against the wall, trying to ignore the handprints smeared on the window. "You didn't have to say a word." She smiled. "You're so immature. You're going to be a mom and you can't even tell your own mother that you're pregnant?"

"Right. No way." January shook her head. "Would you want to?"

"God no. That's the worst. It's like saying, 'Hey Mom, just wanted you to know I have sex.'"

January giggled.

Katie smiled, but her words felt hollow. She looked at her sister, sitting on the floor in a square of cold sunlight, her pale hair unwashed, the soles of her feet dirty. Her eyes had the look of blank patience they often had when she was a child and would sit on her bed for hours watching the sun slide across her hands, or on one of the candy-striped swings in the backyard, falling backward, watching as the sky rolled by. Today she looked ready to lounge on Katie's dining room floor all day, waiting. But waiting for what? Katie felt a flash of annoyance. January had no drive, no gumption, no get-up-and-go—what the hell was she going to do with a baby?

But if you thought about it, who *should* be entrusted with a child? To Katie, everything seemed filled with brokenness. She saw it everywhere and she hated it, hated the haunted house she grew up in, flooded with moonlight, with blue light from the TV, filled with voices, laughing and chattering, until the set was clicked off and the silence set in. Outside, old oaks curved into tunnels. Lawns seeped into the streets like stains. There was her father, floating out the front door, off to tennis, off to the golf course, off to the club. And January, silent, asleep at her side like a dead child, the bones of the canopy unmoving. What had she known? Had Larry Johnson gotten to her? She claimed to remember nothing of her childhood, nothing until she was twenty-five, she'd laugh, brushing away your question with a flick of her hand. And Iris too, floating, all sky and rushing, a lilac-colored cloud flitting toward the horizon, no longer real, no longer the color of dirt, her black hair no longer fragrant with oils and spices, and her body no longer warm, rooted firmly in the wet dark earth that was Katie's home.

A neon rose bloomed, dissolved in the gray winter sky.

In the OB's waiting room a sculpture sat on a pedestal—a creamy shell sheltering in its belly a large orb. The orb had one eye, etched closed as if it were sleeping.

Rose couldn't keep her hands off it, returning to pick it up as soon as her mother's attention faded.

"Just pet it," Katie said for the millionth time, sinking into the silence of the room. The walls were, of course, vaginal pink, and covered with great dilating Georgia O'Keeffe blooms that made her feel like squatting and giving birth, right there on the pink carpet. Paul was busy collecting all the pamphlets in the room—*Why Not to Smoke in Pregnancy, The Truth about Preeclampsia*—as Jake, home from school after a half day, slumped in a chair beside his aunt, looking bored and annoyed, his chubby cheeks flushed, his black hair sticking up in a gorilla-like crest that Katie found charming.

"I've noticed something about you," January said, leaning back and stretching out her long legs. She still wore her pajama bottoms, tucked into Katie's best sheepskin boots, but she'd replaced the top with a long purple T-shirt, the pale sweatshirt she'd arrived in, and Wilson's old jacket, the one he wore when raking leaves, gray with an orange lining. Purple lipstick set off her crooked white teeth. The cold air had brightened her pale cheeks.

Watching her sister sitting there in the old-man jacket, waiting for her first appointment with the OB, Katie thought she looked pretty. *Unique*, that was the word, just as she'd looked as a kindergartner when she'd dressed in all the clothes she could find on her bedroom floor and declared herself "fancy." Not sad, unique, and once again Katie was surprised at the fluidity of the past, the way it shifted like a cloud into a completely different animal, every time you looked.

"You're either totally helpless or a complete know-it-all," January continued. "Like with Wilson, you can't do anything." She mimicked Katie's nagging tone. "Wilson, will you please change this light bulb? Wilson, Rose is poopy. Wilson, will you please put the kids in the car? Wilson, will you please feed the dog?"

"Right. I'm not going to pour anything." Katie made a face. "I told you about the mice."

"Yeah. But most of it's because you're lazy."

"Ha." Katie smiled.

"And then, with everything else, you're a total know-it-all."

"Yeah, you are, Mom." Jake sat up eagerly. "You think you know everything: Go to bed. Brush your teeth. No more Game Boy. Turn off the TV. You even boss Dad, and I know he gets sick of it, because he tells me." He sighed with boyish frustration, looking up at his aunt for approval.

"Exactly." January winked, ruffled his thick hair.

"What does Daddy say?" Katie was amused.

"That you're bossy. And that we should hide or pretend we're asleep when you come home from the store so you won't make us do anything."

"Poor Daddy. Poor put-upon Daddy." Katie reached out and grabbed the clipboard her sister held, scanning down the medical history sheet until she came to the question she was looking for: *List all legal or illegal drugs you are currently taking, or have taken in the past.* On the space provided, January had listed a cornucopia of pharmaceuticals, including but not limited to pot, hash, coke, LSD, ecstasy, quaaludes, opiated pot, and crystal meth. "Oh my God," Katie said. "January, no. You're way too honest. You can't be so honest. If you write all this down, you're going to look like a total junkie."

"But it's true. They said the past, right? I don't do any of that stuff now." January's voice was indignant. "I'm not stupid. Nobody wants a baby with two heads. And all I've done since I was eighteen was a little pot, like twice—"

"Shhh." Katie nodded at Jake who was sitting very still, all ears.

"A little pot," January continued in a loud whisper, "and I didn't even like it."

Katie pointed at the list. "Crystal meth, crank—aren't those the same thing?"

"No. They're totally different." January paused. "I think. They have different names, right?"

"How the hell should I know?"

"What, that they have different names?"

"No. That they're different drugs."

"Oh, sorry, I forgot. You're so innocent." January rolled her eyes.

Jake was watching his aunt intently. She turned to him and playfully grabbed his shirt. "No matter what, never be like your auntie Jan," she warned, her voice dark. He pushed her away, and she tickled him, making him giggle.

Katie looked again at the clipboard. *List all STDs you have had in the past or currently have now.* January had written chlamydia and PID. "When did you have this?" she said, curious.

January's face flushed. She took back the clipboard, slipping it between her hip and the chair so Katie couldn't get it again. "None of your beeswax. God, it's like you're in my body, in my head." She laughed shortly. "Get out. Leave me alone."

"Whatever." Katie glared, her feelings hurt. January had always kept parts of herself private, whereas she was the opposite, nosy and intrusive, she knew, but it wasn't malicious. She just wanted to know people, to connect, but was never quite sure how to go about it. She was like a cat with a mouse, batting away the thing she wanted most.

"'Dere." Rose had succeeded in retrieving the egg-like thing from its shell. She dropped it into Katie's lap with a grunt, brushed off her hands, then trotted across the room to play with Paul and his pamphlets, turning to squat and grin at her mother every few steps, curls spiraling from her head like rays of sunshine. A nurse appeared in the doorway and called January's name.

*But of course,* Katie thought as her sister stood without speaking and disappeared down the hall, *the reason the cat wants the mouse is to kill it and eat it.* Maybe she didn't love people at all. Maybe she hated them, hated them for their ease and comfort, their sense of belonging in a world that, to her, often felt far too difficult to manage.

They were invited to hear the heartbeat. Katie and the kids crowded around January, lying on the exam table, and waited as the doctor found first January's pulse, slow and jaded, and then the baby's, lightning quick, its watery whoosh filling the tiny room. Katie closed her eyes and the world turned inward, dark and red-veined. She felt her own heart fall open, like a tulip in sunshine, full of gladness.

"It's so fast," January said. "Is that normal?"

Dr. Hookjendjyke—a blond woman with pert, beauty queen curls, an immaculate white coat, and a glittering chunk of ice on her left hand—nodded. "You're thirteen weeks along, and your due date," she quickly twirled a circular card, "looks to be August 1. Any questions?" She wiped the goo off January's flat stomach, off the tattooed spiral whirled around her belly button, and helped her sit up.

"I guess I should eat healthy?" January adjusted her layers of clothing, pushed her spiky hair from her eyes. The small scar on her cheek caught the light, gleaming like a fishhook.

"Yes." The doctor stretched out the word as if January were stupid. Katie was surprised at her rudeness and instantly defensive. Her sister had asked rhetorically, the way people do—obviously she knew a healthy diet was important.

"Which she does. Eat healthy, I mean." Katie grabbed January's hand, warm in her own. "She's a vegetarian," she lied. "And she doesn't like chocolate at all. Which is weird, don't you think, for a girl?"

"What do you mean?" The doctor didn't smile.

"And not smoke, of course." January, who had never smoked a cigarette in her life, smiled, and Katie realized she was playing along, making the doctor think she was stupid, something she did when she felt threatened and wanted to be left alone. "Drink a lot of water. Avoid caffeine?"

"Yes, yes, all those things." The doctor tapped her pencil impatiently. "I take it there's no father in the picture?"

"Oh. No." January looked at Katie. "I mean there is one, obviously, but he's . . . not here."

"She's got a huge family, though. Lots of support: me and my husband. Our mom . . ." Katie trailed off, unable to think of anyone else. January giggled, and Katie stifled a laugh, thinking of the dubious support Wilson, who couldn't stand January, and Iris, off on her cloud of denial, had to offer.

The doctor looked annoyed. "How are you going to handle this alone?"

She touched January's wrist, her voice softening. "It's not easy. Raising a child is the most difficult job there is. And to do it all alone . . ."

"Yes, I know. But I had a dream, or a vision, I guess it was, and I was in it, and the baby and—"

"She's around my kids all the time. She knows how hard it will be, and she's great with them. She's a wonderful aunt, they adore her." Katie bit her cheek, remembering her sister's words of wisdom to her son: *No matter what, never be like me.*

"But daddies are important," Doctor Hookjendjyke persisted, her blue eyes wide. "A child needs a daddy."

"Right. I know." January's cheeks were hot, the tops of her ears red. "What are you saying? What do you want me to do, Doctor . . ." She stumbled over the doctor's name, and Katie laughed, stopping when she saw the hurt look on the doctor's face.

"It's just something to think about." The doctor's voice was light as she busied herself gathering files, tucking away her pencil.

"Thanks." January looked anything but thankful.

"Stay away from drugs, of course. Prescription drugs. Street drugs. The teratogenic effect on the fetus can be profound." The doctor paused at the door, and Katie was struck by how perfectly her cool beauty fit the antiseptic chill of the room. "Profound and irreversible. And we don't want that." She touched her curls as if reassuring herself of something then disappeared into the hall, her white coat fluttering slightly behind her.

January sat slumped on the table, her smile fading. "What did she want me to do?" she said, pulling on her boots. "Kill myself, right here on the table, because the baby doesn't have a dad?" She stuffed her pajama pants into the boots. "Go find one in the waiting room? Have an abortion?"

"Right. I'm sure she'd be all for that."

"She wasn't nice, was she, Mom?" Jake said.

"I don't know. I mean we were the ones that were laughing. How nice is that?" Katie knelt to zip Paul into his coat. He grabbed her ponytail, smoothing it with his hands.

"But the way she said 'daddy.'" January shuddered.

"I know. Baby talk. 'Daddies are important. Baby needs a daddy.' She was a total bitch, but you have to realize that not everyone's like . . ." Katie thought a moment. "Like us."

"What do you mean?"

"Most people think you should get married first, then buy a house, then have kids. You have heard of the *normal* way of doing things?" Katie raised her eyebrow.

"You didn't know whether to shoot her or change her diaper." January ignored her sister, her voice cheerful as she dug a jar of hand cream from her pack, rubbing some into her hands. "I'm such a loser and I never even knew it. I'm glad I had Dr.—"

"Wait. What is that?" A familiar smell filled the cramped room.

"Hand cream. Cocoa butter. The water here is awful. Why?"

"I smelled it before," Katie said, excited. "The exact same coconut smell. In the living room, the day before you arrived. It was driving me crazy, I couldn't figure out where it was coming from. I thought Wilson was grooming or something, but he wasn't—"

"Oohhhh." January waved her arms in a ghostly way, and Rose started to cry.

Katie picked her up, wiping her tears, giving each wet cheek a kiss. "It's not funny." She grabbed her sister's arm. "It was like déjà vu before the fact. I smelled you. Part of me knew you were coming. Don't you think that's weird?"

"Yeah." January grinned. "I think we should get you on *Oprah*."


Katie had often imagined giving birth at home. Pregnant with her own children, she'd lie in bed at night, picturing it as an underwater sort of experience, the air in her bedroom thick with silence, vibrating slightly with each contraction as moonlight poured through the windows onto the bone-white island of her belly, onto Wilson's strong hands, waiting to catch the new child. Then it would be time, and the baby would come, rushing from her in a rush of waters, rushing to Wilson who would place it on her belly, a briny washed-up creature, its sea-kissed face surprised and sleepy, as she gathered it into her arms and up to her breast, awash herself on a tide of mother love. They'd nurse and sleep and sleep and nurse, getting to know each other, alone together in the seclusion of her room, lost in the twilight world of *after birth*, the moon rising and the moon falling, the baby warm and dry, its hair still caked with blood, its creases still waxy and white from the womb.

Half here, half not—this was what she fantasized in a good mood. The other side of the coin was less pretty: She is in labor in her bedroom. It's a mess and she can't get her mind off the fact that she'd cleaned it just that morning and already it is trashed, Underoos and socks thrown everywhere, the bed covered with wet towels, graham cracker crumbs on the sheets, books—an explosion of picture books—making it hard to walk without slipping. And it's not the heart of the night, it's a busy bright

Saturday afternoon, and through the wall the neighbor guy's stereo is blasting, annoying rap music vibrating and thumping around her room, vibrating and thumping around her already too finely tuned body. Wilson is losing it, yelling at the kids to stay out, wrestling with Lovely who is barking, howling, scratching at the door because he only wants to get in. Every fiber in his doggie being wants only to *get in*, and why can't his owners understand this? Everything is covered with dog hair—is it even sanitary to bring a new baby into this mess?—and the neighbor kids are at the smeary windows, peering in, hands shading their eyes, knocking, laughing, shouting, wondering why on earth, on today of all days, they are not allowed to come in and play.

The baby is born. Lovely bursts in, leaps about the room like a bucking bronco, sniffs disinterestedly at the new baby, then makes off with the placenta, the cord trailing behind him like the tentacles of seaweed he used to love dragging around on the beach in Oregon.

"I'm not going back," January announced as they drove home, winding through a grove of naked winter trees. "I'm going to find a midwife and have the baby at home. Like the lady that took Pearl said."

"Do they even have midwives in Luna? It's so small."

"What?" January looked at Katie blankly.

"Luna? Midwives?" It wasn't lost on Katie that she spoke in the same rude tone as Dr. Hookjendjyke. Thinking of the name, and of the way January had mangled it, made her smile. "Ho-ken-dike, that's how you say it, by the way. You don't pronounce the *J*s."

"I'm not pronouncing anything. I'm having the baby here."

"You can't do that." Katie continued along the familiar roads, roads she'd followed for years, day in and day out, wearing a groove in them, it seemed, a groove that led her from home to the grocery store, home to the library, home to the gas station, the oil-changing place, and the video store. She sighed, tired. After the visit to the OB, they'd spent a grubby hour in the lobby of the Family Independence Agency, waiting as January applied for pregnancy Medicaid. Now she wanted only to put the little ones down for a nap, send Jake out to play with a friend, slip into her bathtub, and disappear.

She passed Jake's school, where a jungle gym like a plated dinosaur, cherry red, stood alone in the frozen yard. For some reason, she couldn't get the doctor out of her mind. As she drove, she kept picturing her, standing in the doorway of the exam room, with her curls and her coat and her white-hot ring, all of it—all of *her*—caught in a silvery net of . . . of what? Of misery, it had seemed, misery like droplets of mercury, netting her pretty face, and seeing it, as plain as day, Katie had thought, *Wow, I know exactly how you feel.* It was the feeling of doing everything right and still feeling as if everything you did was wrong.

She looked at her own ring, thistle-blue, harsh in the bright light. She looked at her kids in the rearview mirror, and at her sister, eating the hand-sized gummi rat she'd bought at the hospital gift shop. She was doing everything right, wasn't she? Getting married, staying home to mother her kids. But where had it gotten her? She often felt like a fraud, waking in the middle of the night to look at her sleeping husband, her sprawled and snoring kids, her beloved dog, and think again, *My God, what have I done?* And, *Who the hell am I to be in charge of these precious souls?*

"You can't fly past your eighth month, how would you get back?" she said now, irritated by her sister's loose grasp of reality. "And that," she nodded at the floppy rat, "is totally disgusting."

"What do you mean?" January giggled. "Katie, I told you, I'm staying here. I'm not going home. I'm staying here. I'm having the baby here, with you guys." She looked at her sister, amused, the purple tail of the rat hanging from her mouth. "What aren't you getting?"

Katie stopped at a red light, surrounded by snow-covered cars, clouds of steamy exhaust. She looked at the guy in the SUV beside them, watched as he took a bite of something sloppy, didn't chew until the light changed. *Here, with you guys.* That did not sound good, not at all. In fact, it sounded ominous. Yes, she'd wanted a tribe, she'd even cried about it to Wilson the night of their awful hike, and yes, she'd wished that her sister and mother lived closer (she even vaguely remembered harassing him about *that*, too), but never had she said that she wanted her sister, her fellow tribeswoman, so close she was actually living in her own home. It didn't sound good, not at all. Her plan, formulated over the last few days, had been to fly out to Luna with the kids a few weeks before January's due date, help her prepare for the baby, be with her for the birth, then help her settle, *in her own home*, after.

*Here, with you guys.* Well, there was no way *her guy*, Wilson, was going to go along with that. They'd barely seen him since January's arrival, but that couldn't last forever. He'd have to come home sooner or later and then January would get on his nerves and . . . "Wilson will freak," she blurted. "It won't work. You need to go stay with Mom—"

"You go stay with Mom."

"What, and let you stay here with Wilson and my kids?" Katie laughed. As they passed the credit union, she automatically glanced up at the sign, black and tilted against the sky. The temperature read 12 degrees, and she made a mental note to find Jake an indoor playdate. "What are you trying to do, take over my life?"

"Yes. And your dog, too. Haven't you noticed that Lovely's been sleeping with me lately? Come on. I need to be with you. Please?" January looked at her, eyes wide, hands clasped in prayer. Her blond hair was a spiky mess, her mascara smeared, and when she leaned closer she smelled of coconut hand cream and grape rat. "Don't make me go home alone. You're a great mom. I want to be here, to learn how you do it—you heard the doctor, it's so hard and I need help—and then I'll go, as soon as the baby comes, I promise. OK?"

"No. Not OK. You can't just make a plan and do it without consulting anyone."

"Why?"

"I don't know why. Because that's not how it's done. Wilson's right." Katie scowled, confident in her superiority. "You have no boundaries."

"Ha," January laughed. "And you need to get out of the Midwest. *Boundaries. Not everyone is like us. Do things the normal way.* My God, you're turning into Grandma Edith."

Katie thought of their grandmother, standing in her kitchen, in her long yellow apron, her rolls of iron-colored hair hornlike against her head, *shocked and appalled* by one or another of their childhood crimes. Did she want to be like that? No, she did not. Therefore, she must let her sister stay. She shook her head, annoyed at the way January's broken logic always got her exactly what she wanted.

"Please? I need you. Don't make me be alone."

"I don't know. If I let you stay, and it's just an if, you'd have to do something for me—babysit, maybe."

"Whatever."

Katie hesitated. "And you have to tell me who the father is."

January was silent. She looked out the window, traced a crooked heart in the fogged glass. "He could be one of a million guys. Really, I have no idea."

"That's so charming. And I know it's not true. Come on, tell."

"I don't know, honest." January affected a dramatic tone. "I'm like *la Virgencita*, born again, I'm—"

"Will you stop with the Mexican crap? Who are you, Frida Kahlo?" Katie laughed. "Do you want to stay or not? Because you're not unless you tell."

"OK. I'll give you one important detail, and then you have to promise to leave me alone." January paused, milking the silence until Katie reached over and poked her in the ribs. "I think, and other people do too, it's documented, that he looks like the guy in Soundgarden. Or Audioslave now. You know the singer? Chris whatever-his-name-is?"

"Really? Cute. With the long hair like when he was cutest, or short like it is now?"

"Long."

Katie nodded approvingly. "Nice. And the full lips, the sexy goatee?"

"Exactly."

"Wow. That's good. At least we know the baby will be cute." Katie paused, flicked up the heat a notch. "What's his name? Is he smart?"

"Nope. That's it. Not another word." January turned so that her back was to her sister and she was hunched, staring out the window.

Katie started to speak then stopped. January's posture was familiar. She was *watching*—her old habit from childhood. Back then, it was an unspoken rule that no one was to disturb her, for then as now she had two ways of being in the world—off in her mind, absent and dreamy, or in your face, a holy terror.

No, she wouldn't ask any more questions, she'd let her sister be. Katie knew she'd get the information she wanted sooner or later—it was only a matter of time. She glanced into the rearview mirror, pleased to see that Rose and Paul had fallen asleep in their car seats. And Jake looked itching to get out of the car and go play. Her peaceful afternoon was close. She could feel herself sinking into it. "Jan?" She spoke quietly, not wanting to disturb her.

January turned, her face serene.

"When you said you'd have the baby at home, you didn't mean my home . . . did you?"

"Yes. I'm not going back to that doctor, or to any doctor. It was stupid. I felt like a bad teenager, like she was going to go and call my mom."

"So you're going to stay here and have the baby . . . here . . . in my room?" *Not bloody likely*, Wilson shouted in Katie's head.

"No. In Jake's room, where I'm sleeping now, where I'm comfy. Jakey, you don't care, do you?" January turned to Jake, hanging her arms over the seat.

"I guess not." Jake looked doubtful. "But I'm not going to be in there."

"Wilson is going to freak," Katie said, but softly this time, the idea not quite so worrisome. Inside, a part of her was growing excited. She could feel dullness slipping away, like a beauty queen's fur cloak, like a shroud. And beneath it, she stood naked and new. Wilson would freak, and she would let him, because part of her knew it was exactly what he needed, what they both needed, to freak, to let some air into their stagnant lives. She pulled into the Reserve, sliding on the icy road, nearly hitting a car that someone had parked in front of the mailboxes, far too close to the security gate—the useless security gate, for it had been frozen open all winter. She jerked the wheel and laughed, exhilarated.

"Stop. Oh my God, stop." January's voice was urgent.

"Why?"

"Stop now."

Katie pulled to the curb. January opened the door and hung her head out, breathing hard. "Oh shit, I'm so sick," she groaned.

"You're pregnant." Katie waited patiently as her sister puked onto a dirty mound of snow. "Methinks the pregnant lady should go easy on the gummi rats."

## Katie
1973

It's the strangest thing, bad luck. It marks you, becomes you—or you become it. After a while, you're no longer a person that something bad has happened to, you are the bad thing, and there's no going back.

We'd always been a lucky family, always. Iris was beautiful, like an Indian princess, like Cher, and my father was a king, his golden brush cut waxed into a perfect crown. He was the champion golfer at the club for years and years and years. We lived in the haunted house, statuesque and dignified atop the steep, rain-washed hill, the sky tilted and streaked behind, and some afternoons, out of the blue, my mother would leave work early to take me shopping. We'd go to Lloyd Center where she'd buy me caramel corn and a brand-new fluttering top that made me look like an angel, me, grubby Katie, with the orange hair and the ears like a chimpanzee. I became pretty, me, Katie—my third-grade teacher, Miss Moss, had told me so.

"You look just like an angel," she'd said, "and I want you to come and live with me. I'll be your mom, and every day we'll drive home from school in my little yellow bug, read *Ramona the Pest* and *Ellen Tebbits*, and for dinner we'll have pizza and orange pop, how's that?" Then she smiled, showed her guinea pig teeth. She patted her beehive that I imagined felt rough, like the fur on the guinea pig's back.

We were lucky. Once when I was seven, we ate at the A&W down in Sellwood. My dad ordered a Papa Burger, my mother a Mama Burger, and January and I both had Baby Burgers, with root beer floats for dessert. The carhop brought the food on an orange tray that she jammed onto our car window. We ate our burgers and then our floats, and when I'd sucked all the root beer from mine and was spooning up the remaining ice cream in the bottom, I found money. The bottom inch of my mug was filled with money! I couldn't believe it. "Look, Mom, money," I cried, pouring the sticky pennies and nickels and dimes, even a quarter or two, into my palm.

"How about that." She smiled at my dad, who was busy wolfing down the rest of our Baby Burgers. January tried to grab the coins, but I held my fist up and out of her reach. I knew—I was certain—that I had been chosen to get the root beer float with the money in it because I was special.

"Give that girl with the orange ponytail the float with the surprise money—I can see that she's neat," I imagined the boss of the A&W saying. And when my mother said something about kids keeping their tips in the mugs and not looking when they grabbed, I didn't listen because one, I didn't understand, and two, I knew it wasn't true. We were lucky, we were special. Good things came to us, they surprised and delighted us, and that was the way it was.

Even at five, surprises happened. For example: the spoiled Pixie Tanner's fifth birthday party. When all the presents had been opened and Pixie had cried because she "hated it all and hated all of us," her mother, Mrs. Tanner, a harried smoker in a baby-blue pantsuit, with skinny shoulders and an eye that twitched, presented us with a chocolate cake. It was a big cake, layered and tilting, its sprinkled face ablaze with five fat yellow candles. We sang, we clapped, we said yes or no to ice cream, and then we dug in. I took a bite, humming, swinging my legs, bouncing on my seat, enjoying myself. I loved birthday parties, loved everything about them: the cake and the candy and the punch and the favors, and especially, I loved the drama of the birthday girl, the question of how she'd act when stuck in a room for two hours with everything—sugar and presents and friends—a kid could want. Most girls wept, some threw things. I found it all terribly exciting.

"Eat up, eat up," Mrs. Tanner cried. Eagerly, I took another bite. At first, I tasted chocolate, rich and dark and smooth, but then, surprisingly, another taste came through. It was a hard coppery metallic taste that seemed wrong, very wrong, in my mouth. I froze. There was something else wrong, too, something besides the taste, some *thing* that hadn't dissolved in my mouth with the frosting and the cake. It was a round disc, cool and heavy on my tongue. I resisted the urge to spit. Instead I considered the strangeness of the situation, the strangeness of the thing in my mouth. Was it supposed to be there? Was there something about birthday cake I didn't yet know? Was it a candy, a nut, a tiddlywink Pixie had thrown into the batter when her mother wasn't looking? I sat, disturbed and unmoving, looking at the clown-covered paper tablecloth, the pin-the-tail-on-the-donkey game that had been half ripped off the wall earlier, when the birthday girl had thrown her fit.

When I could stand it no longer, I spit the thing into my hand. It was a penny! The incident at the A&W had not yet happened, so I truly *could not believe it*. The other kids were making faces, opening their mouths to let big chocolaty blobs fall onto their paper clown plates. One girl gagged, another started to cry. But I was excited, thrilled—Pixie Tanner's birthday party was the best birthday party yet. I took another bite, and a moment later, spit out another penny, and then another, and another. *Like magic*, I thought. I couldn't wait to run home and tell my mom.

"It's a surprise cake," Mrs. Tanner crowed, clapping her skinny veined hands, her eye twitching happily. "Pennies in the cake, pennies in the cake. Now, isn't that exciting, kids? Did you ever imagine that anything that exciting could happen to you, here, today, at Pixie's birthday party?" We looked at each other, the bewildered guests of the spoiled Pixie. No, we could not.

Very soon it was time to go. Kids skipped home in pairs, or ran to the curb where their mothers waited to walk them. No mothers came to the door. No mothers wanted to get caught chatting with Mrs. Tanner. All her loneliness poured out onto you, my mom said, and it was impossible to escape. I stayed. The table was empty now, a sticky clutter of pointed hats, melted ice cream, and smashed paper cups. Mrs. Tanner sat at the far end, smoking, tapping ash onto a clown plate, having just sent Pixie to her room for refusing to thank her guests. I could hear Pixie banging away over our heads, as if she were throwing large pieces of furniture. I looked at Mrs. Tanner and smiled. She returned my smile, then went back to her cigarette. I sat quietly and finished a second slice of cake, not stopping until I had a good bit of change in my hand, thirty cents at least, enough for a Hostess Fruit Pie at the little store should I want one, later. Although I didn't think I would. I was feeling a bit sick.

When I was done, I stood and cleared my throat, carefully pushed in my chair. "Thank you, Mrs. Tanner," I recited, clutching my money tightly in my fist lest she try to take it away before I was safely out the door. Who knew what the rules were regarding money found in birthday cakes? Maybe she considered it hers, and the fun was just in the finding it and not in the taking it home.

"Katie." Mrs. Tanner smiled sadly. I knew why she was sad. She was divorced, and she worked in an office. She smoked. And every one of her polyester pantsuits matched. They came in pastel colors, mint-green and yellow and lavender, some with belts, some without, and to me, it looked like a very uncomfortable, matching, icky way to live. Everything about

Mrs. Tanner was hard, her elbows and shoulders, her zigzag shag and black-tipped eyes. She wore pale wigs with names like Champagne and Flirt, and they lived, when they weren't on her, on Styrofoam heads that she lined up on her bedroom windowsill.

Pixie's Siamese cat, Vivian, was not allowed into Mrs. Tanner's bedroom. If Vivian should get into Mrs. Tanner's bedroom, there was a good chance the cat would go berserk. She liked to leap onto the windowsill and wind her way through the wigs, sometimes knocking them down, sometimes ripping them off their heads, T-pins flying as she rabbit-kicked them into submission.

"See this?" Pixie said once, grinning mischievously, her pink nose running as she showed me a drool-covered ratted mess she'd retrieved from beneath her mother's bed. It was after school. The babysitter, a lady who read magazines at the kitchen table, was there. "Vivie got it." Pixie's voice was dark. "It's going to make my mom cry." She grinned again, her pixie hairdo sticking up in wicked peaks, and I was excited because I could see that she loved the fact that when her mother got home from work and found her mutilated wig, she was going to cry.

Mrs. Tanner clucked her tongue now, blue smoke streaming from her nose. "You have frosting all over your face, on your nose, even, and your hair is an absolute mess." She beckoned me closer, and I went, fist behind my back. I stood before her, as still as I could, resisting my wiggle-worm tendencies, and watched as she dipped a napkin into a cup half full of water and began to wash my face. But it wasn't water in the cup. As she scrubbed at my nose, dipped the napkin into the cup again and swirled it into my ears, I smelled bubbles and lemon and lime, and realized that I was being washed with 7 Up. Mrs. Tanner had rules in her home that were unlike anything I'd ever known. But what was I to do? I didn't want to make her angry by bolting—she might chase me down and make me give back the pennies. So I stood, not wiggling, and let her wash my dirty face with pop.

"There," she said when she was done. She licked her thumb, swiped my eyebrow, then sat back and nodded, satisfied. "Now run along home." She gave me a pat on my butt and nudged me in the direction of the front door. "And have your mommy give me a call sometime," she yelled in a high, cheery voice.

I did as she said. I ran all the way home, and when I told my mother about the money—*pennies in the cake, pennies in the cake, Mrs. Tanner clapping, twitching and happy*—she didn't believe me. "But you must," I said in my best spy voice as I opened my fist to reveal the sticky, fudge-stained coins within, warm now from being held.

"And she wants you to call her sometime," I said as my mother sniffed at the coins, tasted one even, to confirm that indeed they had come from Pixie Tanner's birthday cake. "Maybe she wants you guys to be friends."

"Ha." Iris snorted. "The woman is a lunatic." But she was happy, leaning in to inspect my pennies, specks of water from her freshly washed hair spattering my bare arm. When I told her how Mrs. Tanner had washed my face with soda pop, she was delighted and held my sticky cheeks in her warm brown hands and told me that it was the best thing she'd heard all day.

Luck followed me, it rained down upon me. Which was why, when I followed Larry Johnson into his bedroom, the day I visited Number 15 at the motel with the blooming rose, I was shocked. In less than a minute, I had become very unlucky indeed. I had become marked, and I was no longer an angel, fancy, fluttering and free. I had stumbled onto a problem, a big problem, one far too large for an eight-year-old to handle, and there was no escape, no way to make time stop and start over again, back in the moment when Larry Johnson had pulled up to the curb as I walked home from school and told me to hop on in.

I'd thought of birthday parties.

"Come on, I'll show you where I sleep," Larry said in the strange voice, the one that sounded as if he were trying not to shout. He closed the pink Barbie doll case, latched the black plastic latches, and carefully returned it to its place in the center of the coffee table. He ran his hand through his slick hair. His cheeks were dark and hot looking, and he loosened the top button of his shirt, flapping it a bit to let some air in. "Ready?" He smiled, showed his teeth.

I nodded, got up, and stumbled along behind him. I wasn't thinking of anything. I was a stupid kid; I was thinking of candy.

Sometimes now I replay the moment in my mind, that precise moment, and make things turn out differently. "Ready?" Larry asks, and I shake my head no. *No, I am not ready. I will never be ready for my life, my self, my body to be torn apart.* And so I shake my head no. I sit on the itchy couch and watch as his silky, flowered back disappears into the bedroom, never to return.

But the truth is, I was greedy and hoping for candy, and I went.

The bedroom had the same charred, wet-earth smell as the rest of the suite. It was an ugly room, not much of a room even, but an alcove, just to the right of the front door. A single bed hunched in the corner with a bedspread that looked to be made of the same itchy plaid as the couch.

On the cheap bedside table was a small brown lamp, a candlestick—the kind with a spike on it to impale the candle—a square green candle, and a scattering of face lotion samples: clear plastic ampules full of the same pink stuff Larry had squirted on me earlier. *Real mink oil, that's the kicker.* The window was small and set high, like a window in a basement.

Larry wasn't talking. I thought it was strange. What was unique and wonderful about this room? What—like the tiny fridge, the Barbie doll case, and the Velvis—was this room's secret? He stood beside me near the door, but he wasn't looking at me, he was looking out the window, or more accurately *at* the window, as the blackout curtains were drawn. I didn't like the quiet, and I didn't like the dark. Something felt wrong.

No, that's not true. I'm lying. It was a dark room, maybe, but I didn't care. I wasn't scared, and I wasn't thinking of anything. I was simply existing—existing in the greediness of an eight-year-old girl with candy on her mind.

No. The room was dark, too dark (I can control this; I know . . . I knew . . . I had some hint . . . I could have stopped it), and I felt as if I were in a cave, like the Indian Caves at the Enchanted Forest, far below the earth's surface, and I couldn't get my bearings. I was about to turn and leave when Larry grabbed me. At first I thought he was hugging me, but it wasn't like any hug I'd known, it was more that he had *captured* me, forcing me into his silky sweaty chest, into his aura of perfume and animal stink, my arms pinned tightly to my sides, my feet inches off the ground. I tried to breathe, tried to speak, but before I could catch my breath, he'd thrown me onto the bed, pulled off my tennis shoes—tossing them, *clunk, clunk*, against the ugly wood-paneled wall—jerked me out of my pants, grabbing them at the cuffs and shaking me as if he were shaking a cat from a burlap sack, and yanked my undies down around my ankles.

I froze, terrified. I could sense him behind me. I heard him breathe, in and out, in and out. I heard the clink of his belt buckle, the soft *whisk* as something—his pants?— slid to the floor. And then he was on me, his flesh hot against my back. He'd taken off his shirt. I never heard it. It must have fallen silently, and for some reason this scared me the most, the fact that he'd taken off his shirt without my knowing. The bed shuddered beneath his weight. He grabbed my ponytail and wound it tightly around his fist, shoved my face into the itchy bedspread, forced my thighs apart with his knees, and sodomized me.

Of course, I had no idea what he was doing. I had no words for what was happening. I had no way to shape it in my mind. It was so out of my grasp that nothing—not the smell of sweat and fear, not the pain, not the rhythmic slamming of my body into the lumpy mattress (I was certain he was killing me)—made sense. And for a long time after, I felt as if I were walking around with holes in my brain, literal black holes that contained a lost part of my life, a part that had happened outside of time and been frozen there, hidden away even from me. I could see the holes in my mind's eye: a big one in the left side of my head and several smaller ones up front, behind my forehead.

I smelled beer, smoke on the bedspread. Larry pushed into me and pain shot into my gut. The worst pain I'd felt up to then was when I stubbed my big toe running barefoot around the block, or when Missy Price accidentally whacked me in the head with a baseball bat. This didn't compare. It belonged in another world, one of hopelessness and rage. I couldn't breathe, couldn't move. The pain grew enormous. It overwhelmed me. Like a dark shadow, it blotted me out.

Outside, rain hissed. Crouched in a corner of my mind, I could see it. It soaked the earth, soaked the beds of mud beneath the windows of Number 15. The rosebushes, bare and stubby when we arrived, began to grow. They wound up the walls of the building, covering the windows, blocking out the light, creating around me and Larry, locked in its mildewed heart, a cage of twigs and thorns and sap-sticky leaves.

I was suffocating. Larry had wrapped his hands around my neck, his big fingers pressing into my throat. What if I didn't make it home? What if I never saw my mom again? I started to black out, bright sparks shooting across my field of vision. Again I shrank into my mind. I saw roses bloom: opal roses, smelling of candy; roses with yellow petals fluttering; roses with pink petals, veined in orange. They grew full, heavy heads nodding, then fell to the ground like overripe fruit.

In the sky, a neon rose bloomed and disappeared.

The earth tilted. In Number 15, I felt myself rise from the rough bedspread and hover near the gold-flecked ceiling. I slipped from my body as easily as I slipped from my nightgown in the mornings. "Skin the cat," was what Iris always said. I skinned the cat and the pain was gone. I could have been in heaven, a speckled gold heaven, as I hovered, angelic, near the ceiling and watched as a girl, a very unlucky girl, was raped in a rose-adorned motel, not too far from home, but not too close, either.

• • •

In an instant, I was small again. Walking was new. I could feel the jerk and wobble of my babyish steps as I toddled down a long tunnel, at the end of which was a brilliant light, one I moved toward intently, knowing that in the light was the Big Daddy, sparkling like Elvis, it was where he lived, and no matter what, I had to get to him. I picked up my pace. I hurled my tiny body toward the light.

Before I made it, however, the scene changed. *The end of the world is coming; the end of the world is near.* But no, I wanted to tell my mother, the end of the world had already happened, there in Number 15. It was morning and I was snuggled in her lap. She was rocking me, holding me close and telling me things. I was five and January was new, and I hated her, hated the way she'd taken over my world, taken over my mother's lap. "You're a big girl now," Iris would say, pushing me down when I brought her a book to read. I couldn't stand it, the way the boiled-looking thing was keeping me from my mom. No plastic tea party set, the consolation prize given to me the day Iris brought the intruder home, could ever make up for it.

But this was heaven, and January was nowhere to be seen. It was morning in paradise, and I rocked with my mother in the old green La-Z-Boy, the pretty one with the gold swirls. Iris was warm in her silky nightgown, and I sank back, burrowing into her body that was still a part of me, I felt, because the dreaded baby sister had not yet come and it was simply us—me and my mom, a single being not yet broken. She smelled of flowers freshly yanked from the earth. She smelled of the coffee she drank, as it was morning still but dark and raining out as we sat inside safe, the hated baby gone, my father off at work, or at tennis, or jogging around the club.

My mother was telling me about her dream—the best dream she'd ever had, the one that made her happy. "I'm in a jail cell," she said, shifting me to set her cup on the floor.

"Like with bars?" I was intrigued by the idea of my mother, or anyone's mother, in jail. It didn't seem possible.

"Yes, exactly," Iris said.

"Were you bad?"

"No, just trapped."

"Like someone got you?" I knew that people could be *gotten*, captured or caught in a trap. I'd seen it on TV. Batman and Robin were trapped often. Monsters got you, and bad guys too, although unlike monsters, which I knew ate you, I wasn't sure what the bad guys did.

Iris tried to explain the feeling she'd had in her dream. "Angst," she said. "A metaphor," she said, but I couldn't understand and quit listening, closing my eyes until she was quiet.

"Were you bad?" I said when it was my turn. I pictured her dressed in robber stripes, a black mask tied around her large, dark eyes.

"No," she said. "I was trapped . . . by being alive. But you're not going to get it, so let's go on." She picked up her cup and drank. "I'm in a jail cell, with bars, but I wasn't bad." She smiled. "And then there's this light. This gorgeous light, pouring into my cell, pouring all over me, all over my face and my hands."

I looked at her. It was like her dream was happening again there in the dim living room, rain making wiggly shadows on the walls. Light poured from my mother. As if she were a saint, pretty white light streamed from her face and fell onto me. I leaned back and smiled, pleased with her prettiness.

"And," she said, grabbing my hands. "Guess who it was?"

"Who *who* was?"

"The one who brought the light."

"I don't know. Dad?"

"No." My mother paused, squeezed my hands. "It was Jesus."

"No," I gasped, thrilled with the turn her story had taken. "The baby Jesus?" I loved the baby Jesus. That year, I'd started going to Bible class in the basement of the old lady down the block. Other scruffy kids on 31st Street went, too. We talked a lot about the baby Jesus, and I'd become entranced. I wanted to hold the baby Jesus, love him, stroke him, pluck him from his manger and take him home, feed him and rock him and touch his sweet face. In the old lady's basement, we memorized Bible verses. *For God so loved the world* . . . I knew mine by heart. I recited it perfectly. "Hooray." The old lady clapped her hands together, delighted. As the other kids fidgeted, bored speechless, she bestowed upon me my reward: a paper Dixie cup full of Hi-C punch. "Scamper on home," she said when I finished drinking, and I did. I thumped up her dark basement stairs, past her clean sunlit kitchen, out her back door, past her poodle drowsing on the porch, and into the sun-drenched yard. I left the disgruntled neighbor kids behind. I burst into the light.

. . . *he gave his only begotten son* . . . *Jesus. The baby Jesus.*

"No. Just Jesus—the grown-up Jesus. And then," my mother rocked faster, "he came in. Jesus came in, right into my jail cell, pushing aside the bars, and he freed me—"

"But you weren't bad, right?"

"No, Katie. I wasn't bad. I wish you would listen."

I closed my eyes, waited until her annoyance passed.

"Listen. He set me free. And I knew then, in my dream—although it wasn't even a dream, it was much too real, it was a vision is what it was. I knew in my vision, as certain as I know that you and I are sitting here now, in this green chair at seven on a Monday morning, I knew, absolutely and positively, that the world would come to an end *while I was still alive.*" She looked at me, cocked her head. "What do you think of that?"

I didn't think much of it. I didn't like it. I squirmed, uncomfortable. I hated things to end. I never wanted anything to end, not ice cream, not candy, not cartoons, not the mornings I spent sitting on my mother's lap, rocking in the chair, reading books or telling stories or just being quiet, watching the rain splash against the windows. I certainly didn't want the world, the big blue ball spinning in the sky, to end.

"We would all be saved. Do you see how exciting that is?" Iris said. The look on her face was blissful. She smiled, showed her chipped front tooth. "I would be saved, and you and Daddy and January. Jesus is coming, and all of us, we'll all go to heaven with him, and have everlasting life forever and ever, amen." In the next room, a baby began to cry, a thin cry like the wail of a troubled cat. The cries grew louder and more insistent. My stomach tensed. Finished with her story, Iris dumped me off her lap.

*. . . that whosoever believeth in him should not perish, but have everlasting life . . .*

*Jesus loves the little children, all the children of the world . . .*

I was back in the tunnel, moving toward the light as fast as my chubby little legs would go. It was an awesome light, the essence of life, a living light, full of goodness and peace. Finally, I made it to the end. I came upon a small door, the light I'd followed pouring from the cracks around it. I pushed it open, slowly, stepping into a room full of warmth and light and the faint scent of lilacs. I knew I was home. Relief flooded my frightened body, and I sank to the ground, happy. Someone spoke my name. I looked up. Sitting cross-legged before me was the Big Daddy, sparkling like Elvis, too bright to even see. He held out his arms, and I climbed into his lap, tears of joy spilling down my cheeks.

After a while, he spoke. "Go back," he said. His arms encircled me, warming my cold body. I felt his kindness, filling up my heart. I felt pretty, noticed and adored. "It's not your time. Go back now. I promise, no one will ever hurt you again." He pushed me from his lap.

I was furious. What was he thinking? How could he send me away? I did the only thing a toddler can do when crossed—I threw a fit, a screaming, crying, kicking-on-the-floor fit. There was no way I was going back to that horrible place. I would stay there with him, where it was safe, forever.

My temper tantrums got me what I wanted with my mother. With the Big Daddy, it got me nowhere. It got me back in the tunnel, slinking away from the light, heartbroken. I'd never felt so sad. The farther I went, the more I felt as if a huge part of me were tearing away. How could he send me away from the only place I knew I truly belonged?

A moment later, with a sickening jolt, I was back in my body. In the black heart of the cage, neon-swept, singing with insects, I was me again, eight-year-old Katie, only not the me I'd been ten minutes earlier, my hair tangled, my ponytail ruined, my spine trembling in deep, rhythmic spasms as I sprawled half-naked on a bed with a rough plaid cover, in a run-down motel room, much too far from home.

# Seventeen

## Katie

Happiness is a hot bath. *There should be a song about that*, Katie thought as she soaked in her tub with a Diet Coke and the new *Us* magazine, Jake off at a friend's house, January and the kids asleep in her room. *I am steeping in happiness.* It was late afternoon, the doctor's visit, the grubby wait at the Family Independence Agency, January's puking episode, done. Wind whirled around the condo, rattling the chimney, gusting through the cracks beneath the windowsills. Katie sighed, content. She turned on the tap with her feet, let hot water pour over them. She'd just settled back to read when there was a knock at the front door. She ignored it, thinking it was a neighbor kid, but when it persisted, she got up, wrapped herself in a beach towel covered with giant slices of lime, and padded into the hall.

As she opened the door, Lovely shoved his way past her legs, his paw pads making blossoms in the fresh snow on the porch. Katie looked up. Steven stood before her, dressed in pumpkin-colored sweats and a gray stocking cap, his beard stubbly, his brown eyes sleepy, as if he'd just woken from a nap.

"I'm in the bath," she said, hiding behind the door, embarrassed. The last time she'd seen him had been before January arrived, and it seemed like another lifetime. She'd been unkind about his engagement when he announced it at the coffee shop . . .

"Your cheeks are pink," Steven said.

She touched her cheeks, made a face.

"How are the mice?"

Yes, the mice. He'd saved her, she'd thanked him, and then there was Lucy's remark: "You two talk like you're lovers." Was that what she'd said? Something of the sort, something embarrassing and thrilling at the same time, because Steven was so, so . . .

Lovely scrambled back onto the porch and knocked past her, making a beeline for his spot on the couch lest Steven claim it first. "The mice are fine." Katie shivered, remembering the flying dark bodies, the horrible skittering. "I truly believe they're gone. I think they made their way back to the garage, and from there, the first chance they got, they hightailed it off to the field, back home, where they belong."

Steven smiled. "I'm sure they did. Rodents always like to leave the warmth, head back out into the cold."

"I truly believe they're gone." Katie raised her eyebrow, her voice firm.

"If you believe it, it must be true." Steven paused. "Katie?"

"Yeah?"

"Can I come in?"

Katie hesitated, touched her hair. "I'm in the bath, I—"

"It's OK, we can talk in there." Steven grinned. Gently, he pushed open the door. Behind him, a blizzard was kicking up, the world hidden by a blowing mess of snow.

What had possessed her to bathe in front of Steven? It had felt like a dare, as if both were seeing how far the other would go. "I don't want to ruin your alone time," he'd said. "Go on, get back in." He nodded at the tub, smiled. She looked at him like he was insane, then did as he said. A shred of modesty remained. Katie added bubbles, locked the door, made him turn around until she was in. She was embarrassed at first, lying naked and exposed before him, but she soon got used to it and was now enjoying herself. Her breasts bobbed in the water, full and round, with no gravity distorting their pleasant shape. She rested her hand on her belly—flat as she was lying down—and stretched out her long legs. *Fuck it*, she thought. *Am I supposed to live like a nun?* She wasn't doing anything wrong. It was the same as if January were sitting on the toilet seat across from her, telling her about her day.

It wasn't, though, she knew it wasn't. Wilson could come home at any minute, but that just made it all the more exciting, and she was tired of being bored, tired of being good. She watched Steven watch her, felt a tingling of pleasure between her legs. Maybe she was disturbed. Maybe she needed help. But more than that, she needed to feel alive, to feel as if she were more than just a *mom*, taking care of everyone, when no one noticed her or thought that maybe she might need care, too.

It was peaceful in her lemon-colored bathroom, no one whining, no one pulling at her clothes, criticizing everything she did.

"Lucy wants you guys to come to dinner," Steven said, Katie's watercolor of a seed-speckled strawberry bright on the wall behind him.

"Why?"

"How the hell should I know?" Steven rested his chin on his hand, his eyes merry. "I'm just following orders. Are you coming?"

"No. You don't like Wilson and Lucy doesn't like me. Why would that be fun?"

"It won't. Are you coming or not?"

Katie shrugged. "I guess so."

Steven sat back on the toilet seat. He took off his cap, ran his hand through his hair. "Howard Stern's back on."

"Really?" Katie and Steven had been depressed when Howard Stern moved his show to satellite radio. Katie had always loved Howard, had listened to him during the early mornings in New Mexico when baby Jake had woken before dawn, ready to nurse one last time before the sun rose. Sure, Howard could be disgusting, but he was smart and hilarious, and anyone who could make her laugh, first thing in the morning, she was all for.

"Wait." Steven looked confused. "I think I dreamed it."

"You dreamed it?" Katie laughed.

"I don't know. I remember finding it, and I was so psyched, but now I think I was dreaming." Steven sighed. "I'm not sure. I was in my mom's salon, sweeping . . ."

"Dreaming of Howard." Katie flicked water at him. "That's so funny."

Steven got up and knelt by the tub. He touched her hair where it had come loose from its clip. "You're so mean," he said softly. "Why is that?"

Katie sat up, crossing her arms over her chest, uncomfortable. "I'm not mean, I . . ." She looked away. What the hell was she doing? Her ring sparkled against the dull bathwater. This was wrong. She was married. If something happened, she'd feel guilty for days.

"I've got to get to the gym." Steven smiled sheepishly. "Lucy thinks I'm fat."

"Really?" Katie was intrigued. "What did she say?"

"That I'm fat. That I've got a gut and I'd better lose it before the wedding."

"Or what?"

"Or else." Steven's voice was dark. Katie giggled.

"Let me see."

"No way."

"Come on. Let me touch it." Katie reached for his sweatshirt, but he quickly moved away.

"No. I'm sensitive. I'm shy." Steven stood against the wall, arms crossed protectively over his middle. His sweatpants were too short, the hair on his ankles gold. Katie imagined sliding her hands up his legs, over the strong muscles, to the place where the hair grew thick and dark. She looked at him, slumped against the wall. He *was* sensitive, he *was* shy—it was what she liked about him, the fact that like her he felt the need for protection, the need to keep the freakish events of life at a minimum. Plus he was grubby. The sagging sweats, the stocking cap, and worn tennis shoes—grubby was a turn-on for Katie, it always had been.

"Steven." Katie leaned her elbows on the edge of the tub. "I think you have a great body. You're big, like a bear." She smiled. "It's sexy."

"A bear. Please." Steven knelt beside her. "I'm off," he said, not moving. "Bye."

He touched her hair again, let his hand fall to her neck, drawing her close. Katie moved her cheek against his. She loved the way his stubble felt, softer than you'd think. She inhaled his clean laundry smell, the salty smell of his sweat. She had the urge to pull him into the bath, pull him into her. Steven moved his lips across her throat, up to her mouth. As he kissed her, she twisted her ring around, thoughts of her husband falling away.

"We can't do this," he said, sitting back on his heels, cheeks flushed.

"Not good." Katie shook her head. "Yes. No. I know. I feel exactly the same."

When he was gone, Katie sat at the kitchen table wrapped in her beach towel, replaying the moment in her mind. She thought of his touch, of his lips on hers, felt it in her body, in the weakness of her thighs, the heat between her legs. She felt light and pretty sitting at the ugly card table, as if she were the thinnest shell of glass, filled with rolling balls of light, everything inside her alive. *Yes*, she thought, shaking out her damp hair, remembering the warmth of Steven's lips against her throat. *Exactly what I needed.* She could go back to her life now, noticed, touched—feeling as if she mattered.

January stumbled out of the bedroom, sank into the chair opposite Katie, rested her chin on her hand, and stared.

"What?" Katie looked away.

"I'm not awake yet."

"Then what are you doing out of bed?" Katie tapped her hand on the table, annoyed. She wasn't ready to let go of her moment, to lose it to daily life so soon.

"I was having the strangest dream. Did you dream a lot when you were pregnant?"

"Yeah." Katie wrung the last drops of water from her hair, pulled it into knot. "And when I took Zoloft. I dreamed all night long. I hated it."

"When you had the breathing thing?"

"Panic, yes. Why are we talking about this?" Katie didn't want to talk about her failures, the long year after Jake was born when the minutes, the hours, the days, moved by in a slow, torturous crawl. She wanted to talk about her recent success in the bathtub, her kiss—the moment in which someone she liked had held her, had asked her why she was so mean in the kindest possible tone.

"I was dreaming of possums. Isn't that neat?" January vigorously rubbed her nose, wiped her mascara-smeared eyes. "Possums everywhere: hanging from the ceiling, lined up on the fence in Mom and Dad's back-yard, leaping over the moon, swimming on their backs beside me in a lake. They all had the sweetest little Kabuki faces, pink tails, pink noses, hands like little pink stars." She sighed. "It made me so happy. I was in possum heaven—" She broke off. "What is that?" She nodded at Lovely's food bowl, sitting a few feet away on the kitchen floor.

Katie stiffened. "What do you mean?"

"In the bowl, there's something weird in there." January stood up, inspecting it more closely. "Ooh." She crossed her arms, moved back a step.

"What?"

"You don't want to know." January headed to the bedroom, pausing at the door. "I'm going to sleep some more. Call me if you think you're going to freak."

"Don't leave me," Katie cried as January shut the door behind her. Alone at the table, Katie forced herself to look into the bowl, blocking the image of the skittering, the flying dark bodies, from her mind. *Please God don't let anything move*, she prayed. Thankfully nothing did, but there was indeed something weird in there, something other than the brown nuggets of food Lovely had poked his nose at moments earlier and found wanting. It was a grayish-brown lump, and it looked like a pom-pom—holy shit, a fur-covered pom-pom—plopped, unmoving, in the middle of the bowl.

# Eighteen

## Wilson

Katie hadn't gone berserk, and that was precisely what was bothering Wilson as he sat at Steven's oversized dining room table, poking at a shockingly bad low-fat dish his sexy fiancée had just served, leaning over him, ample breasts brushing against his shoulder. Thick lemon-scented candles burned in the center of the table. A blues CD played softly in the background.

"You have to check the fucking dog food before you bring it into the kitchen," Katie had said when he arrived home from work, but nicely.

"You can't bring dead mice into the kitchen where we live," she'd said, but again her voice had been kind, and it had freaked him out. She'd found a dead mouse in the dog food bowl, one that had somehow infiltrated the hermetically sealed Rubbermaid garbage can in the garage in which the dog food was kept. Wilson, the pourer of the dog food, the man in charge of household rodents, had unwittingly brought it into the kitchen to surprise—no, scare the hell out of—his wife.

Strangely, it hadn't. When he walked in the front door, she'd kissed him pleasantly, then reported the incident in a mature and matter-of-fact manner. She'd taken him by the hand and led him to the kitchen to point out, calmly, the dead rodent in question. Finally, after gently admonishing him, once again, to "check the fucking dog food" before delivering it to Lovely, she'd grinned and suggested that after he disposed of the body—a fat ball of a mouse, it looked as if it had eaten itself to death—they go into the bathroom and have sex, quickly, before everyone woke.

Wow. His head had spun around twice. Had he entered the wrong condo, the one on Chablis Lane, perhaps, where the good Katie lived, the Katie *without* the hysterical mood swings? He'd taken her up on her offer. They'd done it, happily, on the bathroom floor, and as he moved into her, burying his face in her sweet-smelling neck, careful not to make a sound lest some child—or God forbid, the sister-in-law—should wake, he'd thought of the Stepford wives, the husbands of whom he'd always secretly admired. Wouldn't life be easy if women were always nice? Wouldn't it be nice if when it came to women, there were no surprises?

He'd come quickly and sunk onto Katie, then just as quickly hopped up, wiped himself with a towel, adjusted his pants, and neatly tucked in his shirt. Glancing in the mirror, he was surprised as usual by the sight of his long hair. He'd grown it long per Katie's suggestion, and secretly he hated it.

"You look just like Jesus," trembling female students often told him. That was nice, of course, there was nothing wrong with Jesus, but hadn't Jesus been the kind of guy that long hair fit: gentle, peace-loving, a laid-back, live-and-let-live, savior-of-mankind kind of guy? And wasn't he, Wilson, nothing of the sort? With his unruly curls, sun-bleached a million shades of blond, with his *ponytail* for crying out loud, he felt like a fraud.

"I'm not some happy hippie," he wanted to tell his young students, innocent girls mistaking him for someone wonderful just because he happened to resemble the Son of Man. "I don't even like people. They're too difficult, too unpredictable. I like to smoke, nap, and avoid all members of the human race whenever possible." Instead, he said nothing and continued to live his life as a fake, spending too much money and time on a hairdo he found ridiculous. The truth was, he was afraid to cut his hair, afraid Katie would find him ugly. If he didn't at least look like the kind of guy she wanted, what was to stop her, like Divinity, like his mother, from walking away?

"Is this ham?" he said politely to Steven's fiancée, pointing with his fork to a chunk of something pink and meat-ish on his plate. All through the meal, Lucy had been watching him. He'd felt her cool blue eyes on him, assessing him, it seemed, although he had no idea why. When he looked up, she gazed back, unsmiling, and when he looked down, he felt her eyes boring into the side of his head. Her attention was discomfiting, while at the same time it gave him the overwhelming urge to please, which was why he'd spoken instead of simply biding his time, mouth shut, until Katie gave him the OK to go home.

"Nonfat ham," Lucy said. She glanced at Steven, who was freshening his drink in the kitchen. "He's getting super fat," she whispered. Wilson nodded gravely, as if he, too, had noticed the change in the clown-across-the-street's physique. What he had noticed was that the clown in question, Steven, dressed in a fuzzy brown sweater flecked with pink, was a drinker with a capital *D*, refilling his tumbler with what looked to be nine parts rum to one part Coke, skipping the ice, then sloshing in a final splash of liquor before returning to the table. *Why not just drink from the fucking bottle?* Wilson thought, relieved that he was no longer that person. At the same time he felt a grudging if envious respect. He had no patience for girlish drinkers, drinkers like Katie who took one sip from a glass of wine before pushing it away, done.

Tonight Katie drank water, sitting beside him, chatting happily with January who sat across from her, her hair wrapped in a silky purple scarf, feet propped on a chair, eating an apple and sipping Sprite, having refused Lucy's "ham" dish with a "God no, I'm pregnant, if I even look at it I'll be sick." She'd made a face, covering her nose with her hand, and Lucy had laughed as if she'd just done something delightful.

The women began to talk excitedly about the pregnant lady's heightened sense of smell. "Every foul stench, each one worse than the last," January cried. Katie nodded in agreement as Lucy gazed adoringly at Jan.

Wilson felt his eyes glaze, his mind begin to drift.

"The bathroom, a normal clean bathroom, had about a thousand horrible odors," Katie was saying when he came to.

"You guys are freaking me out," Lucy said with a laugh.

Steven gulped the rest of his drink, set it down with a thump, then got up and turned the music loud. Stevie Ray Vaughan's "Little Wing" filled the room, and everybody froze, smiling politely, until Lucy grimaced and told him to turn it down. Did he think he could just *rock out* whenever he wanted? Did he not notice that other people were talking? Wilson sipped his Coke, amused. *Rock on, brother,* he thought. *Now, while you still can.* Steven was only . . . what? Twenty-three? He had his whole life to be married—why now, why so soon? Sure, Lucy was hot, but once he was hooked, it was all over. Despite the past, Wilson almost felt sorry for the guy.

*The past, the past, the jerk had dared to put his hands on his wife, when* . . . Wilson looked down at the rich oak table, the delicate violets on the china, feeling the anger rise. Quickly he shoved it away. It was ancient history, why should he care now? Wasn't he larger than their stupid behavior? Hadn't she ended up with him in the end, anyway?

Besides, it wasn't the past that was nagging at him, it was the present— earlier in the evening to be exact. In a marriage, the smallest of moments took on weight, became fraught with the fears and neuroses of the husband and wife. For example: Why was he bothered that Katie hadn't flipped out about the dead mouse? It had been a normal exchange, ending in quick hot sex, between two mature and peaceful adults. What was so bad about that? Nothing, he knew, but it had scared him. He looked at Katie, shining the way she did when she was happy, her eyes pretty, her long hair a clean ruby-red in the light of the candles. If he didn't want a calm and sensible wife, what *did* he want? He thought of Alice Cherry's hat, curled in the backseat of his car. Dirty, smelly, the tiny gleam of a glass eye in the dark. Did he only want what he couldn't have? Was it as murky, and as clear, as that?

"Where did you find nonfat ham?" he said to Lucy, taking in her elastic top, purple and cropped, the twinkle of her belly-button jewel when she raised her arms to stretch.

"It's Tofurky ham, or Tofam, or something tofu-ish like that." Lucy shrugged. "It's super good, don't you think? *I* taste ham. And I'm not going to get fat eating it. You could eat tons of this stuff and never gain an ounce." She filled her plate with seconds, smiled, picked up her fork, and dug in.

Katie nudged him, a smirk playing across her lips. Across the table, January rested her cheek on her fist, her eyes falling closed. Lucy asked her a question, and she started, a look of fright briefly flickering across her face. "I'm half-asleep," she said, smiling, purple fringe from her scarf falling across her forehead. "What did you say?"

"I asked how long you plan on staying."

"Oh, till the end." January leaned back in her chair, resting her hands on her still flat stomach. She wore several chunky rings—*like Wilma Flintstone,* Wilson thought—the bright stones glowing in the light of the candles. "I'm staying until the baby is born. We're having a home birth, maybe even a water birth, right there across the street." She motioned vaguely in the direction of Wilson's home. Wilson, his mouth full of Lucy's gluey concoction, nearly choked.

"Hold on," he said when he'd recovered from his coughing fit. "You just don't . . . You just can't . . ." He didn't know where to start, it was all so wrong, but when he looked around, nobody was listening.

"Wow." Lucy was excited. "I'll be there. You'll have to let me do the pictures—"

"Lucy," Steven chided. "You don't just go to someone's birth. It's called being invited?"

Lucy made a face.

"She's taking photography," Steven explained. "Last week she had to do textures. We did some hair, at the salon. And then we did . . . what did we do? For smooth? Hon?"

Lucy ignored him. "We'll use black-and-white film," she said, turning to January. "It'll be amazing. You'll treasure these pictures for the rest of your life."

January looked across the table at Katie. "OK." She hesitated. "Do you want photos, though, of that kind of thing?" She was still looking at her sister.

"Oh my God, yes." As Katie began to gush about the wonders of the birth experience, the primal mystery of it all, the way the pain tears you open, transforms you into someone new, Wilson felt himself growing more and more resentful. January was staying how long? She was having her baby where? And nobody had bothered to consult him, why? *Over my dead body*, he thought. Pregnant women scared him. He could still remember the moment this particular fear had been burned into his psyche.

Katie was pregnant with Paul, caught in the throes of morning sickness, and one afternoon she'd asked—no ordered—him to get her French fries from the mall, immediately, as they were the only thing she could hold down. It was a Sunday, he was relaxing, watching the US Open on TV, and there was no way he wanted to drive to the mall, of all places, for French fries, of all things, so he'd foolishly suggested she try something healthier.

"How about some soup?" he'd said, knowing there were several cans conveniently stacked in the cupboard.

"What did you say?" she'd asked, and when he repeated the word, tentatively, all hell broke loose. "Never say *soup* to a pregnant lady," she'd screamed before racing to the bathroom, barfing violently, then collapsing in a sobbing heap on the sticky floor.

When he tried to touch her, she kicked him away. "You have destroyed my life," she cried, her body wedged between the toilet and the wall. "My life is over because of you." He'd never seen anything like it. She was a two-year-old, a madwoman. Where was his happy-go-lucky Katie, the roller-blader with the scabbed knees and the penchant for dirty talk during sex? And who was this monster, this vomiting, raging, sorrowful *mother* who hated him with every ounce of her being? The incident had so shaken him that, after fetching the fries and depositing them silently on her kitchen table, he'd retreated to his bachelor pad, keeping his distance until the final days of the pregnancy.

What had he known? There was no manual, nothing to guide the expectant father through the long months of insanity. With Rose, it was easier. And now, post-vasectomy, he knew many things, chief among them: Never say *soup* to a pregnant lady, and, no matter how large, even if she's the size of a linebacker with a temper to match, a pregnant woman is always gorgeous.

In any case, there was no way he was going to play host to his lazy little sister-in-law, with her lounging and moods, for the next six months. When Katie paused for breath, he spoke.

"Are you all insane?" he shouted, quickly modulating his tone. "You don't just have a baby, in a bathtub, in someone else's house, without asking first—"

"You use a kiddie pool," January said. "Ladies do it every day. It's perfectly natural."

"What are you saying?" Katie gave him a look, the one that said, *You are such an ass, I'm dumbfounded.* "Do you want her to have the baby alone, with no family around? Do you want her to squat in the dirt, all by herself? Is that what you're saying?"

"No, I—"

"Does he not like you?" Lucy asked January, giggling.

"Lucy," Steven warned.

"What?"

Steven frowned and shook his head, then knocked back the rest of his drink, the food on his plate untouched.

"Wilson adores me. He just doesn't know it yet." With that January winked, shoved back her chair, and announced she was going home, promising to pick up Wilson and Katie's kids, plus Abby, from the neighbor girls' on her way. "You decide," she said to Wilson, pulling open the front door, cold air blowing in around her. "If you want me to go, I'll go." She hesitated, touched her cheek. "It's not a problem. I'll be fine."

Wilson didn't believe she'd be fine, and by the look on her face, he didn't think she did, either. She looked forlorn, standing there in the cold in her fluffy bedroom slippers, her silk scarf making her head look too big for her body. He immediately felt a pang of regret. "Jan," he said, before he could stop himself.

"Yeah?" She continued to gaze outside, her hand on the doorknob, shoulders hunched, chin bravely raised, milking the moment for all it was worth, like the annoying little drama queen she was.

"I don't want you to . . ." He sighed. "I don't want you to . . . squat in the dirt . . . alone."

Katie poked him in the ribs.

"I want you to stay," he said, making his voice bright. "I want you to have the baby here, with us." He took a deep breath. "Here with your family."

January turned to him and smiled, her hands clasped at her chest. He was surprised to see tears in her eyes, and immediately congratulated himself on his well-timed burst of generosity. Who knew they meant so much to her? He looked around, pleased with his good luck. Steven nodded manfully. Lucy gave him a thumbs-up. "Hooray," she said. "We'll do before and after pictures. I'll get out my camera and bring it over, first thing tomorrow morning."

Katie squeezed his hand beneath the table. "See?" she said. "See how nice it is it be nice?"


"I love your sister," Lucy announced when January was gone. "She's so skinny."

"Yeah." Katie smiled. "She's always been thin, even as a little kid."

"I bet you wish you got her genes." Lucy returned to her food, apparently unaware that she had just destroyed Wilson's weekend. He felt Katie freeze beside him. She set down her fork, pushed her plate away, her cheeks pink, eyes shiny with tears. Damn it. Why had Lucy said that, why? He could hear it already; let the litany of insecurities begin: *Am I fat? Do you think I'm fat? I know I'm not as skinny as Jan, but why would she say that? Why would anyone say anything so cruel? How can people be that way? Do you think I'm fat? Do you? Do you? I know you do. You do, don't you? I'm never eating again.* With one stupid line, Lucy had destroyed Katie's confidence, and who was going to have to pick up the pieces, soothe the tears, endure the endless hours of grouchy depression? He was.

"Skinny is not all that." Steven leaned back confidently, if drunkenly, in his chair. He looked at Lucy. "Skinny is not all that," he said again, and by the belligerent tone in his voice, Wilson figured he'd be slurring his words by dessert.

"What are you talking about?" Lucy looked annoyed, or maybe defeated, Wilson thought, her shoulders slumped, her pale hair shoved awkwardly behind her ears.

"Guys like something to grab onto." Steven demonstrated, grabbing an imaginary ass in the air in front of him, hefting it slightly before giving it a few good squeezes. His crew cut came to a bristly peak at the top of his head, and his eyes were shiny with liquor. "I'm just saying, skinny is not all that." He looked at Wilson. "Right, my man?" He didn't wait for an answer. "Yeah, you know, *you* know," he mumbled, smiling to himself, shaking his head.

Katie giggled. "Steven, settle down."

Wilson smiled through clenched teeth. *If you're thinking about my wife, prepare to die.*

"Anyone want dessert?" Lucy said brightly.


"She's perfect for him," Katie whispered, ever the martyr, when Lucy and Steven went to the kitchen to fetch dessert. The candles had collapsed into hot yellow puddles, hissing in their saucers. "So bright and clean, so simple and nice." She bit her lip, touched his hand. "Are you having fun?"

"Are you drunk?"

"I'm just saying that she's normal," Katie said tightly. "More people should be like that. *We* should be like that. It's an underrated way of being, that's all I'm saying."

"If she's marrying this clown, I guarantee you, she's not normal."

Katie ignored him. She stuck her finger in her water, held it to her lips.

"I think I need to go now." Wilson was careful to sound nonchalant.

"What?"

"Katie." He took her hands, looked into her eyes. "I really need to go." He lowered his voice further, making his lie sound as sincere as possible. "It's the drinking, Steven's drinking. I don't think I should be around it—"

"Bullshit," Katie hissed.

"Just fifty feet from here," he said, desperate. "I could be lying on the bed, watching TV, in total peace and silence. You stay, you have fun—just let me go, please?" He was begging, but he didn't care. January had left, no problem. Why couldn't he? "And you owe me," he said, pulling out the big guns. "You never told me that she was staying, you two never even thought to ask—"

"Stop."

"I'm going."

"If you go," Katie looked at him, her eyes hard. "If you go, I don't know what."

"I know." He paused, hung his head, truly sorry for what he was about to do. "I know you don't know what." With that he got up and left. He did something bad. He left his wife sitting alone and unconfident at the table. He left his hosts Steven and Lucy bickering about the whereabouts of the nonfat Cool Whip in the kitchen. "I know I bought it," Steven was saying. "I had the list, the list you gave me—"

"But where did you put it?" Lucy snapped. "That's the question, if you weren't wasted—"

"But I had the list . . ."

Wilson walked, no ran, to the front door. He let himself out, silently, and from there, he ran home, not stopping until he was safe on his own porch, crouched on a pile of chunked-up ice, against the brick wall and behind the fence, hiding from his wife, should she attempt to pursue him.

She didn't. Steven's dark green door remained closed. After a minute, Wilson relaxed and lit a cigarette, inhaling deeply. He'd left his wife at the dinner party. He'd put his own selfish needs above hers and there would be hell to pay, he knew, but for the time being, he was free. He couldn't take any more, not another second of husbands and wives and the politics of marriage, of Steven and Lucy and the way they acted out their obnoxious roles like . . .

No. No more. He was done; the party was over. He sank back on his heels, the brick cold through his shirt. All around night glittered: the ice on which he crouched, the stars overhead, the snow and the rock salt and the sheen of ice on the windshield of his car—everything glittered, hard, beneath the cold eye of the moon.

Punishment was swift. After hustling little Abby back home—racing off as she tripped onto her porch in pink-feathered Hello Kitty mules—Wilson spent the next two hours coaxing his kids into bed. It wasn't an easy task. Megan or Mandy's bulldog, Cleopatra, had bit Paul, and the excitement level was high. "The bull-poochie got me, Daddy," Paul kept saying in an awestruck tone, carefully pulling up his pajama pants to reveal his unscathed ankle.

"And then she got the big swat," Jake said, demonstrating dramatically on his own behind, after which all three collapsed into giggles.

Wilson sighed. He was alone in his bedtime plight, as January was asleep in Jake's room and Katie was still at the party where he'd stupidly left her. He began enthusiastically enough. He patted backs, sang the Pokémon song in a solemn, dirgelike tone that made everyone laugh. Jake was given permission to play his Game Boy in his sleeping bag, a luxury strictly forbidden by his mother, and the book with the weird photos of the Weimaraners was read several times in a row. He brought water—three cups on three separate occasions—and told a story about a bunny named Stu who kept falling off his bike. Thirty minutes into the proceedings, however, as things were starting to settle, Rose threw a fit.

"What does she want, what does she want?" he cried after his daughter had screamed the same unintelligible words again, this time near hysteria.

"A cookie," the boys shouted in unison, and Wilson, relieved to have an answer—although he would've preferred it ten minutes earlier—expanded the bedtime ritual to include a brief cookie break—anything to make Rose, with her tear-stained face and furious clenched fists, *stop*.

The cookie break was a big mistake. It stretched on and on and on. Requests were made for more, requests that were swiftly denied. The children were invigorated by the sugar. Rose and Paul would not sleep. They popped their heads up, they laughed; they jumped on the bed and ran squealing from the room. An hour into the insanity, Wilson lost all will to live. Knowing he would die if they weren't unconscious within the next minute and a half, he insisted in his most authoritative tone that *sleep must happen now*. Nothing happened. His demand was met with giggles. Sleep remained elusive.

He wheedled, he threatened. He enlisted Jake in a game of good cop/bad cop against the little ones, all to no avail. Wiggling kids were returned to the bed. Kicking and screaming kids were returned to the bed. Then, just when he thought he would have to crawl back across the street and fetch Katie, on his knees and sobbing, it was finally over, and all three children—two his own, one he'd lucked onto—were asleep. Sleep had come; he'd done it, ushered them all safely into the Land of Nod. He touched Paul's hand, smoothed Jake's hair, kissed Rose's cheek, then stumbled to the couch in the living room, sank into its velvety depths, and cried.

At least he tried to cry. His frustration was soon forgotten, however, by the operation he found when flipping channels on the TV. It was a breast reduction procedure, and he was instantly absorbed, although he forced himself to get up and pop a tape into the VCR, thinking he would record the thing, show it to his students at the final class meeting Monday morning. *Perfect*, he thought, stretching out on the couch, resting his head on his arm. He'd let the intro class watch it, the class that hated him. Like a lion tamer throwing hunks of meat at his snarling charges, he'd toss the surly students this gory bone in the hopes that the graphic excitement of it all would finally make them like him.

As the show faded into a commercial, he congratulated himself, for the second time that evening, on his foresight. Genius, he was beginning to see, was always on. Genius, he realized, never slept. And wasn't that a good title for the memoir he would one day write, at the end of his long and illustrious career, books published, awards won, chairs endowed, women conquered? *Genius Never Sleeps* by Wilson A. Lavender, genius extraordinaire.

When the show returned, the doctor was explaining that depending upon the amount of tissue removed, the woman might not be able to nurse her young. "It's not a concern," the lady told the camera. She was a youngish woman with a frazzled perm and enormous drooping breasts. "I want to be able to jog, and I want to look good in my clothes. That's all I care about." She smiled, showing her bottom teeth, crooked and small. "I mean, how am I going to meet a guy to *have kids with* looking like this?" She smiled again, but it was a pained smile, and she quickly looked down at her hands.

Wilson wondered if he'd ever been nursed. It was more likely his mother had dangled him by his toes over a boiling cauldron. He pushed away an image of her lying on the old green couch, hating her life, hating their town and everyone in it, hating *him* it seemed, for how else to explain the long afternoons of crying and sorrow, when even the cartoons on the TV, turned to the lowest possible volume, made her angry? "The good Lord gave them to you, and the good Lord can take them away," his grandmother always said when his mother complained about her kids, and to his young mind, it had sounded as if his mother wanted him dead, and it was only by his grandmother's random intervention that he was saved.

The woman lay unconscious on the operating table. The shot moved over her still face, her eyes closed, lashes dusky against sallow skin, hair hidden beneath a paper cap. From her open mouth sprung a length of thick tubing. *It really is obscene, isn't it, students?* Wilson murmured in his head. *The lengths women in our society go to, simply to fit into the elusive shape the media has deemed pleasing.* The camera zeroed in on the woman's naked torso, draped in blue surgical sheeting. Her breasts looked like two snub-nosed sea animals, nestled comfortably in her armpits. Gloved hands picked one up. It was marked with black hieroglyphics—lines and circles and arrows. The knife slipped in, as if into water. Blood welled, flesh was cauterized, and the offending breast was gutted, fat and tissue scooped out and plopped into a scale. "Five hundred grams, about a pound," said the smooth voice-over, "the amount most insurance companies require be removed before they will cover the procedure."

*It's sick.* Wilson continued his silent narration. *The violence, the act of voluntarily amputating a part of one's body. And not just any part but the most womanly part of all, the part intended to feed and comfort one's young. What about her sexuality? Nipple sensation may be lost—you heard the doctor. With this procedure* (here he would pause, glowering darkly) *the subjective is made objective, the subject object.*

After another round of commercials, during which Wilson rooted in the fridge for something to eat, coming up with a deli carton of mini-meatballs, which he dumped on a plate and nuked, the woman's nipples were excised and repositioned to fit the new, smaller breasts. She was stitched up. A final shot lingered on her torso, her breasts now perky, her chest covered with a prickly black bra of sutures. The show ended with an image of the woman, happy now, bouncing in a bikini on a mini-trampoline. *A pretty thing, her breasts no longer her own.* Wilson finished on a solemn note. *Pleasing to society perhaps, but absent from herself.*

Credits crawled over the bouncing woman. She leapt into the air. A handsome man caught her around the waist. Freeze frame: the woman captured, her head thrown back in ecstasy. Wilson muted the TV, went into the kitchen to find something more to eat.


*If you go, I don't know what.* It was close to midnight, and Katie still wasn't home, although Wilson expected her any second and had taken pains to prepare for her arrival. All the lights were off, the windows locked, blinds drawn. He was on the couch, watching *Saturday Night Live,* a cup of coffee with four spoonfuls of sugar warming his cold hands, as he'd just smoked his last cigarette of the night outside. He stared at the flickering screen, one ear cocked for the sound of Katie's footsteps on the porch, at which point he planned to click off the set, move swiftly to bed, and feign sleep should she still be angry.

But the coffee—he'd missed a step. He hadn't thought of the coffee. If he left it on the table before fleeing, Katie would feel its warmth when she tidied up—something she did every night before bed—and become suspicious. Knowing he was awake, she'd want to bitch him out for leaving her. It could go on all night. Would he have time to make it to the sink, dump it, and disappear, before she came inside? Should he go to bed and fake sleep now? What if she didn't return for hours? He'd be lying there, wide awake, as he'd just gulped a cup of coffee.

He sighed and tried to relax, realizing for the millionth time that he put far more energy into life than was needed. He sipped his troublesome brew, wondering when it was he'd slipped over the line. For instance, when had he begun watching TV all the time instead of enjoying only his weekly dose of *Cops*? When had he lost control, napping and staring at the tube with abandon, no longer caring that he'd sunk into the annoying mire of American trash culture? It was, he knew, the day the sister-in-law—like the mice—infiltrated his life. On a pink winter morning, clouds jitterbugging on the horizon, Wilson A. Lavender had begun to sink.

The phone rang. He scrambled to find it, his heart crashing in his chest, as it seemed to do a lot lately. It had become tricky, going wild at unexpected events, like when Katie yelled at him from the bedroom, or the heat roared on, or when Lovely, who never barked, barked, for no reason and at the most random things: the wall, the bed, a balled-up pair of socks someone had dropped on the floor.

Wilson needed a drug, something powerful to keep things flowing smoothly. His perfect drug would be a cross between a muscle relaxant, a tranquilizer, and a major anesthetic. *Skelarid,* he would call it. *Rid yourself of that pesky skeleton once and for all.* He pictured the print ad, a limply blissful executive splayed across his desk. *Come with us, puddle a while,* the copy would read.

He finally found the phone shoved down the side of Katie's big pink chair. Who could be calling this late? Was it the Queen herself? Had she finally decided to leave him? Was she phoning to inform him that she'd be moving in with the goon across the street, effective immediately? Did she want her kids, her contact case, and the book she'd been reading, pronto?

*And then it would all be over.* Wilson took a deep breath, forgot to let it out. When he spoke, his hello sounded strangled.

"Hello, Wilson."

It was Alice Cherry. He recognized her voice immediately. It glowered. It glowed in the dark, urgent and hot, tense with pent-up lust. At least that was what he heard, and he was immediately turned on. "Why are you calling?" he said. His voice sounded choked, juvenile. He bit his lip to keep from saying more.

"Right." Alice was all business. "I talked to that chick, Suzanne. Remember? After you dropped us at the office, I went back, and guess what?"

"I don't know." Wilson hated guessing games. "She put a hit out on me?"

"No. Why would she do that?"

"I was joking." He had forgotten that Alice was humor impaired.

"Oh." Alice paused. "Well, guess again, for real this time. And hurry because I'm on my cell. I don't want to waste my minutes."

"Alice. I have no idea. The dog was there? You got the dog?"

"No. But almost."

"You almost got the dog?" Wilson's heart leapt. If she'd almost found the dog, then that meant the dog was around to be found, and who would finish the job? He would—Wilson, hero in residence. He'd fetch the canine Pearl and present her to her mommy who would no longer be alone, who would now have her precious pal to squat in the dirt with her when she gave birth at home—at her home, not his. They could put her on a plane and send her on her pretty little pregnant way tomorrow. Adios, Mommy.

"Get this." Alice lowered her voice as if they were going over the details of a murder case. "The lady and her baby and the dog, they were all at the shelter when you called, only Suzanne didn't think it would be right to tell you, and by the time we arrived on Monday, they were gone . . ." Alice trailed off. "Maybe it isn't the best news."

"They didn't say where they were going?"

"No. Nothing. They just left. I guess the woman got mad at Suzanne for telling her she couldn't smoke—you know, get high—on the premises, and so she left. After telling Suzanne to fuck off, of course."

Wilson was silent.

"Are you there?"

"This makes me very sad." A wave of disappointment crashed over him. "Things have been . . . how do you say . . . *hellish* around here lately." He laughed, but his laugh was bitter. He remembered a comedian he and Katie had watched the night she gave birth to Rose. They were lying together on her hospital bed, the baby, unbelievable and new, asleep in Katie's arms. The comedian was talking about marriage. "Let the joylessness begin," he'd cried, and they'd laughed because it was funny, and because, at the moment, the joylessness seemed very far away.

"I can't believe you're sad." Alice spoke as if she truly did not believe him, as if she thought he was lying.

He didn't answer. *Save me*, a small voice cried in his head. He rested his hands on his chest. His heart hurt.

"If it's any consolation," Alice began, "Suzanne is devastated by the whole thing. She wants you to know that she's going back into therapy—"

"Does she want me to pay for it?" Wilson's voice was flat.

"I don't think so."

He didn't tell her he was joking.

"She also wanted me to tell you that the woman was kind to the dog," Alice continued. "It slept with her, and they did this trick where the woman held a treat in her mouth and the dog took it, gently. They were a happy team, Suzanne said. Or trio, I guess, because there was the baby—"

"Where are you?" Wilson could hear loud music thumping in the background.

"I'm at work." Alice's voice dropped.

Wilson sat up, his sorrow forgotten. "At the . . . at the place?" He too spoke in a hushed tone, so excited he could barely get the words out.

"Yes. I go on in twenty minutes."

"What are you wearing? I mean . . ." He didn't know what he meant. He meant, *what do those luscious breasts look like naked, and when can I bury my face in them?* He couldn't believe he was on the phone with his colleague, the humorless Alice Cherry, and that said colleague was about to strip down to nothing. His finger hovered near the flash button ready to hang up the second Katie's foot hit the porch. For this was wrong, very wrong. Katie would not appreciate this at all.

"I'm wearing a cop getup," Alice said. "With handcuffs, the hat, a nightstick I do some really naughty things with."

Holy shit. Had she really just said that? Wilson was on his feet, pacing the small room.

"You said you like *Cops*, right?" Alice said. "That day in the car?"

"Yes, yes. It's my favorite show." He tried to breathe slowly. "I try to watch only that, but I've been backsliding lately, I don't know why." *Shut up, shut up, you moron.* He bit his lip, forced himself to quit babbling.

"Then my routine is for you." Alice was silent. When she spoke again, her voice was fierce. "I want you to come and see me."

Wilson was silent. He could hear the music roaring and receding. He thought of the lines from Eliot's "Prufrock," the saddest lines of all:

I have heard the mermaids singing, each to each.

I do not think that they will sing to me.

"Wilson?"

"Uh-huh?"

"Will you come and see me?"

"I don't understand," he said, suddenly understanding everything—his entire life—quite clearly. This mermaid was singing for him, goddammit. Was he going to stay in his pink shell, afraid of life, forever? Or was he going to get in his car, drive to the Mermaid Lair, and watch his naked office mate do naughty things with a nightstick as quick as humanly possible? The question, he realized, as he slipped on his boots and patted his pocket for his cigarettes, wasn't why, but why not?

"Will you come? Now, tonight, in twenty minutes?"

"Uh-huh." It wasn't a yes and it wasn't a no. He picked up his car keys, checked his wallet for cash. It was a neutral response. He'd done nothing wrong—yet.

"Good." Alice was all business. "And don't act like you know me. Remember, I'm *undercover*. This is a *front*. I'm gathering information— *covert* information I wouldn't normally be able to get. You can't ruin it for me. Do you understand?"

Wilson nodded.

"I'll be waiting."


Often when drinking, Wilson would go into a free fall. Things would happen—bar fights, wrecked cars, sex with women whose names he didn't know—and they would happen as if underwater, everything pretty, exciting, violent even, but he wouldn't feel a thing. He'd coast, slide like the liquor sliding down his throat, slide through the night and into dawn, the sky wet and smoky, the color of bourbon, the sun a slick maraschino cherry bobbing on the horizon. Slick and liquid, he'd coast, bumping up against things like ice in a drink, numb, frozen, another person, not himself—not anyone really. He'd watch the world slide past. Takeout food would appear at his door, food he rarely ate and never remembered ordering. Sometimes the screens would be torn off his windows. Big holes appeared in his apartment walls. Some nights his car disappeared. He often woke in clothing not his own.

You might say he had a problem.

But it was the problem that led him to his dissertation, which, eventually, put him on the pathway to sobriety. On a grim Sunday afternoon, hungover, sick as shit, he'd read *The Bell Jar* for a class and had immediately felt for Esther Greenwood. Like Wilson, she was juvenile, awkward, much too finely tuned for her own good. Things happened, but seemed to hit her only in a fractured way, while some essential part of herself remained tucked away, watching. Of course in the novel, she is sliding into insanity, but how different is that from drinking? Esther undergoes shock therapy. Didn't he use alcohol to the same effect, to stun himself into nothingness? Was alcohol then, in some sick way, his cure?

He found himself wondering about the author. Who had written such a thing? The first images were of death by electrocution, of a cadaver's head like a balloon—jarring when found in the psyche of a "good girl" circa 1950s America. The writer was on intimate terms with the damage life could inflict. Surely she'd sustained damage herself. Over the next weeks, he read the *Letters Home*, the journals, and the collected poems, each work revealing another facet of Plath, a brilliant writer who, at the same time, seemed to be barely hanging on in a world Wilson found disturbingly familiar, one of perfect surfaces, one in which mothers broke.

He'd never say so to the guys at his meetings, but the chance reading of *The Bell Jar* had stopped him drinking for good. It took a few tries, and one disastrous blowout in Chicago when he attended a David Mamet play and afterward told strangers in a bar that he *was* David Mamet, but eventually he'd quit, and shortly thereafter met Katie, became a father, became good. He'd only needed a friend to help him make the leap into sobriety, a fellow genius that saw the world as he did: dangerous in its beauty, a place but not a home. He'd found that friend in Ms. Plath, and now, years later, needed only to finish his tribute to her: *The Lost Journals of Sylvia Plath* by Wilson A. Lavender, fellow writer and a big fan. *Felt like singing today!* It would all be over soon.

Sobriety had lifted his bell jar. The problem was: He wanted his bell jar back.

Wilson in liquid, vodka skies, the sweetness, the sheen, the ease and the falling, falling into Alice Cherry, his colleague with the nightstick, a girl he didn't particularly respect, but it was easy, like the drinking. There was the anticipation, the ache in the throat, the wanting . . . and then the first drink, knocking you back in your seat . . . and the relief, the wonderful fucking relief.

His life with Katie and the kids was good—if you could call something that felt like it was killing you good. He didn't know how much longer he could take it without something, anything. He wasn't going to drink again, he knew you weren't supposed to say that—*one day at a time, one day at a time*—but it was true, it wasn't an option, not with the children, asleep like weary puppies in the next room. One drink and he'd lose everything.

He stood at the front door, his hand on the cold knob, considering his next move. When one disappeared, into liquor, or drugs, or off to the Mermaid Lair, across town and much too far from one's bed where one belonged, there was always the shock of the next day, the hangover. There was the sick pounding, the dry heaves in the shower, the payback of too much when even that was not enough. Wilson jingled his keys. He looked at Jake's bedroom door, scarred with strips of Scotch tape, a hole from a hockey stick some kid had jammed through it. Behind the door the sister-in-law slept—the sister-in-law who was arguably an adult and could be there for his kids in the brief window of time between his departure and his wife's arrival home.

Still he didn't go. He thought of Plath, of her many faces: the perfect daughter portrayed by her mother in *Letters Home*; the disturbed Esther Greenwood; the writer of the journals, witty and competitive and mean; the cool, primeval persona of the *Ariel* poems. Who was Sylvia Plath, really?

And, even more interesting, who was he? A broken drunk with huge chunks of his life lost to alcohol? Or a genius, writing a bold and exciting dissertation, a work no one had dared attempt before? *Felt like singing today!* Was he the hip teacher, hundreds of impressionable young women squirming in the palm of his hand, thinking he was Jesus, thinking he held the knowledge their budding souls craved? Or an idiot, urging everyone to follow him down his happy feminist path when he himself knew nothing about women? There was the child he'd been but barely remembered, living submerged and furious and dangerous. And there was the father he was now, safe in the sweet company of his kids.

He opened the door. Cold air blasted his face, and he quickly pushed it shut. The problem was the usual: He needed more. He needed something easy, like the drinking, but without the disastrous repercussions. An image of a dead baby popped into his head, the bad dream of the world swirling around it. Maybe he was still in the bell jar, just a bit, and he liked it and wanted more, a thicker more impermeable layer between himself and the world. But did a part of him, the smallest part, the lost submerged boy, perhaps, want out—could that be it? Did he want to be touched, to breathe the fresh air, to feel for the first time in a long time what it was like to be alive?

And what exactly was a bell jar? Wilson had no idea—about anything. The fact was, he didn't know who he was or what he wanted, and at that moment, he didn't care. He turned and laid his palm on the cheap wood of Jake's door, felt the silence of the condo shimmering around him. He only knew that he must go to the obnoxious girl with the red-tipped curls, who had dedicated her "Cops" striptease to him. The hangover was hours, days, maybe even months away.

He opened the front door once again but hesitated, listening to make sure no one was awake. Jake's bedroom door had drifted open in the breeze, and he looked in at January asleep on the narrow futon. She'd surrounded herself with stuffed animals, plush pets encircling her like blossoms, as if she were a sacrifice, laid out on a flower-bedecked bier. The room smelled strongly of crushed grass and lemons, and he wondered if she was burning incense, if they should review the rules of fire safety before she set the place ablaze. He didn't trust her with matches in his home, but in other regards, was it really so bad having her there? He took in her pajama pants, slush-stained at the cuffs, her Oregon Jam '79 T-shirt, held together by a motley collection of safety pins. Wasn't it almost like having a nanny?

"I'm going now," he whispered, freedom strange and unexpected on his tongue. He felt unmoored, as if he were hovering two feet above the carpet, something Katie would love, as it would save her from vacuuming. January remained motionless, her face sweetly composed, like a doll with its eyeballs clicked shut. Should he check her breathing? It wouldn't do to leave his kids with a dead girl. "Thanks for helping," he murmured as he quickly picked up her wrist, found the slow warm flutter of her pulse.

Having ensured that she was, indeed, alive, he quietly shut Jake's door. Her warmth lingered in his palm, and he felt, for a moment, merciful. As annoying as January could be, she was just a kid—at least she acted like one—and she was pregnant and alone, with no one to depend on but herself. As he zipped his leather jacket, flipping the collar up around his chin, Wilson vowed to be a better brother-in-law, to support her throughout her pregnancy and quit making fun of every ridiculous thing she said. And while he was at it, why not be a better husband, too? He could nap less, resist the urge to flee every time Katie plopped into his lap and tried to start a conversation.

Secure in his goodness, Wilson hesitated no longer. He left, he *rocked on*. Drifting out to his car, he started it and drove, away from home, away from Katie and the kids, away from the Reserve—snow-swept, lights sparking in its pine-rimmed bowl—and out onto the road, gaining speed as he entered the freeway, on his way to the Mermaid Lair. If he had bothered to look, he would have noticed that Lucy's truck had disappeared from Steven's driveway, and that behind Steven's drawn blinds, the rooms of his condo were dark. But in his excitement and haste, in his *drifting*, Wilson hadn't looked. He'd smelled Divinity. The sirens were singing his name.

# Nineteen

## Wilson

When Wilson walked into the Mermaid Lair on a sleeting winter night—no, *drifted* was the word, for he was there but not there, strictly an observer, he had a hat to return goddammit—he found his colleague, Alice Cherry, naked on her knees, whacking the stage with a nightstick. It wasn't quite the nasty image he'd conjured, but it was enough to make him crave a drink.

He watched from a table in the back, *there but not there*. It was hardly proper to leer at your office mate from the lip of the stage. Ogling her from afar, however, seemed OK. Alice's breasts were big and bouncy, her bottom jiggly, and she'd shaved *down there*, a sight that made Wilson uncomfortably hot. A fringe of bills stuck out of her garter. She wore a policeman's cap pulled low over one eye, and heavy black boots that, frankly, looked hard to dance in.

Wilson sipped a Coke, delivered by a waitress in a bunny-pink halter. A pale butterfly glowed on her suntanned hip. The club was close and hot, but with a strangely cool undercurrent. It smelled wet, of ancient air-conditioning, of alcohol and fruit and melted ice. The surface vibe was tropical—girls, drinks, *fun fun fun*—but beneath it all, there was the sense of being underwater, as if the Mermaid Lair had long ago sunk to the bottom of the sea. Wilson looked down, half-expecting to see salt water slosh over his ankles. Had he turned to bone? Was sand sifting from his eye sockets? There were no windows in the place; the outside world had disappeared.

He returned his attention to Alice. She was dancing to an old Metallica song, which seemed odd. Something was off. Alice was a shade behind the beat. Wilson willed her to catch up. It was one of his pet peeves—bad rhythm—left over from years of playing clarinet with the idiots in his high school band. Alice did not catch up. A few blockheads made asses of themselves near the stage. An older man in big black glasses sat quietly nursing a drink. He had the word *sales* written all over him. Alice spread her legs, flashing the college yahoos. They roared in appreciation. Alice looked bored. After simulating masturbation with her nightstick in an incredibly realistic manner (Wilson made a note to compliment her on that later), she rolled into the splits, hopped up, and skipped offstage.

That was it. Wilson was shaking inside. *This is my girlfriend, the stripper.* The words ran through his mind as he lit a cigarette, inhaled. The butterfly girl slid by, depositing the second Coke of his two-drink minimum. Wilson dug in his wallet for a tip. "Peace," she said, moving swiftly away. Wilson watched as she chatted with the frat guys across the room. Their table sat under a black light. When the waitress smiled, her teeth glowed blue. *Alice Cherry, stripper/scholar—Wilson's new love.* Katie would freak. Thinking of his wife, home by now from her ridiculous dinner party, probably asleep with the kids, made Wilson feel bad. What was he doing? Nothing—he'd done nothing wrong yet. *Of course you have, you idiot!* What if Katie found out and sent him away?

A jolt of panic shot through him. He got up to go, shoving his smokes into his jacket pocket. He'd explain it all to Alice on Monday morning. "It's like this," he would say. "I'm in love with my wife, I'm afraid of my wife, and I can't live without her." It was as simple and as complicated as that. The thought of losing Katie terrified him. What if he never recovered?

Still the genius drifted. Alice appeared behind him. She wore a ruby-red G-string and bra. She smelled of sweat and tequila and yes! there it was, a hint of powdery pink Divinity. Wilson tried not to swoon. He forced himself to keep his gaze above her neck. *This is a supremely awkward situation*, his mind observed from afar. When Alice spoke, her voice was terse. "I'll meet you outside," she said, cutting her eyes to the left. Wilson remembered that she was undercover. How ridiculous it all was. "I'm done. I can go home and work on my . . ." She made a scribbling motion with her hand, mouthed the word *notes.* "Can I get a lift, did you drive?"

*No, he'd drifted.*

Alice didn't wait for an answer. "Good. I'll meet you at your car. The green one, right?"

Wilson nodded, watched her go. His legs had grown heavy, his arms weak. He could feel the water rising, tugging at his hips, lifting his feet off the ground, rushing him away.


He'd slipped beneath the crust of a frozen lake and, once immersed, no longer had the strength or will to pull himself out. On an icy winter night, Wilson sat with Alice Cherry in his car, in the parking lot of the Mermaid Lair. Snow pelted the windshield, enormous flakes, soft and white like the bodies of moths. Beneath the syrupy glow of the neon sign—a sly mermaid with zipping pink breasts—he caught a glimpse of himself in Alice's eyes. *Skeletal* was the word that came to mind. He was a tiny creature, floating on an ocean of black.

Something—lust, loneliness—had washed him away from the warm banks of his home. "What's your real name?" he asked, unsure what to say. He started to light a cigarette, then thought better of it. His hands shook. He reached into the backseat and retrieved Alice's hat (*that* was his mission, nothing sinister, only returning a hat). The fur was silky in his hand. The minute she took it, he regretted letting it go. He missed it, his driving companion of the past month. ("Why is that hat in our car?" Katie had asked. "Get rid of the skanky thing.")

"You mean my slave name? The name my father gave me, marking me as his property?" Alice was sweating. She twirled the hat on her finger. Its beady eyes spun. Her own eyes were large and dark, burning in her pale face. Her curls were sweat stained, snaking down her back like flames. Wilson sensed danger, as if he were in the wrong place with the wrong stranger at the worst possible moment. At the same time, he never wanted to go home. "My slave name," Alice repeated softly.

"Whatever." He briefly wished Katie were there, sitting in the backseat, so he could turn to her and smirk. So he could say, "See? Some women find me irresistible." Alice, it seemed, wanted to believe everything good about him, while with Katie the X-ray had flipped and only his faults were apparent.

"A goddess never invokes her slave name," Alice breathed. "It's unspeakable." Snow pelted the windshield. Wilson wondered if the Marilyn Monroe voice was a part of her act. It was a little unnerving. They sat in a cocoon of fogged windows and glowing pink light. He was unsure how to proceed. Maybe, he thought, rubbing his eyes, he would *not* proceed; he would let the story spin itself out. Just this once, and then he'd go home and sweep out the garage, something Katie had been nagging him to do for months. "Come on," he said for want of anything better. "Alice Cherry can't be your real name."

"Of course it is." Alice took a notebook from her pack and began jotting notes. She glanced up. "Why would I lie?"

Wilson shrugged. She seemed smaller than she had onstage. Her ripped jeans revealed faded blue long johns. Her boots were tall and fleecy, like something a trapper might wear.

"Can we go?" Alice looked annoyed. "I really can't be seen with you. You *look* like a grad student. You're going to blow my cover." She zipped her baggy black sweatshirt, pulled the hood over her head, and jerked the strings tight.

Wilson started the car, relieved. The show was officially over. The Alice he knew—humorless, paranoid, more than a little self-involved—was back. He drove along slick winter streets, heading downtown per her instructions. The snow slowed. The sky was full of watery black holes.

Alice looked up from her scribbling. "This is it. Stop. Back there."

Wilson drove in reverse for half a block, then parked in front of a small brick duplex. Alice's home wasn't far from the battered women's shelter. Bare winter trees crouched low over the building. The apartment next to hers was boarded up.

"Where does your son go when you work?" Wilson asked as Alice tucked away her pen, dug in her pack for her keys.

"Oh. He's living with my mother." Alice shook her head, still searching. "While I get established as a . . . you know . . ." she sat up, dangling the keys, "writer."

"That must be hard. How can you stand it?" Wilson thought of his own children, their sweet faces, their personalities blossoming like flowers. He pictured them walking away from him. His heart hurt.

"It's OK. Stuey is hard to handle."

"What's his name?" Wilson laughed. "Suey?"

"*Stuart.* Stuey. And really, it's OK. He's wild and I'm a shitty mom."

"No," Wilson said, although he figured she was correct. Hadn't she had the kid on a leash once at the office? Stuey was a chimp-like fellow, cheerful enough, Wilson remembered, but definitely out of control.

"No. Yes. I'm a horrible mother. Some women are, you know."

"I *do* know."

"So why inflict your poor skills on an innocent child?" Alice looked at him for a long moment. "You don't seem to have been mothered very well. You're sort of tense. You're itchy and sarcastic, and the smoking is a dead giveaway. You obviously never got that cushion, that buffer, to carry you through life."

Wilson nodded, excited by her analysis.

"There's a reason moms get fat."

"I'm not following." He was still caught up on "the buffer." What was it and where could he get one for himself?

"Mothers are vast." Alice looked at him with big guru eyes. "They fill up, billow out, become this entire universe for their children to draw from." She frowned, pushed her hair behind her ears. "Case in point: After Stuey was born, *I* got really skinny. My mom made me go to the doctor, and they thought I had worms. I had to drink this Ensure crap. Like a little old lady. But it was a sign. A month later, I turned him over to her—to my mom. It was the best thing I ever did. Of course, she won't keep him all the time." Alice rolled her eyes. "He visits some weekends. But now he's like a little brother. And I'm a good sister. I've always been a good sister."

"Hmmm." Wilson waited for more of her theories on *him*, but Alice was zipping her notebook into her bag. As she climbed out of the car, he wondered why she'd invited him to her show. He suspected he was a part of her story. He had to admit he'd make a great character in her exposé. Wilson A. Lavender: quirky genius of a colleague. He appears just when the undercover stripper least expects to see anyone she knows. Her two worlds—one seedy, the other ridiculously underpaid—collide. Chaos ensues. Life-changing lessons are learned. Everyone hugs in the end. The buffoons at the stage? They were her students. Come and see your teacher naked. Who could resist that extra-credit assignment?

"Later." Alice leaned into the car. "Don't forget: *Do not* mention tonight to anyone, not even your wife."

Was she serious? Wilson nodded gravely, waved good night. He started his car, then watched as she shambled up her walk. The sleeves of her sweatshirt hung over her hands. With her hood up she looked like a tired burglar, come to halfheartedly rob the run-down place, or perhaps just climb through the window, sit on the couch, and stare. Alice fumbled at the door, slammed it shut behind her.

As he pulled away, Wilson thought again of Alice's exposé. Katie the psychoanalyst said that humans create their stories—the stories of their lives—subconsciously, choosing just the characters needed in order to learn and grow. Alice, it seemed, had created her story on a conscious level, before it even happened. Setting, character, tension—everything was in place. How did it all turn out? Was Wilson the romantic hero? Or a minor character—odd, flat, and meaningless? The thought made him sad. As he turned on the radio, he noticed Alice's hat on the floor. He leaned over and picked it up. The fur was warm from the heater. Without thinking, he jerked the wheel, circled the block, and returned to her apartment. He turned off his headlights, sat in the darkened car. Now what? Light spilled from Alice's front window onto the snow below. It was a purplish light, as if she'd thrown a scarf over a lamp, at once warm and bewitching, dangerous and cold. Wilson clutched the fur hat more tightly. His heart raced. He tried to breathe slowly. After a moment, he pulled the keys from the ignition and headed up the slippery walk. He had a mission to complete.

# Part Four

## California Girl

> "What a strange thing!
> to be alive
> beneath cherry blossoms."
> —Kobayashi Issa

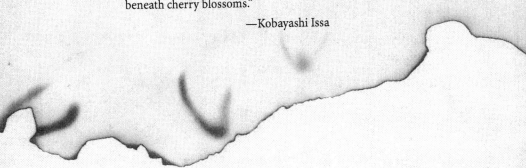

# Twenty

## January

Spring had arrived in all its sticky budded sweetness, and still January dreamed of the Rock Star. In the green room she was a seed, swaddled in a green Winnie the Pooh comforter, surrounded by all of Jake's junk: a rock, a crab claw, six crushed bottle caps. Outside the world was green. A storm had blown in, thunder rolling around the sky, the sky itself an egg, incandescent, lightning cracking its shell. Forsythia burned, tulips bobbed their candy heads. The wind picked up, shaking the lilacs in their trees. A dragonfly appeared in the window, its belly bottle-blue.

In her dream, the Rock Star stood before her. The energy that made her so fucking happy flowed around him in waves, electric, the color of orange juice. They'd had a baby. He held it in his hand, a yellow creature sloshing in a beaker of green liquid. "It's a boy, but we're going to train it to be a girl," he was telling someone.

"No," January protested. "It's a girl. It smells exactly like a girl."

They stared at the baby. It undulated. It had evil little teeth.

"I don't know what it is." Stevie shuddered.

"Get rid of it," January cried.

# Twenty-one

"Pull your shoulders back so your boobs stick out," Lucy ordered, crouching beside January with her camera, Santana blaring from the boom box behind her. "They're so much bigger now; do they hurt? I can't wait to be pregnant. I want seven girls, all in matching fluffy dresses. Like daffodils."

An image of the scary twins in *The Shining* popped into January's head. She didn't say anything, just stuck out her boobs and tried to look exotic. She was sitting near the tulips behind the library. It was three a.m. They were documenting the pregnancy. January didn't know why. It passed the time.

It was their fourth session. The early ones were all about flatness, Lucy had said, angles and bones—and grief, too, because Pearl was newly gone. In one, January lay naked in the snow, an empty snow angel beside her. "One of the more ridiculous things you've done," Wilson remarked. He was no longer allowed to see.

January lounged in the tulips, perky bobbing things, pink and yellow and grape. Why did she pose nude? Because it was fun. Because Lucy was fun. January called her the Corn Queen. She seemed so silky and pure, but the truth was, she wasn't. Katie was jealous for no reason.

"She's everything I'm not," Katie would say, "so untouched, so easy."

It was an illusion. Lucy was as fucked up and annoying as anyone. She sold weed, not a lot, just a little here and there. She LOVED to take naked pictures of people. She had lots of video of Steven, hidden in a Hello Kitty box in her closet. "If he cheats, I post," she warned. She got into her role. She was *mean* about it, which turned January on. "Do this, stick this out, spread this, be SEXY, Jan," she ordered. January did and it was fun.

After their sessions, Lucy would come over with a couple of Mountain Dews and the contact sheets. They circled the ones they liked, x-ed out the ones they didn't, like January was some SUPERSTAR. Lucy developed the photos. January filled her book—a portfolio with a purple-furred cover, a gift from Lucy. Could it be more exciting?

Tonight they were doing black and white. January sat on one hip, mermaid-style behind the flowers, gazing up at the sky. The pictures would be the best yet: the tulips fleshy, like pods of seaweed guarding January, her breasts black-tipped, her belly a smooth boulder, her eyes like black stars. She was a sea goddess in a watery world, the baby snug in an aquarium of its own.

Lucy did the makeup. Tonight she paused to trace a line of black liquid liner into the crescent of January's scar.

"Why?" January asked, touching her cheek.

"Because it's *you*. Because I'm working with *brokenness* and *roundness*, and it's none of your beeswax anyway. *I'm* the artist. *I'm* the boss. You just do as I say." Lucy's voice was plaintive. January wondered if she'd had any friends as a kid.

"Don't smear it," Lucy added.

She was the Corn Queen, sweet and smooth as taffy. And January was the Queen of the Nighttime Tulips. Of course it was all an illusion. That was the point. That's why it was fun. In reality, January was pregnant—in the third trimester, there was no denying it now—and she couldn't remember Pete's last name. The other day she'd called the gas station back in Luna only to find he'd been fired. "He comes to work, he drags around like a sick dog—what did you do to the man, *mija*?" his boss said.

January asked a friend to find Pete. Luna was small. *Follow the seeds*, she urged. *Follow the scent of the yellow cherries.* The truth was, she was scared. Wouldn't Pete like to know he was going to be a dad? She thought of her father, busy in his garden, awash in a whirl of apple blossom and bee balm, possums like geishas crouched on the fence around him. Wasn't he nice? Hadn't he taken them to Disneyland? And once, to the casino like a castle in Lake Tahoe?

She couldn't do it alone. She had no idea how to be a mom, let alone a mom alone. Her dad had bought them Adidas. He'd let them watch him play tennis. The evil doctor was right. She needed a dad *now*.

January pictured her house in Luna. The back steps were sticky with watermelon juice, seeds like sequins scattered here and there. But Pete had disappeared.

Lucy beckoned her to a patch of grass beside a cherry tree, the blossoms silvery and aflutter in the moonlight. They took a smoke break after Lucy promised not to tell Katie. Besides, it was just a hit now and then. January certainly wasn't like Sophie, the psycho bitch that had stolen her dog. She didn't *live* to get high.

January drank from her water bottle, feeling pure. The weed burned her lungs, made the purplish night smell sweeter. She looked down at her hands resting on her thighs. There was the moon of her belly, the swirl tattoo, the faint purplish scars. Everyone should be naked all the time. It was calming, like being a rock, or a bunny, sitting quietly in the night, rivers of stars trickling overhead.

"Is it kicking?" Lucy rested her hand near January's belly button. "It's perfectly round," she said, cupping her belly. "Some chicks, like my sisters, just get fat. But not you, you're perfect." She lay her warm cheek against January, listening.

## 1987

Dirty blond hair littered the kitchen floor. It was Stevie Flame's birthday, and January was beautiful; he'd cut her hair, dyed it a baby-chick yellow as she sat on a folding chair in the kitchen of the studio apartment (*their* studio, he'd moved in! six months, four days, and counting), cockroaches crawling up the wall, slowly, as if the heat, so dirty and obscene, was getting to them, too.

Swarms of cockroaches—January had never seen so many. They'd all of a sudden appeared. It was early afternoon, morning for Stevie and Jan, the windows smeared with white sunlight, the kitchen floor a sticky mess of coffee-colored linoleum and . . . what? Filth, January guessed, but none of it mattered. It was August, and at exactly 11:51 that night, Stevie Flame would turn twenty-five.

There would be a party. January, now eighteen and no longer the puppy she'd been, following Stevie around all these years, couldn't wait. She had a new dress, skintight sheer black lace, cut high on the thigh, pulled low off the shoulders, and in it she was curvy. No longer a skinny kid, she was a woman now, and tonight, at the party, in the dress, she would be THE GIRLFRIEND. THE GIRLFRIEND of THE ROCK STAR, 100 percent official. They *lived together* for God's sake—how much proof did a person need?

The one. The only. They were so close he even did her hair, putting the finishing touches on the cut right that very second, roughing it up, the small sharp scissors skirting her neck, her fragile ears. "Your little wrist," Stevie said, his voice mournful and happy as he picked it up, gave it a little kiss.

"Are you sure it'll look good?" January was nervous. She'd never had short hair before; what if it turned out ugly? What if he didn't want her anymore? She looked down at her hands clasped tightly in her lap. She watched the cockroaches, tiny ones and enormous ones, all of them moving together, a big swarm of icky bugs, emerging from a stack of boxes some earlier squatter had left sitting on the kitchen floor, up the wall and across the stove, disappearing down behind. There were so many; where were they all coming from? It was so gross it was fascinating. You couldn't look away.

"It'll be cool," Stevie was saying, bangle bracelets clanking. "Only don't wash it, you need damage, you need . . . shit." He laughed shortly, rested his hand on her head. "Otherwise you're going to look like someone's grandma."

Jan giggled, but inside she tensed a little more. Stevie was always saying they needed to "dirty her up." She didn't understand; what else could she do? She'd gotten the tattoo, the spiral on her belly that had hurt so badly she'd run to the bathroom and barfed when it was over. And she never did her laundry, she barely knew how. At home her dad did the laundry. Her jeans were filthy, she hadn't washed them all summer—was that what he meant? But it wasn't, she knew; it had more to do with her hair, her makeup, but even more than that it had to do with who she was deep down. He was always calling her an angel, which was good, most of the time, but sometimes she caught him looking at the dirtier girls, girls that were grimy through and through, from their dyed purple hair to the cold sores on their mouths to the filthy torn fishnets hanging from their legs. Girls with unwashed bottoms. Girls that didn't care about Ten-O-Sixing their faces or curling their hair, something January couldn't fathom.

"If you try to *do* this hairdo, you're going to look like Carol Burnett," Stevie warned.

January chewed the inside of her cheek. "I don't know . . . all my hair." But she stayed in the chair, careful not to move as he pulled out a razor blade and started hacking. The kitchen window was jammed open with another of the ex-squatter's boxes, and the air was murky, swampy really, there were bugs flying around! A big cloud of bugs, humming over the dirty dishes soaking in the sink. Dishes that had been soaking far too long, months maybe. They should clean the place, January knew, but she had no idea how to begin. It was the same in the bathroom. Somehow the tub had gotten clogged, and there was a foot of standing water. Dangerous water, for one afternoon January had the bright idea to use Drano. She dumped it in, never bothering to read the directions, not knowing you were supposed to bail first—*bail* like they were pioneers! So now you couldn't take a shower. If you did, your feet would be eaten off. They never washed the towels. Sometimes, after she cleaned up in the sink, Stevie said he could smell them on her ears.

So she *was* dirty; only at her core, she was not dirty. She was an angel, innocent, only fifteen when they met, how could he have expected her to know anything about anything back then? And even now, what did she know? She knew him. She was an expert on *him*. She worked at the juice bar at the fitness center down the street, and beyond that, her life was all Stevie Flame. Which was why she sat in the chair, unmoving. He could do anything, anything he wanted, that was how in love she was, change her, mold her, whatever. Just last night he'd mentioned putting her hair in a coffee can with gelatin, shaping it into a Mohawk, dyeing it with Jell-O, pink or purple, raspberry or blueberry, could life get any better? What were bugs in the face of that?

"I'm not sure I'll be pretty," she said, making a face, trying to look like she didn't care.

"Hon, you're gorgeous. Look at your lips. I love your lips. You're an angel, you look exactly like an angel." Stevie set down the razor blade and knelt before her, holding her face in his hands and staring intensely into her eyes, a move of his that always scared her to death. She had trouble looking a person in the eyes, it was too . . . extreme . . . and she couldn't be looked *into* that deeply, either, it was as if he were staring right into the center of her soul, to the place where the real January crouched, the nothing Jan, scared and alone. And if he knew her, if he discovered the real her . . . But she never looked away; she stuck it out, holding her breath, her cheeks flushing a bright red. "You act like one, too," Stevie said. "An angel." He released her.

She breathed a sigh of relief, looked down at her bare feet hooked behind the legs of the chair. Stevie moved away. He wet her down with the spray bottle, then pulled out his hair dryer, stuck in his belt like that guy in the movie they'd seen, the hairdresser that slept with all of his clients.

"Not even," she said.

"Yeah. You never bug me, you never even ask about the . . . you know . . ." his voice dropped ominously, "*things* I do."

Was that good? Maybe she should bug him, get under his skin, crawl into him the way the cockroach crawled into his mouth that time he was sleeping, the way the bugs crawled into his soda can during the night, and then floated into his mouth when he took a swig first thing in the morning. Causing him to freak. Every time.

"What do you do? Don't tell me," Jan cried, closing her eyes and holding her hands over her ears. Of course there were other girls, millions of other girls, he was in a band, he was beautiful, deep down she knew the guys used girls to eat, to buy them groceries and to cook for them, to "loan" them money for guitar strings and all the rest. And she knew the girls expected something in return. "Stevie?" She looked up at him, helpless. "I don't . . . I just . . ."

"Look." He picked up the hand mirror and held it in front of her face.

"Yes, it's—"

"Hot." Stevie pronounced. "Totally fucking hot."

"Yeah." Her voice sounded weak, and she wondered why she felt like crying.

He ruffled her hair. "You're such a California girl. You look like a little surfer chick, a dirty little surfer chick." He grinned. "I love it, I can't wait to show the guys."

January stared into the mirror. The cut made her eyes look interesting, brighter somehow. Yellow feathers of hair stuck up, framed her face. She looked new, clean and new, blond like a child, like someone nice. And punk, too, a little tough, like the kind of girl Stevie Flame would like.

# Twenty-two

"It's the '70s bush," Lucy said, nodding at January's crotch. "It's got to go. I'm thinking modern California girl for the next session, like Pam Anderson, something neat and tan, with the big blond hair, the false lashes. You need to get a wax. You need to get a Brazilian."

"I don't think so." January was tired. It was close to morning, and she was done, ready to go home, crawl into the green pod of Jake's room and sleep the day away. She pulled on her flannel shirt, shivering, then jammed her legs into the scary Goodwill stretch pants and found her flip-flops. The soles of her feet were green from the grass. "What exactly is a Brazilian?" she asked, buttoning her shirt.

Lucy didn't answer. She was busy gathering her things, humming to herself. January could sense her happiness, her satisfaction with the night's work. She leaned back on her hands and waited. The earth rolled its way toward dawn. The horizon was indigo. Birds chattered like monkeys in the trees.

They walked down the block to Lucy's truck. Lucy nodded at a used condom floating in a puddle near the curb. "Fuck and chuck," she said.

January laughed, jumped away.

As they climbed into the truck, a police cruiser pulled up beside them. A cop got out, slamming his car door. He was young, with cherry-colored hair cut short like a scrub brush. His cheeks were ruddy, as if he'd just spent the weekend snowboarding.

"Shit." Lucy sighed loudly.

"What is it—" January began, but Lucy shushed her and hopped out of the truck. January followed.

"Chad," Lucy said, her voice cold.

"Lucy. Lucy Johnson." The policeman grinned, moved closer. January got a whiff of cologne, something cheap and disco-y. Which seemed wrong. Were cops supposed to smell good?

Lucy leaned against the truck, hip cocked, arms crossed over her chest. She looked tiny next to the rangy policeman. Her jeans were too long, the frayed hems pooling on the ground.

"Whatcha doing here, Luce?"

"A photo shoot." Lucy's voice was casual. "An assignment for *Photo* magazine," she lied. "I'm a photographer now. I have shoots."

"Cool." The policeman smiled, wiggled the flashlight in his hand. He had a big smile. His lips curled. He looked like he'd like to eat Lucy alive. "So what the fuck are you doing marrying Steven James?"

"None of your business."

"The drunken leprechaun. You're marrying the drunken leprechaun?"

Lucy didn't answer. She stared at her feet, tapped her foot. Her thin hair hung in her eyes. January could see by the tension in her shoulders that she was pissed. She could see that she and Chad had a history.

"He got his arm stuck in the pop machine at school," Chad said after confirming that January did know the drunken leprechaun in question. "They had to call the paramedics. Or, Luce, remember when he moved Dean Hosey's car onto the lawn? And took a crap in it?" Chad laughed. "Holy shit. The guy's *unruly*." He paused, mouth open. "And you're marrying him. Well, good. Good for you."

Lucy looked horrified. "He doesn't drink. No one calls him that. It was like a million years ago—"

"Don't make me come out there on any domestics." The cop winked at January. "Dude is *insane*," he continued. "One night he drank an entire fifth of Jack Daniel's by himself. We're at this party? At this house? And he beats the crap out of me. We're wrestling, but the guy won't stop. He takes it too far, dragging me up and down the stairs like a caveman, punching me in the chest until I puke." Chad took a deep breath. He looked thrilled.

"One more word and you die," Lucy warned.

The policeman gave January a quick ninja bow. The sky behind him was yellow. Black tree fingers seemed to shoot from his head. "I assure you: The guy is certifiable."

## 1987

It was bad luck to be so pretty. This she thought later, when everything had ended, fallen apart like a song.

After the haircut, after making love in the stifling apartment, their bodies slippery with sweat, a baby cockroach smashed between their bellies (they found it, stuck like a bindi on January, after), they decided to drive to Disneyland. Stevie wanted fun on his birthday. The day should *kick ass* was what he said. They would buy mouse ears, he announced as he pulled out of her, falling onto his back. Mouse ears with names on them, but fake names, fake and funny names, like Irving for him, and for her . . . he thought a moment, tossing their stuffed dog into the air . . . Fern.

January had smiled, lying naked on the bed, sweat cooling her skin, the taste of him still salty in her mouth, while inside she'd cringed, knowing she'd be too embarrassed to wear in public the ears of Fern. He should find someone who was better at having fun, she thought, getting up, plucking a towel from the bathroom floor to wipe between her legs. *And he would.* She looked at herself in the mirror, touched her hot cheeks, the harsh voice echoing in her mind. *Of course he would, was she stupid?* She let the towel drop without using it. Like wiping it off would help. They never used protection. Stevie was sure he couldn't get a girl pregnant, sure that he was sterile (why did every young, healthy guy think this?), but January knew it couldn't be true . . . no, she *hoped* it wasn't true.

Traffic wasn't bad. They listened to the radio the whole way. AM radio. It was awful. January could only get AM stations in her old beater of a car because when it had belonged to her mother the teacher, a disgruntled student had snapped off the antenna. The orange Pinto wagon with the wood paneling—it was such an embarrassment. One night at the Rainbow, after the valet presented a red Corvette belonging to none other than Rudy Sarzo, GUITAR GOD, formerly of Quiet Riot, now with Whitesnake whom January worshipped, the awful orange Pinto was brought around. And nobody claimed it! Not Stevie, not Jan, not even Rose Red's singer, Animal, who was hanging around that night with a stomachache, hoping for a ride home. They all pretended they didn't notice the beast, chugging horribly, leering its woody leer, there in front of the crowd of rockers and groupies and genuine STARS, milling around on Sunset Boulevard.

Stevie was the one who was brave, January remembered. He'd walked right out into the middle of the street, bowing and waving, shouting insults at the jeering crowd. January followed (Animal had gone back into the club to use the bathroom), relieved that Stevie had taken over, pleased with the whistles and catcalls she got, and she'd thought then, with the hot lights of the club pouring down upon them and the stars barely visible in the purple smoggy sky: *This is how it will be when he's HUGE, everyone watching him and me right by his side.*

A sign for Anaheim flashed by. "When Doves Cry" came on, and she turned it up loud. Stevie didn't like Prince. He thought he'd faked playing the guitar in the movie, but January adored him. He was the first star she'd spotted when she arrived in LA three years earlier, right there on Hollywood Boulevard, getting into a car, wearing a ruffly white shirt and platform heels, and she'd been amazed at how tiny the guy was. But that was the thing about stars. They always looked smaller and older in real life; they were always kind of shrunken and disappointing.

Not so with Stevie. He was exciting to watch onstage, sweating behind his drum kit, his soaked hair blown back by the fans, making him look as if he were being electrocuted. Lit up, glowing beneath the lights, a furious fireball of thundering drums and twirling neon sticks. Still, January liked it better when it was just him: Stevie in the daylight, his long hair pulled into a messy ponytail (the only kind guys seemed to be able to manage), the stubble on his jaw, smoking a cigarette, in baggy gym shorts, his skinny legs, his skinny chest and arms. He was a real man. She'd never been with someone so manly before. Other boys had wispy mustaches; Stevie could shave every day if he wanted.

"Stevie?" she said. "Did you like it . . . you know . . . earlier? At home?"

"Fuck yeah." He tossed his cigarette out the window. Outside everything was ugly, the cement walls of the freeway, a row of dilapidated palms, ugly buildings, the sky on top, yellow and close. Stevie pulled her to him, kissing her passionately, careful to keep an eye on the road. "You're the only one that makes me feel good. You're the only one I give a shit about."

"You do?" She smiled, tried not to smile, pleased. "You give a shit about me?"

"You know I do. I love you."

January waited for more, her heart dancing in her chest, but Stevie looked away, embarrassed, fiddled with the radio. The Thompson Twins' "Hold Me Now" came on, and she sat back in her seat, the ugly vinyl seat she'd ridden in as a child, amazed. He'd said it! As casually as the time last spring when he'd announced that they were fucked, that they were about to run out of gas on the 101, and they did, less than a minute later. He'd said love, and then there was love, she could feel it, filling up the car. But what did he mean? Had he loved her all along, or not until just that very second?

She leaned over, buried her face in his neck, breathing him in, letting his smell weaken her like a drug. Was it forever love, or a passing feeling of *hey, you rock*? She rested her hand on his bare stomach, slid it into the waistband of his shorts, felt his wiry hair, his penis silky and warm against her hand. The details, when or why, weren't really important. Because if he loved her, wasn't it more proof? That she was the one, the only one that mattered? She sat back and closed her eyes, felt him tapping out the bass line of the song on her bare thigh, the Southern California sunshine warm upon her face.


"Have you ever woken up in the middle of the night and everything looked small?" Stevie rubbed his eyes, making a smudgy mess of his eyeliner.

January giggled. It was evening. They were sitting in the car parked near the band's apartment on a quiet, leafy street, the noise and stink of nearby Hollywood Boulevard a world away. Inky shadows stretched across the pavement, and January could feel fall in the air, a hint of cold, a sense of electricity, the night like a black cat, its fur standing on end. Stevie was about to go in, to prepare for his birthday party, while she went home to change. Her mouse ears were gone, having thankfully blown out the window, whirling up into the sky on the drive back from Disneyland.

"Or close your eyes and see something, like a person?" Stevie continued. "Like one day every time I shut my eyes I saw that guy on that show, the one in the wheelchair, Ironside, was that his name? The fat guy?"

January shrugged. "My sister ruled the TV." She hesitated, wanting to tell him something good, to make him laugh for once instead of the other way around. She crawled onto his lap, straddling him on the seat. He worked his hands down the back of her shorts. She took off his mouse ears, threw them in the way back.

"Hon," he complained.

"Listen," she said, burying her face in his hair, his earrings sharp against her cheek. She sat up, leaned back against the steering wheel. "One time, this weird thing happened. There was this guy that hung around, I guess he was a friend, I remember he sold stuff door-to-door, meat I think. Larry something or other. And we're sitting at the dining room table, eating fondue, and he tells me this horrible story."

"Yeah?" Stevie squeezed her ass, adjusted her on his lap, pushing his hard dick against her. It was strange to see him quiet, listening for once (when he wasn't humping), and she liked it and continued, warming to her story. "So the guy was like, 'Do you know who Dick Van Dyke is?' And I'm like, 'Yeah, on that TV show.' And he's like, 'Well, that guy's going to prison.' I think I was about five when he's telling me this, and I'm like, 'Why?' And he's like 'He killed his wife and cut her up into pieces, like hamburger, and wrapped the pieces in white paper and stored them in the freezer of his rumpus room.' And I was like, 'Oh,' and didn't think any more about it, you know how kids are. But then when I got older I thought, wait a minute, Dick Van Dyke didn't do that, did he? I mean he was still on TV. I think I even asked my mom if it was true."

Stevie laughed, and January stared at her hands, pleased. "Did you know . . ." he began.

She looked up expectantly.

"Did you know that your mouth twitches when you talk? When you get excited and talk a lot, it twitches," Stevie crowed. "I never noticed before, Jan, it's so funny, it's so cute."

January was horrified. She scrambled off him, her cheeks burning, but Stevie caught her, pulling her close, kissing her, still laughing, and she kissed him back (of course she did, *don't act like you care or you'll lose him for good*), tears seeping from her tightly closed eyes.

On the way home, alone, Santa Monica one long smear of yellow light, and all the stoplights haloed, she thought of her punch line: *I didn't know what a rumpus room was, but I remember thinking at the time that if I ever came across one, I should stay away.*

Screams of laughter. *Jan, you are so fucking funny!* She said the words aloud, heading up La Cienega—*and the whole time he's telling me this, he's dipping his meat in the oil, sizzling it, scooping up big hunks of the cheese, eating like it's no big deal, like he's telling me about a movie he saw or something*—watching herself closely in the rearview mirror, looking for signs of a twitch. Her new hair stood on end, making her look shocked. She hated it. Like there was no place to hide.

# Twenty-three

Steven's mother's hair salon was called Pink. Haircuts were $12.95. A shampoo and set would run you ten. The salon was in a small bungalow the chalky pink of baby antibiotics, set back from the street and surrounded by enormous black pines. The lawn was littered with needles and cones, the front stoop sticky with fragrant sap.

Minutes after leaving the library, January sat on the steps waiting for Lucy, who'd decided to make a quick run inside for beauty supplies.

"What'd you do, rob a bank?" she asked when Lucy returned, a bulky canvas bag jammed under her arm. January glimpsed a black-and-white poster on the wall behind her—a mother and child with sun-white hair, a father that resembled Satan—before the door swung shut.

"Of sorts." Lucy knelt to lock up. She slipped the keys into her pocket and sank to the step beside January. "I cleaned out the safe." She lit a cigarette, exhaled with a sigh. Her pale hips curved over her low-slung jeans. Her belly-button jewel disappeared as she leaned forward, hugging her knees to her chest.

"What is it really?" January poked the canvas bag with her foot.

"Money." Lucy pulled her hair back into a ponytail. With her clean curve of jaw and blue-pooled eyes, she hardly looked like a thief. "I told you: I cleaned out the safe. I'm going to triple it when me and Steven hit Vegas."

"Right."

"Or maybe it's just makeup." Her voice was coy. As if to demonstrate her innocence, she pulled a lipstick from the bag, popped off the lid, and rolled it up to reveal a pretty hot pink shade.

January was lost in thought—what kind of mother-in-law-to-be gives you free beauty supplies?—when Lucy stood and knelt on the step before her. She pushed January's knees apart, catching her cheeks in her hands. "Let's try it on. For the California girl shoot." Her eyes were bright. She ran her finger across January's lips. "You'll be pink and tan and waxed. We'll put daisies in your hair."

January closed her eyes and waited, excited. And sad, too, because thinking about California always made her sick. "I think about *you* all the time," she wanted to tell Stevie. "*You* kick my ass. It's *you* I eat." Whatever that even meant. "And I'm bleeeeding." No, she was dead. Because she'd never see him again.

As Lucy arranged her hair, she talked about the policeman, Chad, whom she'd had the misfortune of dating in high school. "He ate all the meat," she said, raking January's bangs across one eye. "He'd come over after school and want to eat everything in the freezer. I'd cook him steak or pork chops—stuff that was supposed to be for dinner, it wasn't like we were rich—and then tell my mother that the dog got it."

"How would the dog get the meat out of the freezer?"

"It didn't. That's not the point. The point is: My mom knew I was lying. 'You're a beautiful girl and you're giving yourself away,' she'd say, this awful disappointed look in her eyes."

January didn't answer. "Moms can mess with a person," she mumbled, loving the feel of Lucy's hands in her hair.

"Right. It was like she could see this . . . this *awful girl-ness* in me, something she'd known about all along, and now I did, too. It was this horrible club—something so ugly we weren't even going to mention it." Lucy shuddered.

January reached out and touched her hand.

Lucy picked up January's hand and dropped it back in her lap. "This isn't a sob story."

"Do you have video of Chad?" January squirmed on the cold cement.

"Ugh. Are you kidding? We'd watch wrestling in his room. Have bad sex. Stinky-sock sex. Freshman sex. He'd eat tuna fish and clam chowder, drink a huge glass of milk, and then expect me to kiss him."

"Yuck."

"Yes, yuck. I'd like to erase him from my mind."

January opened one eye. "Didn't you say you guys had pugs?"

"Close your eyes. I'm composing your face in my mind."

"Pugs?" January whispered. "Didn't you have pugs, growing up?"

"Yeah, so?"

"Well . . ."

Lucy unbuttoned the top button of January's shirt. January lost her train of thought, captivated by the warmth of Lucy's hands, lingering near her heart. Movie stars must feel this way, she thought, breathing in the pine-soaked air. Movie stars and dictators . . . and dogs . . . cats, for sure . . . babies, old ladies. "Aren't pugs little guys? Do they even eat meat? I mean they're not like German shepherds. Those I can see wolfing down a big, bloody steak—"

"Will you let it go?" Lucy eased the shirt off January's shoulders. The breeze was cool against her breasts. "It's not about pugs, or meat, or what kind of dog eats steak. It's about me, why I fucked a guy, *repeatedly*, that I didn't even think was cute."

January didn't answer. What was there to say?

"Why do you think I did that?" Lucy asked.

"I don't know. Why did you?"

"Why do you think?"

"I'm not thinking, I'm—"

"Don't move." Lucy sat back.

January opened her eyes as Lucy picked up the lipstick and made two bright Xs on her nipples. She jerked away. The lipstick was cold. "Now you're mine." Lucy smiled. "And never be nice to jerks like Chad again."

"Like I was." January could barely remember Chad. She could barely remember anything before this moment.

Lucy leaned forward to smooth the lipstick onto January's lips. It was cool and soothing. It smelled sweet, like bees. Lucy sang softly to herself, an old Zeppelin song, "Castle wind tail wind leave the day far away . . ."

She had the words all wrong. For some reason this made January happy.

"Let's see how it looks on me," Lucy murmured. She kissed January, her lips fat and warm, soft against January's own. Like that, they were back in the tulip world, the world of illusion, in which Lucy was the Corn Queen, smelling of blue sky, and January was on a rocket ship ride, swooping low over a mud-soaked county fair, trying to catch her breath.

Lucy kissed her again, deeper this time. She whispered in January's ear, her cheek hot, telling of how she hated her life and everyone in it, Steven like a drunken sucking baby, and how was she going to go through with it, how was she going to get out of that one?

"Plus he's getting super fat—" Abruptly Lucy moved away. She stared out into the ring of black trees, hugging her knees to her chest.

January waited, but Lucy didn't move. After a moment, she buttoned up her shirt. Lucy didn't say a word—was she crying? Her face was tilted away. Screams faded in the night. Neon light dripped to the ground.

## 1987

She knew him, inside and out, knew every word by heart. *Soft*, the way his skin felt under her hands at night, like the time the helicopters woke them, sweeping the apartment with their blind eyes, and she'd crawled onto him, onto his skinny pale chest, and he'd opened his arms like, *come on in*, and she had, staying there safe for the rest of the night. And *hard*, the way he fucked her, hard the way their hearts locked together, their bodies writhing, hard the way he made her come. And *lost* because where the fuck was he? She looked at the wall before her, spattered with something black. Once again, Stevie Flame had disappeared.

January was outside, having been forced into the hall, the party exploding from the tiny apartment, people shouting, screaming with laughter, the Scorpions blaring and Stevie lost somewhere, the Birthday Boy who never drank or did drugs drunk off two beers, his mouse ears traded in for a crown. A golden plastic crown! With fake jewels some idiot girl had given him. But the Birthday Boy was sexy, the Birthday Boy was wild, wearing purple leopard spandex and January's black shirtdress, falling open to reveal his bare chest, the line of hair that ran from his belly button down (she liked to trace it with her tongue). Earlier, Animal, seeing them together—Stevie holding her close, his arm around her neck, hers wrapped around his waist—had shouted, "The king and queen of the fucking prom."

"And here's the little jester," Stevie had replied good-naturedly, everybody laughing, January thinking that Animal was right, though, wasn't he? Stevie 'n' Jan: hot, a matching pair, Stevie in his spandex and her like a model, with the legs, the hair, the gentle sexy curves.

Now everyone was excited, everyone was freaking out. Right before the party, the fat roadie was saying, the SWAT team had arrived! The guys in Rose Red had been hanging out in the kitchen, goofing, wasting time, when someone—the fat roadie remembered it as being Ben, the angry bass player—got the bright idea to shoot at the people on the street. Squirt guns were brought out and filled, plastic weapons that looked exactly like Uzis and M-16s, and everybody had a fine time, dousing unsuspecting passersby, until one of the victims was scared shitless and dialed 911. "The SWAT team, can you believe it?" the roadie crowed, wringing his hands, shuffling his small feet, his eyes inexplicably sad. "Like a fucking TV show, out there on the street, rifles cocked, wearing the bulletproof vests—"

"Well this is Hollyfuckingweird," someone else said dismissively. January craned her neck to see. It was the short Japanese girl who did graphics for the band. The one who spoke incomprehensible English slang, and always seemed too cool to have any fun.

Not like Stevie. If nothing else, Stevie Flame knew how to have a good time. January sighed, wishing she had been there the time the SWAT team arrived to take Rose Red down! Where was he? He'd been gone nearly an hour. Smoke burned her eyes, and everyone was shoving her around. She elbowed an innocent girl with bangs, then gave up, letting the crowd move her, down the hall, over the rusty carpet scarred with cigarette burns, up a narrow stairwell, and out onto the roof.

Where she could breathe. The sky billowed overhead, a big black circus tent, gouged with broken stars. And far below, the street: slick pavement and naked trees, Hollywood Boulevard an eerie glow, several blocks away. January sat on a rise, beside something jutting like a chimney (unlike Stevie she never knew what anything was), asphalt shingles rough beneath her thighs. She'd picked a spot in the middle, away from the edge.

She looked up at the moon, wishing she knew how to use it to tell time. Stevie had not been in the hall, he was not on the roof—didn't he want to find her, too? The moon was empty, a face with nothing to say. She thought of the song "Eyes without a Face." They played it for the cooldown at the fitness center sometimes, and it always made her happy. She imagined going home, just getting in the Pinto and driving, leaving Stevie to wonder. He was a jealous guy, something you wouldn't think when meeting him, stunned as you were by his ego and frantic light. But every once in a while, January had learned, it worked to make him sweat. Like the time the singer of Whitesnake bought her a drink at the Rainbow to celebrate her eighteenth birthday. David fucking Coverdale, and Stevie had shit, screaming that Whitesnake sucked, that they were just copying Led Zeppelin who *fucking sucked* to begin with, before he started to cry, there at the club, January standing before him, the word in her mind: *Success*.

Or the time when she had an earache and thought she was going to die, and had walked all the way down La Cienega to the ER at Cedars-Sinai, a trip that seemed to take days. That afternoon, Stevie, who never called when he said he would, had called when he said he would and continued to call long into the night, *freaked and stunned*—that was what he said later, when he found her at home after the long walk back, holes worn in her pink flats, curled up in bed, comforted by the kindness of the doctor, a hot towel pressed to her crackling ear—*freaked and stunned* that she'd just taken off and never bothered to give him a call.

January looked at her hands. It was quiet on the roof, and the air smelled good, like heat that had disappeared. She glanced up, spotted Animal, who gave a little wave and made his way over, sitting at her feet. "Short," he said, nodding at her hair. His own platinum do was huge and reeked of Aqua Net. His makeup was dramatic—smudged eyes, full red lips, a slash of black war paint on his cheek—but he looked sad and uncomfortable, like a girl on a disappointing date. "Someone was thrown off the roof," he said, leaning back and nodding at the edge, the place where the sky and nothing met.

"Just now?" January was alarmed, and glad she was safe in the middle. She hated edges, never went near them. When she was a kid she had an awful recurring dream. In it she and her mother were driving in the old blue Chevy, the one that rolled down hills—sometimes with the girls in it—because the emergency brake didn't work. In the dream January and her mother had been to a party and were late, it was much too late, daylight seeping into night, and they needed to get home fast. Why? *Because something really bad was going to happen.*

The old blue Chevy snaked over a mountain pass, over jagged cliffs, the road falling away into nothingness, inches from the car. Next was always the same. January would glance out the window, and there, hanging in the sky beside them, big and blue and horrible, spinning like on her mother's soap opera, was the world, the planet Earth. And the terrifying part was this: The world was spinning without them. They'd stayed out too late, daylight watery and weak, pouring now into night, and they'd missed their chance to return, to get back on the planet.

January had once tried to tell Stevie about the dream, but it had sounded idiotic, and he didn't get it. *You rarely make sense, I love it*, was what he cried. It was the feeling that mattered, she knew, the part she hadn't been able to get across. The feeling you had when you'd messed up, when you'd gone too far and fucked up, and it was too late to fix things, over, the damage done. And also the feeling of being suspended . . . somewhere *wrong* . . . lost and alone and scared.

Then there was the time a couple of years ago. At a bar in the mountains north of LA, January—devastated that Stevie had encouraged her *not* to attend Rose Red's gig that night (and of course she knew why)—snorted coke off the back of her hand with a construction worker named Ty, much too far from home. It was a cowboy bar, or a biker bar, nothing like the glittery rock dives she was used to. Everything was raw wood, heaps of sawdust on the floor. She'd used her fake ID, drinking rum and Coke until she could no longer feel her teeth. Or maybe it was that she could *only* feel her teeth, she was all teeth, giant frozen choppers, getting in the way of the important things, like breathing or being able to maintain. They drove home near dawn, January staring out the truck window, grinding her teeth and paranoid, over mountain roads exactly like in her dream. The road fell away. Ty pulled over to puke. January tried to breathe.

"Or the guy jumped," Animal was saying, "but I think he was thrown." He sighed. He didn't offer any more information. January didn't ask.

"You look pretty," she said, touching his glittery hair.

Animal gave her a hurt look.

"I mean in a guy way," she said reassuringly. "Totally rockin' and hot."

"Thanks, I feel like shit." Animal touched his hair as if it pained him and sighed once again.

"Why? What is it?"

"My stomach hurts, I think I'm dying." He hesitated. "You know . . ." He grabbed her bare foot (she'd kicked off the fake snakeskin stilettos; she still couldn't feel her baby toes) and gave it a little shake. "He really cares about you . . ."

"Yeah." January smiled, wiggled her toes. That was the thing about love, everyone knew, it was everywhere, like sunshine—you couldn't hide it if you tried.

"But—"

"What?" She tensed, moved her foot away.

"It's just that . . . Jan." Animal picked at a hole near the crotch of his jeans, his face serious. "I think you could find someone better—"

"No I couldn't. How can you say that? There's no one better. You should know, Animal. No one better in the world." Her voice sounded shrill, and a girl standing nearby, the same girl she'd elbowed in the hall, her bangs hanging in her eyes, turned to look.

Animal continued, looking sick but determined. Why wouldn't he stop? January wanted to kick him in the head. "Someone who . . . you know . . . is . . ." He cleared his throat. "Someone that wants just one chick, you know what I mean? Only one chick and that's it, leave the rest for someone else."

"I'm not even listening." January's cheeks were hot, and she was shaking deep in her spine. "You're making me so mad I'm not even listening."

They were quiet.

"I hope I do it onstage," Animal said after a bit.

"What?" January was confused. Why didn't he just go away and leave her alone? She used to like Animal, but now, she was deciding, she hated him, and was glad Stevie called him a pussy behind his back.

"Die." Animal leaned back on his hands and stared up at the sky, his long hair brushing the roof. "I hope I do it onstage. I'll be legendary, like Bon Scott or Randy Rhoads, the only way to go. You know: Live young, die fast; it's better to burn out than fade away." He got up, hesitated a moment, sat back down. He held her feet in his warm hands (her baby toes tingling now), then rose to his knees and kissed her.

January wasn't surprised. She kissed him back. Unlike Stevie, Animal didn't smoke, and he tasted nice, young and clean, like air. His kisses were softer, and she liked the way he was so pretty, made up like a Cosmo girl, but manly too, his black-painted nails short and chipped, the stubble on his jaw rough against her cheek. He smelled faintly of musk cologne, which made her think he was trying too hard, which made her sad. Unlike Stevie. Stevie didn't try at all. He was a plain old stinky rock 'n' roller. And if you didn't like it, well, he could always go fuck someone else.

What if she was with Animal? He was the quiet one, she knew. Like Stevie, he didn't drink or do drugs, but unlike Stevie, he liked to read, to hole up in the closet for hours, sometimes the whole day, in his sleeping bag, lost in a book he'd borrowed from the library. She knew this because Stevie was always having to evict him whenever they wanted to have sex, the closet being the only place in the band's apartment you could go for privacy. It was kind of a joke that Animal was always in there.

"It's live fast, die young," she said, but Animal didn't answer.

He moved his lips down her neck, his tongue lingering on the sensitive part below her ear. It tickled, and she raised her shoulder, pushing him away. He sat back on his heels, holding her hands in his. "If you were my girl," he began, staring at her lap, "I'd want you to look the way you do in the mornings, after you guys crash here. Just plain. None of the fancy shit, just you, pretty in your T-shirt."

Tears sprang to January's eyes, and she bit her lip hard. "This is me," she said lightly, pulling her hands away.

"But it isn't," Animal protested. "You're so young, and everything about you is good. Sure you look hot all done up, but who you are, *just you*, is so much better—"

"No. It's not." January smiled, but inside she was furious all over again, with no idea why. Did she ever know anything? How could you go through life knowing nothing, and when was it going to stop? Stop, just like that. Like a heart, stopped. All the confusion, all the . . . She didn't even know what. "It's not better, *I'm* not better, don't talk to me like you know me, this isn't school, you're not my boss." She tried to laugh, but could only make a face, her heart racing in her chest.

People were screaming. Someone was pouring beer on someone else's head. The guy being soaked was jumping in place, laughing so hard he was crying. "The fuck you will," some girl shouted. The helicopters were out, dancing in the sky, disappearing into the billowing black hills of Griffith Park, before reappearing, swooping so slowly you could feel the slap of their wind.

January sat back and closed her eyes, making Animal disappear. Stevie wouldn't like it; Stevie wouldn't like him kissing her one bit, and what if she told? He'd probably be kicked out of the band. She took a deep breath, got up and walked away, moving fast, searching for the stairs. Animal stayed where he was, stretched out flat on the roof as if flung there.

She'd left her shoes behind. January fought her way back inside the apartment, Robin Trower on the stereo, the carpet gritty beneath her bare feet. The fat roadie whistled, giving her ass a pat and a shove as she moved past. And there was Stevie slouched near the bathroom, talking to a girl, someone January had never seen. The girl (or woman, for she looked at least thirty) wore a beige corset trimmed in ribbon, her spray of lavender hair washing the color from her face. She had large hands, a hawk-like nose, and bright beady eyes. If you looked closely—as January was—you'd think she was the female version of Stevie Flame. Only hideous and horrible, talking to him as if she owned him, Stevie backed into the corner, the girl leaning in, their heads together as if they were lovers, as if it were only those two.

"Hon, this is Dizzy." Stevie jumped at her touch, his voice enthusiastic.

Did he seem guilty, too excited to see her? January couldn't tell. She said hello, her voice sounding high and foolish in her ears.

Dizzy (or had Stevie said DZ?) didn't answer, only smiled, as if something about January amused her. She smelled of bitter herbs and licorice. Her corset looked old, as if it might crumble at a touch. Her black lips, her bloodless skin. She'd had acne—January could see the scars. And no boobs at all (not that she had much) . . . Her lips were definitely funny, thin and long and droopy, like a Muppet's.

*I hate you.* January smiled big, asked if she'd ever seen Rose Red live.

The woman raised an eyebrow.

January's heart sank. Nervously she reached for Stevie. "I need to talk to you." She grabbed at his shirtdress, but he deftly moved away. "I wanted to tell you—"

"Dizzy's off to London," Stevie interrupted. "She was there this spring, and now she's off again." He set down his beer, removed his crown to muss his mane of hair. "She's going to bring our demo around to the clubs, our pictures to all of the magazines. *Melody Maker* and that other one . . ." He glanced at the woman, who gave him an encouraging nod. "She says we're the next big thing. Punk is dead and glam is going to rule."

Stevie went on. *Dizzy is London, Dizzy is punk, Dizzy is going to make us huge.* January tuned out. Her chest ached. Everyone knew what a fame whore Stevie was, that the easiest way to get him to sleep with you was to tell him he'd be a star. Dizzy knew, Dizzy wasn't stupid, and now Dizzy was the next big thing. It was perfectly clear. Look at her, watching Stevie ramble, as if she adored him, as if she even knew him at all. They lived together,

Stevie and Jan, did she know that? Did she know that he loved her, that *she* was the one good thing? January chewed the inside of her cheek. The night was ruined. Here she was, in the dress, with the hair, the GIRLFRIEND for God's sake, and nobody seemed to care.

What she was beginning to understand was that status didn't matter. What mattered was what Stevie wanted. He was the one that got to choose.

"She's a dominatrix," Stevie finished, looking at Dizzy proudly.

What had January missed? Someone slammed into her. Cold beer splashed down her back. She ignored it, staring at Dizzy who stared back, a small smile flitting across her lips.

"Crazy, huh?" Stevie's voice was lame.

Dizzy still hadn't spoken. Beneath her smirk, she was beginning to look annoyed, as if January were some groupie who needed to disappear.

"Stevie. I wanted to . . . On the roof, there was this—"

"Hold on, Jan." Stevie sounded peevish. "We've got to get our plans straight first. We're busy." He noticed her hurt look and softened. "Just for a bit. London, you know. Fucking rocking babe."

"But—"

"Hon."

"I just—"

"Hon!"

January stared at her feet, unable to move, to walk away and leave him standing there with her.

After a moment, Dizzy spoke. "Your feet!" she cried. "You have no shoes!" Only she mixed up the words, and it came out: "Your shoes! You have no feet!" Her voice was high and thin and girlish. It wasn't the voice January had expected, and its wispiness made her sad.

"Jan!" Stevie checked out her feet, then shook his head, dismayed. He replaced his crown. It was askew. Instinctively, January reached to adjust it. He flinched, took a step back. And then it was gone, Dizzy had grabbed it, she'd plopped it onto her own head, she was pulling him down the hall, laughing, her black lips curling, her black heart pulsing, Stevie was shouting something in her ear, his hand on her waist, they were swallowed by the crowd.

"Like you pee on people? Like you spank them? How is that even fun?" January shuddered, standing in the bathroom with Melinda, poor chubby Melinda who could only get the ugly guys in the bands to sleep with her, usually the drummers. Stevie Flame being the exception to the rule.

Meaning he was a drummer, but not ugly. Had he slept with Melinda? January didn't even want to know. But she suspected. Melinda sometimes had that look. That secret smirk, the one that made you panic.

January stared at their reflections in the mirror, mottled in places where the silver had worn off. Poor Melinda. Her long black hair was shaved close on one side and hung in her face on the other, the new asymmetrical cut that on her looked neither New Wave nor sexy. Only silly. Because her face was as round and sweet as a baby's, chubby Melinda who would do anything to be a part of things, sleep with anyone, let them throw bologna at her naked body, whatever. Her life was spent in service to the guys in the bands. And she always had drugs, as she did now, laying out thick waxy lines on the mirror of her Clinique compact. Melinda was rich. Just sixteen, she lived in the Valley with her mom and three badly behaved standard poodles. January had gone with her once to feed them.

"I don't know what you're talking about." Melinda's eyes were blank, her skin a beautiful creamy pink. "Who peed on whom?"

January sighed. "That girl. Dizzy, DZ, whatever her name is. She's out there with Stevie, right now, acting like she owns him."

"Oh, her? They're always together. She works at Duke's, at the—"

"No, they're not."

"Yeah." Melinda's voice was stubborn.

"No. Not." January kicked at the pile of girlie magazines at her feet. The bathroom was clean and smelled of mint. Its green ribbony wallpaper made her feel wrapped in a little package. "Because he's always with me, so how could they always be together, or even be together at all? He doesn't even know that girl—"

"*That* girl? The one with the purple—"

January cut her off. "You're tripping. What do you know? You're still in high school." She laughed shortly.

Melinda shrugged.

"Talking about this is only going to piss me off," January warned, leaning in to wipe eyeliner goo from her eyes.

Melinda shrugged again. "You're the one that brought it up."

January didn't answer. She sat on the toilet, inspecting the bottoms of her feet. They were filthy from the carpet, and Rose Red vacuumed all the time.

"I like your haircut." Melinda tousled January's hair, smiling. She had a pretty smile. Her teeth were perfect and white, her gums a bright pink. The poodles all had nice smiles, too. Melinda's mom brushed their teeth, something January couldn't believe. Melinda hated the poodles. She called them "the little bitches" and shoved them whenever they came near.

"I like your haircut, too," January lied. "It's black."

"Blue black." Melinda leaned over, rolled bill in hand, the long side of her hair hanging in her face. She snorted a line off the compact. "This is from Uncle Fester," she said, standing motionless, pinching the bridge of her nose.

"Huh." January closed her eyes. She should have gone home. She should go now, just get in the Pinto and drive. But how could she? How could she give up so soon? It was his birthday. He'd declared his love as they sailed along the freeway that very afternoon. The night was momentous, he just didn't understand.

Melinda handed her the compact. "Uncle Fester?"

"Yeah?"

"They're bikers. This guy I know? He sends me stuff. Leathers, crank."

"You got this in the mail?" January stared at the neat lines, doubtful.

"Yep. It's crystal. And go easy on it." Melinda sniffed and wiped her nose. "He said that. He wrote it on the note. Here." She leaned close. She smelled of hot dogs. "Two lines for me, two for you. I already did one, so . . . Hey! What the fuck, Jan?" Melinda pulled away the empty compact. "That was mine. That was fucked. You're so greedy." Her dark eyes flashed. "You've always been greedy, did anyone ever tell you that? Like the time you had the leftover pizza and I was starving and you wouldn't let me have any?"

"Sorry," January mumbled. She'd taken it all, all three lines, waxy stuff, yellowish, ugly, ugly, like how she felt inside. Stevie hated it when she got high, hated it. "That's the one thing about you I can't stand," he'd said, so why not make him mad? Why not take it, take it all, take all of Melinda's drugs, it was so easy, and she was so pitiful, standing there with her splayed feet, her pink zebra jeans and leather jacket. Bubblegum pink, just like Stevie Flame's, a fact she was proud of and told everyone, making January cringe. "Why is it so easy," she said now, her heart racing, hands tingling, the chemical drip in her throat. "Why is it so easy to take everything from you?"

Melinda didn't answer.

"It's so easy," January went on. "To take all your shit. You're so easy, you should stop, you know, stop someone once in a while."

"You're fucked." Melinda's voice was hateful, the one she reserved for the poodles.

"I know, but guess what? Nobody cares." January let herself out of the bathroom. She leapt from the pretty package. Here I am! Naked, in my birthday suit, a toy for the Birthday Boy! She'd find him. She'd make him play along.

. . .

"You disappeared," Melinda yelled when January ran to the car, hours later. "I've been waiting out here forever. You said 'meet me out front,' and I did, but you disappeared."

Where had she been? January sat in the front seat, the sky purple and fuming, everything going up. It was almost morning, and she'd somehow disappeared. She gripped the door handle, fighting the urge to barf, focusing on the light in Rose Red's window, far away, way up at the top, the building cindery and gray, lurching over the sidewalk. Think back. Focus. Take a breath and stop.

She was on the roof, kissing Animal—someone had just been thrown off. She was in the party, watching Stevie and Dizzy dance away. And in the bathroom with Melinda . . .

X. She was here: flat on her stomach in the parking lot of Rose Red's building, over behind the dumpster, gravel up her nose, in her mouth, the fat roadie on her, his hand between her legs, shoving her face into the sharp rocks. DID SHE GET IT YET? And she did, she totally did.


After snorting Melinda's meth, January wandered the party, searching in vain for Stevie Flame. She found Ben, the grouchy bass player, taking bong hits in the kitchen. "Hey, Ben," she said, and he gave her a surly nod. Ben, aka Smokin' Ben Wa, didn't like her; she had no idea why. One night he was making Potato Buds and chicken for the guys in the band—he'd been a fry cook once at Perkins—and he wouldn't let her have any. Mean Ben, shirtless and tattooed, scary in his hairnet. "She's not eating, no fucking way, there's barely enough for us," he'd told Stevie. As if she were a begging dog, as if she weren't standing right there.

She found Dale, the band manager, staring out the living room window, neat in his shiny shoes and suit. Dale was to be avoided at all costs. He was usually coked to the gills, his skin fishy-pale, and insisted on asking her fatherly questions, like when was she going to quit acting like a fool and do something with her life, while at the same time leering, as if he could see right through her clothes. January crept past. Dale caught a glimpse of her reflection in the glass. "I see you," he said without turning. January scurried around the corner.

In the bedroom, she found Crystal and Mimi making out on a sleeping bag, a group of guys crouched around watching. Crystal looked up, gave January a wave. January smiled back. Crystal had lanky blond hair and owned just one pair of sweatpants, as well as a single pair of jeans that weren't cute. She was a runaway from Arizona. She told everyone she was sixteen, but January knew she was only thirteen, and that her real name was Mary. Her parents had somehow found out where she was and called Stevie every Sunday night. He gave them updates; it was all very hush-hush. The police were supposed to have picked her up a week ago, but they hadn't. January wondered if Crystal knew that the party was about to end.

"Are you leaving or staying?" one of the crouching guys whined, because Crystal's attention was still on January while Mimi, with her droopy cat eyes, had already taken off her top.

Out in the hall, as January headed back to the roof, somebody grabbed her by her skirt. "You," the fat roadie said, pulling her around and backing her into the corner. "Why'd you cut off that long pretty hair?"

January was surprised and tried to walk away.

"Why'd you cut off that long pretty hair?" he said again, moving to block her path.

"Sorry." January smiled, tapping her foot, she needed to go, couldn't he see she was about to explode?

"I know something about you."

"Yeah?"

The fat roadie nodded, smoothed his short hair. His Nazareth T-shirt rode up, and he pulled it back down over his gut.

"Well, what?" January's eyes roamed the murky hallway. Orange lights like lanterns glowed every few feet. She bet Stevie was up on the roof, and if not, maybe Animal was still there, and if so, maybe she'd make Stevie pay.

"You fucked a nigger," the fat roadie said.

"What?"

"You fucked a nigger. I can't believe it." The fat roadie wrung his small hands, danced from foot to foot as if he had to pee. His face was fat but elfin, his eyes big and sad.

"Whatever."

"What do you mean?"

"What do you mean, *what do I mean*?"

"What do you mean, *whatever*?"

"Whatever. I don't know what you're talking about." January laughed shortly. She didn't walk away. Maybe she should have, but she didn't. It was obvious the poor slob was in love with her, he was always staring at band practice, the time she sunbathed on the roof. Let him drool, let Stevie walk by and see what he was missing.

"I can't believe it, I'm so disappointed." The fat roadie shook his head as if he knew her, as if he were her dad. "You seem so sweet and innocent."

"He was in the Commodores," January lied.

"I used to think you were hot, but after Stevie told me that." He sighed, dismayed. "I just don't know—"

January needed to stop grinding her teeth. "He was in the Commodores," she said again, grimacing, being nice. "He was a great—"

"It really brought you down in my eyes," the fat roadie interrupted, his voice rising.

January was silent. "Then I guess . . ." She hesitated. "I guess you're . . . kind of a . . . racist asshole." She laughed, shocked. What had possessed her to say such a thing? He was a guy. Guys were intimidating. Around guys, gross roadie or no, she was only ever nice.

"Ha." The fat roadie nodded approvingly, as if she'd made a joke. He stuck out his hand. "I'm Bomb. I don't know if you know . . . I mean we see each other, but you probably don't know my name."

"Yeah. No." January took his hand reluctantly, her eyes on the stairwell.

"I know who you are. January. Like the month."

Melinda ran up and grabbed her around the waist. Her hands were cold, and her hair smelled of the outdoors. "You're not going to believe it," she said, ignoring the fat roadie. "Guess who I was just making out with on the roof?" She didn't wait for an answer. "Animal, that's who. Can you believe it? Totally fucking hot, I'm going back up there right now. I just had to pee first, super bad." Melinda made a face, moved away, a ribbon of toilet paper trailing from her heel.

"Wait."

She turned around.

January took her keys from her purse and tossed them. They landed at Melinda's feet. "Will you . . . Do you want to stay at my place tonight? Melinda?"

"But, Animal . . ." Melinda shook her hands, impatient.

"But that's just going to take a minute. Please? Meet me out front when you're done. We can drive to my place. Melinda, I'm just really freaking out." January hadn't known she was freaking out until she said it, but she was, the drugs weren't working, she was coming down, she wanted to go. She wanted Melinda, calm, placid Melinda who was always exactly the same. They could lie in bed together, be close and quiet, it would feel just like being home, like being a kid again, snuggling up to her mom after a bad dream. "Please? I don't want to go home alone. I need you."

"Shhh." Melinda held her finger to her lips. She giggled. "Jan. Maintain, OK? First let me go meet Animal. Then we'll go, I promise, OK?" She picked up the keys, then turned and ran swiftly down the hall. Melinda was surprisingly fast. She sometimes parked blocks from clubs and ran just for the fun of it.

"Maybe we can go feed the poodles," January called. The door to the stairwell whooshed shut.

Bomb was looking at something through the open door of the apartment. January followed his gaze. Just inside, leaning against the back wall, was Stevie, smiling at someone, his shirtdress gone, his skinny torso covered with bright stripes—was it lipstick, paint, what on earth had he been up to?

"I've got to go," January began, excited. She bent to retrieve her purse, but Bomb grabbed her arm. He was still staring into the apartment, a smirk on his fat face. "What?" January pulled free. Bomb nodded at Stevie, still in the apartment, a glittery ragged figure against the beige expanse of wall, but kissing someone now, kissing Dizzy, who clung to him dramatically, her lavender hair gone flat, hanging in her eyes.

January caught her breath. Her body felt strange, as if it had disappeared, and she stamped her foot, gave her arms a shake.

"Hey, I forgive you though," said Bomb. "Let's go outside and have a smoke." January hesitated, then followed, down the hallway and into the stairwell, the image of Dizzy stuck in her mind, Dizzy not old and horrible at all, but young and pretty and excited, crushed in Stevie's arms.


There was a smashed Yoo-hoo can inches from January's nose. Bright yellow, the chocolate-colored swoop. Stevie drank Yoo-hoos. She'd never heard of them before she met him. She wondered if it was his.

There was no joint. Nobody was going to get high. Once they were in the parking lot, out of sight behind a dumpster, ancient eucalyptus trees blocking the neighboring building, Bomb had grabbed her from behind in a bear hug, shoved her to her knees, and pushed her face into the gravel.

She tried to scream, but he covered her mouth with his hand. She tried to struggle, but already he'd jerked up her skirt, slapped her hard on her bare ass—she hadn't worn underwear, why would she, hadn't he heard of panty lines?—and thrown his weight on top of her. It was impossible to breathe, much less move. He grabbed her hair and held her face to the ground, his forearm on her back, his full weight bearing down, as he shoved his other hand into her, tearing her dry flesh.

January concentrated on the can. Chocolate pop—was there anything more disgusting? Stevie had wanted her to try it, but she'd refused.

"No panties, fucking slut," Bomb said, smacking her again. Shame filled her, burning her face and ears. Why did he sound so cheerful? *I fucking hate you*, she thought, *you're going to fucking die.* She repeated the words like a mantra, grinding her teeth, trying to breathe, until they no longer made sense.

*I . . . hate. I . . . die.* The grizzled trees shivered in the wind. They smelled like medicine. And the rocks smelled exactly like blood—she'd never known that before. Panic coursed through her, while at the same time, she was totally numb. *Comfortably numb*, like the Pink Floyd song? Not quite. It was like a dream, being out there in the night, squashed like a bug on the ground, but it was real life. Or maybe it wasn't. Maybe it *was* a dream, was there really any difference?

Bomb jammed his hand into her. He was hurting her. She was dry. His hand was too big. She could feel herself tearing. Or was it his hand? Was he raping her? Was she being raped, right that very second? Was tonight, the night of Stevie Flame's birthday, the night she was to be raped? It was an ugly word. And not true. She'd simply fucked up, big time. She'd failed to maintain. She was on the roof. Someone had just been thrown off. Or maybe they fell. Maybe *she'd* fallen, ventured too close and toppled over the edge. Landing here, in the lot, behind the dumpster, beneath the fat roadie.

"Do you get it yet?" he said, breathless, shoving into her, the slamming, the horrible rhythm. But she was busy, she was thinking of corsets, of the bones in them, all the pretty bones, the bones on the outside, holding you in, and she wished she had one, a corset, wished she were all bones, a pile of bones, gone clattering off the roof, landing here, in the lot; a pile of bones that didn't move or talk, that had no stories to tell; he could hurl her into the dumpster for all she cared, or a dog could carry her off. She giggled. The fat roadie squeezed her neck and grunted. She was choking. Was this it, the end of her stupid life? Stopped, like that, the silence after a bad joke?

"Do you get it yet?" he asked sadly, collapsing in a heap on top of her. January waited. After a moment, he sighed and clambered off.

"Why did you do that?" She scrambled up, coughing, pulling down her skirt. The fat roadie wouldn't look at her; he was staring at something behind her left ear. "Why did you do that?" This time she shouted it, her face hot, her legs wobbly as she backed away. The fat roadie had no answer. He shrugged, helpless, rocking slightly from foot to foot. "WHY . . .

DID . . . YOU . . . DO . . . THAT?" she screamed once again, her lungs burning as she turned and ran for the street.


Melinda couldn't drive a stick. The Pinto lurched and bucked, squealing in the quiet night. Melinda laughed, rolling through an intersection as January opened the door and puked. She got it. Dark asphalt moved swiftly beneath her—nothing flowing into nothingness.

They sat in the car outside January's apartment while she searched her purse for the security card that opened the front door. Across the street a fancy restaurant nestled into a hotel, its windows dark, the silvery swoop of its neon sign dull in the early light.

"C'mon. We'll just wake up the old man." Melinda tapped her cigarette out the window. But the window was closed and orange sparks showered onto her jeans. She shrieked, slapped her thigh. "Let's go. The old man loves you." The old man lived in 9C. He was always happy to let January and her friends in, no matter what the time of night. He'd shuffle down the hall in his neat robe and slippers, wide awake and cheerful, as if he'd been sitting in 9C, waiting just for them.

The security card was blue; January could never find it. "It's fucking lost," she cried, throwing her purse into the back.

"Calm down." Melinda giggled. "Where were you, anyway? And why are you bleeding?"

"What?"

"Your face. Did you fall?"

January looked into the rearview mirror. There was a trickle of blood on her cheekbone. She wiped it off. She was shaking, although it was stuffy in the car.

"Your shoes are gone and you look like a doll," Melinda pointed out.

January looked into the mirror again. She did look like a doll. Her pupils were enormous black pools, like something you could fall into. And her face was waxen, two bright spots burning on her cheeks. She imagined Stevie behind her, caressing her doll face. "*Exactly* what I wanted," he murmured, turning her around.

"You look like night," she said. She looked at Melinda. It was true. She was all black, and there were stars in her hair, bright shining stars, shimmering like a crown. "You're all covered with stars." January sighed, started to cry.

"You idiot." Melinda glanced over her shoulder. "It's the lights, the reflection on the glass. Come on. We'll wake up the old man."

The front door was ajar, no need to wake the old man. In the lobby, masses of impatiens cascaded over cement planters. Petals, dark and grapey, littered the Mexican tile. Melinda and January stood in the elevator, arguing over who cared more for the human race. "I give money to every bum I see," Melinda said, rubbing the plush half of her head.

"You *sleep* with every bum you see," January retorted, meaning *them*, the guys in the bands. Meaning Stevie, the GOD no longer hers. "And it's not about giving, it's about caring," she continued. "I *care* about whether people like me or—"

"That's not caring, it's just selfish," Melinda snorted.

The elevator doors slid open. Flowers, purple petals—they were right where they'd begun.

"Fuck." Melinda laughed, headed for the stairs. January said nothing. She was thinking about work. Saturday was a big day at the fitness center. She started early, eight a.m., taking the towels to the Laundromat down the street and later washing the mirrors with water and wadded newspaper. She liked her job. She'd never missed a day, not even when she was still drunk from the night before and hadn't slept a wink. Her bosses loved her back. They called her their "little punk rocker" and spoiled her with sweet potato pies from the Fatburger next door.

In the apartment, she was sick again. Filthy water stagnated in the tub. There was a cockroach stuck to the bar of soap. She brushed her teeth, wondering aloud when her pupils would go back to normal. Melinda didn't answer. She was on the phone with a high school friend looking to score some downers. "We're never going to sleep," she kept saying, her voice awed, as if she were on a roller coaster, about to drop. January hadn't felt high earlier, but she knew she was coming down hard. She was nauseated, shaky. She could sense black clouds gathering on her horizon.

"Because it's shocking. I would be scared looking at me," she said.

"Wear sunglasses," Melinda hissed, turning to face the wall.

Perfect attendance, something January had never achieved in her life. She stepped out of her party dress, leaving it in a heap on the bathroom floor, then pulled on shorts and a cut-off Betty Boop T-shirt, found some flip-flops, and left.

"I'm walking," she said, slamming the door behind her

She should have worn sunglasses. The sun was impossibly bright, making her hunch and squint, stumble on a buckle in the sidewalk. Across the street, a waiter in a black apron arranged baby sunflowers on the restaurant's outdoor tables. January leaned against a wall, shading her eyes from the sun. The wall was stone, with bright bougainvillea draped across its top. The waiter gave her a questioning look. She smiled, turned away. After a moment, she continued on. The sidewalk seemed spongy, giving with every step. She kept sailing off in her head, slamming back with a start. *Way too fucked up to work,* she thought. At the corner she turned and ran home.

Someone had propped open the front door with a rock. The flowers in the lobby were brighter now, the wash of Mexican tile cracked like a riverbed. She took the stairs, everything blue in the cool stairwell, and out the landing windows the blue expanse of swimming pool, shimmering in the morning sun, so pretty it made her ache. It was reassuring somehow: all she needed was sleep, a good day's sleep to wash away the night. Like diving into achy blue depths, rising to the top, alive.

In the apartment, January curled on her bare mattress, the lumpy beige comforter pulled to her chin, and tried to sleep. But she couldn't sleep, couldn't even breathe. She tried to breathe, sighing, looking for a rhythm. Nothing worked. It was as if her brain, the tiny reptilian part that kept a person alive, had quit, and it was up to her to keep herself breathing, to keep herself alive. Her lungs felt full to bursting. She was suffocating, about to pass out.

Melinda was no help. Melinda was a distraction. "Fuck you if you can't follow along," she growled, slamming down the phone. Poor chubby Melinda, gnashing her teeth, flipping the pages of her sequined phone book. She was scaring January because she seemed basically OK while January was so *not*. What was in those drugs? *Go easy on the shit*—wasn't that what the biker guy had said?

Drenched in sweat, January couldn't stop shivering. Her arms and chest began to tingle. The muscles in her hands tightened spasmodically, pulling her fingers into claws. She closed her eyes, willing herself to sleep. If only she could knock herself out. Or die, there on the bed, for something was horribly wrong. And not just with her body, but with her self—her very soul, she guessed—the broken life that spun from her spinning from something broken, and there was no way to fix it, no way to get it right. Or at least she couldn't figure it out. Better to die. And let Stevie find her body; let him suffer for the rest of his life.

The breathing, the clenched hands, her heart rattling in her chest . . . In an instant, the black clouds burst. If she was dying, she'd really rather not. Why would she, she was only eighteen. Fuck Stevie Flame. What about her, what was happening to *her*? Breathing, clenching, pounding . . . It was like the movie where the guy devolved into an ape. It was a seizure, a heart attack. "I'm dying," she gasped. "Call an ambulance now."

Melinda laughed. "Jan, hype down." Her cigarettes were gone. She poked in the ashtray for something to smoke.

"Now," January cried. The world was closing in, couldn't Melinda see?

"You need to quit trying to sleep." Melinda flicked her lighter. She took a drag off a butt, smashed it into the ashtray. "You're not going to sleep. You probably won't sleep for days. Just accept it and you'll be OK. Get up and we'll clean, OK? Or we'll walk, all the way to the beach."

"Are you crazy? Not OK. No. I'm dying. Look at my hands." January didn't move. She stayed in her fetal position, hoping Melinda would look for herself. Any movement, any change—talking even—brought fresh waves of panic.

Melinda didn't move. She was silent, tracing the kitty on her book. "*How* are you dying?" she said after a minute. She sounded skeptical.

"My heart." January knew Melinda's dad had died of a heart attack, sitting in an ER, waiting to be seen. "Pain in my chest, down my arm. I have a sense of . . ." she hesitated, remembering Melinda's words, "impending doom, GODDAMMIT, CALL AN AMBULANCE NOW."

"If you're lying . . ." Melinda sighed loudly. She sat a moment, then picked up the phone and dialed. "My friend's freaking out," she said flatly, handing the receiver to January.

*I will kill you when I'm OK*, January vowed. She took the phone, reported her symptoms—the breathing, the clenching—then waited on the line with the dispatcher. In her mind, the woman was a trucker, smoking a menthol cigarette, the *Enquirer* spread out before her, sympathetic in her padded plaid jacket. "There's this edge," January wanted to tell her, "this place where things are . . . awful . . . and I've fallen, I've gone there, and I need help . . ." But she didn't. She waited. Soon there was a soft knock at the door.

"Don't say anything about the drugs," Melinda warned, getting up to answer it, kicking over the ashtray. "If we get busted, I swear to God, you're dead."

January looked away.

"If you tell, Uncle Fester will kill you," Melinda hissed. She picked up a pile of clothes and threw them on the bed, opened the door wide.

The EMTs were young and good-looking, with the competent air of construction workers. January felt a tiny bit better. "Your elevator's busted," one said. She nodded in agreement. They took her pulse and blood pressure then loaded her onto a gurney. They lifted her. A radio crackled, and they set her back down. One of the men spoke into the radio. After a moment, they lifted her again. She began to move, down the hallway and into the stairwell, the pool outside winking in the sun, dirty palms encircling it, their shadows black and still. She floated into the lobby where the old man from 9C waited, clutching his mail, smiling, as cheerful as ever, his skinny legs, his big white tennis shoes, his silver hair combed, a cowlick sticking up in back. "January! Hello. Good-bye," he cried, waving as she sailed past.

The doctor was less than impressed. "You hyperventilated," he said, a wry look on his face. "Your friend should've given you a paper bag to breathe into, then you—"

"There was no friend," January interrupted. "I mean, *I have no friend.*" She laughed at his confusion. It was important that no friend be mentioned, but she couldn't remember why.

The doctor raised an eyebrow. He was young, barely older than January. His dark hair was curly and neatly parted on the side. He had once been an Eagle Scout, he'd said, but she wasn't sure why he told her this. Upon her arrival in the ER at Cedars-Sinai, they'd shot her full of Mellaril. And just like that, the fear, the breathing and the clenching, had disappeared. She was only bliss now, a purple puddle of bliss.

"That thing you said . . ." She tried not to speak so slowly. "Is that like a Cub Scout? The Eagle Scout?"

"Kind of . . ." The doctor hesitated, taking a seat beside her. "It's kind of like a Cub Scout, but way more advanced." He was smug, his curls tamed into perfect black poufs, a large one on one side, a smaller one on the other.

January smiled, pleased to have made a friend. She was quiet, thinking of scouts, of eagles and soaring poodles, their pretty yellow talons. Melinda's mother sometimes painted the poodles' toenails—blood red, like her own.

The doctor marked in January's chart.

"I hope this scared you," he said, snapping the lid on his pen. He looked up, his eyes dark and serious. "You never know what's in that street shit—PCP, LSD. You could be chewing off your thumbs in Bellevue as we speak." He gave her a look that said, *And how would you like that?* "And you got this garbage from bikers?" he went on. "In the mail?" He sat back, too flabbergasted to continue.

"But I'm OK? Am I OK?" January tried to look interested, not really caring at all.

"Maybe better than OK." The doctor smiled. "Because now you're scared, am I right?"

She tried to shrug, but it was almost impossible to do so, lying down. She didn't move, didn't say a word. Was she afraid? She didn't know. The drugs had washed everything clean. If anything, she was a husk . . . a shell of something, or someone . . . floating. How could that be scary?

"I'll bet before, you were too stupid to be scared," the doctor continued. He stood up, leaned against the bed. "Am I right?" he asked again. He smelled nice, like Coca-Cola and ink. His eyes were a beautiful dark brown. "January?" When he spoke, his voice was soft. He rested his warm hand on hers.

January started to cry. *Fix me*, she wanted to scream. "Right, you're right," she said. Tears seeped from her closed eyes, dripped into her ears.

A perky woman from social services paid a visit. She made herself comfy on the end of January's bed, wiggling like a child. "*Why* did you try to kill yourself?" she asked when settled, her voice dramatic and low.

"I didn't. I just couldn't maintain." January was shocked at the woman's rudeness. They'd barely met. The woman was *sitting on her feet*. She wore a necklace of gigantic wooden beads that she kept clacking against her teeth. Her hair was a colorful red, fluffed like a bird's crest.

"I wonder why someone so pretty would want to die?" the woman asked, her eyes turned heavenward.

January didn't answer. It was a stupid question. Pretty people killed themselves all the time. Hadn't she heard of Marilyn Monroe? And a, January wasn't pretty. And b, she didn't want to die.

She wanted to go home. The curtain around her bed was blue. Ripples like cold flames moved up its folds. She thought of the doctor's words: *It's scary to be stupid. It's stupid to be scared.* Before Stevie's birthday party she was stupid, and after she was scared. And now she was nothing, which seemed easiest of all.

The woman began to hum quietly. January wondered if she was insane, if she'd escaped from the crazy part of the hospital and was only pretending to be a social worker. *If anyone belongs in the loony bin, it's not her*, said a voice in her head. The voice was gleeful. January shut her eyes.

They sat in silence, the woman humming, January drifting. January drifted, the woman hummed. At some point the woman must have gotten bored because when January looked again, she was gone.

Stevie Flame had arrived! He stood beside her bed wearing a plain white T-shirt and jeans, his face unshaven and pale. "Jan, what the fuck?" he said in a low voice. He looked scared. He touched the ID bracelet on her wrist, stood nervously in the corner as she signed the discharge papers the nurse presented.

January threw back the covers. "You need pants," he said. They'd taken her in her underwear! "She needs pants," he shouted, running after the nurse.

In the parking lot, January's knees gave way. She sank to the ground in blue paper scrubs under a boiling ball of sun. The tar was soft and hot beneath her bare feet, the air wavering with fumes. She laughed. Stevie Flame had come for her! Melinda had called him; he'd arrived in the old orange Pinto.

"This is so fucked," he cried, reaching to help her up. There were dark circles under his eyes, and his hair was a mess, half in and half out of a ponytail. He looked like he'd been crying.

January laughed again. *He's scared, he cares, he's mine*, she thought, taking his outstretched hand.


She slept for two days straight, after which they pooled their wadded bills and quarters and drove to a cheap motel in Manhattan Beach, making love and watching professional wrestling on TV, late into the night. Cyndi Lauper was on the show, and January couldn't figure out why. Everything was surreal: Stevie's naked body entwined with hers, her fingers, his feet, the room like a 1950s den. Their flesh was blue in the light of the TV. *Like we're aliens*, she thought, resting her head on his chest. *Or married and normal and this is how it will be from now on.* It was scary without all the noise of home. Everything felt raw. They were both self-conscious and polite.

Around three in the morning, Stevie told her he'd written a song for her. They went outside, sitting on a log in the parking lot. Waves exhaled. The air was salty and close. "There are no words," Stevie said. He hunched over the guitar he'd brought, concentrating on the chords. The song was surprisingly upbeat. January listened, tracing a drip of black sap, wondering how the happy melody connected with her.

"You're such a loser." Stevie set down the guitar, tousled her dirty hair. "Fired for overdosing on company time."

"Shut up." January smiled, looked up at the sky. It hurt that her bosses hadn't cared about her bad night, that they'd told her to never return. She fell back off the log, her arms flung out, stars like pearls glowing in the misty night.


In the morning, they drove farther south. "Can you do it?" Stevie yelled.

"I'm fine," January shouted back. Her voice was lost in the roar of the wind.

They scrambled down a cliff side to a deserted stretch of beach. "Body-surf. Rock 'n' roll," Stevie cried, already halfway to the shore. The waves were ferocious. They knocked January down, sucked her under, spat her out. It was nice, like playing with a friendly beast. Salt burned her eyes. Tendrils of seaweed stuck to her bare legs.

"Something's wrong," Stevie said later as she searched the sand for her shoes. He pulled her close. Foam swirled, sand sucked. His skin was cold beneath his soaked clothes.

They left the beach and drove to the free clinic in town. It burned when he peed, Stevie said. They gave him a prescription, said it was probably an irritation of the urethra but to call later for test results. January was examined, too. The doctor pronounced her OK (call later for test results), but with a lot of sand up there. "Cans?" she asked, or maybe she just thought it, for the night of the fat roadie was gone, shoved to the back of her mind like a scary movie she'd made herself forget.

On their last night of vacation, Stevie and January went out for pizza. *Just like a normal couple*, she thought again, *and this is how it will be*. They sat at a long wooden table, *family-style*, everyone crowded together, bikers and grandpas and grandmas and kids. January sat next to a hard-looking woman in a worn leather vest. Across the table was the woman's boyfriend—or husband—or maybe he was just a friend. The man wore his hair in a long, gray ponytail. His leather vest matched the woman's, only his looked brand new. Maybe it was vinyl. Stevie was in a sullen mood. As he stared at the menu, January eavesdropped.

The woman, Kay, told a story of the time she was jumped by a group of "drunk chicks" at a party. They beat her, blackening her eyes, kicking her in the ribs. The cops arrived, and for some reason (January didn't hear, they were ordering their pizza) Kay was hauled off to jail. Upon her release, she went straight to another party and came across the same drunken women.

A lady with long black hair—*Elvira hair*, Kay called it—came up and apologized for the group. "We got the wrong gal," was what she said. Kay's dilemma was this: Should she befriend the woman who'd apologized as they obviously ran in the same circles? Or should she just kick her ass?

"Be cordial, but don't get too chummy," the man advised.

"But I like her," Kay protested. "She's got a lot of spunk, like me."

"Don't get too chummy," the guy warned. He flipped his ponytail over his shoulder and dug into his salad.

Listening to them talk was depressing. Kay and the guy were old enough to be her parents. Was it always the same? Did anything change? January looked at the woman sitting beside her. There were dark smoker's circles beneath her eyes, but no visible bruises. How had it felt to be attacked in such a way? Had Kay fought back? Had the idea of death crossed her mind?

Their pizza arrived. January reached for the peppers, knocked over her Coke, and started to cry. Something let go, or broke inside, and she couldn't stop, couldn't speak.

"What is it?" Stevie cried as she sobbed, her throat aching. Tears dripped onto her pizza. Coke ran onto her bare leg. The guy in the leather vest got up, returning a minute later with a box. His girlfriend helped Stevie pack up their food. "Take it," she said, handing January a new Coke in a Styrofoam cup.

Another part of her had taken over, and January couldn't believe what she was doing. "It's over," she told Stevie in the car. They'd parked too close to the bushes, leafy black branches scratching at her window. The pizza sign hovered overhead, a red moon, flooding the car with its rosy glow. January's words were bad lyrics: *I love you too much. It hurts too bad.* "And you said stuff about me," she said, angry.

"Like what?" Stevie pushed his hair behind his ears, confused.

"Things about me, things about the people I've dated, personal things that are nobody's business but—"

"Like what *exactly*?" Stevie grabbed her arm, annoyed. "Tell me what I said."

January hesitated. "Forget it." She pulled away, stared out at the leaves, little flat hands, slapping at the window. "And you slept with Melinda." The accusation came out of nowhere. Her voice was cold, but she was shaking deep inside. *Please don't let it be true,* she prayed. She looked at Stevie. His face was flushed. He shook his head, opened his mouth to speak. "Don't try to explain," she lied. "Melinda told me everything."

"But—"

"Everything." January closed her eyes. She pictured her heart cracking, scarred now with an ugly black fissure.

They sat in silence. Stevie smoked, nervously tapping out a rhythm on the steering wheel. He was so tall, so loose-limbed and skinny, he seemed to take up the entire car. But it wasn't just his size; it was his presence that was larger than life. It was what she loved about him, that he was so *here* when she often felt *so not.* His arms were jammed with rubbery bracelets, hot pink and green, black and yellow like a bumblebee. His tangled hair hung in his eyes. He'd added pink and black streaks the day before. She reached out and touched one. The pink looked sticky, but it was soft; the black was slippery and smooth. He was so vast, even his hair was its own universe. Glitter sparkled on his stubbly cheek, having worked its way into his pores after Rose Red's last show. There was always life, zipping through and around him. Something was always catching the light—a sparkly purple lip print here, a stray sequin there—as if he never truly left the stage. Was she insane, telling him good-bye?

"She begged me," Stevie said after a moment, tossing his cigarette out the window. "And it was nothing. Shitty sex with a stupid little blabbermouth."

January was secretly pleased. *Take that, Melinda*, she thought. "My best friend," she lied again. "How could you? I hate her. I hate you both."

Stevie looked at her, surprised. "Melinda's your best friend?"

January didn't answer.

"She's not your best friend . . . is she?"

January closed her eyes.

"She was begging—"

"So what," she cried, turning on him, slapping him away when he reached for her. "*I'm* begging. I'm always begging. And you don't care. You do what you want, you never think of the people you hurt."

Overhead, the pizza sign hissed and went dark. Silence filled the car.

"I'm sorry. Jan. You don't know how sorry I am." Stevie hesitated. "But try to understand. When you're a guy . . . like me . . ." He squinted into the distance, fluffed out his hair. "A guy in a band is what I mean . . . And there's all this . . . *temptation*. How can a guy say no? I know it's messed up, I'm just trying to—"

"Stop talking," January said. She leaned over, searching the floor of the car for her keys. She was sure she'd flung them there, but they were nowhere to be seen, and neither was her purse. She had the sinking feeling she'd left it in the restaurant, she could see it, the worn denim bag covered with pins and patches, plopped on the floor beneath the bench.

Stevie touched her back. "What about the song? The one I wrote for you?"

January laughed, scornful. "There are no words!"

"It's the feeling—"

"It's a happy song." She wanted to hit him, hurt him the way he'd hurt her. For none of it was about Melinda. It was that he'd left her, alone and unprotected, on the worst night of her life. And the awful part was this: He didn't even know. He'd never know—that was the truly fucked part. When he'd danced off with Dizzy, she had disappeared, and it would never be a story because there were no words. "Your song is like: All right! I'm gonna fuck everyone I see because January is so stupid, she'll never figure it out—"

"No." Stevie's patience was wearing thin. He shook out another cigarette, clicked his lighter, inhaled fiercely. "It's how you make me feel: happy. Happy January; January happy. And then there's the sad part at the end because I make one stupid mistake and you're fucking dumping me." He slammed his fists against the steering wheel. "For no reason. There was nothing wrong, we never needed to go to that fucking clinic in the first place." He punched the dashboard, started to cry.

January watched, tried not to smile. She loved it when people freaked out, especially if they were freaking out because of her. It made her feel light and excited, as if she were floating several inches off the ground. Stevie cried silently, his thin shoulders shaking. A siren wailed in the night. Headlights slid across the windshield, touched the bushes, and disappeared.

"And you know what?" he said, wiping his eyes, blowing his nose on a rag from the gas station. "You're not nice, you're not an angel. You'd have everyone believe you're this helpless, sweet girl, but you're not. You're a devious little brat, a real pain in the ass. I mean, who gets high and ends up in the fucking hospital?"

January was shocked. "Me," she wanted to cry. "That's me, exactly who I am." But how had he seen inside? And why was he still hanging around?

Stevie ran his hand over his eyes as if exhausted. He sat up straighter, pulled off his Rose Red T-shirt. It was his favorite shirt, his official shirt; a work of art, he'd spent hours getting it right. The lettering was scarlet, the soft cotton shredded, held together with a hundred tiny safety pins. January was never to touch it, but now he tossed it into her lap. "It's yours if you want," he said, studying the gearshift.

January frowned, pleased. She slipped out of her Betty Boop T-shirt. It was filthy, stained with dirt and soda, reeking of salt and dampness and sweat. She hadn't taken it off since the hospital, and it was strange—painful even—like peeling away a layer of her own skin. She wadded it and threw it into the back. She sucked in her stomach and arched her back, offering herself to Stevie. He smiled sadly, pulled her close. His bare chest was warm; she could feel the outline of his ribs beneath her hands. "Only us two," he said. "I promise. Only me and you."


Her purse and keys were discovered on the roof of the car. Love was declared once again. Their STD tests came back negative, Stevie even added words to her song, but nothing was ever the same. The band got their record deal, the huge advance—unheard of in the business, everyone said—and went to work on their first album. Stevie morphed into a star, or maybe it was that his inner star came leaping to the fore. His outside turned cracked and golden and hard. Platinum extensions were added to his hair. He obsessively shopped for stage clothes (he had a budget!) and took to wearing platform boots like a member of the KISS Army.

January, without her job at the fitness center to hold her down, felt herself growing lighter and wispier by the day. Was she dirty now? An angel? She had no idea, only that the days shifted, and she drifted along.

"You talk slow, you walk slow, you move slow," Stevie announced one grubby fall afternoon. "You're so slow I can't stand it. And what do you do? Nothing. You were going to take those art classes up in the hills, and what did you do? Nothing. You were going to work at that day care center, and what did you do?" The answer was left unsaid. "You're always going to do something, but you never *do* do anything." He was angry because he was late to rehearsal and January, who was driving him, had decided to quickly blow-dry her hair while he searched for his cigarettes.

"I'll do stuff," she said, throwing down the dryer, scrambling to find her purse.

"It's not that easy."

"Let me do stuff with you . . . *for* you." She shook the comforter from the bed, dug in the space between the mattress and wall for her keys. "I'll help with band stuff, anything you want."

"I'm not having one of *those* girlfriends." Stevie found his cigarettes beneath a pair of her discarded panties and shoved them into his waistband. His jeans were new and skintight. Enormous black sunglasses made him look like a fly.

"What girlfriends?"

"*Those* girlfriends." Stevie shrugged on a leather jacket the color of grenadine. He hesitated. "Maybe you're not even my girlfriend."

"How can you say that? We live—"

"Maybe we don't." His voice was ominous.

"What? Live together?"

"Maybe we're just seeing each other. Maybe that's all it is." With that, the Rock Star plucked the car keys from the dusty TV set and left, not bothering to shut the door.


A week later he went out and never returned. It was over like a song that had ended, done, he'd put her away. Like a child with a doll, he'd taken her out and played with her, made her pretty, and put her back. That was life, get over it, did she get it yet, would she ever?

# Twenty-four

"Not good," Katie said the next morning. "Not good at all. It's a horrible story, I don't even know what to . . ."

January's body was so heavy with sleep, she could barely move. She lay in Jake's bed, listening to her sister chatter. The blinds were closed, tendrils of sunlight probing the green room. She shut her eyes, felt herself drift and sink back to sleep. The humming of a million bees filled her ears, and her body was weightless, like water flowing into water.

In a waking moment, she realized Katie was on the phone with Steven, and the night came rushing back: Lucy, Chad, the tulips, the salon.

Sleep whirled her away. She was dreaming of big green feet crashing through a garden, and then she was awake for good, staring at Katie's bare feet planted beside her futon. She'd gotten a pedicure, her toenails a shiny tomato red.

"Pretty feet." January's voice was a slurred mumble.

"It's three in the afternoon." Katie poked her. "Even pregnant ladies need to get up and play."

January curled inward. Her body felt rested and well-used, and she was starving, the baby thumping away in her belly like a song.

Jake and Paul and Rose huddled around the TV, lost in a video game. "Slippy's dead," Paul said, his voice matter-of-fact. Nobody answered.

January sat at the table eating cold pizza as Katie rinsed lunch dishes at the sink. "You look like a raccoon, and you have black stuff on your cheek," Katie said, wiping a plate with a sudsy cloth.

"Hmmm."

Over the clatter of dishes, she started to babble something about Steven. January automatically tuned out. Lovely walked under the table and flopped onto her feet with a groan.

"The dog's getting so skinny—" January began, but her sister interrupted.

"Did you hear me? Someone robbed Steven's mom's salon. Last night." Katie busied herself cleaning the counter, but January could tell she was excited, her face serious and smiling, the way it got when she talked about Steven. "I guess she got to work this morning to open up—she was going to take the money to the bank; Steven says she always goes on Monday mornings—and the safe was empty."

January coughed.

"You annoying little fly," said a voice on the video game.

"Jan? Did you hear me?"

"Yeah." She swallowed. "Wow. So it was an inside job?"

"What do you mean?" Katie gave her a quizzical look.

"Right?" January tried to sound casual. "You said the safe was empty, so it must've been someone who knew the . . . whatever you call it . . . the code, right?"

"I don't know. I don't know if it was forced open or not." Katie squirted lotion onto her legs and rubbed it in, the smell of lemon filling the steamy kitchen. "Poor Steven, though. He's all freaked out. He can't believe anyone would do this to his mom, and they don't know who to suspect, everyone who works there has been there forever . . ."

January rolled her eyes.

"He was calling on his cell phone, on the way to the airport. Did you know they were going to Vegas?"

"Yeah. Lucy said something—"

"What were you two doing last night?" Katie gave her a sharp look.

January shrugged.

"Come on. Wilson said you didn't stumble in the door until almost seven in the morning."

"Just some pictures."

"That is so weird, Jan. You hardly know Lucy. Don't get people to do your weird things with you."

"She—"

"And don't do naked pictures, period. Jeez." Katie laughed. "Do you want them to get stolen? Do you want us to end up looking at them on the Internet?"

*Yes*, January thought. And then Stevie Flame would see them and he'd hunt her down and her life would be ROCKIN' once again. But she didn't say anything. When she looked up, Katie was staring at her chest.

"Is that . . . did you paint your boobs?"

January covered herself, ignoring her sister.

"Jan?"

"It's art," she shouted. "And I didn't 'stumble.' God! Your husband is a catty little bastard."

Katie laughed.

January picked up a sippy cup and drank warm Diet Coke.

"Your boyfriend's coming here." Katie bent to whisk a pile of dirt into the dustpan.

"What?"

"Stevie Flame. Rose Red. They're coming to the county fair. I heard it on the radio this morning."

An explosion sounded in the living room. The children whooped.

# Part Five

## Ectomy

"Ah! When the ghost begins to quicken . . ."
—William Butler Yeats, "The Cold Heaven"

# Twenty-five

### Katie

*And one day, all the guinea pigs in the world went away . . .*

Something had shifted, something had gone horribly wrong. Katie woke in the middle of the night in a panic, her heart racing, her mother's clear voice ringing in her ears. Icy terror—the opposite of a feverish flush—poured down the back of her neck. She tried to breathe but couldn't, all the air in the room, the city, the universe, it seemed, gone. Shadows bloomed on the walls like malevolent flowers. She lay motionless, drenched in sweat, praying for the attack to pass.

It was hot—maybe that was the problem. Early August already, and so steamy, there probably *wasn't* any air in the condo. She squinted at the bedside clock. It was three a.m. Without her glasses on, the room was murky, the fabric on her ceiling gray and lumpy, bulging like a large cocoon. *Like in a monster movie*, she thought, *The Body on the Ceiling*. And in the fragile nest was the other Katie, the one that had gone away when she was eight, a fetus-like bundle of bones, sleepy and innocent, haunting the woman she'd become.

*Morbid thinking.* And tomorrow she'd be shaky, and things would seem surreal, as if tinged with a high gloss. Panic wasn't unfamiliar, although it had been years, not since after Jake was born when it was bad, and she'd taken the Zoloft and after a time was OK. But now, like a demon that never dies, only shifts shape, it had returned. Life would never end. She would die; she would never die, every moment, every breath, endured in a state of agony. It was torture. She wouldn't wish panic on her worst enemy. Staring at the shroud above her bed, she swore to never make fun of Wilson and what she called his "benzodiazepine ideation" again. "Skelarid," she'd scoffed, but now she wished the pill (or was it a shot?) upon him, her husband, tortured genius that he was, spending entire days in his office, pounding out his ridiculous dissertation.

She closed her eyes. A wave of fear washed through her. What if it didn't pass? What if she were never normal again? She was so cold, as if her vital organs had been removed, replaced with freezing water. Was this it? Had she snapped? Was life as she knew it over? *Please God please God*, she prayed, struggling for one deep breath. The only way out, she knew, was to be good. Or *perfect*—maybe that was a better word. And she would be, starting now. Katie Jane Lavender: the kindest, prettiest, skinniest mom in the history of moms.

Wishing peace on Wilson wasn't enough. Anyone who knew him, who knew the way he twisted his psyche through the wringer on a daily basis, would do the same, out of basic human decency. She wished peace on the entire planet, on every lost and suffering soul. Why, oh why had she gone along so arrogantly, so sure of her place in the world, her security and sanity? It was all just an illusion! To have judged others: her lazy sister, boring Lucy from across the street—how had she had the nerve? And the things she'd done with Steven, oh, she was being punished. This moment now, pinned to the bed in a black web of fear, was hell, and hell, as she'd always known, wasn't a place you went to, it was a beast that came to you.

Outside, a breeze rustled past, knocking the heavy heads of the sunflowers against the window. Katie bit her lip. Her stomach was cramping. She needed to use the bathroom but was too scared to move. Should she call Wilson, asleep in the living room, have him take her to the mental hospital, which was where she surely needed to be? And then what? Suffer for the rest of her life? Did they drug you, fix you, put you out of your misery? Her eyes filled with tears. She was too scared, even, to call out for help.

The bedside clock, a squat pink thing with a luminous green face, read 3:04. She couldn't believe it had only been minutes. How long could it last? She couldn't take the psychic pain much longer. Every cell in her body screamed at her to flee, but to where and from what? The *thing* on the ceiling swayed as her promises grew heated. She would be kinder, more empathetic, more patient, and less selfish. She would slow down, really listen to her kids and Wilson. She would devote her life to being good, if she could only—please God—feel OK again. Worrying about her body and health (she obsessed over every disease she read about in *People* magazine, convinced that she had it), her boobs for God's sake . . . what a luxury it seemed when one was lying in bed at three a.m., feeling as if her life were no longer her own.

"Sand," Paul said in his sleep. Katie looked at him, surprised. He turned over with a sigh, and she rested her hand on his back, felt the ribs beneath his soft skin. He was so skinny. It made her sad. The other kids were chubby. Why was he so thin? Holding him, she always felt the need to be careful lest he break. Was she doing something wrong? Had she missed the one vital thing he needed to thrive?

Rose—robust in the ruffled pink bikini bottoms she'd insisted on wearing to bed—kicked off her covers. Katie pulled the sheet back up over her, moving away so she wouldn't try to nurse. Outside the open window, directly behind her head, a scratching and snuffling started up. It was the raccoon, or badger maybe, that came nightly to eat the stunted corn in their garden. She listened, feeling a little better, knowing in the morning she'd find a nibbled cob, a trail of kernels and husk, left by their messy friend. The creature scrabbled busily. Katie could feel her body beginning to relax.

Peace—thank fucking God. "The monkey has landed," was what her childhood friend, Kelly, also plagued with panic attacks, would say after one had run its course. She equated panic with how it would feel to be one of the flying monkeys in *The Wizard of Oz*: evil, itchy, trapped in an ugly body, ridiculous in your little hat. Thinking of Kelly, gleeful and crazy in the best possible way, made Katie feel almost normal again.

She tentatively stretched her legs. Nothing. She was panicked out; she was done. Curling into a ball, she inhaled the sleepy smell of her little ones, let the sound of their steady breathing soothe her. Moments earlier, it had seemed foreign, filling her with loneliness and grief. She'd looked at their sweet sleeping faces. *That was me*, a voice inside her had cried. It was where she'd been, what she'd lost . . .

Katie sighed, refusing to think any further. She rose to her knees and opened her window wide. The air was wet and fragrant, as if night had sucked up everything—earth and grass and pollen, sunlight and sweat and the mist from a thousand sprinklers—and was now, through the screen, through her thin T-shirt, exhaling the glorious day.

After using the bathroom, she examined herself in the mirror. It was her, whoever "her" was. Encircled by movie star lights, she looked OK, her eyes bright, her hair slightly wavy, stained dark from sweat and humidity. If nothing else, a full-blown panic attack made you look good—thinner somehow, pale and sort of smoldering. Her new aqua shower curtain reflected brightly in the mirror. She was wide awake. It was useless trying to sleep. Filling the sink with hot water, she sat on the pink-veined counter and soaked her feet. It was a weird habit—at least Wilson thought so—but comforting, something she'd done as a kid to warm up during the wet Portland winters when her father had kept the thermostat at a steady fifty-five degrees.

Ribbons of steam snaked up the mirror. A strange electronic sound pulsed through the wall, coming from the neighbor's bathroom. Katie dipped her fingers in the hot water. She concentrated on the sound, which disappeared with her attention. Her submerged feet were wobbly and white. She closed her eyes, leaned her cheek against the mirror. Now that the panic attack was over, she could examine it objectively. They'd begun last spring, occurring at first every couple of weeks and then more often, always at three a.m. They started with the baby bird.

She'd heard it first, in the birdhouse hanging on the front porch. The previous tenants, a minister and his wife, had left it behind, a white chapel of a birdhouse with the words *God Keeps His Promise's* painted on it. One morning, out of curiosity, she'd pressed her ear against it and was surprised to hear the baby birds inside. It was a faint sound—*eee eee eee*—like small hearts (if hearts had a sound) pulsing in the straw.

"What moron thinks *promises* needs an apostrophe?" Wilson said when she told him, but she'd been thrilled with the new life on their porch, flickering and wild.

Her nearness must have spooked the mother. She was so stupid, why hadn't she known? The next morning she found the baby bird. It was lying on the porch, alive but struggling. A thumb-sized pink thing, its perfect yellow beak was flat and wide, its black eyes the size of pinheads. Its feet, too, were exquisitely formed, its head a purple dome, naked and translucent. She stared, unsure what to do. Pick it up? Get a spatula from the kitchen and scoop it back into the nest? It moved its legs fitfully, weakening. Then Jake had come outside in a rush, looking for his basketball, and stepped on it, and it was gone.

It wasn't his fault the bird was dead. It was hers. She'd gotten too close, polluted its world with her scent, and the mother had flipped it out into the world, done.

Or maybe it had simply fallen, the unlucky one, edged out by its growing brothers and sisters.

Either way, it was dead. They buried it in the garden beneath the sunflowers. It was early June then, and they were just baby shoots, a fresh yellowish green, bursting through snow-soaked soil, curling into two leaves on top.

Now in August, they towered overhead, bug-faced and fleshy, peering in her window like curious, floppy-necked aliens.

Katie added a few drops of jasmine-scented oil to the water. Her freshly painted toenails were pretty, a clear Jell-O red. Why panic now, when she had everything a person could ask for? With her children, all that Larry Johnson had taken—her innocence, her sense of belonging in the world—had been returned tenfold. Hadn't it? Why then, with the arrival of spring, had the urge to ruin everything appeared? Winter had melted, things had begun to thaw, and it was then that something inside her began to grow, slowly at first, and then faster, until it threatened the rightness she'd made of her life, the good shape she'd forced it into, like a pillow beaten into shape. Now she wanted to tear things apart, to rip open seams, undo stitches, and start over. Her life was a pretty dress she'd made herself, homespun, not too flashy, modest and sensible, a dress you'd call *kind*. But it was too small, too forced, and it was suffocating her. She was dying. How long could a person be good? With the advent of mud season, she'd become bad with a vengeance.

Water swirled down the drain. Katie dried her feet with a fluffy almond-colored towel (aqua, almond, and "cupcake" were her new bathroom colors). She hurried to the kitchen, careful not to disturb Wilson and Jake, camped out on the living room floor. Months ago, Wilson had refused to spend another moment in the Lavender family nest. "The family bed is a hoax," he'd hissed in the middle of one particularly bad night, when Lovely had stepped on his nuts and Paul had woken him with a swift kick to the face. "We're not fucking Korean. This is America. I have the right to sleep." He'd gotten up, jerking away the blanket, muttering that she'd see him when the kids were grown because that's how long it would take to get them to sleep in their own beds.

"Fine," she'd replied. "More room for me." And that was that. Wilson had retired to the couch and bought a sleeping bag the next day. Katie hadn't minded. For months it seemed, entire worlds had been coming between them: his dissertation, her "experiments" with the guy across the street.

In the living room, Jake and Lovely slept together on the couch. Wilson, however, was gone, his purple sleeping bag, wadded near the fireplace, empty. Obviously he wasn't sleeping in Jake's room with January, his archenemy (*Are you really wearing my boxers?* she'd heard him yell that morning). Katie hurried to the front window—past the turquoise kiddie pool propped against the wall awaiting January's home birth—and raised the blind. Wilson's car was gone. Maybe he'd woken with an idea for his dissertation, raced off to his office to get it down. It was odd, but he *had* been obsessed with his work lately. Steven, she noticed, was home. His lights were on, and a couple of cars were parked in his drive. Katie's heart quickened, this time in a good way. She'd pay him a visit as soon as she took care of business.

In the kitchen, she grabbed the phone and fled, afraid to linger a moment longer than necessary. The rodent was still with them, leaving its droppings under the microwave and, strangely, on the narrow top of the oven door. "How the hell does it fit?" everyone wondered. Katie cleaned up the poop daily with bleach water, scrubbing up to her elbows like a surgeon after. A month ago they'd set up a live trap, but so far the mouse had managed to not only steal the peanuts they baited it with, but to scoot out before the trapdoor shut. It had kept its promise though: Katie had never seen or heard it again.

She sat on the bathroom floor in the dark, the face of the phone glowing in her hand. Quickly she dialed the number she'd looked up on the internet, her heart pounding so hard she could barely sit still. After several long rings, there was a fumbling at the other end. "Hello." It was a man's voice, a Larry Johnson, possibly *the* Larry Johnson, guarded but cheerful, even in the middle of the night. Katie held her breath. She thought of all the things she might say. A feeling like water, like a massive wave, came crashing down upon her, and she felt herself tumbling in an ocean of time. She was twenty-seven, flying on her bike down the steepest hill in Luna beneath a hot blue sky, Anthony close behind, shouting something that was carried away by the wind.

She was fourteen, running with Kelly to some boy's house, dizzy in the cool fall air, the taste of the ouzo they'd stolen from Iris cold in her mouth. It was evening, and she ran, her lungs burning, the licorice burn of the ouzo in her throat, like water and something awful. Running, scared, for tomorrow was the first day of high school, and who would she talk to, how would she ever find her way around? Running, past Reed College, past the rhododendron gardens, down behind the 7-Eleven where the semis parked, then hitting a cold pocket of air, chilled and electric like the ouzo. But more than the physical thrill, there was the happiness of the moment: racing with her best friend through the deserted lot, surrounded by the trucks they used to break into as kids (they'd once stolen a roll of toilet paper and a plastic hula girl), the twilit sky the color of blueberries, the gravel gray as rain, laughing, shouting, Kelly's long legs, her faded jeans and feathered hair, as familiar to Katie as her own.

She was eight, walking home from school, the paper May basket she'd made for her mother clutched in her hand. "Fill them with flowers on your way home," Miss Moss had urged. "Leave them on the doorstep and run, run away." But to where? And why? Katie's May basket was empty, the way she felt, empty, tears heavy in her heart, for the guinea pig was gone. Miss Moss had found it a permanent home with Linda B. after it had bitten several of the kids in the class (never Linda B.). Katie popped hard buds off a camellia bush—the dark green wrapping, the tiny pink tuft—and dropped them in her basket. The loss of all chances, her stupid hopes gone.

"Hey," the man on the phone said. His voice was happy, reproachful.

*So cheerful*, Katie thought. *Always ready for a party.* She remembered the first time he'd taken her to Number 15, the three happy beeps of his car horn, the way he'd made it sound like a birthday party was going on. She started to speak, realized she was about to cry. Quickly she hung up. In her darkened bedroom, she found her shorts and pulled them on, wound her hair into a ponytail. After making sure that January was still home—and she was, asleep in Jake's room, snoring, her belly enormous, she was nearly two weeks overdue—Katie left the quiet condo.

## Katie
1973

There was blood on my flowered-spotted underpants. After Larry Johnson dropped me several blocks from home, I went inside (discovering the blood), then walked to the corner and hid them in the neighbor's rockery. Does anyone know what a rockery is? Was it a word only people in Eastmoreland used? It's a hill, but instead of being filled with flowers or grass, it's full of rocks, in this case porous boulders, gray and jagged-edged. I shoved my bloody underwear beneath one of these rocks, pushing them firmly into the wet earth. If you turned the rock over, you'd find a mess of slugs and worms and slick brown beetles. If you turned the rock over, you'd find my panties, flowered, Girls Size 8, circa 1973. Were they ever discovered? Almost thirty years later does a shred of soft cotton remain?

It was nearly dark, but it had been nearly dark all afternoon, and I wasn't sure of the time. Was it the same day or years later? Was I still eight? Was I still alive? My certain world—home, Miss Moss's third-grade class, gymnastics once a week, treats as often as I could get them—had become watery, as if at any moment, things could be washed away. I looked at my hand and wondered, *What is a hand? A body? A person for that matter?* As I walked home, a ray of sunlight broke through the clouds, falling in a pale golden column somewhere far away. The air was heavy with the smell of rain, although it wasn't raining. It mixed with the animal stink of Larry Johnson, and I began to run, letting the wind wash me clean.

That night I ate dinner. We had creamed chipped beef on toast: lunch meat and white gravy on a slice of Wonder bread. I watched *Happy Days* with my mom and January. Then I went to bed. "No arguing, no hassles? What's wrong with my little monster?" Iris joked. The next morning I woke up. Before I could *not think*, I was thinking. I was thinking of the lady baboons at the zoo. My bottom felt funny. It felt *red* and big like theirs. Shame filled me; my spine began to shake. Everyone laughed at the lady baboons. *Hide it all away*, said a voice in my head. It was a commanding voice, like God, or Dr. Winters, our principal with the pouf of violet hair.

Miss Moss said the principal was our "pal," but Dr. Winters—an old lady, yet so much taller and skinnier and manlier than your ordinary old lady—terrified me. I stared at my bare canopy, at my flowered sheets, stained in spots where I drooled in my sleep. My neck hurt, and my throat felt thick when I swallowed. After a while I got up, dressing in checked pants and my Cindy Brady shirt. Flowers and checks, orange and green, cantaloupe and honeydew—I wouldn't know this was wrong until months later, when I met Kelly with her superior fashion sense (her family was rich, and she had two older sisters). I purposely didn't look at my underpants, or between my legs, afraid of what I might find.

Downstairs, my mother sat in the old La-Z-Boy, faded green with the worn gold swirls, rocking and drinking coffee. I crouched by the heating vent, behind the squat armchair, the same velvety gold as the swirls on the rocker. It was raining, and I couldn't get warm. My body felt cold, as if it had been filled with ice water, and the water was sloshing around, making even my brain cold—cold and sad and dull, and like nothing was pretty, and everything was rain—rain dripping, rain misting, rain pouring down onto the old Victorian that let everything, every draft, every tickle and whisper and lick of cold wind, into my bedroom at night, chilling me as I slept.

"Mom?"

"Yes?"

I wanted to tell her, but what could I say? I didn't know the words, didn't know, really, what had happened, only that it was bad, so bad it was worse than the worst nightmare I'd ever had. And if it was bad, then I, the one who'd gone with Larry Johnson when I'd been specifically told to go to the babysitter's after school, was even worse. If it was bad, I was badder, the baddest of the bad—the worst, probably, of all. "It hurts when I breathe." That I could say. *I have a tummy ache. My head hurts.* Those were things moms knew about and could fix.

"What do you mean?" Rain spattered the window. It was still dark even though it was morning and it would be time, soon, to go to school. I lifted my shirt and let the heat from the vent warm my side. My back hurt, and it hurt between my legs, but it was a pain that didn't seem quite real. It was like I was one thing, and the pain was another, and the two didn't fit together. Crouched behind the chair, I began to notice my breathing. It was strange the way it went—in and out, in and out—without my even trying. What if it stopped? Maybe I should pay more attention. I focused on the pain, concentrating intensely, with all the powers of Samantha on *Bewitched.* To my surprise, it disappeared. When I lessened my attention, it returned.

"When I breathe, it hurts in my back. When I breathe in."

Iris was silent. "Does it hurt bad?"

I shrugged.

"Katie?"

I didn't answer. If I didn't answer and she didn't ask again, which she didn't, maybe I wasn't really there, or maybe I was as small as one of the Borrowers, the little people in the book I'd just finished. Or maybe I was enormous, larger even than the universe, and my mother couldn't see me. I turned around, warming my other side. Soon it would be time to go, to eat the Cream of Wheat that, on the best of days, made me feel sick; to walk to school, put my Partridge Family lunch box on the back shelf, look at the guinea pig or not look at the guinea pig depending on whether or not the kid that had hosted it for the weekend had arrived yet, his mom in tow, swinging the cage, the triumphant return of the rodent, and sit and learn and listen and wonder when the time would come when suddenly, with no notice at all, I simply floated away, up and out of my chair, out the door and down the hall, out the big double doors of Duniway Elementary School and up into the sky, moving fast, a bright spot lifting, rising, fading, until I disappeared, like a balloon, into the rainy sky.

I rested my forehead against the vent, pulling down a book from the bookcase on the wall. It was the one the Hare Krishnas had given my mother, with its glossy pictures of elephants and other fancy deities. I loved the gods and goddesses. They were all bejeweled; they all had lots of arms. I examined the pictures intently, as if it were a normal day and I was still a normal girl. A feeling of calm, like a butterfly, touched me and disappeared, leaving one clear thought in my mind: I would be OK. Nothing strange would happen. I wouldn't suddenly fly off down the hall, or start babbling in tongues like I imagined the creatures in the book might do. I'd stay put. No one would ever know. My visit to Number 15 was like a dream, and dreams, as everyone knew, were invisible, and not really real at all.

# Twenty-six

## Katie

Katie ran barefoot into the jungly night. Her garden was in full bloom, masses of flowers—dahlias and daisies, petunias and poppies and phlox—spilling onto the lawn, overflowing their whiskey barrels, soaking the air with their dizzying fumes. The moon was halved, green in the misty night, and all the street lamps, up and down Merlot Court, stood knee-high in yellow puddles of light. The world was perfect: dark and hot and silent but for the bee buzz of traffic on the interstate. Wilson was gone and Steven was home and Katie was free—free to do whatever she wanted.

She stubbed her toe but kept running, ignoring the pain shooting up her leg. Steven would be drunk of course. His friends were over. It was a Thursday night, his regular party night, the end of his week at the community college. *And aren't you a loser?* Katie's conscience chided. For it was so much easier when he was drunk. Sober, he felt guilty. Sober, he thought of his insane fiancée. Sober, he didn't care as much about her. But when drunk, oh it was glorious. She could get him to do anything. He loved her, told her she was beautiful, hated when she had to go. It was like being in a dream world. But one she controlled and could easily leave behind.

She skirted the parked cars, practically leaping onto his cluttered porch. Something moved in the darkness, and she jumped back, stifling a scream. "Cleopatra!" The neighbor girls' bulldog glanced at her briefly, then went back to rooting in the McDonald's bag it had found wedged behind Steven's gas barbecue. Katie sank to her knees. "Cleo. Come here, girl. Come here, big, chubby girl." The bulldog clamped down on her bag, growling slightly as if Katie, too, rooted for garbage on porches at night and was about to steal her spoils. "Bad Cleo." Katie made her voice sharp. The Queen of the Nile wagged her entire back end, as if Katie had praised her.

Katie glanced at the neighbor girls' place. It was dark. There were no cars in the driveway or for that matter the garage, which she could see into as the garage door was conspicuously gone. A drunken Mandy had taken it out a few weeks earlier with her convertible. The Reserve had yet to replace it, as punishment perhaps—the girls hadn't paid their rent in months and didn't plan to. "We're taking advantage of the Wait-Six-Months-until-the-Sheriff-Moves-You-Out savings plan," Megan had said the other day. It was a dry, fiery afternoon, and she stood in their shared driveway, smoking, her long dark hair newly frosted, wearing nothing but a teeny-tiny leopard-print bikini. "So we save on moving costs, too," she joked, blowing smoke at the gas-blue sky.

"You idiot." Mandy, surly and skinny in a matching shorts outfit, shook her head. "They don't move you to your new place, they put your shit on the curb. I know because it happened to me and my mom. It was blizzarding out, and everything was ruined because we didn't know anyone with a truck. We had to leave our stuff on the street—our couch, my bed, all the dressers and shit—and every day, a few more things would be gone, until, by spring, all that was left was our moldy old couch that the neighbor kids would, like, jump on." She paused, looking miserable. "And then someone set it on fire," she added, a touch of surprise in her voice.

"Oh my God, that's like your whole life story." Megan laughed. "Like Katie cares."

"Oh I do," Katie said. She'd smiled reassuringly as Mandy, the not-as-pretty friend, glowered. What she'd wanted to say was "Can I have your dog?" Because the girls neglected the uncivilized beast, and she was sure she could do better.

Lately, Cleopatra spent most of her time at Katie's anyway. Megan and Mandy would let her out in the mornings and then take off, sometimes not returning for days, knowing she'd waddle over to Katie's, hurl her bulk against the door and be welcomed in, in order to wolf down Lovely's food, growling if the elder dog came near, attack the vacuum cleaner, chew up toys, chase the kids, and generally terrorize her hosts.

Katie loved her, mainly because everyone else—Wilson and Steven and even January—didn't. How could you not love a beast that, Katie knew, wanted to be lovable but had no idea how to go about it? She was so ugly—fat as a piggy, with her drooling Lon Chaney face, underslung jaw, and monster-sized feet. Katie couldn't resist. The dog just needed a friend, someone to counsel her *against* barking viciously at the neighbors as they stood on their own lawns, *against* heaving all sixty-four pounds of herself through the air like a cannonball in order to send Jake flying, then steal and pop his soccer ball. (Jake hated her, too.)

Earlier in the winter, Cleo had undergone surgery for a trick knee. The girls had to work and couldn't care for her during the day, so she'd convalesced at Katie's. Poor doggie! Drooling and out of it, her stitched-up leg so swollen it looked like a small ham, her nose hot and dry, her breath reeking of anesthesia. Katie had moved her by sliding a towel under her dead weight and pulling. She'd given her her pills every four hours, made sure she had water, rubbed her tummy, and tried to comfort her, for the poor thing was obviously in pain—psychic as well as physical, as she couldn't be up and about *destroying* the way she liked.

"Let's keep her, let's not give her back," she'd said impulsively when Wilson came home from school.

"Are you insane?" he growled, not in a good mood. "If you keep that dog, I'm gone. I mean it. I'm out of here. It's me or the dog, make your choice now."

They'd been getting along horribly at that point—as they had at almost every point in their tenure as a couple. Katie was about to say "the dog," when Wilson beat her to the punch.

"On second thought," he said, throwing back his arms in supplication, "take the dog please. Pick Cleo and set me free. Or just stab me now. Kill me and get it over with, and then we'll both be happy."

"Such a drama queen." Katie had laughed, liking him again for a brief, shining moment.

Now as she sat on Steven's porch watching Cleo shred, she wondered where her husband had gone. He was always disappearing, taking off without telling a soul. Once he'd called her on his cell phone, halfway to Indiana. "Why?" she'd ask, but he never had an answer. That trip he'd returned with a trunk full of illegal fireworks. Then there were the gambling trips to the riverboat casino in Illinois. At least these she knew about. He'd set off, armed with gaming books and a travel cup of strong coffee, convinced he was going to beat the house. "No one beats the house," she'd said. It was a sultry afternoon, a month into his life as a high roller, and he was practicing counting cards. She was the dealer; he was the poker-faced pro.

"It's probably not a good idea if they can see your lips move," she counseled.

"Thanks for fucking jinxing me," he replied, throwing down his cards and walking away. It took him several months and a couple thousand dollars to realize that, indeed, no one beats the house, not even a genius such as himself.

Katie sighed, looking at the mess of cigarette butts and pale green packing peanuts in Steven's flower beds. A familiar refrain ran through her head: *If we could only get along.* Lately, things had devolved to the point where neither of them tried. They fought over everything. To the "whose family is worse" argument, they'd added a litany of disagreements: *Who lived in the past? Who lived in the future? Who lived in reality at all? Who was the laziest lover? Who was the most selfish lover? Who even knew what love was? Who was acting out childhood traumas in the relationship? Who* loved, who hated the other more? Who was the smartest, the nicest, the funniest? Who was the grouchiest, the most in need of anger management? Who did the dishes "correctly"? Who was more rigid, and who floated around with no boundaries at all? Who followed the "house rules," and for that matter, why did Katie get to set the house rules in the first place? Who yelled more, and what, exactly, was the definition of "yelling"? Who had endured a rougher childhood? Who did the dog, the kids like best? Then there was Wilson's favorite: Who would survive in the event of the apocalypse? He was convinced that, like a cockroach, he'd skitter on, only strengthened by the poisonous atmosphere, while Katie, weak and whiney princess that she was, would immediately expire. Never mind the fact that she had body fat enough to live for months, while he had virtually none. "You want the world to end," she'd accuse. He wouldn't disagree, and they'd be off on the next argument: Who wanted to live to a hundred and twenty, and who would be fine with the world imploding next week?

Cleo swallowed the last of her trash, stalked over, and plopped herself onto Katie's lap. "Hey, fancy lady." Katie rubbed her blocky head, her funny naked tummy—pink with liverish spots. What a bad person she was, unable to get along with the one man on the planet it was vital she get along with. For the sake of the kids, for the sake of the kids. For the sake of the kids—what? Mommy should be a raving bitch? Daddy should be poised to flee at any given moment? Wilson was a great person, a wonderful dad, she knew. She also knew that they brought out the worst in each other. When they were together, caught in that awful blue fist of fate, struggling for—for what, superiority?—she hated herself. He felt the same, meaning he hated her, too. How was that for a happy home?

Why did she stay? For one thing, she no longer had any money. Grandma Edith had cut off the girls a month ago, saying she wasn't "seeing any progress."

"What does she mean?" January had wailed to Iris on the phone. "We're having all these babies. Isn't that progress? Between Katie and me we'll have a whole baby farm. Life begetting life—what could be more progressive than that?"

After another round of phone calls—made by Iris, the go-between in such matters—it was still a no go. Apparently Grandma Edith had seen the movie Reality Bites on cable. It had made her think of the girls and the way they, like the characters in the movie, "dressed like bums and had sex like it was going out of style." Sitting in her living room in Bremerton, watching the ferry float across the glass of Puget Sound, she'd decided right then and there to put an end to the "hippie nonsense" by no longer funding it.

Ironically, the girls' cousins in Seattle, Mark the Deadhead and Mia the corporate coke fiend, had *not* been cut off, as they had both bought houses and SUVs with their money, as well as showered Grandma Edith with letters, cards, and plenty of Whitman's Samplers. Katie and January, lazy and selfish slackers that they were, had sent only thank-you notes in the minimalist style, and that, Katie knew, was the real reason they'd been cut off. They'd neglected the grandmother that didn't like them but liked to give them money. It made Katie feel bad, and only partly because her income had disappeared overnight.

"But money is only energy, fleeting and abundant," the wealthy ladies in her goddess group would trill. "Never, never let it stop you from living your life." In that case, why else did she stay with Wilson? Because to leave would mean putting her kids in day care and going to work, something she couldn't bring herself to do. Mainly because, who wanted to work? She'd never had a job that hadn't felt like it was ruining her "real" life: lounging, eating chocolate, and reading *People* magazine. But it was more than that. It was the feeling when she was small of coming home to an empty house. And the joy when her mother finally arrived, in living color, not quite to be believed, wearing her turtleneck and chunky macramé necklace, smelling of pencil shavings and the plastic of overhead projectors, bearing treats from Kienow's—lemon turnovers or chocolate éclairs. As if the sun had roared back on. Wonderful, yes, but Katie didn't want her kids to live that way, in alternating worlds of dark and light. So she'd sit with them, like a mother bird in a nest, until it felt safe to shove them out—when they were thirty-five, perhaps.

Cleopatra yawned, her jaws gaping like those of a small hippo. Katie stuck her hand in her mouth. The dog seemed to like it and gnawed gently on her fingers. Her tongue was velvety, the insides of her cheeks slick, her teeth pleasingly hard. After a few minutes, Katie got up, resting her drool-covered palm on Steven's door. A thrill of anticipation rushed through her. She knocked gently and, when no one answered, let herself in, Cleo scrambling over her feet to enter first.

The condo was dark. The dining room table was littered with beer bottles, some toppled and dark brown, others glowing amber in the light from the street. Framed posters of boxers in black and white sat propped against the walls, and the air smelled thick and stale like a gym. The place was a mess, dishes on the counter and clothes all over the floor. There were boxes, too, Katie noticed. Was Steven moving? Was Lucy moving in? The boxes sat alone or in stacks, a few blown open, towels and silverware spilling over their tops.

Katie was nervous. What was going on? She heard a noise and looked into the living room. A lone figure sat on the couch, his shoulders hunched, his mouth slack, concentrating on a video game. It was Steven's friend Jay, jamming the buttons on the controller, cursing under his breath. Katie sighed, relieved. And a little excited, too, for Jay had recently ended a stint in the army, returning to Kalamazoo older if not wiser, and irresistibly cute.

"Hey," Katie said, but Jay didn't hear. He continued to play, bouncing slightly on the oversized couch.

Jay was the friendly fuckup in Steven's "posse" of friends. He was a sweet guy but an alcoholic, always in some kind of trouble. As a teen, he'd been sent to the Oregon desert, to a wilderness camp for bad kids. After becoming deathly ill from a spider bite, he'd escaped and hitchhiked home. When he turned eighteen, MIPs became DUIs, and bar fights and petty thefts were taken more seriously. He spent time in county, sporting the orange jumpsuit, and more time in KPEP, a place that was like jail except you were expected to work, to pay your debt to society. As a member of the KPEP team, Jay had poked up trash along the highway, dug actual ditches, and even spent a day scooping up poop at the annual Doggie Walkathon. Due to a paperwork error, he'd been featured as one of Kalamazoo's Most Wanted, getting his picture in the *Gazette* and nearly giving his grandmother a heart attack. Next came the army where he'd dealt meth and been crowned PT champ. Home now, he was no longer the scrawny punk in the hooded sweatshirt, a backpack of beer on his back, playing bombardo with the kids in the street, that Katie remembered. The army had turned him into a man. He was bigger, both physically and in his personality. The PT had filled him out, and the dealing had given him confidence, nice clothes, a new car, and money in the bank. Always painfully shy, he looked you in the eye now when he spoke.

"Jay," Katie said, this time a little louder.

Jay jumped, startled. He looked at her then did a comic double take. "Jakie's mom? What the fuck?"

"I'm sorry. I didn't mean to scare you. I just needed to talk to Steven . . ." Katie blushed, thinking it probably did seem odd for Jakie's mom to appear in the middle of the night, half-dressed, her big toe bleeding, a slobbering dog not her own in tow. "I had this . . . panic attack . . . thing. And then I couldn't sleep, so . . ."

Jay nodded, his dark eyes sympathetic. His buzzed black hair gleamed in the light of the TV. His skin was a soft caramel color, set off nicely by his pale button-down shirt. As Katie looked at him, she realized he was almost the spitting image of Jake's dad, Anthony. They were about the same size, barely taller than she was, with slight but muscular builds. They both had big noses and a shy, gentle demeanor. "Steven's in his room, on the phone." Jay laughed nervously. "What are you looking at?"

"Nothing." Katie smiled. "It's just that you look exactly like Jake's dad. Down in New Mexico. I never noticed before. It's weird . . ."

"Oh."

"He was PT champ, too."

"Yeah? Who told you that? It's embarrassing."

"No, it's not. It's neat. I wish I were in that good of shape." Katie wrapped her arms around her waist. "You could be on *Survivor*," she added, crossing her legs and resting her weight on one foot.

"Cool." Jay nodded. "I love *Survivor*."

"Oh so do I. I love that show."

There was an awkward silence. To Katie's ears she'd sounded loud and way too enthusiastic. *Oh so do I. I love that show,* mocked a voice in her head. She pulled her hair from its ponytail, letting it fall around her shoulders. She looked down at her bleeding toe, then knelt and wiped it with the tail of her T-shirt. Cleopatra sniffed at the wound, gave it a tentative lick.

"Your hair's so long." Jay leaned forward, resting his elbows on his knees. It was a girlish, eager pose, and it made Katie like him. "You're like Ariel in *The Little Mermaid*."

"Shut up."

"Why? It's nice. You usually wear it up, though, don't you?"

"I have no idea." Katie stretched her arms overhead, enjoying the attention. Her T-shirt rode up, and she bent her head to arrange it, letting her hand rest on her bare stomach. When she looked up, Jay was watching, an appreciative look on his face.

"Anyway." He blushed, nodding at the bedroom door. "Steven's in there on the phone, fighting with his girl. She left a while ago. They've been going at it all night."

"Why?" Katie was intrigued.

Jay shrugged. Behind him on the big-screen TV, two man/beast creatures roared and beat their chests. As if hypnotized and the roaring a secret signal, Jay returned his attention to the set. He clicked a button. The man/beast with the red-veined wings sank to its knuckles and galloped away.

"Steven didn't say why? Jay? Why they were fighting?" Katie was annoyed. She hated video games. People disappeared into them. One moment you were talking and the next—poof—they were gone.

"Nah. He didn't say. But the wedding's off—again." The man/beast with the dripping yellowish horns snarled, moving quickly through a series of bodybuilding poses. Jay picked up the controller and was instantly sucked back into battle.

Katie sighed. "Maybe I'd better come back . . ."

Jay didn't answer.

Katie made a move to go and tripped over Cleo, idling by her feet. This set the bulldog off, and she began to growl and bark at Jay, whose fault it obviously was. "Cleo!" The dog barked louder, dancing to and fro like a crazed boxer.

"Shit." Jay dropped the controller and held up his hands, looking amused and scared at the same time. "I didn't even see the little fucker. He doesn't bite, does he?"

"It's a girl, and I have no idea. Cleopatra!" Katie clenched her teeth, resisting the urge to kick her canine friend. Cleo was now officially berserk, snapping at Katie's hand when she tried to grab her red rhinestone collar.

"I've seen that dog around." Jay got up and began foolishly edging around the love seat, toward them. "She's a crazy motherfucker. The other night I went out to my car to get cigarettes, and she was hiding in the bushes. When she heard me, she came barreling out and chased me all the way to the mailboxes."

"Katie," Steven shouted from the bedroom, his voice almost drowned out by a fresh volley of barks. He sounded angry. Katie looked at Jay helplessly.

"Watch this. Dogs love me." Jay knelt and flipped Cleopatra onto her back, vigorously scratching her belly. She shut up immediately. Katie glanced at Steven's bedroom door, then back at Cleopatra. The fickle thing had gone limp, drooling with pleasure.

"Will you two be OK?" Katie touched Jay's shoulder. She could feel the heat of his body through his shirt. He smelled faintly of cologne. Katie always thought of smells as colors. "It means you're autistic," Wilson had said. Jay smelled green, a soft fuzzy green, like a fern nestled in a woodsy bank. Larry Johnson had smelled brown. Brown was . . . just awful. Most girls she knew smelled pink, or sometimes various shades of blue. Jake was a reddish cinnamon, Paul a deep-space blue, and Rose the pinks and yellows of sunlight, with touches of salty sea green. Wilson wasn't a color. He smelled sad, of smoke and coffee and aloneness. Katie looked at Jay kneeling before her, his head bent, the nape of his neck exposed. Steven bellowed again from the bedroom. She wondered what she was doing.

"Go on." Jay broke her reverie. "Me and crazy are going to hang out. Aren't we, crazy?" He grabbed Cleopatra's jowls and gave them a gentle shake. She closed her eyes, groaning happily.

. . .

Steven sat on the edge of his bed facing the wall, a bottle of whiskey in hand. He wore plaid pajama bottoms and a faded Mickey Mouse T-shirt stretched tight across the shoulders. His room was a disaster, littered with boxers and dirty socks, men's magazines and—for some reason—several crushed vermilion carnations. Like all of his belongings, his bed was enormous, a tangled mess of pale satiny sheets and fake fur comforters. "Katie," he shouted again, setting the bottle on the nightstand. He sounded like a lazy teenager, summoning his mom. Katie laughed, jumped on the bed, and grabbed him from behind.

"I'm right here, you idiot." She kissed his neck, watching herself in the mirrored headboard. She flipped her hair so it fell across his chest.

He made a spitting noise. "Ugh, it's in my mouth." He turned around, pushing her away. "Why'd you bring Cleo here? I've told you, that's not a nice dog. She's going to wake up Abby."

"I'm sorry. She was on your porch eating garbage. She forced her way in, I had no—"

"OK, OK. Whatever."

Katie lay back on his bank of pillows—he had six—quiet. "I guess you're in a bad mood," she ventured.

Steven sighed. He found the phone, buried in the sheets, and threw it across the room. It hit the wall with a sharp crack. "She fucking hung up on me," he said. "Lucy. All we do is fight. The wedding's off again. I swear I'm moving to China."

"Good thing you speak the language."

"Right . . ."

"Say something. Please? Just once. I promise I'll never ask again."

"Fuck off."

"That doesn't sound like Chinese."

"Katie. You don't understand." Steven looked tired. His beard was scruffy, and his hair stuck out on top of his head. His shirt, Katie noticed, was a watery pink, as if it had been washed with something red.

"What don't I understand?" Katie closed her eyes. She stretched out her leg, finding his lap with her foot. His pillows smelled of him. It was a summery smell: hot glittery pavement, beer and salt and sweat. She turned her head, inhaling deeply. In the living room she could hear Jay talking to Cleo in a soft, soothing voice.

Steven grabbed her legs and pulled until she was lying beneath him. Katie sighed. The thrill of his manliness, his red beard, the sexy twinkle in his dark brown eyes! He fell on top of her with a grunt, slipping his hands down her shorts in order to get a firm grip on her ass. "This," he gave an emphatic squeeze, "has got to stop. Me and you. Like now. Like tonight. For good and forever. It can't happen again."

"OK. Fine." Katie's tone was agreeable. They'd had the same conversation many times since the night last winter when Wilson had abandoned her at Steven's dinner party. Lucy had left for work, and as Katie was getting ready to go, Steven, lounging on the velvety couch, had grabbed her hand and pulled her down on top of him. They'd only kissed then, but as winter thawed, their strict parameters—kissing only, which didn't mean a thing—had, too.

Sex with Steven was like a drug, something that had little to do with her normal state of consciousness. She'd experimented at first: If she kissed him, how intense would the hangover (the guilt) be? Not too bad. And so kissing became the gateway drug to *everything but* and, soon enough, *everything else.* Was it worth the price of the hangover? Maybe. It made her happy. She had more energy and no longer felt numb. She was thinner and prettier and a lot nicer to be around.

Sex with her husband was actually more satisfying physically. With none of the dreamy bullshit, it was an intense experience, like going to war. They crawled into bed naked, but clad in full emotional armor. Their coupling was quick and to the point, their orgasms powerful, their moves honed to perfection over the years. They got in, got the job done, and got out, all in the three minutes allotted them before the kids started pounding on the door. Like all kids, the Lavender kids had radar. They knew when their parents were doing it and instantly set out to put a stop to it. Even Lovely got involved, whining at the door to alert the household that *something was going on.* "It's in the DNA," Wilson had said. "It's a survival mechanism to keep the number of offspring low and therefore insure more food for those lucky enough to have been conceived."

"Once again, I'm stunned by your brilliance," Katie had replied.

"We have to quit putting ourselves in this position." Steven reached over and turned off the light. He wrapped her hair around his hand and gently pulled, kissing her neck and lips. He tasted of whiskey. The heat and weight of his body made her dizzy. He lifted her shirt and licked her nipples, grabbed her shorts and panties, pulling them down around her ankles.

"What position is that?" Katie kicked off the shorts and wrapped her legs around his back. "This one?" she asked, her voice innocent. "Or is it—"

"Stop." Steven shook himself out of his pajama bottoms. He pinned her wrists over her head and slid inside her. Katie caught her breath.

"Never again." Steven's voice was resolute, even grim. He pulled out, spent, and flopped onto his back. A cricket had crept in through the open window and was chirping its heart out beneath the bed. The bedroom was dark, the living room silent, and Katie worried that Jay had let Cleopatra out to roam. Greenish moonlight poured in through the window, floated across the carpet and out the crack beneath the bedroom door. "I mean it. This can't happen again." Steven looked at her, assessing her reaction. Finding none, he pulled her close, kissing the top of her head. Katie rested her cheek on his chest. His body felt like a part of hers still, utterly familiar, yet foreign and exciting at the same time. She opened her mouth, flattening her tongue against his sweaty chest. "And what if you get pregnant? Wilson would kill me—"

"He'd kill us both, it would be a disaster, my life would be over, how can you even . . ." Katie wished he'd shut up. But she was the one going on, wasn't she? Still. Real life was not supposed to intrude—didn't he know that was one of the rules? She never, ever mentioned Lucy, not even the time she'd found her bra at the bottom of the bed, tangled around her ankle. It was an annoying bra, like Lucy herself, padded and perky and petite, and it had made Katie feel huge. She closed her eyes. It was strange being in Steven's room, a bedroom like hers only the exact opposite. Lying together, their feet pointed in the wrong direction. The window was on the wrong side, and so was the bathroom. The noisy guy behind the wall was not *hers*.

Steven sipped his drink, a Jack and Coke so strong Katie could smell it from where she lay. "Why don't you get on the pill?" Ice clinked in her ear. The bass beat of a car stereo bounced down the street. "Not for us, but for your own—"

"Who am I going to be with?"

"Or get your tubes tied."

"Right. That would go over big. 'By the way, Wilson, I'm off to the clinic to get sterilized. I know you had the vasectomy, but I wanted to be extra sure.'"

"I guess it doesn't matter. You're still sort of on your period, right?" Steven tilted her chin and kissed her. "Katie." His voice was a dramatic moan, his eyes squeezed shut. "This is wrong. I'm in love with someone else. I'm engaged to be married, I can't fuck it up."

Katie bit her lip. "Fine. You say this every time. 'I'm in love. I'm engaged.' I get your point. How many times are you going to say it? Just . . . fucking . . ."

"Fucking what?"

"I don't know. It's just not very fun to hear how in love you are with . . . her . . . every time *we* get close. You're saying one thing—you're always saying one thing—but for years your body has been saying another." She made a face. "Not to sound like a soap opera."

Steven sighed. He smoothed her hair, switching to his martyr tone. "It's because I care. I don't want to hurt you; you're my best friend. And I've only ever been honest. I've never lied. I respect you too much—"

"Jesus God, would you stop." Katie slid on top of him, kissed him on the lips. "If you're going to be bad, just do it. Go with it and have fun and quit crying about Lucy. She's not here. I am. It's not the worst thing that could happen to a person."

Steven laughed. "You're so mean." He grabbed her ass, rubbed his flaccid penis against her. "It's hot. It turns me on."

Katie rolled off him. She closed her eyes, burying her face in his side. The night was beginning to feel long, and she wished she were home in her own bed where she belonged. Facing the correct way. Usually she left quickly, for it was dangerous and stupid lying there with him. Lucy could drop by at any moment. Wilson could put two and two together and storm the quiet condo. Katie touched Steven's stomach. "Fat," he mumbled, moving her hand away. She pressed her ear against his chest, listening to his heart. What if this was her life? Would she be happy, sleeping beside him, night after night until the end? Or would she tire of the partying, the coming and going of his goofy friends? What about Abby? Could she love her like her own? It actually seemed easier than loving Steven. Steven she loved the idea of. She loved what radiated off him—the heat and electricity and fun. The guy beneath the sexy vibes—the one that numbed his feelings with alcohol, struggled with schoolwork, worried too much about his mother's opinion—she usually ignored. No, that was a lie. She loved all of him. He, in turn, loved Lucy. Outside, across the grassy yard, the neighbors' front door slammed. Katie sat up. It was time to go. Remembering the boxes in the living room, she asked Steven about them.

"We're moving. Me and Lucy. We bought a house."

"What? Why didn't you tell me?"

"I'm telling you." Steven finished his drink, ice clacking against his teeth. "I didn't want you to get all emotional."

"That's what girls do. They get emotional. You can't *fuck one* and then not deal with the—"

"See?"

"When are you going? I can't believe it. You've always been here. I'm really sad." Katie turned away, unable to leave just yet.

"It's not like we're moving to Mars. It's ten minutes from here. Lucy and I are starting our life together. It's a good investment. For me, and now that she has her winnings from Vegas and the settlement money—"

"Do you know how she got them? Her winnings?" Katie stared into his darkened bathroom, feeling mean. Last spring, when January told her the story of Lucy's heist, she hadn't believed her. But then she'd started to think. Was it possible to win as big in Vegas as Lucy had—nearly fifty grand, she'd bragged to Jan—without playing big to begin with? And why *hadn't* Steven's mother pursued the case with the police? Had she suspected the truth but not wanted it confirmed? If so, why not? Why not get rid of stupid Lucy?

"She won," Steven said.

"No. I mean the seed money. The money she *used* to win. If you don't know, you should ask her sometime—"

"What are you talking about?" Steven sat up. "Katie, this is not a bad thing. It'll be easier this way. Lucy is flipping out. And part of it's because of you. She doesn't care if we're friends, if Jake and Abby are friends. 'You can't have some girl over there when I'm not.' That's what she said tonight. That's what we were fighting about."

"What are you saying?"

"She doesn't want us . . . hanging out . . . ever. Unless she's here, too."

"We can't even be friends?"

"No. Unless she's here. That's what she said. She said she was *feeling things*. She was having dreams and shit."

"That's insane." Katie turned around, looked into his eyes. "You're breaking up with me."

"Katie. We're not going out." Steven gave her a pitying look. "I'm engaged to be married. I'm in love with someone else. I—"

"I. I. I. If you say it again, I'm going to hurt you. I mean, as a friend. You're breaking up with me as a friend?"

Steven nodded. "Don't put it that way. It had to end sometime."

Katie closed her eyes. She was so stupid, what had she expected? Sleeping with someone engaged to someone else—did she think it would be lasting, meaningful, and good? She hadn't wanted that anyway, had she? Of course she had, what else did a person want? Getting up, she stumbled in the dark, banging her shin against the bedpost. Her underwear had disappeared (Good, let Lucy find them. No, don't. They were big and ugly and period stained). She grabbed her shorts and pulled them on backward. Her shirt was nowhere to be seen.

"Don't put it that way," Steven repeated.

"Don't put what *what* way? Where are my clothes?" Katie found his Guinness T-shirt on the floor and slipped it over her head. He was leaving? Fine. Then she'd keep his favorite shirt. Under the bed, the cricket trilled its valentine. She stepped on a carnation, its body cold and squishy beneath her bare foot. "I'll see you when Lucy's around." She paused at the doorway. "It'll be fun. We can talk about how skinny she is. We can talk about low-fat food."

"You talk about that stuff all the time."

"But with you it means something." Tears welled in her eyes.

Steven sighed, threw his arm across his face. Katie shut the door behind her.


"Hey, Katie. Can I holler at you?"

"I don't know what you're saying." Katie watched Jay get out of his car and amble across the court. She sat on her porch with Lovely and Cleopatra—found wallowing in her flower bed—and drank from a bottle of water. Her insides still stung from Steven's rejection. She was such a liar, to herself and everyone else. She'd always told herself he was a treat, like a latte or chocolate. Would she feel the same desperate hollowness if all the lattes in the world went away? Probably. But the truth was, he meant more than a four-dollar coffee drink. When they were close, she felt safe. He enveloped her, created a space in which she could rest and feel loved. With him she felt like a child again, rocking in the old green La-Z-Boy with her mom. Who would want to lose that?

Jay sat down beside her, a bottle of beer and a cigarette in his left hand, a new six-pack dangling from the other. Cleo dragged herself onto his lap, reminding Katie of a swamp beast, slithering out of the muck. She was such a prehistoric, freaky creature—with dogs like that in the world, you knew God had a sense of humor. The night was hot and still, stars barely visible in the hazy sky. They sat in silence, both dogs snoring. After a bit, a truck roared up the lane, blaring country music. The engine died, ticked in the heat. Out hopped Lucy.

"You left in the nick of time," Jay said under his breath.

"Hey, partiers." Lucy sauntered across the street. She wore tight ruby velvet jeans and a camisole, a jeweled barrette holding her bangs off her face.

Jay nodded and swigged his beer. "How's the lawsuit coming?" he asked, nudging Katie with his elbow.

"Oh, those fuckers are going to pay. We were out dancing tonight, and every time I twirled, I was dizzy." Lucy demonstrated. She pirouetted awkwardly, lost her balance, and stepped on Katie's zinnias with an orange stiletto. "Things still aren't right. They need to be held accountable. You can't have a restaurant and have shit falling on people."

On the last day of Lucy and Steven's trip to Las Vegas, a crime had been committed against her. According to Steven, they'd been sitting in the restaurant of the Hard Rock Hotel having a quick bite before heading to the airport. "Up around the ceiling there were these decorations, these angel baby things," he'd said, filling Katie in upon his return to Kalamazoo.

"You mean cupids?" Katie had sipped her coffee, bored already with the details of his vacation, as well as jealous of Lucy's big win.

"Yeah. But they were Elvis. Elvis cupids, I guess you'd call them. And he was holding a guitar instead of a bow and arrow." Steven looked confused. He took a huge bite of his peanut butter cookie. "I think. Maybe I'm wrong."

"Anyway," she prompted.

Apparently, one of the Elvis cupids, "the size of a house cat and heavy as a cinder block," had been loose. In one horrible instant, it fell from its perch and knocked Lucy unconscious. "Like that." Steven snapped his fingers. "One minute she's eating her fries, bitching about the fact that they're cold and they forgot the ranch dressing, and the next she's out cold, sliding from the booth, this big plaster Elvis thing rolling on the floor beside her."

Katie laughed, horrified. Seeing the look on his face, she slapped her cheeks. "Oh my God, oh my God!" she said, contrite.

A waiter not their own had dialed 911. Lucy was rushed to the university medical center, already mumbling in the back of the ambulance about a lawsuit. A CT scan and MRI checked out OK, and she was diagnosed with a concussion. "They said she'd be fine," Steven said. "But she's not. She's had headaches since it happened, and they're getting worse. If she flips her head forward, it feels like her brain is whooshing around. She said that. 'Like my brain is a bunch of raw eggs and they're whooshing around.' I told her to quit flipping her head, but that only made her mad."

A week after the assault, after the Hard Rock had comped their room and cold fries, Lucy found a lawyer and filed suit. Since then, she spoke incessant legalese and crowed about the "seven-figure settlement" that would soon be hers. And her symptoms—she obsessed over those, too, a new one plaguing her every month. In June she saw spots floating before her eyes "like thin slices of zucchini, only purple." In July, she had a strange taste, "like lettuce," in the back of her throat. "What, is she turning into a salad?" Wilson had asked.

"Jess was looking for you," Lucy said now, smiling coyly at Jay. She stood over him, towering in her heels, and he seemed to shrink back into the shadows, Cleopatra dozing protectively on his lap.

"What did that ho want?"

"You know what she wanted." Lucy turned to Katie. "Jessica is our friend, and she stalks Jay. He hates her—"

"I do, I fucking hate that bitch," Jay interrupted.

"But Jess doesn't care. She waits until he's drunk. And I mean really drunk, like blacked out, and then she gets him to . . . you know . . ." Lucy broke off purple zinnias and stuck them in her barrette.

"She waits until I don't know what I'm doing, and then she pounces, like a ninja."

Lucy laughed. "She stalks him, waits until he blacks out, and then gets him to sleep with her. Every time. It's been going on for years. You'd think he'd be smarter." Lucy nudged Jay with her foot, rolled her eyes at Katie. "I think he's secretly in love and doesn't want to admit it."

"Yeah. Sure I am, Luce. Look at the girl. Please."

"That's so sexist. Because she's fat, she's not attractive?"

"Yeah!"

"It's not like you're powerless." Katie shifted uncomfortably. She and Jessica had a common ploy—how humiliating. "Maybe you shouldn't drink when you know she's going to be around."

"He's an alcoholic, Katie," Lucy said. "It's not exactly an option."

"Not drinking is not an option," Jay concurred.

"Well then, quit sleeping with her. I mean, if you quit giving her what she wants, she'll quit hanging around. Right?"

"No." Lucy shook her head.

"Nah," Jay agreed. "This has been happening since like eighth grade."

"Then I guess you're stuck." Katie laughed. "Such a funny problem to have." She stretched out her legs, rubbing Lovely's stomach with her foot. Steven had dealt with his stalker; he'd cut her out of his life. Thinking of him made her chest hurt, and she forced the thoughts away. Beside her, Jay leaned forward, setting his empty beer bottle on the windowsill. As he sat back, he briefly brushed Katie's calf with his fingertips. She jerked her leg away, embarrassed (she hadn't shaved), and excited too, a shiver of electricity rushing up her thigh. What was wrong with her? He was so like Anthony—soft-spoken and shy, dark and sexy, a trained soldier that could kill with his bare hands anyone that dared mess with her—she was finding him irresistible. Which was odd, as she'd easily resisted the real Anthony for years. All of it—the nonsense with Steven, the phone calls to Oregon and panic attacks, and now the attraction to Jay—was proof that she was 100 percent out of control. She was a mom. Moms that can't sleep stay in bed. They dream up cookie recipes or read about how to cook a roast.

She didn't even know, exactly, what a roast was. Her specialty was garden burgers and those she often burned. She never prepared meat. The slimy raw stuff was disgusting to handle, although if Wilson cooked it, she had no problem eating.

Lucy kicked off her heels and squatted before Katie. She wore fuchsia eyeliner and her blue eyes were luminous. She smelled of spicy flowers and smoke. Katie was nervous. Was Lucy going to hurt her, confront her with the feelings and dreams she'd been having? Guilt gnawed in her gut. She could feel Steven, his warm wetness inside her, traces of his heat shimmering all over her body. What a bad friend and neighbor she was. And he was leaving—she could hardly bear to think of it. "When's Jan going to have that baby?" Lucy rested her fingertips on the ground. She squatted easily, like a yogi. Katie was impressed. The chunky jewels and blooms in her hair were like a ceremonial headdress. She radiated good health.

"I don't know." Katie shrugged. She leaned back a bit, as Lucy was in her comfort zone. "It could be any second. She's getting restless and more emotional, and all she wants to eat are Junior Mints and Coke. Those are signs. Not the Junior Mints and Coke, specifically, but—"

"And she's huge." Lucy's eyes lit up. "It's not that cute pregnant mama look anymore. It's more . . . monstrous, I guess, is what you'd say."

"Well . . ."

"I can't wait to have kids." Lucy threw her head back, the golden twinkle lights Katie had strung from the eaves dancing in her eyes. "I want seven, all girls, all of them in matching fluffy dresses, like little daffodils. A whole fancy bouquet—all cute, all mine—I guarantee you I get pregnant on my wedding night."

"I thought the wedding was off," Jay said. Lucy ignored him. She was looking expectantly at Katie. There was yearning in her eyes, as if she wanted something Katie had.

Katie didn't know how to reply. "Leave me alone," she wanted to say. And, "Why do you get to start at the beginning? Why do you get Steven?" But all she said was "Wow," as she reached for her water.


"Lucy's fucking nuts," Jay announced, treading water, shivering in his boxers. "'Seven babies, all in daffy dilly dresses,'" he mocked. Droplets of water sparkled in his hair, and the lake spread black and glassy around him. It was near dawn, the pines to the east lined in metallic pink. Katie had agreed to go for a quick swim as long as she maintained complete control by driving them in her own car. Why not be crazy, impulsive, and fun?

January was home. And she'd be back before anyone knew she was gone. As for Wilson, if he asked—which he wouldn't as he'd then have to explain where he'd been half the night—she'd tell him she'd had a panic attack and gone for a drive—practically the truth. At the last second, Cleopatra had hopped in her car. No amount of coaxing could get her to budge from the floor of the backseat, so they'd brought her along. Katie could see her now, pacing near the shore, a ghostly blot, barking at the nothingness that had swallowed up her friends.

"No." Katie lifted her hair off her neck and wrung it out, careful to keep her breasts underwater. She wished she'd thought of putting on a bra before they left. And why were they talking about Lucy? Who cared about the silly thing? "She's just young and pretty and used to ruling the world. I was the same way when I was her age—the queen of the universe, the princess at her ball."

Jay dove under and came up spitting water. "You still look good. I wouldn't have wanted to hang out with you if you didn't."

"How shallow of you." Katie smiled.

"I mean it. Your body's tight."

"Like strong? You've never even touched me. I guarantee you it's not—"

"I mean *tight*. Like, good. *Tight*."

"Hmmm." Katie floated on her back, pleased, her nipples hard in the cool air. The lake water was cold and seemed to penetrate even her bones, making them clean and new. She dove into the murkiness, flipped onto her back, and drifted. The sky overhead was a luminescent green, slightly wrinkled in places like the skin of a newborn baby. She swam over to Jay, then stood up, making a face when her feet touched the slimy bottom. "What I'm saying is when you're a girl, like maybe eighteen to twenty-five, you can get whatever you want, just because you're cute. You can wriggle out of speeding tickets, buy beer before you're twenty-one, get into clubs free—whatever. But then—because nobody stays young forever—you're closer to forty, and maybe you still look good—*for your age*—but all of a sudden you're invisible. People are calling you *ma'am* or *that lady*, and they're no longer carding you, and you're like, 'Wait a minute, I thought it was all about me.'"

Jay looked disturbed, as if he'd suddenly found himself in the middle of a consciousness-raising group, a circle of women gazing at their vaginas. "Lucy's still insane," he said after a moment. "She hates me—"

"No, *me*. She hates me." Katie leaned back, letting the water slick her hair. "She told Steven she didn't want us hanging out anymore. Unless she was there, too. Can you believe it? It's ridiculous."

"I guess." Jay laughed. His teeth were crooked and white, and his smile was familiar in a way that made Katie feel as if she'd found a lost friend. "But . . . I mean, you are fucking her man. You can't blame her for not liking that."

"Oh my God, no. I'm not. Not anymore." Katie dove under, her words lost in the dark water. She emerged as Jay picked up a rock and skipped it toward the shore. The rock bounced one, two, three times before sinking. Smooth ripples flowed outward. It was the same lake Katie brought her kids to, although it was nicer now, the families that squawked on its surface like gaudy birds gone. She loved the way it welled out of nothingness, deep and soothing, quiet in its semicircle of pines. Lake Michigan, a half hour away, she found depressing. It always seemed to be gray there. And the way it was like an ocean—with waves and undercurrents, an opposing shoreline too far away to see—but wasn't, bothered her. The real ocean for her was the Pacific, raging against the Oregon coast, icy cold and foaming, filling up the Devil's Punchbowl, spewing out starfish and sand dollars and those blue glass floats her mother always seemed to find. Lake Michigan reminded her of her life in Kalamazoo. In the same way it was "like an ocean," her life here often felt "like a life," as flimsy as the paper-thin walls of their condo.

Jay ran dripping from the lake. He spread his shirt on the sand and sank to his knees, shaking water from his hair. His body was perfect, smooth and brown and slender. Katie felt like she was in high school again, the same hot anticipation, the same dizziness rushing through her veins. She watched as he pulled a beer from the six-pack and opened it with his teeth, spitting the cap into the sand. Unbelievably cool! He had a dirty toughness Katie loved. Beneath his shy demeanor, he was a cowboy, filthy and nasty, and she could feel her legs growing weak. She was free—of Steven and Wilson and her entire tangled-up life. She was naked in the big black world, with no one to tell her no. "Turn around," she shouted, lying on her stomach near the foamy shore, letting the water move her. She might feel like a teenager, but she no longer had the body of one, and there was no way he was going to watch as she emerged from the surf like a middle-aged Venus, belly jiggling, saggy boobs swaying.

Jay liked to talk, much more so than Wilson and Steven. Sitting in the sand, he told Katie stories of the guys he'd known in the army, of the time his lieutenant had snorted a bunch of meth, gone for a nine-mile morning run, returned to Jay's bunk, and had a heart attack.

"Yikes," Katie said. She picked up handfuls of sand and drizzled it onto her legs. She thought of what it would be like if people's bodies were coated with sand, pretty colors like lemon and aquamarine. Jay's talk was soothing; it was almost like hanging out with Steven. For the first time in weeks, she felt good—clean and clear and serene. She watched as the sun touched the surface of the lake, left its glimmering thumbprint. The pine trees were shaped like party hats and filled with crazy birdsong.

Jay's dream, he said, was to be on *Survivor*. His ultimate dream was that they do a reality show all about him. "Because my life is a total fucking show," he said, hugging his knees to his chest, rocking slightly in the cool air. His ears stuck out and he looked like a little kid. Cleopatra, romping nearby, began to dig a frantic hole.

*My life is a total fucking show.* Katie found herself memorizing the line in order to tell Wilson later. It struck her as funny and kind of sad. *And you were diagnosed as a sociopath with narcissistic tendencies when?* she thought she might say. Who would she attribute the "show" line to? Jay, of course, but she'd have to invent the context. "Do you mean it's false?" she asked. "Like you're acting in a way that isn't really you?"

Jay gave her a quizzical look. "No. I mean my life is a fucking show. Like all the drama and shit. Every time I go out I get into a fight. I've been kicked out of every bar and nightclub in this town."

"You must be proud."

Jay laughed. Cleopatra, still digging, began to fling sand onto Katie. The sand smelled cold and elemental. They got up and walked to a battered picnic table, tilted on the edge of the beach, chained to a cement block. As he settled on the table, Katie on the bench at his feet, Jay launched into a story about the time he was involved in a drive-by shooting. Late one night, he said, he and a friend were driving on the north side of Kalamazoo, where the streets all had old-timer names: Lulu and Ada, Willard and Bessie and Frank. At a stoplight, a dented silver Chrysler pulled up next to them. And then, *blam!* Before Jay knew what was happening, the passenger window was blown out, glass everywhere, and his friend, sitting in the seat beside him, had been shot twice in the head.

"Did he die?" Katie asked, horrified.

"Nah. But he's fucked up."

"What did you do?"

"I got out of the car. I'm running around, and everything's weird, like bright even though it's dark, like I'm in a fucking movie. I'm pounding on doors, trying to find help. And no one will answer. It's the middle of the night, it's a bad neighborhood, they'd probably heard the shots . . . So finally I run all the way to the police station. It's blocks away. I can't hardly breathe. My chest feels like it's going to explode . . ." Jay paused. He took a deep breath.

"Jeez," Katie said.

"Yeah," Jay agreed. "So I get the cops. We go back. My boy's bleeding all over the seat. The ambulance comes . . ." He stopped, shook his head, his face tense. After a moment, he picked up a beer cap and flipped it toward the lake.

"Is that it?" Katie was disappointed. What about the blood, the pieces of skull stuck to the windshield? What had the friend said right before he was shot? Were they talking about donuts or something equally mundane? What had he said after being shot? What did *anyone* say after being shot in the head? Disbelief, Katie thought, would be the predominant feeling, utter and total disbelief. Because how could something like that happen to *you*? What had it smelled like there in the car in the middle of the night on a deserted street in the bad part of Kalamazoo? Was it summer? Was it unbearably humid, the kind of hot that made you want to kill? Did it smell metallic and wet and raw? Or was it winter, the air icy and dry, so cold it burned when you breathed in? Did droplets of blood spatter Jay's cheek? Did they freeze as he ran for help?

"I peed," Jay offered. "When it happened. Just like that, right in my pants. I didn't even know I'd done it until later." He grinned, staring at his hands. "It's so weird. You read about shit like that, people pissing in their pants, but you never think it really happens until it happens to you."

"Do you think you're still freaked out? Like traumatized for life?"

"Because I peed?"

"Yeah." Katie hit his leg. He grabbed at her hand, but she pulled it away. "No. Because your friend was nearly murdered."

"Nah." Jay shook his head. "I mean, I wasn't the one that got shot," he pointed out.

Katie smiled. She moved up onto the table beside him, dangling her legs off the edge. The grass edging the beach was wild and thick, dark green blades tangled. "Did they ever find the guy that did it?"

"It was a drug deal gone bad . . ." Jay gave her a sideways look. "You don't want to know. But then the fuckers put a hit on me! I had to go live in Kentucky with my uncle. This tough backwoods motherfucker. The first night I'm there, we go to get beer, he hits a possum, pulls over, picks it up off the road, swings it by its tail, and flips it into the back of the truck. 'We got supper,' he says, grinning like a maniac."

"Ugh. Yuck. That's so sick. You didn't eat any, did you?"

"Hell no." Jay laughed. He took her hand in his, his dark eyes bright. "Katie," he said, his voice soft. "Do I look like the kind of guy that eats road kill?"

She shook her head. His hands were hot, and she was nervous, her own hands cold. A shiver ran up her spine. What was she doing so far from home? But the lake was just five minutes away, she reminded herself, and her life wasn't going to stop, was it? Just because Steven had dumped her? She cleared her throat. "So your friend, he's OK? The one that got shot?"

"Yeah. But he's fucked up."

"Like how? Define 'fucked up.'"

"Like fucked up. Like he doesn't think right anymore."

"Oh." Katie moved closer. "Your life is crazy . . ." she began. She touched his leg, the denim of his jeans rough beneath her hand. She could see the bulge in his pants . . . and the glint of her wedding ring, which she turned around.

"Like a show." Jay leaned in to kiss her. It was an awkward kiss. Katie's teeth bumped his, and she sat back, embarrassed. She wanted him, she thought. Her cheeks were flushed, her body hot, and she was finding it hard to sit still. But what if he found her old, or flabby, or disgusting in some way she'd never even thought of? That was the thing about casual sex: It made her feel anything but casual. It made her feel almost unbearably intense, as if her very existence depended upon Jay's reaction—to her, to her body—nothing short of enthrallment, she the magician, Jay the drooling subject, being OK. She sighed. What a fucking psycho she was. But enough thinking . . .

"You should pick better friends." She traced the inside seam of his jeans. "It sounds like you're running with the wrong crowd."

"Nah." Jay kissed her again. He tasted of beer, his tongue warm in her mouth. "That's why I like you," he said shyly. "I've never been with a girl like you. You're smart and nice. You think about things and you know where you're going. You're not like the hos I usually . . . you know . . . fuck."

Katie laughed. "Such a compliment. But the thing is I'm not nice. Or smart." She tried to smile, but it felt forced. "At least not about the things that matter."

Steven always said that Jay would end up drinking himself to death. Or that he'd end up in prison or killing himself in a car wreck. Jay agreed. He had terrible blackouts; trouble stalked him. Katie's grandmother would say that he *lacked common sense*. Iris would call his behavior *acting like an ass*, and Wilson would deem him a *drunken clown*. Katie agreed with them all, but it didn't stop her from wanting him. In fact, it made her want him more. There was a damage there that she could sense. She could feel it, as if it were a palpable thing, and it was familiar, even a turn-on. "I know you," she wanted to say as they kissed on the picnic table, Jay's hand down her shorts, Cleopatra gnawing on the leg of the bench. "I know all about this. I am it and you are me and I want to fix it, fix me, or just rest in it—this brokenness that's so familiar—just rest for a while in what is real and the opposite of what the rest of the world says is true." You made it up. You imagined it. It was a bad dream. Don't talk about it; it bothers your mother. Quit fussing. *But it was true.* But it couldn't be. No person could be that bad. You must be crazy, delusional. Why don't you just get over it and get on with your life?

She wanted to scream that she couldn't, that it wasn't OK and it never would be. Not until that person had suffered the way he had made her suffer. Not until everything good had been taken away, leaving him lost and alone. She believed in ultimate justice, of course; she knew that if there was a hell, Larry Johnson had a particularly fiery spot reserved just for him, but she wanted justice that she could hear and smell and taste. She wanted to terrorize the bastard. She wanted to laugh at him the way he'd laughed at her every time she'd cried, every time she'd screamed for her mom. She wanted him to be afraid to look another person in the eye. She wanted him to feel the filth he'd shoved onto her. She wanted him to know the depths of hopelessness. The feeling you had when God no longer cared. When he'd turned his back on you, sent you away, promising it would never happen again, when it had—it had gone on and on and on.

Katie put her fingers in Jay's mouth. He sucked on them, and she slid them down his pants. "You're so hot," he said, his lips against her neck. "I can't believe this. The other day I was like, 'Jakie's mom, she's so fine. I'd like to get with her.'"

"When?" Katie pulled at the buttons on his fly.

"You were outside, picking flowers. I was talking to Ron, over at Steven's . . . And Ron was like, 'It ain't gonna happen. One, you have to go through Steven'—"

"What?" Katie sat back, intrigued.

"He said, 'One, you have to go through Steven. And two, he'd say no.'"

Katie frowned, pleased. "Like I'm his. Like I belong to him—"

"That's what I said. And Ron was wrong; it wasn't true. I was like, 'Steven, man, I'd really like to get with her, Jakie's mom, she's looking fine.' And he plays it up, thinking hard, you know, like he's the fucking Godfather. And then after he's made me sweat, he's like, 'OK.' So . . ." Jay smiled, shook his head. "I'm sorry, I'm drunk. I'm saying way too much here."

"No, no. It's all right . . ." Katie tried to think of something witty to say but couldn't. It felt as if someone had kicked her in the chest. She bit her lip. Tears filled her eyes. "It's just so . . . I don't even know . . ." She looked away, out at the empty lake, at Cleopatra, attempting to drag a tree branch across the beach.

Jay moved into her, his bare chest hot against her own, his lips on hers, his mouth open as he breathed into her, pushed into her, his hands tangled in her wet hair. She didn't want to think, only forget—the way Steven had shrugged her away, the "love" between them something she'd conjured on her own, delusions of a bored housewife, and the phone calls to Oregon, the fear and the craziness and still she couldn't stop, dialing the number she'd memorized sometimes three times a week, the panic, the dead bird, the way she could sometimes feel Wilson's dislike for her, as if it were a separate entity, sitting in the living room watching TV with them—and so what if she felt the same way toward him, it still wasn't fun to be hated in your own home. But now, as her car windows grew steamy, wind whistling through the cracks, it was all falling away. Jay slid deeper inside her, his skin damp with sweat, smelling of the lake, mossy and musky, and her body grew hotter, softening, her heart racing, the wonderful rhythm pulsing in her belly, until she wanted to cry out, "You see, you stupid fuck, you didn't take anything away."

Beside her, in the passenger seat, she glimpsed a man, barrel-chested and short, the scarred leather jacket, the slick and hopeful hair. He sighed heavily, an acre of empty parking lot visible through his bulk. Katie closed her eyes. "Jay," she said, her voice cracking. She grabbed his neck, felt his plush hair, the tops of his naked ears.

"Oh yeah, oh yeah, oh Katie . . . shit." Jay shuddered, collapsed against her. He kissed her. "Just give me a minute," he mumbled into her mouth.

They began again. Outside, the sky was fractured, one side darkening with clouds, the other pressing bright pink against the smeary windows. Katie needed to get home. She glanced at the passenger seat. Nothing. Nothing—wait a minute, where the hell was Cleo? She tried to focus, but after a while it was obvious Jay was done, and she couldn't come the first time, anyway—she was always too tense to let go. Jay sat back, sweating, breathing hard. "Hold on, I need to rest." He jerked up his pants and moved to the other seat. Katie opened the car door. She leaned out, breathing deeply the fresh air as she looked around for the dog. The gravel lot was empty, the path to the beach, the beach and the lapping lake, deserted.

Jay leaned over her legs and grabbed the last bottle of beer. She closed her eyes. The water sounded like laughter, soft and far away.

"Wait, where's the condom?" Katie remembered how impressed she'd been when he'd taken it out earlier, ripping open the wrapper with his teeth, expertly sliding it on. It was bright red, and flavored she saw on the metallic wrapper, cherry, maybe, or strawberry, which was really disgusting if you thought about it, which she hadn't, she hadn't thought at all, only been proud of herself for being safe. But when he'd pulled out, it wasn't on, of that she was sure. And where was the dog? Damn. They'd put her out, she'd whined, wanted to sniff at the garbage in the lot, root in the damp sand. "Why did you come if all you were going to do is complain?" Katie had asked her, annoyed, shoving her out the door.

"Where is it?" Jay said now. He sat back in the seat, eyes closed as he drank his beer. His body was wonderfully brown and solid. Katie touched his tattooed bicep, a feeling of relief fluttering through her. She put on her shorts, attempted to smooth her tangled hair. It felt spongy and sticky at the same time. She pulled down the lighted mirror, resting her hands on her flushed cheeks. Did she look pretty? Was she frightening? She had no idea. Her eyes looked sad, like how she thought gorillas in the zoo sometimes looked, as if there were someone else—a mute and frightened other—trapped inside. She flipped the visor shut. The Guinness T-shirt smelled of Steven, momentarily confusing her. "Wait, where's what?" she said. "The dog or the condom?"

"What do you mean 'the dog'?" Jay smiled like she'd made a joke he didn't get.

"Did you take it off, did you drop it on the floor?"

"What? The condom?"

"Jay." Katie was getting irritated. "Where is the condom?"

"I don't know." He looked around the seat, on the floor of the car, even in the clean ashtray and cup holder. His chest was smooth and hairless, his arms covered with blue and black tattoos—a mermaid with big breasts, the Tasmanian devil, a tribal band, a character that looked Chinese. He touched Katie's thigh. "Is it still in you? I think it's still in you."

"Shit. Shit." Katie slid two fingers inside her vagina, feeling for the condom. *Charming*, a voice in her head hissed. *Two in one night, you're really on a roll.* She turned her face away, her legs open, the breeze cool against her cheek. *And such a ladylike position.* Everything felt the same. She didn't know if she was touching the condom or not. She plucked at spongy flesh, found nothing. She remembered how she'd felt as a kid—her whole life really—as if her "down there" was a gaping hole that anyone could invade, as if there were no *down there* at all. And then she'd had Rose and been amazed and happy to see her girl's little bottom, how pink and puffy and perfectly enclosed it was . . . "It's not there," she said now. Panic welled inside her. To have something stuck that you couldn't find, couldn't get out . . . "Are you sure you didn't have it on when you pulled out?"

"No. Yes. I'm sure. I didn't." Jay shook a cigarette from its box and lit it. He inhaled deeply, blew smoke out the open window. "I think it's still inside you. I came—I couldn't help it, you felt so good—and then when we started again, it had probably already come off, and so when I was . . . you know . . . fucking you again, it just sort of . . . got lost."

"Lost? Jay, that's not OK. We have to find it. Wilson drives this car. If he finds it, if he finds a used condom *in this car*, he is going to freak. And the dog rides in this car. If the dog finds it, or one of the kids . . ." Katie trailed off, the thought too awful to voice. "He will kill me, we have to find it now." She was stammering, her vision blurry with tears. What was wrong with her? Get a grip. Find the condom. Go home where you belong and *never be this stupid again.* She took a deep breath, forcing herself to calm down. "Can you help?"

"Yeah." Jay shrugged as if it were an everyday request. He flipped his dog tags behind his neck, took a final drag off his cigarette, and flicked it out the window. Dutifully he bent toward her, his dark head between her legs, his hands heavy and warm on her thighs. He lifted his head, exhaled smoke. Katie looked away, out the window at the lake, cloud shadows sliding across its surface. She closed her eyes, listened to its hum. She felt Jay's fingers slide up inside her. He poked and prodded, gently at first and then more vigorously. It didn't feel good, which was funny, as the same movements earlier had made her tremble. It was uncomfortable now, and humiliating too, the "hookup," as Steven would call it—the hookup he'd condoned—having turned into a gynecological exam. She felt Jay dig deeper. "Shit. I think I have it." His voice was tight as if he were holding his breath. *Please God,* Katie prayed. She had the urge to drive home and tell Wilson everything. "Can you believe it?" she'd cry as he laughed at her stupidity.

"Now why did you think it was a good idea, to fuck one drunken clown and then his friend?" he would ask. She would shrug and shake her head. She'd say, "So Steven would know I was someone to be missed." She'd tell him how Jay's talk was so full of slang, she hadn't known what he was saying half the time. And how Steven was clueless to the fact that his perfect fiancée was a drug-dealing, safecracking thief, as well as a professional malingerer. "But she's hot," Wilson would say. They'd laugh about the indignity of "the exam." And when things had calmed down, she could tell him about the anger, about how lately she couldn't stand the thought of that man, Larry Johnson, walking the streets, never having had to pay for the damage he'd done, damage so intense that like a mushroom cloud it grew larger over time, billowing into her life, poisoning every corner. "And what do you do with that?" she'd ask, helpless, her arms limp, hands open, tears running down her face, and Wilson could comfort her with his pessimism, he could shake his head and say, "Not a thing, there's not a damn thing a person can do, and that's why the world is fucked." Because the anger scared her. It felt larger than she was, and like it could dismantle a person, reduce them to nothing but smoke.

But of course confiding in Wilson, her best friend and nemesis, was out. "Got it," Jay cried. With a final jab he pulled the condom out of her, limp and spent, a slick and cheery red.

The look was what panicked her. It was the blank and disengaged look of a man who had gotten what he wanted and no longer wanted any more, only wanted to get away, to walk the block or two to his buddy's house—a cop, Jay had said, he worked the seven to seven and would just be getting home—and crash. It was the slightly sick look one had after too much birthday cake. It was Larry Johnson's face after her visits to Number 15, when he'd dropped her near the golf course, practically pushing her from the car, then pulling the door shut and driving off before she'd found her footing. You were no longer useful. You were a thing nobody wanted. And not just a thing, but a repellent thing, like a dirty diaper or a dead cat. Like one of Pixie Tanner's mother's wigs after Vivian had gotten her claws into it.

"Cleopatra's gone." The words sounded unreal to Katie, and she was surprised to have thought of poor Pixie Tanner. A wave of homesickness washed through her; tears spilled down her cheeks. "How can you leave? We have to find her. She's not even my dog."

"Damn. Calm down, OK?" Jay sucked irritably on his cigarette. He looked around as if someone might hear them, as if the lot they were standing in wasn't deserted so early in the morning. He tossed the butt into the gravel and started to back away. "I have to crash, I'm sorry. I'm getting sick, I think. My throat is killing me, and I'm hot, like burning up. If I don't sleep now, I'm going to really be hurting later." He jogged backward onto the grass that rolled like green water up and away from the beach, spreading out into the surrounding park.

"Wait." Katie ran to catch up, her arms crossed over her breasts. Rocks dug into the soles of her bare feet. One jammed her stubbed toe, making her wince. Jay hesitated. His yellow shirt was open. His jeans rode low on his hips, revealing his plaid boxers. Broken light moved across him, his face in shadow, slightly clenched fists in pale light. He was so cute it hurt. He'd been so into her ten minutes earlier. She was sure she'd found a friend, someone to talk to, to maybe walk Lovely with—someone new to make her life fun. What had she done wrong? She wiped her cheeks, forced herself to be calm. "Are you mad?" She made her voice light. "It seems like you're mad. Did I do something to piss you off?"

"Nah." Jay looked at his feet. Then he looked over her right shoulder. "This is just a bad idea. It's a messy situation, you know what I mean? You're married. You're Steven's friend, I'm Steven's friend. You're a mom. You're Jakie's fucking *mom!*"

"But . . ." Katie tried to smile, hating herself for begging. "Moms can still have fun."

"I know . . . I don't know . . ." Jay stared at her feet. When he looked up, he was grinning, his eyes slightly wild. "Katie, this is wrong. I have to go. Let me go, OK?" He jammed his shirt into his pants, turned, and ran across the grass.

Katie watched him go. He was surprisingly fast. But he was the PT champ, she remembered, he could run—what, a three-minute mile? He was Superman, he'd said, that's what his buddies had called him, that's how fast he was. Katie watched as he crested a hill, tripped and went flying, righted himself and kept on. She tried to laugh but couldn't. *I repel people,* she thought. *Send them racing off into the world, away from me, as fast as they can go.*

"What about Cleo?" she called. "What if she gets hit by a car? What if she tries to swim and ends up drowning?"

Jay slowed his pace. He hesitated before turning around. "Dogs can't drown," he yelled, bouncing on his toes. "They're natural-born swimmers, don't you know? And why the fuck would the dog go swimming?"

"She might get confused. She might think it's the way home." Katie paused a moment, marveling at the stupidity of her words. She tried to turn her back on him, to let him run out of her life—after all, they barely knew each other—but her anger got the better of her. "It's *fucking fucked,* by the way, for you to leave me here like this. I thought you were nice, but I was wrong. And guess what? You're *never* going to be on TV." She turned away, her body shaking. *Well, that bridge is burned,* she thought. When she looked again, Jay was gone.

A weeping willow rattled its branches several feet in front of her. Its leaves tinkled like chimes in the rising wind. Dry and papery charms, they made her think of the beads on the hippie babysitter's closet. She could see them, clear orange, that dull '70s brown, flowing through her hands—her little girl hands, small and square and grubby—like loot from a pirate's chest. She'd wanted those beads, only purple, and maybe a few silver, to hang on her closet at home. And weeping willows, too, a whole yard full of them, with their soft green-curtained rooms, the perfect place to hide. She thought of a favorite book from back then, about a little girl ghost who lived in a weeping willow. And another book she'd loved, in which a friendless girl finds a best friend in a department store manne-quin—a mannequin with azure eyes. She remembered the word *azure*, how exciting it had seemed, such an exotic, purring way to say blue.

She sat on the grass, the blades sharp against her thighs. It was the dull-ness in Jay's big brown eyes, the complete lack of interest. It had shocked her; she hadn't seen it coming. And then as he ran away, there was the familiar feeling (so devastating in high school) of having fallen for a ruse, of having been the butt of a practical joke. She fell for it—the drama, the heat and the passion—every time. With Jay, she'd felt like a goddess, as if he couldn't have been more entranced as she unfolded herself, wrapped herself around him. Right up until—when? Until the moment he came. She was such a fool. Would she ever learn?

It started to rain, fat drops staining the dry skin on her arms. She plucked at the grass, breathed the dank air. How she hated Michigan. Rain was different here. Instead of washing the air clean, it hung in it, soaked it, creating a big soggy blanket that wrapped itself around you, smothering you as you tried to go about your day. She had the urge to go home to Portland, but how could she raise her kids in a place that, for her, had turned so ugly? Her insides felt hollow and raw; exhaustion sank into her bones. It wasn't from staying up all night—it felt deeper than that—as if her life itself had worn her out. She'd been running since high school: LA, New Mexico, Iowa, even Las Vegas for a short time, when she'd worked as a cocktail waitress, sleeping with every rock 'n' roller that slouched her way. Now, here in Kalamazoo, sitting at the lake, she had the sense of coming to a stop. It was a strange feeling, scary almost, like being at the top of a Ferris wheel, rocking in thin air, not knowing when the creepy guy at the controls would bring you down.

She got up and walked slowly back to her car. Her eyes ached, and her arms felt shaky and light. "Cleopatra," she called. There was no bark in return. She said it again, softly this time, repeating the name over and over, like a mantra, anything to bring the poor beast home.

# Katie
1973

Elvis, the Big Daddy, was a liar. What did he say? *Go back, little miss. No one will ever mess with you again.* Bullshit. It didn't stop. It went on and on and on.

The third grade. We were reading *The Purple Turtle*, and it was boring. I couldn't stand it. It set my teeth on edge when dummies like Timmy Summers stumbled through, taking forever to read one line. I'd read it already, several times, lying on the grass with Lisa Bidwell, the summer before kindergarten started. School was no longer fun. I wished I could stay home and read what I wanted.

It was late November. Christmas was rattling closer. It was cold and rainy most days. The leaves were no longer crunchy; they were soggy and slippery beneath my Buster Browns. I'd leave school, my cheeks hot and chapped from the wheezing radiator in our classroom. That month there was something new. Every afternoon, the eighth graders came around selling fruit from a cardboard box. For a nickel, you could buy a small yellow apple or orange. Sometimes there were green apples.

"Isn't this wild?" Miss Moss gushed. "A healthy snack, right here in our room." She was wearing one of her new dresses, bright pink and purple like the paint you swirled at the fair. And short—so short, Timmy Summers had told everyone he'd seen the teacher's bottom. I wasn't excited. I liked the fruit, but I didn't like Miss Moss anymore. I didn't like her or her dresses or her bottom. Why? Because she didn't care. She hadn't saved me the way I prayed every night she would. And when she told the class she was getting married at the end of the year, that she was marrying Linda B.'s uncle and would no longer be a teacher, but would be a mom and stay at home like our moms, I didn't cheer and clap and hop up and down like the rest of the kids in Room 3. I stayed seated. I thought, *I hate you.* Because she was going away.

Early December, walking home from school. Grandma Edith had sent us Advent calendars. There were doors, and behind each door was a chocolate. I'd eaten all my chocolates by December 3. My calendar sat abandoned on the kitchen floor, in the corner, open doors fluttering. I'd lost interest. That afternoon, however, I planned to eat January's. The whole month. I'd found hers under her bed. It was mine now. What was she going to do?

It was pouring down rain. My plaid pants were soaked to the knees from the puddles, shallow ones on the sidewalks and deep lakes at the curbs, churning over the leaf-clogged grates. My hair was drenched, streams of water running down my face. The rain was slippery and tasted slightly salty. My clothes were soggy, and I knew that once inside, when I started to dry, I'd steam and itch.

It didn't stop. Elvis was a liar. That wintry afternoon, I heard Larry Johnson's car in the distance, the familiar dull rumble growing more intense every time he shifted gears. He pulled to the curb at the corner of 31st and Rex, his tires flinging up fountains of muddy water. It was where he always found me. His timing was precise. Now I realize he must have waited somewhere near the school until the bell rang and the blacktop was flooded with kids. Then what? He must have circled behind the school, staying out of sight, until he "surprised" me at 31st and Rex. It was the midpoint between school and home. Such a clever man—he'd get me when I was as far away from safety as I could be. Toward the end of the year I changed my route. I started walking down Reed College Place, past the house with the big mirror in the living room, the one that reflected you as you walked, one you trotting down the sidewalk, the other floating in silvery air. I didn't think he'd find me, but he did. Most afternoons, when he pulled up and beckoned for me to get in, I did. What choice did I have? Little girls are easy to get. By the time he found me, I would have already heard his car and gone numb. Having disappeared into my head, I'd climb into the rumbly rusty shell like a sleepwalker. He'd drive us to Number 15, rape me or sodomize me or force his penis down my throat, and then take me home, dumping me at the golf course to walk the rest of the way. How was that for after-school fun? The funny thing is: No one ever noticed that there was a problem. After my first visit to Number 15, there were bruises on my neck. Nobody said a word. Not my mom or dad or Miss Moss. It was then that I knew I was crazy, the baddest of the bad.

Some nights I'd sit in the bath, the water gray and sudsy and warm, and wonder: What did you do if you were crazy and you knew it? You kept on, I guessed. You pretended. You acted normal, and you kept acting normal until you were found out. Sitting in the tub, cool air from the open window blowing on my wet head, the shower curtain yellow and mildewed and close, I'd pray that I'd never be found out. Sometimes my bottom stung in the bathwater. I learned not to use soap. My back often hurt, my breath like something sharp and vicious, gouging my kidneys with every inhalation. I ignored the pain, "thought" it all away.

Which worked, for a time. Until it returned, appearing at the corner of 31st and Rex in a spray of dirty water. On that blustery winter afternoon, my pants soaked, my red socks bleeding onto my feet, for the first time since Larry Johnson had taken an interest in me, I ran. Maybe I'd had enough. Maybe it was because I had other plans: I was going to eat my little sister's candy. Either way, before I knew what I was doing, I was running, my feet slapping the wet sidewalk, my chest burning, cold wind roaring in my ears. I crossed Rex without looking, splashed into a puddle, raced up the hill that led home. I could feel Larry behind me as I ran, could sense something wild and hot and dangerous, and my body jerked, as if falling into a dream, every time I pictured him reaching out to grab me.

Little girls are easy to get. I didn't know that then. I ran past Nicky DiMarco's house, my friend since kindergarten with the small mother like a monkey in a housecoat, who didn't speak English, only yelled gibberish at Nicky and his dad. Near the Dooleys' I looked behind me, but I was running so fast everything was a blur. I slowed for an instant and looked again, my heart crashing in my chest, my head feeling like it might explode. Nothing. The wet, leaf-strewn street was empty. I heard only wind and rain and a distant hum, like a cloud of bugs. The hum seemed to be coming from inside my head. I touched my stomach. I could feel my heart pounding there, too, as if I were a bug, full of hot blood.

The Dooleys' cottage was small and blue with white latticework that made me think of the word *German*. Their sloping lawn excited me. Last fall, Mick, the eighth-grade son, had burned the word FUCK onto the grass with gasoline. The letters were ten feet high; they stretched across the entire lawn, bent and surreal. The F-word, the dead brown blades of grass—it was thrilling. No one had bothered to fix it. The word stood. Mick had made his point.

FUCK. Mick Dooley was fearsome. He had close-cut hair, yellow like pollen, and ladybug freckles spattered across his back. He liked to hurt you—he was happy to hurt you—anytime, anyplace, bending your fingers back until you cried "uncle," grabbing your ponytail as you flew by on your bike, forcing you to a painful stop. "Haw, haw, haw, you fucking baby," he'd laugh, poking you with whatever was handy—a stick or a Wiffle-ball bat or one of his long fingers. He didn't care if you cried. He loved it; it made him happy. Mick Dooley was made to inflict pain.

Once, he came up behind me, grabbed the back of my neck, and forced my head down until I was looking at a candy tin cradled in his palm. My face was right next to the crotch of his scruffy cutoffs. They were rubbed white around the fly and smelled of motor oil and pee. I didn't struggle. I closed my eyes and held my breath, trying to figure out how on earth I had gotten myself into the position I was in: trapped, inches from Mick Dooley's crotch. Everyone knew that if you spotted Mick, you ran. You shouted out a brief warning to any kid unlucky enough to be in the vicinity, and you got the hell out of there. But I had been caught unawares, lost in my head as I circled the old oak on our parking strip, humming, trailing my fingers across the rough bark, wondering what it would be like to live inside it.

"Sniff it," Mick ordered, tightening his grip on my neck. I exhaled, my shoulders aching with tension, and did as I was told.

"Not my dick, you moron. In here, sniff it now." He shoved the tin into my face until whatever was in it touched the tip of my nose. I opened my eyes. The lid with the picture of the lemon drops on it was gone. The tin was filled with planty stuff that smelled bad: harsh and stinky and green.

I sniffed loudly. At the same time I tried not to breathe—a nearly impossible task. After a few more breaths/non-breaths, Mick was satisfied. He let me go, shoving me into the tree. "It's a lid of pot," he said, his lip curling to acknowledge that yes, he'd seen me tumble backward over the tree roots, and yes, it was hilarious. "You just smelled marijuana, you little idiot, and now you're going to jail." With that, he leapt onto his Huffy bike and pedaled off, his knees pumping up to his chest, his freckled arms raised, as if he'd just won a race. Mick Dooley: victorious. I was horrified, scared. What had I done? I'd smelled pot was what I'd done, and I got up, cradling my banged elbow, and ran inside before the police could arrive to tearfully confess everything to my mother.

A couple of days later, Mick brought me a handful of bath salts: small fragrant cubes with tiny gardenias and lilacs on the foil wrappers. They scared me, the fancy things Mick had pressed into my hand without a word before fleeing. I watched him run down the street. He'd stuck a cigarette behind his ear. Halfway to the corner it fell out, but he didn't stop to pick it up. His jeans were cut high on the thigh, revealing skinny bowed legs and big knees. His feet slapped the pavement like a jackrabbit's. I waited until he'd crashed through the rhododendron bushes at the corner, presumably to torture one of the Brown boys. Then I ran inside to rid myself of the evidence. I dissolved the salts one at a time beneath the bathroom tap, cubes turning to grains turning to something slimy that I wiped on the towel. The flower fumes made me dizzy. Mick Dooley, nice guy, was far scarier than Mick Dooley, torturer of 31st Street. I was glad when his gift had swirled away.

Months later, however, on that wet winter afternoon, I began to appreciate the dark powers of Mick. I stood in front of his house—the windows like sad dark eyes reflecting nothing—and willed him to appear. For a split second, I considered knocking on the front door. It was hidden at the end of a dank, shrub-enclosed tunnel. Even looking at it made me shiver. Mick Dooley or Larry Johnson. The choice was so awful, I started to cry. Somehow, my world had receded. A shadow world had appeared, and trying to navigate the two was exhausting. I felt as if *I* had split into pieces. There was the "me" I was before Larry Johnson and the "me" I was now, with a hundred different ghost "mes" slipping out my ears. As I stood in front of the Dooleys', nervously shuffling my feet, one part of me was wild with panic while the other was perfectly calm. Or maybe not calm, but numb (which felt dead). Everything is happy! Everything is grand! While inside I was dissolving, flowing away like Mick's salts.

Somebody screamed with laughter. I jerked around. Two kindergartners were chasing each other down Rex. My stomach hurt, and I jabbed my fingers into it. I wished my body—the hateful thing that had turned against me—gone. *Disappear. Disappear.* I prayed for it, standing on the sidewalk, my head pounding, Mick's house blurring blue through my tears. I imagined bursting into flame, spontaneously combusting like I'd read about in the *Guinness Book of World Records.* The wind would blow and poof! I'd be gone. It had happened to a lady in Wales. One moment she was sitting in her easy chair watching TV, the next she was nothing but a spot of grease.

The Dooleys' back door slammed. I held my breath, but nobody appeared. Their Christmas lights were still up, big red and blue and green bulbs, hanging from the eaves. How did they do it on TV, make the bad go away? The Almighty Isis fought evil with good, and she won. I was beginning to see, though, that that was (as my mother would say) a crock of shit. Hadn't I been nice? Before Larry Johnson had taken an interest in me? Maybe not totally, but I certainly wasn't evil. I didn't kill people or burn down my house like that little girl on my mother's soap opera. Where had it gotten me? Nowhere. It had gotten me trapped in Number 15 whenever Larry Johnson had a hankering for little girl.

I wiped my nose. The rain had stopped. The sky was wan and yellow, and everything sparkled with shivery drops. I glanced behind me. No cars, no kids, only the wet hill, swooping down into a cloud of dripping trees. Maybe he'd given up and gone home. Or maybe he hadn't. Either way, I'd had enough. I was done being nice. I was done being scared. From here on out, I would fight evil with evil. I'd march up to Mick Dooley's front door and demand that he walk me home. "And your sisters," I would say. Nancy and Patsy were even scarier than Mick. They were hippo-sized teenagers, one with orange hair, one with black, who'd once trapped me in their garage until I pulled down my shorts. They were eating apples at the time.

I did as I was told. They haw-hawed like Mick, flung up the garage door. Rattle, CRASH! I flew into the light.

"And your dad," I'd order Mick. Mr. Dooley looked like a bulldog. He was squat and barrel-chested, with short arms and legs. His pure white crew cut showed his pink scalp, and he didn't talk, he *barked*—orders and F-words and threats. Mrs. Dooley could stay home. She was useless as far as I could see, a fat flowered couch of a woman with weepy eyes and troubled, fluttering hands.

You think you can hurt me? Well, meet the FUCKING DOOLEYS!

But nobody came out. I was too scared to go to the door. As I started home, I glanced back one last time. As if I'd conjured him, Mick Dooley stood on his front lawn, as quiet as a cat. He had one hip cocked. A long sharpened stick drooped from his hand, touching down in the exact center of the *U*. I started to speak then shut my mouth. Mick stared at me, a hateful look in his eyes. His snub nose and arms were dirty with freckles. His Keep on Truckin' T-shirt was yellowed and tight and torn across the bottom, revealing a slice of pale stomach. Today, I remember Mick's eyes as glowing red, like the pig on *The Amityville Horror*, but they were probably just a plain dirt-brown. Fixed on me. Glowering.

"What's your problem?" Mick hitched up his jeans. They looked new, dark blue and stiff, with deep cuffs.

"Nothing." I bent my head, surreptitiously wiped my eyes.

"What are you, a fucking bawl baby?" Mick jabbed the *U* impatiently.

I didn't answer. I could feel my heart pounding in my ears. His stick was burned black at the sharp end, and I wondered why. I imagined him impaling small squirmy things with it—gerbils and kittens and kids.

"Get out of here," he said.

"No."

"Do you want me to stab you?" Mick's tone was conversational, as if he'd just asked if I wanted milk with my Oreos. His shoulders slumped. A ring of grime encircled his neck.

"No—"

"—with my stick?" He raised his voice.

"No," I said hotly.

We stared at each other. Or rather, Mick stared at me, and I stared at his dirty, unlaced tennis shoes. I sneaked a look at his face. Mick glared back. Deliberately, he covered one nostril and blew his nose onto the lawn. I swallowed hard, disgusted and enthralled. It was a standoff. I was in a standoff with Mick Dooley, and I thought I might throw up. He was ugly and fearsome, as usual. But he also looked miserable, I thought, slouched on his ugly lawn, his curse jutting awkwardly at his feet. I wondered how long it had taken him to create it. Did he do it in the middle of the night? The K was skinny and cramped, which meant he hadn't blocked it out beforehand. How had he gotten all the gasoline? Did Mr. Dooley whip him when he saw?

Behind Mick, his house burned blue against the grubby sky. My hands tingled and I had to pee badly. Still, I didn't move. I don't know why. Maybe I wanted him to know that I understood how it felt to want to tell the whole world F. Maybe he sensed this, and that was why he hated me.

"Run home, fucking bawl baby."

"No." I hesitated. "Make me."

"What?" Mick looked surprised. He quit stabbing at the ground. He squinted, rubbed his yellow head.

"Make me," I said, a little louder. I wanted to sound tough, but it came out lame, like I was a bad actress, reading a line in a play.

"What did you say? Did you say—?"

"Make me," I shouted, startling even myself.

With a fierce "Yah!" Mick raised his stick and lunged.

I turned and ran, tripping over my feet, Mick's hollow laughter ringing in my ears.


My dad was always on his way out, going. He never took off his shoes in the house. He did the dishes in them. He sat in his chair and watched golf and tennis on TV in them. I figured he took them off before bed. He had lots of shoes, hundreds it seemed. Clean white tennis shoes, Converse, Stan Smith, Nikes when they first came out. All lined up in his closet, polished even, and his work shoes, shiny and brown, or black with brown tips, some with tassels or gold bars, some with laces, some you just slipped on. His polish was in his closet, too, his shoe rags and his shoehorns and the wooden thing he called his shoe tree. His funny golf shoes with the fringe. My dad always had perfectly clad feet—shined, immaculate. When I was very small, I'd sometimes play in his closet, looking at the shoes, touching but never moving them, until he told me to get out.

After my confrontation with Mick, I sat on the floor of the TV room, January's Advent calendar in my lap, a coffee mug of orange juice by my side. The Mickey Mouse Club was on. Everyone was hap-hap-happy, cheery and having fun. I watched, skeptical. I no longer believed in the Mickey Mouse Club. A month ago, my mother had bought me the official scrapbook. Halfway through, Larry Johnson (who saw the book tucked under my arm after school one day) told me that Jimmie Dodd, the smiling lanky grown-up, had killed himself years after the show went off the air. I was horrified. I couldn't believe it. It made me sick. I wondered what other horrible things had infected the people on my shows.

On our round orange set, Jimmie danced a soft shoe. His eyes, which had seemed gentle and kind before I read the book, now looked just plain sad. Desperate. Pleading. I wondered if he'd known then how he would die. Did he kill himself *because* the Mickey Mouse Club ended? Did he die *because* the cartoon happiness went away? What grown-up cared about that stuff anyway? I shoved a piece of chocolate in my mouth. "Stupid Jimmie Dodd," I whispered, just to see how it felt.

My fingers were chocolaty, and I wiped them on the rug. My mother hated our wall-to-wall carpeting. "It's been here since the '20s!" she'd cry whenever my dad wondered aloud why nobody ever vacuumed. I didn't understand what the 1920s had to do with anything. I did know that if Iris didn't like something, she pretended it wasn't there. I thought the carpet was OK. It was like the skin of the house. Forest-green and mottled, it clung to the floors, having grown into them years earlier. In places, it was worn so smooth you could see the floorboards underneath. It spread from the TV room into the living room, avoided the kitchen (with its fake brick linoleum and genuine cowboy-bar swinging doors), before creeping up our thirteen steps like the Blob.

Where it stopped. Upstairs, where the bedrooms were, the floors were cold shiny linoleum—pale gray with even paler speckles of pink and brown and yellow—like in a hospital or a school. We had good door-knobs. Iris said that they, too, were from the 1920s. They were sparkling crystal balls on metal sticks that you could take out of one door and put in another. Or you could shut your little sister in the bedroom, remove the doorknob, and listen to her scream, trapped. Once I collected them all and hid them in my closet. "I don't think so," Iris said, holding out her hand for my secret stash.

After a commercial for Hoppity Hops, the familiar music for *Spin and Marty* started up. I ate the last chocolate. It smelled like dirt, like warm dark kitchens and my mom. Bright tin wrappers glinted at my feet. I loved *Spin and Marty*. With Annette and Cheryl and the other big kids, it seemed so grown-up and romantic. I was soon absorbed in the show. My body began to relax. Sitting on the soft green skin, in the protective glow of the set, the walk home from school, with its double threat of Larry Johnson and Mick Dooley, seemed distant and unreal, with no more power over me than that of a scary movie. I was inside, safe, and my mother would be home soon.

I had only to wait and watch: *The Flintstones, The Brady Bunch, Gilligan's Island*, and a little bit of the news.

I gulped the rest of my juice. It was bitter after the sweet chocolate—watery, too, as it hadn't been mixed all the way. I'd seen the lump of frozen concentrate in the bottom of the pitcher but hadn't felt like finding the wooden spoon. I stretched out my legs. My feet were stained red from my socks. My soggy pants were starting to itch, and my sweater smelled like wet dog—like our wet dog, Cinnamon, chewing on himself beside me. One commercial slid into another. "By Wham-O," the announcer said. A ray of sunlight streamed through the window. I wished I had someone to play with outside. The year before, I'd played with the Price girls. Molly and Mary were twins, one chubby, one thin. In their dim living room, pictures of them as babies hung on the walls. They were strange babies, bald creatures in fluffy dresses, with bows taped to their heads so their mother could tell them apart. Once I was familiar with their photos, I could distinguish them by their expressions. Molly always looked sleepy, and Mary always looked shocked.

Last summer, I shoved a Mexican jumping bean up skinny Mary's nose. I don't know why. It had seemed like the thing to do. Molly and I laughed, but Mary went berserk. Her face turned red, her eyes grew large (like the baby in the picture), and, snorting and sobbing, she ran inside to tell. A moment later, her grandfather, who was babysitting, shuffled out onto the porch. "You," he said, pointing a trembling finger at me (or in the general direction of me, as he was half-blind). "Run home now or I'll squirt you with the hose." I ran, shame squirming in my gut. I avoided the Price twins after that. In the fall, we were in different classrooms. I saw them at the first Bluebird meeting of the year and was relieved to see that nothing was growing out of Mary's nose.

*The Flintstones* came on. I wondered if I should hide the remains of January's calendar, or let her see them and throw a fit. I settled on kicking the wrappers toward the couch. It was the show with Mr. Gruesome. His wife, with her big nose and long dark bangs, looked exactly like Cher. During the commercial, I closed my eyes, hugged my knees to my chest, and rocked. It was good. Everything inside, so big and loud and uncomfortable, was stilled by the motion. Standing on my head had the same effect. I'd been standing on my head a lot lately. It felt right, much more so than being upright, which felt difficult, my body large and cumbersome and hard to move around. Sometimes I propped my feet against the dining room wall and ate my cereal upside down. I read upside down and watched TV that way, too. It wasn't so hard. The brain flipped things around, and it was like watching a show upright. Only you felt good: weightless, your head pressing into the ground, everything slow and quiet and calm. It was a way of being and *not being*. Of being, but *being slightly askew*, which fit nicely with the way the world had turned.

Some afternoons at school, as the clock jerked closer and closer to 2:30, I'd daydream about standing on my head. I couldn't wait to get home. I wished I could stand on my head at school: work in my reading workbook upside down, do my math problems upside down, even spell my words for the Friday afternoon spelling bee upside down.

"Why is it called a 'bee'?" I'd asked one dark afternoon a week earlier. Rain slapped the windows. Fluorescent lights turned our classroom into a terrarium.

"Why is it called a 'bee'?" Miss Moss stood at the board, giddy in one of her new dresses, this one black and tightly crocheted, with beelike flowers budding all over it. She picked up two erasers and absentmind-edly whapped them together. A cloud of yellow dust flew in her face. She laughed, waved it away. "Because in Room 3, we're all just *buzzing* with our new words."

I politely raised my hand. "But why is it called a 'bee'?" I asked again.

Miss Moss gave a vague wave. She closed her eyes the way she did when thinking hard. Her fingers were long and thin. There was a little knob on each bony wrist. I loved the color of her skin. It was a pale yellow that went with her brighter hair. Her cheeks were scarred: little divots and discol-orations that she covered with a thick layer of makeup. When you stood close to her, you could smell it. It smelled nice, like sugar and mud. She called her makeup "pancake." This was thrilling, although I was disap-pointed to find that she did not smell like flapjacks and butter and syrup. "Well." She opened her eyes, looked surprised to be there. "We have other bees, too. There are quilting bees and . . ." She paused, touched her beehive. "There's the *Sellwood Bee*, that little newspaper they have down there . . ." She nodded in the direction of Sellwood, the neighborhood on the other side of the golf course.

"But why is it called a 'bee'?" I persisted, without raising my hand. Timmy Summers laughed. Miss Moss told him to shush up, then gave me an assignment. I was to look up the word *bee* in the dictionary, or better yet, the encyclopedia, and report back to the class tomorrow. I tried not to smile. I had a special project! Specially assigned to me by Miss Moss herself. And I could do it. Last fall, my mother had decided that I needed a set of encyclopedias. Lucky me, they were on sale at Safeway. "Here," she'd said, handing me two heavy red volumes. She stuffed a wad of green stamps in her purse. "Soon you'll know everything in the world." Although she forgot about the project after the first purchase, I had the one with the Bs! That afternoon, I practically flew home, the happiest I'd been all year.

During the last half of *The Flintstones*, I upended myself into a handstand. I thought of other special projects I could ask Miss Moss to assign me. I could study the guinea pig, measure how much it ate and drank in a day. Did it like cats better or dogs? What was its favorite fruit? Apples or bananas? Did it enjoy having a bath? I could bring Cinnamon to school, stand at the board, and answer questions. What were his habits, his likes and dislikes? Had he always chased cars? Did I think he was going to get hit? What did he do the day I dropped him down the laundry chute?

On the set, Fred bellowed for Wilma. In the silence that followed, I heard footsteps on the back stairs. Cinnamon perked his ears. "Dad?" I called. There was no answer. A moment later, Larry Johnson appeared in the TV room doorway. I caught my breath. Chocolate and orange juice came up in my throat, and I quickly dropped to a crouch. Cinnamon didn't bark. He got up and waggled over for a pet.

Was I asleep? Was I dreaming? In the same way I never believed it was my mother when she came home from school—she was too good to be true—I couldn't believe it was Larry Johnson, in our house, leaning against the doorjamb, smiling like he was my friend come by to say hello. Only this was too *bad* to be true. He'd never been past the front entrance without my parents around. His occasional visits for a beer with my father had stopped months ago.

"You can't come in here," I said, staring at his boots. He lifted one, shoved the dog away. Cinnamon yipped once, jumped onto the couch. "My dad is coming home. He says 'no one in the house' . . ." I was stammering. My body began to shake.

Larry shook his head and smiled. "Dan's not coming home." He looked bemused, as if he couldn't believe how stupid I was. "He's at the golf course. Just got a bucket of balls." His bulk took up most of the TV room doorway. He wore tight black slacks with a fancy sheen, short enough to reveal his shiny ankle boots. *Like hooves*, I thought. My breath was ragged although I hadn't moved. Beneath his leather jacket, he wore a red sweater over a green big-collared shirt. Only it wasn't a whole shirt. It was just a collar—something Larry called a "dickey." He'd once made me look at him in it, proud as if he'd invented the thing himself. The sight of him, fat and brown and grinning, naked but for the green collar, made me sicker than anything I'd seen. His sweater was too tight. It was covered with snowflakes.

"You have to go now. My dad is almost here. And nobody . . . He says . . ." My body felt weightless. My voice was nothing more than a breath, and I wondered if I'd formed actual words. I looked at my feet. They seemed strange, as if they belonged to someone else. I couldn't remember how they'd gotten so red.

"Just came by for a visit." Larry's voice was friendly and brisk. He spoke not to me but to the TV set.

"I don't want to visit—"

"Just stopped by to see how you're doing." He looked at me then and smiled, showing his white teeth.

I didn't answer. I was confused. He seemed so normal—maybe he *had* just come by to say hello. Maybe I'd made up the other stuff, and it wasn't really real at all. After all, wasn't I crazy? The baddest of the bad?

"What have you been up to? Still doing the gymnastics? Going to be in the Olympics someday?" Larry laughed. He raised his arm and itched the back of his neck, grimacing with discomfort. His dollop of black hair was shiny in the dim light.

"Maybe I'll be in the Olympics." I shrugged, leaned forward, and touched my toes.

"All ready for Christmas? Did you write your letter to Santa?"

I didn't answer.

"What did you ask for? One of those dolls with the hair? You know, the long hair that grows into a ponytail? What are those called? One of my buddies got one for his girl. She's about your age. Not as pretty as you, though." Larry paused. When I ignored his compliment, he continued, his voice loud and bright. "Not pretty at all if you ask me. She's a homely thing. Chubby. Dumb as a fucking post."

I sighed loudly. *Die*, I thought. *And then die again.*

"A Crissy doll," he cried. "That's what they're called. Did you ask Santa for a Crissy doll?"

"There is no Santa Claus," I muttered. "And dolls are for babies."

"Right. And you're no baby. But you are a baby doll." Larry grinned at me, waiting for my reaction. I closed my eyes, blocked him out. Where was my dad? How long did it take to hit a bucket of balls? I listened hard, praying I'd hear the sound of a car in the drive, but it was quiet out, as if the rest of the world had gone to sleep.

"Hey." Larry took a step toward me. I instinctively drew back, but he pretended not to notice. With a grunt, he settled on the arm of the couch. When he crossed his legs, his pants rode up, revealing silky pin-striped socks. His feet were inches from my face. They smelled strongly of baby powder, and I tried not to breathe. Larry rested his chin in his hand and looked down at me. He smiled sadly, his eyes big. "How come you don't have any friends? How come you're never out there playing like the rest of the kids? What are you stuck in here watching TV all the time for? Don't you know the tube will rot your brain?"

I looked away. Shame burned my ears. How did he know I didn't have any friends? It was a fact I kept secret, even from myself. When Iris came home from work and asked what I'd done after school, I'd say "played," adding "with the kids," if she wanted more. This seemed to satisfy her. I couldn't put into words the truth, that I was bad. My hair was too tangled, my head too big, my stomach stuck out, and I wasn't nice at all. School was hard. Kickball was ruining my life. When it was time to play, as we did every morning at ten a.m., I dreaded leaving the fence. To step up to home plate, kick the ball or miss it, and then to run, alone and lonely, all your ugliness exposed . . . I hated it. Being in the outfield was OK. You could disappear. No one ever paid attention to the outfielders. You only had to pray that the ball never came your way. Lunchtime was the same. I wanted the hot lunch. The tacos, the cinnamon rolls, even the mashed potatoes with the hamburger gravy smelled so good, but I was too scared to stand in the lunch line, to show my awfulness to the school, eighth grad-ers included. This, too, was hard to explain. "If you want to buy lunch, buy lunch," Iris would say, giving me the look, the one that said, *Surely you don't belong to me, you silly thing.*

"You must get lonely." Larry leaned forward. His voice was soft, his breath warm on the back of my neck. "All alone, day after day. No one to talk to but this stupid mutt."

"No." I shook my head, bit the inside of my cheek. In spite of myself, tears welled in my eyes. I watched as they dripped onto my red feet.

"Hey. How come you guys never wash this dog? I mean, this is one stinky dog."

I looked at Cinnamon stretched out long on the back of the couch. He cocked his head. Tangled black fur hung in his eyes. Was he stinky? Maybe he was, but I couldn't imagine him smelling any other way. His odor was a part of him, like the chewing and chasing cars. "My dad gives him a bath." I looked at my hands splayed on the dark green carpet. It was normal, I told myself, to be sitting in the TV room chatting with my parents' friend. Kids did it all the time. *I* was the one that was weird. Didn't I know how life went?

"How often? Once in a blue moon?" Larry laughed. When I didn't respond—I couldn't remember what we were talking about—he rested his hand on my shoulder. I froze. His hand was hot and heavy. He ran his index finger slowly across my neck. I jerked away. "Now calm down," he murmured, pulling my head toward his lap.

That afternoon I realized that houses aren't safe. Their walls are as thin as clouds. I'd always wanted to float on a cloud, ride it through the night like a fluffy, magical bed. I was disappointed when Iris told me that a cloud is nothing more than rain, and do you think you can sit on rain? Or air? "No," I said. "You can't." And do you think a house is anything more than a puff of blue air? *No,* I thought that afternoon. *I don't.*

Larry Johnson had wanted in, and he got in. In the monster movies, the vampire always gets in. He's at the window, terrorizing the poor pretty lady inside. Then, in a quick cut, he's at her bedside, fangs bared, ready to suck her blood. How was my life any different? It had turned into a bad movie, and wasn't that what I'd wanted? I'd liked Larry because he looked like the cute doctor on my show. The night of the Renaissance Fair, hadn't I wanted to hug him, to sit on his knee and be jiggled? If there was a vampire in the TV room, dressed in snowflakes and slithery pants, it was because I'd invited him in. Why? Because I was greedy. Because I'd always wanted more of whatever anyone nice had to give.

Larry held my head, his hands tangled in my hair. He opened his knees, positioning me between them. He quickly undid his belt, jerked down the zipper on his slacks. Panic shot through me. *The Brady Bunch* was on the TV, the familiar voices loud in the quiet room. It was one of the early shows. Someone was lost in the Grand Canyon, but I couldn't remember who. Was it Bobby? Bobby and Cindy? I needed to know, but when I tried to listen, to figure out the story, the voices were tinny and made no sense.

Larry pushed his penis against my face. When I refused to open my mouth, he held my nose until I gasped for breath. He shoved himself in, jerking me back and forth by my hair. I gagged, choked. The thought crossed my mind that I was probably going to die—if not that afternoon then soon. I knew he was going to kill me. It was a certain feeling, as cold and hard as a penny in my mouth. Sometimes I thought I was already dead. I figured I'd died long ago and no one had remembered to tell me. How did you know if you were dead? Ghosts were souls that, like bad guests, hung out long after the party was over. Hadn't someone forgotten to tell them, too? Was I a ghost? Me and Jimmie Dodd?

"No." I don't know if I tried to scream or not. I didn't care if God was a liar, if Elvis was full of shit—I was not going to die. In an instant, I wrenched myself away. Larry held on, and a handful of my hair tore out in his hand. I raced from the TV room, my scalp burning, and up the thirteen steps to my room, where it was safe. Where I could hide in my closet, take out the doorknob so no one could get inside. 1, 2 . . . 7 . . . My feet pounded the slippery rug. The windows on the landing grew larger the closer I got, the sky behind them wide and gray and surprised. I'd just stepped onto cold linoleum when Larry caught me from behind. Laughing, he grabbed my ankles, flipped my legs out from under me, and dragged me back down the stairs. *Clunk, clunk, clunk.* My shirt rode up over my belly. The carpet burned my chin.

At the bottom of the stairs, across the narrow hallway, was a closet with no door. It wasn't neat and tidy like my father's closet. It belonged to Iris and was full of mismatched shoes. There were the Dr. Scholl's sandals—clunky wooden torture devices that killed if you accidentally stepped off the back. My dad had gotten several pairs for free. "Grip with your toes," he'd giggle when Iris attempted to walk in them. After badly bruising her instep, she'd chucked them into the closet where they sat, year in and year out, the red pair and the denim pair and the pair the color of bone.

Her shoes from college were in the closet, too—dancing shoes with delicate spiked heels, dyed to match her formals. I liked to wear them around the house. Her feet were so small they almost fit. The colors were exciting: deep jewel tones for winter dances, powdery pastels for spring. How happy she must have felt slipping them on—like a princess at her ball. They sat in the closet now, grubby and mismatched, but hopeful still, like faded valentines.

Larry threw me onto the pile of shoes, facedown, yanked off my soggy pants, and raped me, quickly and triumphantly, pulling my hair as he went, *jerking, jerking, jerking.* "Take it like a man," he kept grunting, and I had no idea what he meant. His voice was clenched and hard, as if he were furious, and working hard to keep all the fury inside.

*Die. You will die. I will kill you when I'm grown up.* The words burned in my mind. I could see them, could feel their heat behind my eyes, and when I focused, when I stared hard into their bright centers, the pain went away. *Die. Kill.* The words split me in two. One me lay limp beneath Larry, my head jerking with his rhythm, as if I were nodding yes. While the other rose silently from my body, a red mist, all terror and rage, becoming stronger by the second, heavier and more real. It was me, only bad—a presence hurtful and unsafe. One day, I knew, I'd grow up. I'd find Larry Johnson with his pitiful pink makeup case, his animal stink and ridiculous little feet, and I would murder him.

Larry slammed into me, shoved my face into the shoes, his breath harsh in my ears. I lost my grip; the words slipped away. I couldn't breathe, couldn't move. Was it possible to be crushed to death in your own hall closet? I could smell the shoes—leather and wood and the faint scent of my mother: hair spray and lipstick and fun. When I looked through her high school yearbook, I smelled her there too, lingering in the yellowed pages, as if a part of her had stayed behind. She'd worn her big black cat glasses then, with sparks of rhinestones in the corners. They were the only kind you could get, she'd explained. "But something so ugly," I had gasped. She'd looked like a cat, quick and nimble and sly in her prom dress, but wearing the ugly glasses still. Those, along with her crooked smile—so hopeful, so familiar, *that skinny girl is my mom*—made me sad.

Larry moved faster. He'd pulled up his shirt, and his body rubbed slick against my back. A wooden sole dug into my cheek. I thought of all the things my mother had told me. She'd played the lead in *Carousel* and had had to kiss a boy—not my dad—onstage in front of everyone. Another boy she hadn't liked used to serenade her in the halls. "You are my speeccciallll angelll . . ." the boy sang. My mother ducked around a corner, disappeared into Home Ec. *Mortified* was the word she'd used. It meant alive and dead at the same time. Dippity-do, black bristly curlers scattered across her vanity, the tiny baby Avon lipsticks, her necklace made of brown seeds . . . What about Cinnamon the day I dropped him down the chute? His ears had ballooned out like parachutes. I was sorry the second I let go, the moment I released his hot body into the abyss, but when he landed on the pile of dirty clothes on top of the old mildewed mattress, he was OK. He stood still a moment, stunned, then shook hard and raced out of sight (I could see only a square of dim basement). I heard him click up the stairs, and then he was behind me, licking my bare calf, wagging his tail, grinning his dog grin, his eyes bright behind his tangled bangs, ready to go again.

Cinnamon knew the meaning of fun. So did Iris. She'd been popular with a capital *P* her whole life. I wondered what she was doing that very second. How ashamed she would be if she could see me now. And my dad . . . I knew he'd never come home and shoot Larry Johnson in the head the way I wanted him to. There are those kinds of dads—like Mr. Dooley, like Molly and Mary's grandpa—and then there were dads like mine, who took their fun seriously. Fun, I was beginning to see, saved you. If you were out having fun, you weren't trapped under Larry Johnson in a closet full of shoes. Fun made you fast and fizzy and energetic. Just try to catch me now!

As quickly as he'd appeared, Larry was gone, leaving the way he'd come in, his boots clomping down the back steps. I quickly pulled up my pants, ran into the TV room. The TV screen flickered. As I stared at it, an image of Larry driving out of the neighborhood played in my mind. He steered with one hand, the other arm draped across the seat. Blood dripped down his chin. The look on his face was smug, all of his appetites fed. And me, who was I? How did I fit into the scene? I tucked my feet under the couch cushions, leaned back, and shut my eyes. Was I the pretty lady, the husk of a pretty lady, who would one day rise from her bed, her bed of broken shoes, and destroy, as easily as Larry had that winter afternoon?

# Twenty-seven

## Katie

Cleopatra sat beside Katie's car, a thin string of drool hanging from her jaws. Sunlight hit the passenger side mirror and bounced off, giving her a crown of crazy light. The look in her eyes was reproachful, and her stout body shook slightly as if she'd been scared. "Oh thank God, thank God you're found," Katie cried, giving her a brisk rub, hefting her hot body to make sure that she was real. Cleopatra bit at her wrist. Katie released her, pleased. Luck had once again fallen into her lap. How would she have explained to Wilson, let alone Megan and Mandy, the loss of the dog at the lake in the middle of the night? She opened the car door. Surprisingly, Cleopatra hopped in without a struggle.

They drove home along empty summer streets. Cleopatra sat in front, peering around the seat in order to stare out the back window. The rain had stopped, and a strong breeze blew clouds across the sky. Sunlight glittered on mailboxes and parked cars. As Katie drove past the custard shop, she felt a rush of hope. Its sign—a fat swirled cone—glowed white in the fluorescent sky. It was soothing, reminding her that it wasn't too late to go home to her family, to her life of walks and naps and trips to the custard shop. Who cared that she'd slept with Steven and his stupid friend? Who cared, even, about the past? She had her family. Wasn't it more than enough?

*Obviously not*, said the voice in her head. She rolled down the windows. It was going to be a hot day. And it *would* be enough; she'd make sure it was enough.

Pulling into the Reserve, she saw that Wilson's car was still gone. She sat in the driveway, thinking. Cleopatra panted on her arm, her breath metallic and hot. Wilson was working on his dissertation, of course. But was he really? Katie rubbed her eyes. The smell of the lake, dank and cool on her hands, surprised her. The night seemed like a long time ago. She glanced in the rearview mirror. Steven's blinds were still drawn. Did he know about her and Jay? Did he regret letting her go? The familiar ache began in her chest, and she forced her thoughts back to Wilson. Something about the dissertation business nagged at her. For one, her husband was lazy. Diving into a project to the point of staying out all night was not like him. It was starving artist behavior, something young, skinny people did, people burning with questions about the meaning of life or, more importantly, the meaning of themselves. Wilson was skinny, but what did he care about life? He didn't ask much from it; he'd prefer that it leave him alone. Katie pulled the keys from the ignition. Jake's school picture smiled up at her from a plastic oval on the chain.

The condo was quiet. Drowsy sunlight fell in thick bars across the living room carpet. Thank God everyone was still asleep. Lovely, resting on the cool linoleum of the foyer, beat his tail in greeting. Cleopatra nipped at his jowls, then scrambled into the bedroom. It was time for the unpleasant houseguest to go, Katie knew, but the neighbor girls were still not home.

In the bathroom, Katie picked Paul's vinyl alphabet letters out of the tub. Her thoughts returned to Wilson. What if he'd come home, found her missing, and stormed out in a huff? How would she explain? For so long, she hadn't cared. Go ahead and go; she'd be happier without him. She turned on the tap. Water tumbled into the tub. Now, however, it felt as if things had gone too far. No more messing around with Steven, no more phone calls to the past. What had she planned on saying to the guy? *I wish you were dead?* Did she think that he would care, apologize and send her a million dollars? Why would anyone want to conjure up that ugliness? It was time to stop, to sit in her nest and be good. Steam filled the bathroom. It seemed urgent that things stay the same.

The phone rang in the kitchen. Katie's heart quickened. She ran to get it, for one crazy instant thinking it was Larry Johnson calling her back. He'd figured out how to use caller ID and was going to sue her for harassment. Or worse. He knew that she remembered, that she had told, and now she was going to pay.

"What are you doing home?" her mother said. Music swelled in the background, then abruptly disappeared.

"I live here. It's seven in the morning." Katie slipped out of her clothes and climbed into the tub, careful to keep the receiver out of the water. "Wait, it's four a.m. there, why are you—"

"What aren't you at the hospital?"

"Why would I be? Did Jan—"

"Your sister's having her baby."

Steven and Jay receded into the shadows.

Katie's clean T-shirt was on inside out and backwards, and damp in back from her wet hair. She slowed the car near the park. Several white ducks—enormous ducks, the size of kindergartners—slapped across the road in front of her. They waddled down the sidewalk before disappearing into a ditch. Maybe they were geese. What was the difference? Katie looked down. She was wearing two different flip-flops, one with orange hibiscus, the other pink striped. She didn't know what to think. Was she happy? Did she feel free? Her sister was having her baby, and Larry Johnson was dead. A car honked behind her. She stepped on the gas, rounded the corner, and steered into the hospital parking garage.

Wilson had freaked. That was funny, the way he'd called Iris at two in the morning West Coast time and asked her to get on a plane, immediately, because January was in labor and Katie was nowhere to be found. The home birth, the aquamarine swimming pool—all of it was forgotten as soon as January felt the full force of the pain, as Katie knew it would be. Wilson had found her in Jake's room, standing by the bed, unmoving, her face flushed, her entire body trembling.

Katie turned off the car and pulled the keys from the ignition. She quickly righted her shirt, then walked through the darkened parking garage to the hospital entrance. As she moved down a glass-enclosed ramp, she imagined the scene between Wilson and her sister:

"Jan?" Wilson's voice is tentative, afraid to disturb his sister-in-law lest he be asked to assist in some disturbing way. "Should I call the midwife?"

January doesn't answer. She is consumed by pain. The outside world, with its silly rituals like answering when someone speaks to you, no longer matters.

"Do you want to go to the hospital?"

January opens one eye.

"Where there are drugs?" Wilson continues. And they are off, the kids gathered and in the car in two minutes flat . . .

In the lobby, Katie pushed the elevator button for the third floor. The hospital was quiet. Sunlight flooded its atrium, warming a jungle of tropical plants so enormous she expected to see monkeys flinging themselves from branch to branch. She stepped into the elevator, the phone conversation with her mother lingering in her mind. They had somehow gotten on the topic of Larry Johnson. Iris had wanted to know where Katie had been. Why hadn't her husband been able to find her so early in the morning?

"I went out for a run. I didn't feel good—"

"You have to tell people where you're going," Iris had chided. "You need to think of Wilson, too, you know."

"I *do* think of him. Why would you even say that?"

"I just hope you're nice." Iris laughed, her voice light. "You know I like him. He's such a good dad. And he adores—"

"I know he's a good dad." Katie had dried her legs, the phone jammed against her shoulder. "You don't have to tell me to be nice, Mom. I am nice. This isn't about Wilson. It's about me and the stupid panic attacks I've been having."

"Uh-oh."

"Yeah. And nightmares, too. Every night. Where I'm calling, you know . . ." Katie lowered her voice. "*That* guy. The bad one."

Iris didn't answer.

*Who cares if you don't want to talk about this?* Katie kicked her dirty clothes into the corner, annoyed. "Part of me wants to do it in real life," she lied. "Call him up and . . . I don't even know. Make him pay. Make him pay for what he did."

There was a long silence. "Ick," Iris finally said.

Katie felt the familiar rage rising in her chest. "I know it's 'ick.'" She forced her voice to sound calm. "Don't you think I know? But just because it's awful, does that mean he gets to get away with it? Why didn't anybody do anything? Why didn't Dad go out and shoot the guy, the minute he found out?" Katie knew she'd crossed a line mentioning her father, and she was right, for Iris's reply was frosty.

"Your dad was very upset about all of this. And the point is moot. The man's been dead for years."

"What?"

"He's dead."

"How do you know?"

"It was in the obituaries."

"When?"

"Two, maybe three years ago."

"Why didn't you tell me?"

Iris sighed. "Why would I, Katie? Why would I tell you *anything* about that man?"

Katie sat on the toilet, wrapped in a red towel. Her spine shook, as it often did when she talked about the past. It was visceral, her body reacting to a long-ago threat while her mind was relatively calm. Who was the poor man she'd been crank-calling all summer? She could have sworn she had the right guy. "How do you know it's the same person?"

"Same name? Hermiston? It's a small town—"

"How did he die?"

Iris hesitated. "I don't know."

Katie knew that she did. She hoped it was something awful, something that made him writhe in pain for many, many months. But what you wish on others comes back on you. She leaned over the tub, squeezed water from her hair. You were supposed to pray for the people that hurt you. *Fuck it. He got what he deserved.* Katie glanced in the mirror. Her eyes looked hard. She obviously had work to do in the area of forgiveness. And really, what was the punishment? Larry Johnson must have been over seventy. He got old and he died, just like most people on the planet. He never paid the price—*she* did, for nearly all of her life. Katie stared at her feet. They were suntanned, striped white from her Birkenstocks. What did you do when the monster that had been dreaming you woke up, shuffled off this mortal coil? Whose dream did you live then?

"I don't know why we're talking about this." Iris's voice was brisk. "Go on. Get to the hospital. Go and see that baby and tell your sister that Dad is calling the airline as soon as I hang up the phone."

"Why won't you tell me how he died?"

"I'm hanging up."


Wilson stood beside a wall of windows in the deserted hospital waiting room, a bouquet of pink balloons hovering over his head. He wore baggy shorts and his favorite David Letterman T-shirt. His thin legs were brown from the sun, and he'd pulled his hair back into a neat ponytail. He looked handsome and capable. His jaw was dark with stubble like the fathers on Katie's childhood shows when they arrived home after a hard day's work. Rose slept in the pack on his back, her sweet face smushed against his shoulder. Katie loved it when Wilson was in "dad mode." It was when he was at his most peaceful, his most alive and kind. It made her proud to know him.

It also made her hate herself. What a cheater. What kind of wife was she? The mass of pink balloons was like a cartoon bubble, filled not with words but with pure pink girly-ness, the kind of thing that made him most nervous. How could she have left him alone, to be Jan's *doula* of all things? And what had he done with the kids? Katie reached up, touched Rose's damp curls. She leaned into Wilson. He smelled good, like a clean hotel room. She had the feeling of being home, right where she belonged. If not with him, then where? Start over with someone else? That didn't sound like fun. "So it's a girl?" she asked, excited despite her guilt.

"No. It's a boy. Otis." Wilson smiled, rolled his eyes. "The kids insisted I get pink."

"That's such a cute name. It's so nice you got her balloons."

Wilson shrugged.

"She's OK? Did she have drugs? How fast was—"

"Stink. Stank. Stunk." Paul raced past, shouting at the top of his lungs. He circled the waiting room, then threw himself onto a waxy-looking couch the color of red lipstick. Jake followed behind, giggling. He wore long board shorts decorated with graffiti and skulls, and Wilson's Midwestern T-shirt, which hung nearly to his knees. They'd obviously been in a hurry that morning.

"Let's get along." Katie impulsively grabbed Wilson's hand. "Let's do things together, like go to the movies. Or we could take a dance class. A couple's dance class like Steven and stupid Lucy did. Doesn't that sound like fun?"

"I'd rather be shot."

Katie smiled. "I know. No dancing. But maybe just . . . OK, I know you don't like walks, but how about bike rides?" She looked up, hopeful.

Wilson was smiling, his gaze distant. He noticed Katie watching and slowly shook his head.

"What? Why are you shaking your head?"

"Because I don't want to . . . you know . . . do that."

"Do what?"

"Swim."

"*Swim?*"

"Or . . . what you said." Wilson looked confused. Or maybe not confused, for that would imply some sort of energy behind the look, but pleasantly bemused.

"Are you *on* something?" Something was off. He was talking slowly. And he seemed to be working too hard to form his words, as if he'd been out in subzero temperatures. "It's like your mouth is frozen. What's wrong with you? Are you having a stroke?" Katie tried to laugh.

"No. Leave me alone. I'm tired is all." Wilson turned away. "I'm going to go home and sleep." He took a step then stopped. "The baby's cute," he added. "I didn't have to be in there at all. It was so fast, but Lucy came . . ." He trailed off. "With the camera." He was halfway out the door.

"Wait." Katie ran after him. "The baby? The balloons?"

Wilson fumbled with the backpack. Katie lifted it off his shoulders and shrugged it on. Rose's warm weight felt good against her back. Her sleepy scent enveloped her, causing her milk to let down, a heavy tingle in her breasts. "*Are* you high?" she asked quietly, grabbing Wilson's shirt. She breathed in. He didn't smell of alcohol.

"No. Katie, I swear." Wilson pulled away. "I'm just tired. Can't a guy be tired?"

Katie looked at him, skeptical. She'd dated many addicts in the past. At first they'd be sober and yes, struggling, and yes, a pain in the ass, but still they were *there*, in all their hypersensitive glory. Then they'd use again, and there was that one moment, like a door shutting or a light going off, when you'd realize that they were gone, without giving anyone a chance to say *good-bye*, or *stop*, or *have you really thought this through?*

But not Wilson. Surely she was mistaken. She'd always believed in his sobriety, had never been able to imagine him as a drunk. The person he described seemed like someone else, no one close to the responsible, faithful man she knew. "Is it really that you're tired? Is that it? You just didn't get any sleep?"

"Swear to God." Wilson solemnly raised his right hand, the hand with the balloons, and swayed with exaggerated drunkenness.

Katie scowled. Fucking liar. He probably had his toes crossed. *Or maybe you're wrong*, her conscience nagged. *Haven't* you *been up all night, too? Playing your own ridiculous games? Couldn't your perception be just a bit off? Do you ever give anyone the benefit of the doubt?* The voice in her head sounded suspiciously like her mother's. Katie bit her lip.

"C'mon. Let me go." Wilson held out the balloons, his eyes pleading. They were glassy, Katie saw, the pupils pinned. Her heart sank. She reached for the balloons, but Wilson let go a moment too soon and they floated to the ceiling.

She looked up. The strings dangled several feet out of reach.

"Mommy lost the balloons," Paul cried, leaping off the back of the couch. His platinum hair was so shiny it looked wet.

"I'll get them, Mom." Jake ran over, jumped fruitlessly in the air.

"No. Let your dad—" Katie looked behind her, but Wilson was already gone.

# Twenty-eight

**Wilson**

It was like drowning. As water fills the lungs, the victim grows sleepy and peaceful, and no longer cares about the self: the poor, hapless, drowning, foolish self. The drowning man becomes other—the self cast off—and isn't this new water-stopped person, in his sleep of death, infinitely more intriguing?

Wilson had held out for as long as he could. But on a midsummer morning, when Alice Cherry showed him what her little brother (arrested the night before on charges she wouldn't name) had left in her apartment, he slipped.

"This is state's evidence." He set down his flyers for the upcoming Clothesline Project, a display of fluttering T-shirts painted by abuse survivors, and grabbed for the large Ziploc bag full of pills. "I'm well within my rights to seize it."

"Go ahead." Alice held the baggie just out of his reach.

Wilson pinned her against the copy machine, glad the women's studies office was empty. Alice's body was hot and damp beneath her sheer blouse.

"Can I at least try one?" he said.

"If you kiss me."

And he did. Why not? He was feeling good. The baby was due any day now, which meant that the baby's mother, January, would soon be out of his life. And he'd just successfully scared a third of his summer school students into dropping after the first day. He kissed his colleague softly. She placed a small white pill—a Xanax—on his tongue, and it was good. Miraculously, after years of misery, he'd found the cushion, the buffer she'd said he lacked due to poor mothering.

The question—to do or not to do the pills—never came into play.


There were no boundaries at home, no edges—hence, the need for the buffer. The buffer was a miracle. It placed Wilson back in the bell jar, in a womb alone, safe from the dream of the bad world closing in upon him. In the vagina, they were all one crazy, amorphous, feeling creature, with no one person separate from the others. Wilson's sister-in-law, for example, had taken to using his toothbrush. Or maybe she'd been using it all along and he'd only just noticed. It was wet when he went to brush his teeth that morning. He confronted her on the front porch. It was early, a little after six, the sun a pink yolk, smeared across the sky. He was smoking before heading off to teach his summer school class, and she was hanging out, bothering him.

"Why?" he asked, when January readily confessed to the crime. She wore a pink halter top and baggy cream sweats. Her belly was once again flat— it was now several weeks after Otis's swift arrival—and for some reason she'd let the children finger-paint it the night before, covering it with bright blurry handprints, a flower, a bumblebee, and what looked like a blue fork.

"Wait. Is it the green one?" January squatted against the brick wall. Her hair had grown out, and she'd braided it, wrapping the braids around her head like Heidi. An evil Heidi, Wilson thought. The ends poked up in back like horns. "The green one with the funny rubber spike on the end?"

"Yes, yes." He exhaled impatiently. "Why? Why would you use another human being's toothbrush? Don't you have your own?"

She shrugged, unconcerned.

Wilson looked at her, at her unwashed hair and dirty feet. "How often do you brush your teeth anyway?" he asked, feeling mean.

"Why would you say that?"

"You just don't seem like the kind of person that . . ." He paused, searching for the right words. "Follows the rules."

January glared. "I groom constantly. And I thought the green one was the extra one."

"Green does not mean extra," he said stiffly.

"Whatever."

"Please don't use my toothbrush."

"Move it then and I won't." January turned and flounced inside, leaving the front door open, the air conditioner blasting.


Hours later, all thoughts of the annoying sister-in-law had disappeared. Wilson had smelled Divinity. He'd smelled Divinity and followed his nose, followed it straight to where it was now, buried not between his wife's legs, but between those of his colleague, Alice Cherry, splayed on a desk in a locked office in the Center for Women's Studies.

He licked gently using the technique Katie had taught him. "Like a cat," she'd ordered. "Use your whole tongue, nice and flat, and then flick it, but easy, easy . . . Wilson!" Stop. He would not think of his wife. This was not about her. He'd stopped going down on her long ago. It was too much work. She was too much work. Sex with her was too much work, and the two of them together, he'd recently decided, was also way too much work.

The dalliance with Alice Cherry was play, done in the name of good mental health. It was a prophylactic measure, for Wilson could feel himself slipping even further. He was in danger of drinking again and needed relief, the kind that only Alice could provide.

She moaned, tightened her grip on Wilson's ears. Why was he thinking of his difficulties now? He was having fun. At least he thought he was having fun. He was feeling a little dizzy. At least he wasn't home. The condo felt unbearable lately, growing more crowded by the day, although only one new person—Otis—had joined them (his in-laws had, thankfully, stayed in a hotel during their brief visit to see the new baby).

His home was full of human beings, the very creatures he had a hard time dealing with. And yes, Katie, he knew he *was* one, but that didn't help. Katie and January were queen bees. Katie had always been bossy, but January, too, had been buzzing around, handing out orders for months: "Wilson, will you go to the store and get me celery juice? The midwife said I might want to cleanse. Wilson, you have to quit smoking, like, yesterday. The midwife says . . . blah, blah, blah . . . and all the gasses get on your clothes, so even though you smoke outside, you should stay, like, a hundred feet away from me at all times."

Wilson believed the birth process should be put back in the hands of women, but January's midwife had driven him crazy—all of her directions seemed to be aimed at him. Did she know January had gotten high during her pregnancy? He'd seen her once through the bedroom window, puffing on a fatty, blowing the smoke into a stuffed monkey.

It was unbelievable. Katie and January were unbelievable. He didn't understand where they got their sense of entitlement. Their father, Dan, certainly hadn't encouraged it. He was pleasant enough, but his daughters seemed to interest him only mildly, the way a cat would interest someone who was *not* a cat person. Dan was not a daughter person.

*Quit thinking.* Wilson was busy, having fun. "You're a lazy lover," Katie sometimes teased, but she had no idea. He was working so hard he felt close to passing out. It was hot in the office. They had no air-conditioning. Outside, the late August afternoon roared. Wilson rested his cheek on Alice's warm thigh and breathed deeply, trying to catch a hint of Divinity. He hadn't smelled the familiar scent since the night last winter when he'd watched her dance at the Mermaid Lair. "Did you switch perfumes?" he asked, working his stiff neck.

"Wilson." Alice gave his head a gentle push. He went back to work. The problem was the usual: He did not understand women. Not his mother, not the mother of his children, and not the annoying little new mother who'd been irritating him for months. Every time she barfed in Katie's car, who had to clean it up? He did, of course, and the whole time he wanted to . . . *Stop.* Concentrate. Gentle, flick, quicker and quicker, insert the finger, another if the lady wants. *Oh dear God, hurry up*, his inner lazy guy groaned. His tongue was numb, his jaws ached, why was he even doing this? Alice he felt no need to understand—it was part of the appeal. Her thighs tensed around his head. His inner lazy guy cheered. She tugged hard on his ears then abruptly shoved him away.

"You're a god," she said in her funny, flat tone.

Wilson wiped his face on his shirt, rested his hands on her shaking thighs. He looked into Alice's black eyes. They were flat like her voice.

Sunlight beat against the office window. Dr. Gold's geraniums drooped on their stalks, dribbling pink petals. Outside someone screamed once—a high, shrill shriek that fit the fiery day. "You're a god," Alice repeated, her panties around her ankles. "Highly skilled. I'd recommend your services to any of my friends."

"Don't. Please." Wilson let go of her thighs. He returned to his desk, satisfied. He thought of fucking her, quickly, just to show her what a god he was, but it seemed too difficult, too emotionally messy. They were safe enough. He'd shoved a chair under the locked door, and no one used the office on Fridays anyway. But Alice wasn't on birth control, and after he'd refused to sleep with her last winter, on the night of the Mermaid Lair, Wilson had stayed strong. The guilt would be unbearable—it *was* unbearable, and all they'd done the first night was kiss. Nonetheless, he'd driven home in the frigid early morning feeling like a troll. An enormous hump grew on his back. Long black hair sprouted from his ears and nose. He smelled of a swamp. He smelled as if he'd been rolling in the carcass of a cow. How would Katie not see the disgusting subhuman he'd become?

She hadn't. That only made the guilt worse.

The second bad thing was that Alice had "fallen in love" with him for one long, uncomfortable week. She was suddenly always in the office, hovering, grimacing, holding her breath, waiting for him to notice her. A nice Alice, he discovered, was a far scarier proposition than a crabby Alice. After he sat her down for a talk—*I'm in love with my wife. What happened the other night can never happen again*—her "love" had flipped into hatred, and Wilson had been relieved. Over time, however, as winter softened into spring and then summer took over, Alice's hatred of him had waned.

Recently, they'd reconnected in a new, warped way. Alice wanted sex (as much as Wilson was willing to give), and he wanted . . . something else.

"I have so much work to do. I'm starting a new project." Alice pulled up her panties but left her pants around her ankles. She leaned forward, resting her elbows on her knees. "Here's where I got the idea. The other day I threw away an entire batch of essays. Just dumped them in the trash. It was so liberating. I recommend it to anyone who teaches. Just toss them. *You* don't care. The students obviously don't care. So get rid of the fuckers. It's a much more honest way to teach."

"Did you tell your students you threw away their papers?"

"Yes, I did. They were excited, jumping up and down. Some were speechless and a few even cried. But we talked it all out. We processed the whole thing. And we came to the conclusion that they will do *no written work for the rest of the semester.*" Alice's voice darkened, as if she were God.

"Which is one week." Wilson tried to imagine the student that would jump up and down—or cry—because a crazy teacher had chucked her paper.

"One very important week. With my new curriculum, I won't have to read a single research paper." Alice paused, her brow knit. It was humid in the office. A halo of orange frizz framed her face. "They should make people in jail read research papers. If I had to sum up the genre in one word, it would be *punishing*. There's a better way to teach—"

"I think—"

"—if we even *should teach*." Alice wasn't through. "Does the social construct of education benefit anyone? Nobody likes it. It's boring, expensive, and causes intense stress for both the teacher and the student."

"Hold on." Wilson propped his feet on his desk, mildly excited by her insanity. "Are you saying that, while you doubt the entire business of education, for now, your students will do no work at all?"

"Exactly. It's radical. I'm starting my paper today. I'm going to send it to *The New Yorker*."

*Why?* Wilson thought. And, *Why don't you pull up your pants?* "Do they publish that sort of thing?" he asked, trying to sound polite.

"They will. It's radical. I might even write a book. My theory of 'academic exhaustion' could change the face of higher education." Alice jerked up her pants, jiggled her breasts back into her bra (she *did* wear a bra, Wilson had discovered, a sheer bra that was more like a shimmering membrane, a garment he found unbelievably hot), then got up to unlock the office door.

Wilson watched as she settled in—curls bobbing, notebook paper flapping, pen whisking—at Dr. Gold's desk. The funny thing was, she was serious. Once again he marveled at her lack of irony. She truly believed that students should do no work, that her essay would be in *The New Yorker*, and that she'd single-handedly change thousands of years of tradition. Wilson didn't know if she was stupid or a genius, although he leaned toward the former. Lately, he'd begun to devise a theory of his own, the result of time spent with Alice. Were very dim yet highly motivated people the most successful on the planet? It seemed so. They weren't smart enough to realize how dumb they were and so attempted anything. Unlike him, they had no neurotic forebrain in place to tie them up at every turn. At the same time, they had an innate ability to believe in their own "genius," without any reflection or doubt. This belief was so blinding, others couldn't help but "see the light."

Wilson sat back, stumped. Had he just described himself? Was his theory as cockeyed as one of Alice's? And she actually finished her work. She'd published her exposé of the Mermaid Lair—which included her theory of "gender hypnosis"—not in the *Trib* but in the *Kalamazoo Gazette*. (He'd been disappointed to find that not a word of it concerned him.) Who was he to judge? In nine months, he'd written exactly one line of his dissertation. *Felt like singing today!* Plus thirty-odd pages of BS, mostly musings on his wife and annoying sister-in-law.

Wilson shoved *his* stack of research papers to the back of his desk. The fact that they were graded and ready to go made him feel foolish. He arranged his sandwich and chips on a napkin, then flipped open his notebook, dread sinking in his gut. *Felt like singing today!* What did it even mean? He took a bite of sandwich. It was icy inside. Someone had "adjusted" the fridge at home. Everything—the milk, the fruit, and leftover pizza—was frozen. As the turkey and lettuce thawed in his mouth, he picked up a pen, set it down. It was hot. He fanned his shirt. Was it proper academic protocol to sit at one's desk bare-chested? Probably not. It was just so hot. He had an entire *book* to write. The thought was chilling. He took a breath, fought the urge to crawl under his desk and stay there. Was it hopeless? No. He simply needed to buckle down. He needed something to help him buckle down.

"Alice?" He spoke quietly so as not to disturb her. Footsteps squeaked in the hallway. Water rushed in the wall. As he waited for Alice to respond, he ruminated on the strange color of her curls. The roots were nearly black, and the ends were—he wanted to say the color of Cheetos. It was not unappealing. She wore pink-and-cream plaid pants, pointy black witch shoes, and a hairy sleeveless turtleneck that smelled of sweat and pepper. Her aura of Divinity—Love's Baby Soft and cherry ChapStick—was gone. Wilson sometimes felt betrayed, as if he'd been lured into their relationship under false pretenses. It also made him sad. Divinity had *not* reappeared but remained locked in his past.

"I'm working." Alice finally spoke, hunched over her desk.

"Do you have anything?"

"I have a paper to write."

"Yes, but . . ." Wilson's voice was strangled. It always seemed to tighten around her. He didn't know why. He wasn't in love with Alice Cherry. She didn't inspire fear and lust and misery the way Katie had—and still could. "What about me?"

"What about you?"

"Do you have anything for me?"

Alice sighed. "Go ahead. It's in my purse." She watched as Wilson dug through her bag. It was an enormous satchel, made of what looked like goat fur. Wilson was hesitant to put his hand inside. He half expected to feel warm guts, to see hooves dangling from the bottom. Taking a deep breath he reached in, rummaged around, and came up with what he was looking for—the large Ziploc bag full of pills.

Alice shook her head.

Wilson selected a generous handful: Vicodin, OxyContin, tramadol, several baby Xanax. He popped three of the Xanax, chasing them with a swig of Coke. It felt good to count out the pills, to drop them into a smaller baggie and tuck them in his pocket. Finally: relief.

Alice kicked her goat bag under the desk and returned to her writing. Wilson could feel his body begin to soften, relaxing into the hard wood of his chair. At least he wasn't drinking. He could—and should—congratulate himself. Technically, he was sober. He could handle the pills. They didn't wreck him the way alcohol had. He no longer had much of a sex drive, but that was good. It made it easy not to cheat, to only service Alice, to keep himself out of the equation. He patted his pocket. He wasn't using or cheating. It was all good.

Thoughts of his dissertation drifted away. He stared at the rug Dr. Gold had brought in to the office. It was like a living thing, glowing ruby flowers floating on a deep purple sea. To know there was a solution was a relief in itself. Wilson's eternal problem: Life did not feel good. In the words of Hamlet: "How weary, stale, flat, and unprofitable / Seem to me all the uses of this world!" With an exclamation point. It was the part Wilson loved most. The tiny mark added such rage and frustration, changing "gosh, I'm depressed" to "this *really* fucking sucks!"

"If you chop up the OCs and snort them, you get higher," Alice said, still scribbling. "You bypass the time-release mechanism."

"So I've discovered."

She swiveled around on Dr. Gold's chair, her pen hovering in midair. The sunlight caught her face, and it was beautiful: heart-shaped, pale, and childlike. With her fierce brows and bright lipstick, she reminded Wilson of Anne Sexton, or of Sylvia herself. If only she had a sense of humor. "What will you do when they're gone?" Alice asked, holding out her hand for the Ziploc bag.

"What do you mean?" Wilson reluctantly turned it over.

"When they're gone. The pills. You seem to be addicted."

Wilson shrugged. He tried not to think of that dark day. "Why don't you just give them all to me now?" he asked for the hundredth time. "They're of no use to you."

"Oh, but they are." Alice cleared her throat. "Because of them, I'm learning how it feels to be the man in our society. To be the one who controls the means, the one who shares those means only if he is serviced sexually."

"Sounds a little sick."

"Exactly." Alice grabbed her pad and made a note. A curl like an upside-down question mark curved across her cheek. "How does it feel to know, intimately, the sexual servitude you inflict upon your wife every day?"

Wilson thought a moment. "I guess it makes me horny." Katie was hardly his sexual slave. Nor did he control the means. Every cent he made went to her for "household expenses," which meant "the bills" and "whatever else Katie wants." He had to beg for cigarette money. Did he think she'd give him money for narcotics? "Just quit," she'd say about his measly pack of American Spirits. "I can't in good faith finance something that's killing you as we speak."

"You're not financing it," he'd shout. "It's my fucking money."

"Of course it makes you horny." Alice grimaced. "You're so corrupted you can't see things as they really are."

"So that's all I am to you, a pawn in your weirdo experiment?"

"Yes." Alice looked sympathetic.

"OK." Wilson gave a manly nod. Of course it was OK. He was like a kid in a candy store. "But . . ." He hesitated. "What *about* when they're gone? Can you get more?"

"I'm not a drug dealer. No. Buy them off the internet. Or don't do them." Alice spun around once in Dr. Gold's chair, then jerked herself another half turn to face her desk. "If you're so worried," she said after a moment, "go over to the north side and buy some heroin. It's cheaper, easier, and you don't have to wait for the mail."

*Aha.* Wilson smiled. There was always an answer. You only had to ask. He didn't question Alice's expertise. Her brother, after all, was in jail. His knowledge of pharmaceuticals had obviously rubbed off on his sister.

The afternoon sun had waned, dusting Dr. Gold's rug with golden light. Wilson was nearly asleep, a puddle at his desk. Wait, was he drooling? He tried to rouse himself. He needed to drive home and crawl into his bed. Bliss was an exhausting affair, he was beginning to see. The office door slammed open. Wilson sat up with a start. Dr. Gloria Gold bustled in, her arms loaded with student notebooks. She wore red stretch pants, a hot orange tunic, and sandals with shiny fake fruit. Her toenails were neon yellow. She hurt Wilson's eyes.

"Hi," he said, trying not to squint. As usual, Dr. Gold ignored him, their tentative friendship forged the day of the visit to the battered women's shelter having never quite blossomed. She was glaring at Alice, busy working at *her* messy desk.

"Hey, Gloria." Alice glanced up, then casually went back to her papers. It was a deliberate dismissal. Wilson sat up straighter, waiting for the fur to fly. He scooted his chair in, giving Dr. Gold room to get by—plenty of room in case she wanted to prep for a flying body slam. As she moved past, he looked back, smiled cordially, then scooted in even more. Wilson A. Lavender: the most considerate office mate of all. Unlike Alice Cherry who hadn't budged, who had refused to defer to her senior colleague. Wilson had just begun to doodle in his notebook, thinking of ways to inform his wife that he would be sleeping the entire weekend, when Dr. Gold exploded.

"Why must you do that every time I enter this office?"

*Let the games begin.* Wilson looked to Alice for her reaction, trying not to smile. But Alice was looking at him, a worried expression on her face. He looked up. Dr. Gold was glaring down at *him*, not Alice. What had he done? Besides going down on his office mate, on the desk, earlier, but surely Dr. Gold hadn't seen that. The bag of pills was safely tucked into the goat bag. What was the problem? He'd been sitting there, minding his own business—planning, obsessing, conniving, yes, but when had Dr. Gold learned to read minds? "What?" he said, wide awake.

"Every time," Dr. Gold breathed hard once out her nose, "every time I enter this office, you scoot your chair in, which is fine, very nice and polite. But then as I'm walking past, you scoot in even more, you suck your skinny little body right up to the desk in such a deliberate, judgmental way," Dr. Gold's voice rose, "as if I'm this enormous . . . hippo, trying to squeeze its way past. It's rude and it's hostile and I've had enough."

"No." Wilson sat back, alarmed. "I was just trying to give you room. It's a small office—"

"And I'm too big? Too big to fit?"

"No, no. You're not. You're not . . ." Wilson lowered his voice, "large . . . at all."

Dr. Gold shook her head. "You have no idea what it's like to be a woman of size in our society. You never will. It's the last form of socially acceptable discrimination, and I will not have it *in my place of employment.*" She leaned close, staring into Wilson's face as if he were a naughty child. He instinctively closed his eyes, holding his breath for good measure. Dr. Gold smelled of vanilla, of cakes and puddings, of the pudding with the flip-top lid—the Snack Pack, his childhood treat of choice. He was a first grader again. His mother had put a Snack Pack in his lunch every day, day in and day out, and then one day she stopped. He walked home from school, a windy afternoon, March roaring like a lion. Where was the pudding, he wanted to know. Where was the pudding, he growled, roaring like the March lion, and his mother had thrown her coffee cup and cried, cried so hard his grandmother had to call his father at work, and his father had come home and whipped him for making his mother cry. Didn't Wilson see that he had work to do, he had a family to support, he couldn't be coming home every time some goddamn kid decided to kick up a ruckus? And his mother, watching from the couch, sniffing, her eyes hard, the hateful look on her face, the look Wilson couldn't bear to see because what had he done to make her hate him so?

He opened his eyes. Dr. Gold had, thankfully, turned her attention to Alice. "And you," she said, pointing a stubby finger. "Out of my desk by the time I get back." With that, she left as quickly as she'd blown in, the cherries on her toes clacking. As she passed, Wilson made sure not to move. Dr. Gold shoved him and his chair out of her way, slamming the door behind her.

Wilson and Alice sat in silence. Alice kicked off her shoes. There were holes in the soles. "That was scary," she remarked.

*Yet I am strangely elated,* Wilson thought. *I now have more than enough reason to obliterate myself.* "When do you think she's coming back?"

"In about five minutes."

"How do you *know* that?"

Alice shrugged. "Just a sense."

"I can't believe she shoved me." Wilson wiped sweat from the back of his neck. "What did she mean by 'discrimination'? Do you think she's going to sue me?"

"Probably."

"Are you going to move?"

"Never."

They sat quietly.

"You're crazy." Wilson laughed. "Why won't you move? Go on. Get up. Get out of her desk. Let's go."

"No." Alice shook her head. "I'm not going to move. For you. Because she was mean." She smiled. She looked young and small, her body dwarfed in the big black chair.

Wilson turned away. Tears burned his eyes. He chucked his sandwich in the trash, quickly gathered his things to go.

# Part Six

## Wildflower

"Bring me the sunset in a cup ..."
—Emily Dickinson

# Twenty-nine

## January

Lucy appeared at Otis's birth after Wilson called her in a panic. She was crying so hard she couldn't work her camera, which was a relief because January had never wanted pictures of the blessed event in the first place.

When Lucy poked her head into the shower of the birthing suite, January barely noticed. Had it been another occasion—one that did not involve otherworldly pain—she might have been surprised. Lucy had been cold to her for months, ever since the night of the robbery. January closed her eyes. *Fuck, it hurt.*

"I was just so jealous," Lucy stammered, mistaking January's silence for anger. She was disheveled in pink Juicy sweats, her face bare, hair pulled back into a ponytail. "You're everything I'm not: exotic, tall, pregnant. And then that Elvis . . . bastard . . . knocked me out. I couldn't quit crying. Everything scared me. I mean everything: the doorknob, pistachios in a bowl. I had raging PTSD. And the thing is, it all happened at once. Elvis, you. I couldn't *not* hide."

January stood motionless, hot water raining down on her back. She didn't care about Lucy's trauma. She was wondering if she was finally having "real" contractions. The nurse with the hot orange lipstick had said that the pains tearing through her—like the force of all hurricanes, tidal waves, and twisters on the planet—weren't real contractions.

"Then knock me out and cut me open now," she'd said, but the nurse had refused. In the shower, the contractions changed. Instead of ripping through her, hitting a dead end, and starting again, these contractions were moving out, down into the earth. Lucy quit crying and looked at January. "What are you doing?"

"Pushing," she muttered. It felt good. She could *act*, no longer at the mercy of the pain.

Lucy ran for the nurse.

"Don't push," the nurse ordered, hustling her back to the bed. "The midwife's on her way." Like January had a choice. It wasn't *her* pushing, it was her body—or this otherworldly force—and she had no power to stop it. In less than five minutes, out flew Otis. The bag of waters hadn't broken, so when he came out—swear to God—amniotic fluid exploded all over the nurse and the wall behind her.

"That's why you guys wear goggles," Lucy cried.

Little Otis, blue and cheesy on January's belly, the cord pulsing like something out of a science fiction movie—it was all so surreal. "Never again," she said and then felt bad, like the nurse would think she was ungrateful. But she wasn't. She was so fucking grateful that she would never have to feel the pain again. Otis glared at her with one open eye. January was sorry that he'd lost his warm, dark world. She was sorry the labor was so fast she didn't get drugs. The nurse asked Lucy if she wanted to cut the cord. Lucy took the scissors, turned green, and shook her head. She handed them back to the nurse. The nurse cut the cord. Something snapped in January then. The girl she'd been disappeared. Nothing would be the same.

The midwife came in and stitched her up. January held Otis in her arms. He squirmed sideways, rooted around, and began to nurse, all on his own. She couldn't believe it.

Lucy sobbed. "Are we friends again?" she asked. She sank to the ground. Just collapsed. January laughed, thinking she was being funny, but she never got up. January called the nurse, who set Lucy in a chair with her head between her knees.

"Are you going to throw up?" the nurse asked, her voice loud.

Lucy shook her head. "Just . . . light-headed," she said in a whisper.

"It's always the friends that lose it," the nurse said to January. "Or the dads." She brought Lucy apple juice and a packet of graham crackers.

# Thirty

January no longer dreamed of the Rock Star. Otis was three weeks old. She rarely slept for more than two hours at a time, and when she did, her dreams were feverish and rushed and the baby was always, *always*, waking her up.

It was the word *monstrosities* that got her. January sat on the floor in Jake's green room—on the Winnie the Pooh comforter that was now covered in spit-up—trying to understand what had gone wrong. Otis lay on his back in front of her, screaming, his knees pulled to his chest, his monkey face screwed up and sad. "It's OK, it's OK," she crooned, trying to sound upbeat. His eyes focused on her face. His dark hair stood on end. He looked horrified. Otis's arms and legs were skinny, and although his diaper was the right size, it always looked too big, which made her sad.

The evil Dr. Hookjendjyke had said that drugs had a teratogenic effect on the fetus. What the hell did it mean? The bitch had cursed her. January ran to the living room, found Wilson napping on the couch, and asked him for his dictionary. Wilson didn't move, only waved at his briefcase sitting by the front door. What was wrong—was he depressed? Sometimes January had a crush on her brother-in-law. *Save me*, a part of her would cry.

She took the worn book back to her room. Otis screamed. Her heart raced. What had she done? What if he never stopped?

*Teratogenic: causing fetal malformations or monstrosities.* Because she'd been stupid enough to smoke during her pregnancy, she'd created a monster. January flipped the yellowed pages, scared. *Monster: an animal, plant, or object of frightening or strange shape . . . an extremely vicious or wicked person.* It was true. She and her son were both monsters. Otis scared the shit out of her. She was an extremely wicked person.

The problem: Otis was colicky. He didn't feel good. January knew it was her fault. She was a terrible mother, a disappointment to herself and her child. Katie had said to quit eating oranges, they were probably giving him gas, and she'd eaten one anyway. As soon as Katie said *don't*, it was like a challenge and she couldn't stop herself—she hadn't even wanted one. Everything she thought she knew about motherhood was a lie. It wasn't any fun. It was awful, like being tortured. She'd pictured them strolling through the nighttime orchard in Luna, plucking at stars. Was she insane?

She couldn't even find time to take a shower, let alone figure out how to get them home. She longed for Pearl, her stolen Dalmatian. Pearl was so quiet, so self-sufficient. January fed her once a day. They slept entire weekends.

Otis was purple now, enraged, kicking his legs as if he wanted to blast off. January yelled for her sister. Katie came into the room and sat beside her, plopping a naked baby Rose on the blanket next to Otis. Just the fact of Katie was comforting. Her body was warm. Her freshly shampooed hair smelled of lily of the valley. January knew it was lily of the valley because before Otis, when she'd still had time to shower, Katie had told her that if she ever smelled her expensive lily of the valley shampoo on her again, she'd be out on the street. It was special, a Mother's Day gift from Wilson.

Rose and Otis were like two different species. Rose was big and bouncy and gleeful. Otis was a goblin. Angry and wizened, he looked like a creature you'd find living under a toadstool. January didn't pity him. She loved that he was a goblin—she just wished he were happy. She felt powerless, like she was back in high school, taking the most important test of her life, and she'd never bothered to study, never went to class—she didn't even HAVE THE BOOK!

Katie squirted a few drops of olive oil onto his belly. "Baby massage is proven to help colic," she said, ultraserious, as if they were about to embark on a top secret mission. "You practice on Rose." January flipped drooling Rose onto her back. Rose giggled, got up, and toddled out of the room. Jake and Paul came in to watch, sitting cross-legged on the blanket. They'd been at the lake all morning with their mother and were shirtless and suntanned, cheeks pink—they still smelled of salt and coconut oil. Katie moved her fingers in a circular motion on Otis's belly. "Touch him lightly, like you're smoothing butter in a tub," she said, her voice serene.

"What do you mean?"

Katie didn't take her eyes off Otis. She paddled at him with the flat of her hands. "Like butter . . . in a . . . tub."

January was about to explode. She was sweating, and a canker sore on the inside of her bottom lip had been ruining her life for a week. She couldn't eat. It hurt when she talked. Otis hated her. Her BOOBS KILLED. "What do you mean? I don't know what you mean," she cried. Tears filled her eyes. "Butter in a tub like that gross stuff we put on crackers when we were kids?"

The boys giggled. Katie looked at her, laughed. "Hype down. Your freaking out doesn't help. It only adds to the problem." She sighed, squirted oil onto her palms, and rubbed them together. "'Butter in a tub' is what the lady in the class I took said. Who cares? Just use common sense. He's a baby. Be gentle."

"Because butter is vague. People don't touch butter. I never should've been a mom."

Katie looked at her, eyebrow raised. "Are you going to try? Or should we put him up for adoption now?"

January sniffed, wiped her nose. Katie set Otis in front of her. January reached out and smoothed her fingers across his oily tummy. He cried, pulled his fists to his chest.

"Here. Let me." Katie grabbed the baby by his ankles and slid him back in front of her. "It's a whole routine . . ." Her voice trailed off. She worked on Otis for a good twenty minutes, pumping his legs like he was riding a bicycle, massaging his skinny arms and hands. She finished up with his chubby cheeks and head. When she was through, he was quiet and—January didn't want to say content, she didn't want to jinx it—but . . . Katie lifted him onto her shoulder. He looked at January, squinting his goblin eyes. His hair was oily, smoothed into a single Kewpie doll curl on top of his head. Katie rocked him back and forth, humming rhythmically. January lay back, staring out the window at the blue sky, exhausted. When she looked at her son again, he was asleep, a droopy little bundle on Katie's shoulder. She wished she were him.

"He's so pretty," Lucy squealed, tossing her beach bag on the bed. "Look how tan he is. Look at that dark hair."

Katie held her finger to her lips, still rocking Otis. The boys got up and ran into the living room. They didn't like Lucy. When January asked why, Jake said it was because Lucy never gave them snacks when they played with Abby. "She wants all the ice-cream bars for herself," he said. Lucy slapped at the boys' butts as they raced past.

"I can see his dad is Pete," she whispered loudly, kicking off her metallic blue flip-flops. "Unless you were fucking a lot of Mexican dudes."

"Lucy," Katie said.

"Like I can even remember." January sniffed the sleeve of her pajama top. It reeked of spit-up. There was gunk in her hair. Luna and Pete were a distant memory. When she pictured Otis's father, she saw only the guy in Soundgarden. She saw cherry pits, watermelon seeds decorating her back steps. If her house was still there. It had probably burned to the ground. But Pete. If she could find him. If she could get him to help. Because she couldn't do it. The rest of her life . . . her boobs . . . her fucking lip. She'd rather be dead. "I can't do it," she blurted, tears burning her cheeks. "He only sleeps for a minute at a time, and he eats constantly, he never stops. I haven't changed my clothes since he was born. He hates me."

"It gets better. I promise." Katie set the baby on the bed, tucking a yellow blanket around him. He curled into a tight ball, bottom in the air, fists under his chin. "I'm going to go wake up Wilson."

"Does your husband ever *not* sleep?" Lucy asked.

"No. If it weren't for me, he'd spend the rest of his life in a coma."

January followed Lucy out onto the porch. They basked in the sun, stretched out like starfish on the warm cement. The sky was blue, and they lay beneath a net of morning glories, twisting from the eaves, creeping down the fence, the bright flowers closed to the hot sun.

"The problem is he's spoiled," Lucy was saying. She took off her T-shirt. Her bikini top was the blue of faded denim. A cool jewel sparkled in her belly button.

"You can't spoil a baby." January closed her eyes, lost in the humming summer afternoon.

"Yes, you can. He cries all the time because he knows you're going to pick him up. You need to put him on a schedule."

"He cries because he's starving." *Please shut up.* "He eats constantly. It's like he can't get enough."

"He probably *can't* get enough." Lucy rolled to her side, her head resting on her arm. Her body was covered with the shadows of vines. "You may not have enough milk. My sisters never nursed, they didn't want to ruin their boobs. Put him on formula and he'll be fine."

"Like you know anything about babies." January pulled off her stinky pajama top and threw it into the bushes. The nursing bra was hideous— beige and enormous—but she was too tired to care. A fat bumblebee hovered near her ankle, buzzing peacefully.

"Excuse me?" Lucy said. "My sisters have six kids between them. I think I do."

"*You* don't have any."

"Yes I do. I have Abby."

"You don't even like Abby. And she's not a baby." January flipped onto her stomach, letting the sun warm her back. The hot cement felt good against her cheek. She drifted off. "Anyway," she mumbled, "I'm supposed to hold him all the time. That's why I have the Snugli. That's why he sleeps with me. It's attachment parenting. Katie says—"

Lucy looked aghast. "Jan, you can't let him sleep with you. You'll roll over and suffocate him."

"No. It makes him secure—"

"Yes. We knew this guy, Chuck? And when he was a kid, his stepdad was drunk one night? And he passed out on the couch and rolled over on Chuck's brother and killed him." Lucy tucked her hair behind her ears, absorbed in her story. "Only here's the crazy part: It wasn't a baby. Chuck's brother was, like, seventeen."

"Yeah, right." January laughed. "Isn't Chuck the guy you said was crazy? The guy that stole your black waitress skirt the night Steven had that party?"

"I'm just saying." Lucy sighed, frustrated. "I feel like you're gone." She leaned over January, her eyes bright. "It's like the fun Jan, the Jan I thought I liked—I mean, *knew*—is replaced by this . . . I don't even know . . . depressed, blah mom. Come on. You don't have to wear that ugly nursing bra. Did you know that? You can still wear hot bras. You can wear a thong if you want." She dropped her body on top of January's. She was heavy; it hurt. January pushed her off and rolled over.

"I had fourteen stitches," she said from her fetal position. "I'm sorry if it's taking me a week or two to get over this . . ." her voice cracked, "disaster."

"Don't start crying again." Lucy's voice was fierce. "Come on. We're going to the Rose Red concert tomorrow night. There's no way I'm going to let you miss. That guy was like your whole life."

"*Was.* I'm not even the same person. And I can't leave Otis. He's nursing."

"My sisters go to the bars all the time." Lucy grabbed January's shoulders. "Listen. Your life sucks. You have to party. Any good mom would tell you that. Otherwise you're going to dry up and cut your hair off and turn into this raging, sexless, cleaning mom that never gets laid and takes it out on her kids—is that what you want?"

"No," January cried. "I hate to clean. I've never cleaned in my life."

"OK. So we're going."


Wilson drove Lucy and January to the Rose Red show, as if they were teen-agers going to a school dance. January had never driven in Kalamazoo, and Lucy's new truck had been impounded. When January asked why, she said she couldn't talk about it, but "FYI: When the cops impound your car, it's because you've used it to commit a criminal act."

"Is it because you bought the truck with the *blank* you stole from *blank's* mom?" January asked.

"That's a lie." Lucy laughed. "Why do you make shit up?"

January closed her eyes. Her arms were floating without the weight of Otis. As they wound through the countryside, she glanced out the window and saw a raccoon emerging from the green, green brush. She'd only seen them lying dead in the road. This one was wild and alive, with bandit eyes and little black hands that pushed the tall grass aside. Its eyes were so intelligent and sparkling in its black mask—the raccoon itself was so awesome—that she didn't say anything, she kept it to herself. It was a good omen. She could feel herself coming back to life, as if the girl she'd been—the one that had disappeared the moment Otis's cord was cut—might still be hanging around.

Lucy sat in front. She turned around, resting her chin on her arm. "Clean is a good thing, right?"

It did feel good to be clean. Katie had even let January use her good shampoo, after agreeing to babysit for the night—if January pumped first. "Then if we run out of breast milk, he can have some formula. One little bottle isn't going to hurt."

"Or you could nurse him," Wilson had joked.

"The day I start nursing someone else's baby . . ." Katie shook her head.

*Please*, January thought. *Take over, set me free.*

When she left for the concert, Otis was in his baby swing. Back and forth he clicked, tinny music plinking. He wore a white nightgown and cap, like the sandman. His forehead was crumpled, and his eyes looked suspicious, as if he didn't know whether to cry or fall asleep.

Fight or let the world sweep you away?

Lucy and Wilson chatted about her upcoming wedding and the house she was renovating with Steven. Or rather Lucy talked and Wilson drove, unable to escape. Tiles, grout, the colors of the wedding (black and white with a splash of blood red; *Nazi colors*, Wilson remarked), landscaping, drywall, chicken, beef or vegetarian? January had heard it all a thousand times. The wedding was called off every other week.


Wilson made a sharp turn. January slid on the slippery seat. She wasn't nervous, she was numb. Sleep deprivation did that to a person. After weeks of hysteria, there was nothing left to feel. *They should keep crazy people up for days at a time*, she thought, closing her eyes. Her body jerked, as if falling into a dream.

"We're here." Wilson joined a line of cars snaking into a huge, muddy parking lot. "Don't talk to strangers. Do not make me have to look for you after the show." He lit a cigarette, rolled down the window. A paperback book sat on the seat beside him. "I can't believe I agreed to this." He caught January's eye in the rearview mirror. "So you think you're actually going to get backstage to see this . . . rocker?" Wilson smirked.

"Don't you mean, is *he* going to be lucky enough to see *her*?" Lucy turned to January. "You look hot."

January shrugged. She felt like an alien in her body. Her cutoffs were tight. She undid the top button and exhaled. She wore a Pucci-print halter with an empire waist that showed off her new boobs. Lucy had ironed her hair flat—her bangs hung in her eyes. Black eyeliner, pale pink lips—she felt exotic, like the raccoon in the ditch. She thought, *This is what I'm meant to do: look sexy, out in the big blue night, going to a show, listening to rock 'n' roll.* It was the only thing that had ever truly made her happy. Wilson turned up the radio. Pink Floyd, "Brain Damage." January felt like a kid again.

Lucy wore jeans and a vintage Heart T-shirt, tied in a knot at her waist. "You don't even know Heart," January teased. "I went to their concert when I was nine. When Ann Wilson was still skinny."

"You're right. I have no idea what you're talking about."

January hesitated. "I just hope I smell OK."

"What?" Lucy laughed.

"—because there was that kitten smell—"

"Kitten smell?" Lucy grinned.

"Shut up." January jerked her eyes at Wilson, who was fiddling with his wallet, one hand on the wheel. "After you have a baby, stuff comes out. It smells like when a cat has kittens. I remembered it. Our babysitter's cat, Trish, had kittens, and we all crouched around this box on the back porch. It was so weird. The cat was frozen in place, breathing hard, its eyes huge. It yowled, this low deep growl that went on forever, and we all squealed and ran away. When we came back, she was having them—none of us said a word—and then she licked them clean, these wet, dark sacs that turned into fluffy, blind kittens, and there was that smell—a kind of salty, bloody smell—and then she ate the—"

"January, please," Wilson said.

She lowered her voice. "So after I had Otis, I had that smell. I remembered it from Trish."

"You're so weird, January." Lucy rolled her eyes. "No. You don't smell like a cat that just had kittens." She looked at Wilson, smiling, waiting for his reaction.

"What I think is so funny," he said, "is that your babysitter named her cat *Trish*."

# Thirty-one

The sun collapsed behind the outdoor stage. It was hot, the air thick with the smells of the fair: mud and manure, sugar and grease and freshly mown hay. The rides in the distance were like dinosaur bones, black against the orange sky. Neon swirls and sparks, rows of glowing gumdrops—January could have watched them spin forever.

But she was at the show. She needed to pay attention to the show. It was loud. She and Lucy stood near the back of the little theater surrounded by a handful of empty seats. Rose Red looked small. January felt as if she were watching from a great distance—like outer space. It was the opposite of before, when she and Melinda had gone wild at the Troubadour, screaming sweaty pigs, smashed against the stage. She was starving—maybe that was why she couldn't concentrate. Rose Red played "Apple of My Eye," the song Stevie had written for her. January felt nothing. The words were hollow, about a girl she barely remembered. Fountains of sparks exploded onstage. Thank God they were almost done. She sat down, exhausted. Motherhood had stolen her mojo.

"Well, that sucked," Lucy said when it was over.

"Shall we go?" January was nervous, her ears ringing. Now came the fun part. If only she could find the energy. What if he didn't remember her? What if he sent her away? "We have to tell Wilson. Should we ditch Wilson?" She laughed, shook her arms.

"No." Lucy tucked her hair behind her ears. She had the look, the one she got when switching into criminal mode. "We're not done yet." She grinned. "We'll meet him when we're *done*, like we said."

A pathway of plywood boards led around the amphitheater to the back of the stage. A tour bus was parked to the side, the words ROSE RED in the front window. Some of the guys in the band—pale, skinny, glittery—stood in front signing autographs for a handful of fans. January hesitated. Her high heels were covered in mud; she thought she might throw up. "Go on." Lucy poked her in the ribs. It was easier to watch. Animal was talking to two overweight girls with dyed black hair. He looked the same only smaller, with a fringy purple scarf tied around his head. Was he still in pain, or had his stomach miraculously healed? Grouchy Ben the bass player skulked off to the side, a cigarette clamped between his lips. He was still a troll only more so, as if all those years ago he was a beginner troll, and now, his face shrunken and creased by time, he'd become the troll he was meant to be. January didn't see Stevie Flame and then she did—signing drumsticks for a couple of boys—and she realized she'd been looking at him the whole time.

The first thing Stevie Flame said to her was, "I love your hair. You look Swedish."

"Thanks."

They stood in the dark, in the shadow of the bus. Roadies loaded equipment. An excitable guy in red basketball shorts kept shouting at a guy named Bob. "Fuckin' Bob." Stevie smiled, shook his head. January thought of the fat roadie, pushed the thought away. Was it possible the night had grown hotter? She was sweating and her legs felt weak, as if at any moment they might give out. A crescent moon hung upside down in the muggy sky. She couldn't believe it was him.

Stevie Flame was a completely different animal. His body was crawling with tattoos: a rat curled on his arm, an angel spreading blue wings on his throat, tribal markings, skulls and geishas and Betty Boop. Each creature morphed into the next. It was hard to see where one began and the other ended. The surface of him was alive, shifting like water. He wore nothing but baggy black shorts, and January was dizzy just looking at him. "It's not you," she cried, putting her hands to her face.

Stevie laughed. "Jan, it's been like twenty years. Don't you watch MTV?"

"Yeah, but you haven't been on—"

He grabbed her hand, pulled her close. "It's a whole new Rose Red. We're punk now. What do you think?"

"I think you look . . . beautiful." January blushed. His long hair was gone, replaced by a Mohawk, bleached blond and hot pink.

He told her how everyone but Animal had cut their hair short, how you had to once you started going bald. "Or you turn into David Lee Roth, afraid to leave the house without a bandanna on your head."

January buried her face in his neck. She'd bumped into David Lee Roth once at the Hard Rock Café, literally plowed into him as she was going out and he was coming in. Diamond Dave with his mane of blond hair had laughed, grabbed her arms, pulled her in then set her free, checking out her ass as she went. She'd *smelled* David Lee Roth—some kind of fancy, fruity cologne you wouldn't expect—it was one of her best ROCK MOMENTS. Her heart had raced; she'd melted on the glittery sidewalk. Stevie hadn't noticed. "*That* ass," he'd muttered, walking ahead of her to the Pinto. "They had to carry him out of the Rainbow the other night, caught him pissing in the corner." He laughed, adjusted his big white sunglasses. The seats of the car were too hot to sit on. They'd stood on either side, looking in . . .

"I never would have recognized you," January said. Standing beside the bus, exhaust warming her bare legs, she knew it was a lie. She closed her eyes. She could be blind and know it was him. She inhaled the Rock Star. Aqua Net and smoke and the sky—all of her dreams had come true.

"Your boobies, Jan. They got so big."

She smiled, covered herself with her hands.

"You were just a baby then. I should have been arrested."

"I know . . . I don't know . . ." January felt breathless. She'd found him. Now what? How did the song end?

"Wanna see where I sleep?" Stevie led her onto the bus. He showed her the bunks—dark curtained compartments—and the half-bullet-shaped room in back where they ate and played video games. Everything was maroon and chrome, cracked and worn, and it made her think of an old casino. The smell of sweat socks and aftershave and stale cigarette smoke hung heavy in the air. "Fucking Monster Wars, man." Stevie backed her into a corner and kissed her.

January was fifteen again, back on planet ROCK. Her legs shook. She stepped out of her high heels. "They're muddy," she said. "It was . . ." She'd lost her train of thought. "What is Monster Wars?"

"Monster Wars is my game. Jan, you're so short. Were you always this short?" Stevie moved his hands beneath her shirt, stroking her bare breasts.

January pushed his hands away. It was too much, breast milk was leaking—fine, let him think she was hard to get. She stepped back. "I'm not short. You're tall. *And* pierced. You *never* had any tattoos. You *never* had any piercings." He had, but only in his ears. Why did it make her sad? She touched his studded ear, the bolt in his eyebrow, trying to hide her tears. "You had two holes. And now you're like a robot, with . . ." She couldn't think of the word.

"Rivets."

"Rivets?" She laughed, wiped her eyes.

"Come to the next show." Stevie kissed her again, his hands hot on her cheeks. "Grand Rapids. Or Detroit, I think. We're leaving in a minute. I don't want to stop."

"I have to . . ." What did she have to do? She should find Lucy. Shouldn't she find her friend? Stevie was so punk. His nipples were pierced. She could hardly believe it was him. It was a new dream, even better than the last. He had wings tattooed on the sides of his head. She kissed him, her hands on his wings. The hair was shaved, plush beneath her fingers.

"Check it out." Stevie turned around. He was still a skinny guy; his shorts were falling off his hips. When he raised his arms to lift the tail of his Mohawk, all of his ribs showed. He had a tattoo of a samurai warrior on the back of his skull. Its eyes were hard and mean. "I call him Earl," Stevie joked.

"Scary. Earl is scary. And you—you're covered. Like those Japanese guys on those shows."

"Right. This *is* the Japanese style. But I'm not covered. Not completely." Stevie moved closer. He lifted her shirt, pressing his bare stomach against hers. "You leave room here . . ." He untied her halter, slid his hands over her breasts to her armpits. "And here . . ." Stevie unbuttoned her shorts and pulled them down, resting his hands in the creases of her thighs. He licked her nipple, pinned her against the wall. "So when you die, your soul can escape."

Lucy had told her about the deep-fried Twinkies at the fair. January had never heard of them. She'd wanted to try one, wished she had one now. She couldn't concentrate on online poker. It was Stevie's new obsession. He was telling her everything about it.

"Do you know about the deep-fried Twinkie?" she asked when he paused for breath. They were lying naked and tangled in his bunk, the maroon curtains drawn.

Stevie laughed. His Mohawk had gone flat; blond and pink bangs hung in his eyes. He pinned her wrists to the bed. "Hon, we're having a poker lesson. Now, what do you do if you have a king, an ace, and a seven?"

*Oh my God, who cares*, she thought. She loved to look at his face: his hawk-like nose, his full sexy lips. His arms were wiry, his chest thin. The line of hair on his belly was just as she remembered. "Nothing. I don't do a thing because I wouldn't be playing in the first place."

"No. Wrong. Think."

"No. I don't want to think." January rolled over, curled her legs to her chest. "I got a royal flush once in Vegas. I won four thousand dollars."

"So you do know how to play poker."

"No. *Video* poker. You don't have to think. You just push the buttons."

Stevie lay back, pulling her on top of him. January let her body go limp. They'd already had sex, and their bodies clung together easily now, their skin sticky and hot. She closed her eyes. She could hear Lucy chattering in the back of the bus with Ben, the bass player. Ben—of all the trolls on the planet. They'd found Lucy in his clutches—sitting on his lap as he ate a ham sandwich—shortly after the bus took off for Detroit. January sighed. Animal shouted from his bunk across the aisle for everyone to shut up. Like a little kid.

"You *exhaled*," Stevie whispered. January giggled. They'd been ignoring Animal for an hour. He was in a terrible mood. He'd been cool to her all evening, as if he held a grudge. Why? Because she'd kissed him and run away that night on the roof? She barely remembered. It was a million years ago. She'd fallen, she remembered that. Animal's girlfriend—a short makeup artist with dyed purple hair—had picked a fight with him and refused to get on the bus. She was probably still at the fair, standing in the lot, her face sour, clutching her big jug of drinking water. She'd taken or hid his noise-canceling headphones; it was part of why Animal was pissed. Smokin' Ben Wa had a wife and six kids back in LA. "Oh my God, *I* want six kids," Lucy had cried before disappearing with him into the back.

January let the rumble of the bus soothe her. She tried to ignore the panicky feeling in her chest. She pictured the bus crawling into the night, and the night itself, a fun house of stars and planets, the funny upside-down moon. There was Wilson, sitting in his car in the now deserted lot of the fair, his silly book beside him. But of course, he'd be gone by now. She'd messed up. He would hate her, and it was important that he care. What about Otis? Did he miss his mother? Was he glad she was gone?

Stevie moved behind her. He ran his hands over the curve of her hip, as if he were a magician, measuring her for some future trick. His sheets were white, covered with scary clown faces. "Are you insane?" She'd laughed when she saw them. Another mistake: She never should have had sex. There were rules to follow. You were supposed to wait weeks—six, she thought—after giving birth. Now she would probably die of a horrible infection. Who cared? It was worth it. "Can I say something now? Can we be done with poker?"

Stevie didn't answer. He was tracing her tattoo—the spiral around her belly button—with his tongue.

"Listen." January played with his hair, sticky with hair wax and sweat. "My baby's head is perfectly round." She didn't say Otis's name; it would feel like a betrayal. "It was never misshapen or pointy, because he came out so fast. And it smells good. Have you ever smelled a newborn baby's head?"

Stevie nodded, moved his lips down her belly. "Ben's babies," he mumbled. "God, you make me hot."

"It's sweet like clover. I can sit there and rock him and smell his little head for hours at a time." That was a lie. She had no patience when it came to Otis and his endless, sucking needs. Why not tell the truth, that she was happy to be going, gone? Stevie's hand grazed her nipple. She winced. It was too sensitive. She was engorged now, her breasts as hard as rocks.

"You're nursing?" Stevie's voice was thoughtful.

"Yeah, why?"

"It's a turn-on, that's why." He lay beside her, his erection pale against his inky body.

"Right." January laughed, covered herself with the sheet. A clown with purple hair leered at her. Another sobbed. A third had Xs for eyes. "I hate your sheets," she cried.

"I'm serious." Stevie whipped off the sheet and lay on it so she couldn't get it. His nails were black, the polish chipped. The pads of his thumbs were raw from playing drums. Earlier she'd watched as he superglued a crack back together. Stevie started to stroke himself. "Can you squirt milk? Squirt milk on me while I look at you and jack off?"

"I'm not going to do that." January laughed and turned away. "You're crazy. I don't even know who you are anymore."

Behind her, Stevie was silent.

January looked over her shoulder, intrigued.


The bus stopped with a shudder. Everyone was quiet. An old Allman Brothers song played in the distance. "Dreams." January had always been in love with Gregg Allman. Did he have a bus like this or something better? Yellow light crept beneath the curtains. She lay in the bunk, wide awake, watching as it moved across her fingers. Stevie slept beside her, a black satin mask covering his eyes. "Hey," he mumbled, pulling her close. "Where are we?"

"I think we stopped for gas." January didn't move. She loved—*loved*—the heat of his body, the rhythm of his breathing, his smell of smoke and sweat. They were like animals in a den. She was in heaven, reunited with the Rock Star, the one true love of her life. So why did she feel trapped? She was starving, for one. And so cold—how low did they keep the air-conditioning?—she knew she'd never be able to sleep.

She wanted to go home and take a hot bath. And eat something (the deep-fried Twinkie). Then she would crash in Jake's green room, like a bug, safe in the folded green goodness of a plant. But there was the rub: Otis was home. Waiting to punish her for her absence, stare at her with those wide, horrified eyes, make her feel like the terrible mother she knew she was. Did she really think she'd have time for a bath, let alone to sleep the day away? Panic swept through her. She was better off on the bus, night ticking into dawn.

"Michigan." Stevie's voice was sleepy. "How the hell did you end up in Michigan of all places?"

"I didn't." January jiggled her leg, forced herself to stop. Her body had been going since Otis's birth, why should it shut off now? But it was more than that. Something—something between her and Stevie—felt wrong. Lying naked in his arms, *on tour with the Rock Star*, was everything she'd wanted. The night was a dream come true. "It was a dream come true," she imagined telling Katie and Wilson. Wilson would scoff, but wouldn't Katie care? Didn't she—January—care, too?

She slid from Stevie's arms, found her shorts, and pulled them on, checking the back pocket for her cash. Her top was twisted. She flipped it right side out, trying to hurry. She wanted M&M's and Mountain Dew. They probably didn't have much time. "I can go, right?" She kept her voice low for fear of Animal's wrath.

"No. Once you get off, that's it. They don't let you back on."

January giggled. "You look like a scary movie star. And *you* know where I live. In New Mexico. In Luna. In the house you bought me there."

"What?"

"The house. A pink adobe like a little old lady—"

"I didn't buy you a house." Stevie pushed his mask up onto his forehead. His eyes were smeared with black liner, the lines at the corners deep. His jaw was dark with stubble, his hair a waxy mess. He kissed the small of her back. January reached behind her, rested her hand on his head. Their bodies still fit together, two halves of a perfect whole. A part of her never wanted to leave. But how long could you stay in someone's . . . cubby? It was like being a pet. "Are you on drugs?" Stevie joked. "Should we do an intervention?"

January laughed. "No. It was your manager. Dale. He—"

"*Dale.*" Stevie said it with the venom he reserved for rock stars not himself.

"What?"

"He stole millions from us. From the very beginning. And his other clients: Bruce Dickinson from Iron Maiden, the guys from Queensrÿche."

"No." January was intrigued. "Whatever happened to Iron Maiden?"

Stevie shrugged. "I know what's going to happen to Dale. He's going to prison. If he doesn't flee the country first."

"Wow." January thought a moment. "So who bought my house? Because I have a house."

"Dale probably did, like you said. *But with our money.*" Stevie shook his head. His eyes gleamed. "Sleazy motherfucker. I can't wait to tell the guys."

"But why did he do it? Just to be nice?"

"I'd say that's pretty nice."

Ugh. Dale, pale and fishy. An embezzler. Why on earth? January shuddered. It was like having a guardian angel—but an icky one in a leisure suit. She pulled up her halter, tied it behind her neck. "Are you mad?"

"At you? Nah. If things don't pick up, I might have to move in."

Her heart leapt. She looked away, tried not to smile.

Stevie patted the shelf behind the bunk for his cigarettes. When he spoke, his voice was thoughtful. "He always liked you. He'd say, 'January, she's a special one.' Stupid, sentimental shit. He said you reminded him of his daughter. Which was weird, because the vibe we got was that he wanted to fuck you."

"Yuck. Stop." January looked down at her hands, small on the ugly clown sheet. She covered a clown with her palm, pressed it into the bunk. She looked at Stevie, naked and sleepy, his body a map of good luck and pain, RIP MOM in a broken heart on his chest, a blue lotus falling open on his belly. There wasn't a trace of her. Not a word. Not even the smallest flower. The realization made her sad. She hadn't left a mark. But Stevie had. He'd shifted the molecules of her body, become the air she breathed. How had it happened? How could one person be so vast while another barely registered? *Leave it alone*, said a voice in her head. *Get your M&M's and stop.* But she couldn't. "Everything turned ugly," she blurted. "At the end. And then you left—"

"Hon, you moved away."

"You told me to go. You said I had no business. You said you belonged there, in LA, and I belonged . . ." January bit her lip. "I belonged way over here, at the bottom of the map."

Stevie laughed. "I said that? I had a map?"

January didn't answer. Her cheeks were hot, her eyes blurred with tears. What was wrong with her? Two seconds ago they were having fun.

"Sweetie. I was an ass. An egomaniac. A joke—I still am. You never should have listened to me." He took her hand, rested it on his chest. "Because I missed you. I missed you when you were gone."

"Then why did you . . . ?" January looked away. He didn't understand. How could he? There were no words. But she could feel it, the pull of the purple night, drawing her closer to the edge, whirling her off into thin air. And in Luna: the desert, the loneliness, sucking you down. The sun you thought was your friend turning you to dust. The boyfriend you thought was a GOD was just a kid, a punk like you. He wasn't your dad. He wasn't your LIFE. He wasn't God or anyone that was going to save you. And from what? Why had she felt the need to be saved? It was the one thing she never understood.

She pulled her knees to her chest, embarrassed. "I never thought you bought me the house." She kept her voice light. "I mean, it always seemed kind of unbelievable. But . . . there it was . . ." She reached for the curtain. Where had she left her shoes?

"Hey." Stevie grabbed her shirt.

"Stop." January smiled, squirmed away.

"Get me some apple juice, will you, hon?" Stevie flopped back on the bunk, clicked his lighter, exhaled smoke with a sigh.

# Thirty-two

Over the woods, across the street from the gas station, curtains of shimmering red light rose and fell in the sky. "What the hell is it?" January said through a mouthful of chocolate. "Because it's really freaking me out." Although it wasn't. She was too exhausted to care. She felt as if she were underwater. The night was black and close. It smelled, faintly, of skunk.

"Calm down." Lucy grabbed her Big Gulp off the curb. "It's just the northern lights. Who cares? If you were from here, you'd know. I think Steven is cheating." She flopped her leg on top of January's. "Do *you* think Steven is cheating?"

"What do you mean?" January sensed a trap.

"Is your sister in love with Steven?" Lucy rested her hand on January's bare thigh, fingers poised to pinch. She was skinny in her T-shirt. Her hair was stringy, and she looked miserable, despite her night in rock 'n' roll heaven. Or maybe because of it. "Let me put it this way." Lucy wiped her nose. "Is your sister screwing my fiancé?"

"No. God, no." January closed her eyes, bracing herself for the pinch. But it didn't come. When she looked up, Lucy was smiling—content, like a cat. She didn't say a word. January grabbed her hand, confused. Lucy's nails were dirty and chewed.

"You're a terrible liar." Lucy pulled her hand away, tucked it beneath her leg.

"No." January hesitated. She sounded like a liar. "I don't know why you're worrying about Steven. You just slept with Smokin' Ben Wa. Gross. What would Steven think of that?"

"We *talked*. And you can do what you want *up until the wedding*. That's when the fun stops—"

January laughed.

"—God, do you know anything?"

*No, I don't*, she thought. "He was teaching her Chinese," she said after a moment.

"What? When?" Lucy narrowed her eyes.

"When she used to go over there, at night." At the fill-up station, insects swirled in a dome of dirty light. The bus sat silently, the driver fiddling with the pump. Two roadies smoked and argued and walked into the store. The bell clanged behind them. Along the highway a river of purple flowers shivered with each passing car. January closed her eyes. The pavement was warm beneath her bare feet. She'd never found her shoes.

"When at night?" Lucy rattled her ice.

"I don't know."

"Where was I?"

"I don't know." January took a guess. "At work?"

"So when I went to work, your sister came over and Steven taught her Chinese?"

January shrugged. The lights in the sky never stopped. They were like nervous angels, looming and retreating. It was exciting in an aliens-invading kind of way. She thought of the raccoon, off on its midnight rounds, the world warping all around him. And of Otis, safe with her big sister, a bundle on her shoulder, his face warm against her neck. Wasn't that where he belonged? With a good mom and dad, three siblings, Lovely the trusty dog?

She gathered her drink, her candy and change, and stood to go. Lucy grabbed her ankle. She was stretched out flat on the sidewalk, the pockets of her jeans bulging with candy. She pulled out a six-pack of gum balls. "Does she know it?" she said, popping an orange one into her mouth.

"Know what?" January sank back to the curb.

"Chinese."

"I guess. I mean, she was learning it. I don't think it's an easy language—" January glanced at the bus. Rose Red could easily leave without them. The strange thing was, she didn't care.

"Have you ever heard her speak it?"

"I don't know. I wouldn't know it if I heard it. I don't know Chinese. Why are we talking about this? Let's go."

Lucy took a deep breath. "Does your sister ever speak in any language—not English—in your home?"

"I have to say no, my sister does not."

Lucy got up and walked quickly toward the bus. January ran to catch up. At the door, Lucy turned around. Her eyes were lavender in the fluo-rescent light. She leaned close, her hands warm on January's neck. January could smell her orange bubblegum. "OK. Here's the plan. We're going to go with these *rockers*," Lucy rolled her eyes, "all the way back to LA. We'll find an apartment in the building Marilyn Monroe used to live in. I'll be a makeup artist, and you," she hesitated, "you can just be you. We'll have Katie send the baby, like UPS or something. Good?"

"No. Not good." January bounced on her toes. She had to pee and Lucy was in her way. Her body ached, and she didn't know who she was any-more. "I hate LA. And you don't just *go there* with Rose Red. You have to have a plan—"

"I do have a plan. Ben's going to set me up. He knows people in the movies—"

"Ben's married. He has six kids. What about Steven? What about all your stuff?" January's anger surprised her. But you didn't just leave people. You didn't just disappear. Plus, why should Lucy run off with the band? What gave her the right? She hadn't been there in the beginning. She didn't *believe* in Rose Red. She'd said the show sucked.

"Wow." Lucy took a step back. "You used to do anything. You were wild. And now you've turned into this . . . *housewife*. It's boring. I don't even want you to come." Her cheeks were flushed. Despite her words, she sounded hurt.

"Well, you're a home wrecker," January said.

"And you."

"What?"

"Your guy's married. Stevie Flame." Lucy smirked. "Ben told me. He and his wife live in the Valley. They have like thirty dogs—a whole dog farm."

January didn't know what to say. She didn't say anything.

"Don't freak out. Time doesn't stop. People don't stop just because you go away."

"I just didn't know about any . . . dogs." In that moment, January hated Lucy.

Lucy laughed. "It's not the dogs, it's the wife." She cocked her head, looked at January like she was stupid.

January didn't answer. After a moment, Lucy sighed loudly and disappeared onto the bus. January watched her go. *I thought we were friends*, Lucy said. Her voice was faint. Maybe January had imagined it. She stood, rooted to the pavement, waiting for the pain: the knife in the gut, the ache in her heart. *Your guy's married. A whole dog farm.* But it didn't come. Or at least it didn't knock her to her knees. She took a deep breath, angry and confused. What the hell should she do? Get back on the bus, watch Stevie sleep, kiss the angel on his throat, see how the song ended? You never knew what would happen. His wife could be a bitch like Animal's girlfriend. Stevie could dump her, pick January. There was always hope. But the truth was, Stevie Flame—the glittering, gorgeous fact of him—hadn't sucked her up and spun her away like he had years ago.

She was tired of hoping. She knew that Stevie was not, at that moment, nestled in his bunk, dreaming dreamy dreams of her. He was waiting for his apple juice (which she'd forgotten) or thinking of Monster Wars, if he was even awake. She needed to go home to Otis. It was what any good mom would do. Even the bad ones—the moms that cursed out their toddlers in the mall—stuck around. She pictured Otis with his big eyes, his soft pink cheeks, peaceful in her sister's arms. A flood of shame washed over her. Katie had eclipsed her. January was a failure as a mother. Thank God he was a lucky baby. He was a seed, blown by the wind into the perfect place for him. Who was she to mess it up?

She took a step back. She could hear the driver chatting on his cell phone in the cab. *You what?* he said in a girlish tone.

Which would it be? Curtain number one or two? The Rock Star or your baby? Heartbreak or torture? *Neither*, she screamed inside. Before she could think, she was running, out of the parking lot and down the highway, away from everything she'd ever wanted. Asphalt tore her bare feet. Her lungs burned. Her breath was ragged in her ears. She'd never run in her life. Yes, she had in eighth grade. Mr. J. had made her run laps because she wore panty hose beneath her gym shorts. But those were slow, sullen laps. She'd spent most of the time hiding behind a tree at the back of the field.

She clutched her breasts to her chest. After what seemed like hours but was probably only minutes, she slowed. Was she going to barf? She was wearing cutoffs and a halter in the middle of the night on a deserted highway in the woods. Wasn't there a scary militia in Michigan? What was a *militia*, anyway? And what about the rapist/trucker? The serial killer with chopped-off limbs in his trunk? January shuddered, thought, *What the fuck have I done?*

She rounded a bend. Civilization disappeared. The bus and the gas station were just a faint glow behind the trees, as if a spaceship had crash-landed. Insects shrieked. Something rattled in the ditch. She squatted and peed, praying that nothing would bite her.

Squatting in the muggy night, sweat pooling beneath her breasts and dripping down her back, she thought of Luna: her cool pink cave, the soothing hush of a Laundromat at night. She imagined a dog, a tiny one this time, one small enough to fit in a pink leopard purse, one that would never go away. She looked up into the sky. The northern lights were nearly gone. They were watery scarves, and she could see the stars behind them. *Wilson will kill me*, she thought, buttoning up her shorts. Thoughts of him, and of Luna, calmed her.

Headlights swung around the bend. January hesitated. *Are you insane?* her brother-in-law shouted in her head. Beneath his voice was a softer, sultrier one: the desert, calling her home. *Follow the river of flowers*, it crooned, *back to the land of enchantment*.

*You were lonely there, a neurotic mess*, Wilson reminded her.

*Like you're not*, January thought. *And maybe this time it will be different. Maybe now the loneliness is gone.*

The car, a shadowy shell of a VW Bug—an old one, direct from the 1970s—rattled closer. January thought she heard music, something jaunty and Dead-like wafting from the open windows. That was a good omen, right? Hot wind rattled the trees behind her. The soles of her feet burned. A deer crashed out of the brush inches from her shoulder and bounded across the road. Her heart pounded in her ears. Another deer followed close behind. The wilderness was random and violent, like the worst nightclub on the planet. Deer were like fierce, flying dogs. What was next, a bear?

January forced herself to quit thinking. She took a deep breath and held it. And at the last possible second, she stepped into the road and stuck out her thumb, eyes shut tight.

# Part Seven

## Edge

"The rest is silence."
—Shakespeare, *Hamlet*

# Thirty-three

## Wilson

On a chilly autumn morning, in a dank downtown apartment, Wilson woke after a solid fourteen hours of sleep. Or maybe *sleep* wasn't the word. The last thing he remembered was shooting up: the belt tight around his arm, the taste of leather in his mouth, the new syringe, one of several he'd bought at the pharmacy near his children's favorite ice-cream place, and wasn't that an uncomfortable thought to never think again? The needle, the poison-tipped stick, and then the warmth, the glorious rushing warmth, enveloping, no *filling* him, enveloping *and* filling him, rushing him straight back to the womb.

He no longer lived in the little pink condo on Merlot Court. Katie had kicked him out. Or he had recused himself—it depended on who you asked. One gray morning several weeks ago, Katie had gone grocery shopping. She'd returned with twenty cartons of yogurt and the Sunday paper. Why? It had to do with his sleeping. Apparently sleeping was no longer an option in her home. "Circle what looks good," she'd said, handing him the classifieds, helpfully turned to the Apartments for Rent section. Dead sunflowers rattled at the window behind her. There was something hard in her eyes, a determined look that scared him, and made him want to push back.

"We can't afford it," he'd said, tossing the paper on the table.

"We can't *not* afford it." Katie's voice was pleading. The strap of her paint-smeared overalls had fallen off her shoulder, and she pulled it back up. They'd been arguing about him moving out for weeks.

"I'm not leaving my kids."

"You'll see them as much as you always do. The only difference will be that we'll no longer have to . . . get along." Katie's voice faltered. They both knew *that* wasn't true. The wall behind her was grubby with little handprints. He could hear the boys outside playing pirates in the empty kiddie pool. Rose and Otis were napping in the bedroom. Who did she think she was, kicking him out of the family he'd helped create?

He spoke the words he knew would set her off: "If you're so unhappy, *you* get an apartment. You go and I'll stay here with the kids. Why should I be the one to leave?"

Katie's breathing quickened. He watched with satisfaction as she fought to control her temper. He hadn't known about her bad temper back in the beginning, when she'd rollerbladed up to his front door, witchy and pale and impossible not to love. No, that was wrong. She'd walked. Walked from the wrong direction; walked *in* the wrong direction. Wilson looked at the newspaper on the table. He felt sad. She'd reminded him of orange juice. Orange juice—how strange everything was. It had all come down to a newspaper on a table. And not even a table, but a card table—they'd never gotten around to replacing it with anything better. Katie was shouting now. He'd better pay attention.

"—and you sleep all the time. 'Genius Never Sleeps'? Genius sleeps all the time. You lie, you're never here, and when you *are* here, all you do is sleep. Sleep and lie—"

Her rants typically went in a circle. Wilson could tune in at any time and hear a variation on the theme. He fought the urge to lie down on the carpet. Soon she'd wear herself out and he could go relax. And why shouldn't he lie down? Just because Katie wouldn't like it? Wilson sank to the ground. He curled into a fetal position then stretched out long, his body limp and still. He was going to be covered in dog hair, but who cared? He was a passive resister. Maybe Katie would laugh and let him go.

She didn't laugh. When she spoke she sounded tired. "Why are you on the floor?"

"You should be a drill sergeant." Wilson smiled, closed his eyes.

"Why are you on the floor? Wilson? Crazy?"

"Have you thought about enlisting? Oh, I forgot, you wouldn't be able to get up that early."

Katie giggled. "I'm serious, though," she said after a moment.

Wilson didn't move. Numbness filled his limbs. He could easily drift off to sleep there at his wife's feet.

Katie lay down beside him, her head on his chest. "You really think the army would kick me out?" She slid her hand inside his shirt. Lovely lumbered over and sank to the ground with a sigh. He rested his chin on Katie's hip, observing Wilson with cloudy brown eyes.

"They wouldn't take you in the first place." Wilson patted the dog. He was grizzled, ancient—he'd be surprised if he lasted the winter. "You wouldn't go. They don't have lattes. You don't get to lounge."

Katie sighed. She moved closer, draping her leg across his hips. Her warm weight felt good. She smelled of cinnamon toothpaste. If they could just be still, if she could just leave it alone. But she didn't. "If you go—" she began.

"I'm not leaving." Wilson spoke quietly. He shoved her off him. It was no use. He couldn't sleep. He was going to be sick very soon. He was sick of being sick. What was the old saying? The problem isn't the drugs; the problem is when you run out of the drugs. He needed money and he needed to score and he'd be damned if he was going to waste money—money he needed—paying rent on another apartment.

Katie was standing over him, sobbing. He'd said something mean. Her face was red, and she looked ugly, her mouth distorted, her hair bunched in a silly pink bandanna. Wilson watched from the floor. He hated her in that moment, hated her for—what?—for not saving him? For not loving him enough? *For never being enough.*

*I'd rather be dead*, Katie had cried on that depressing Sunday morning. *If you don't go*, she'd threatened. So he'd gone. Wilson had gotten up off the floor, picked up the newspaper, and circled what looked good. And now, several weeks later, here he was, waking after a solid fourteen hours of sleep, in his mildewed little apartment on Park Street, not far from Alice Cherry's old digs, wondering why he'd ever resisted moving out. Katie had granted him freedom. It was the best gift he'd ever received.

With freedom came perspective. He understood now that even if Katie had spent every second of the past four years breathing his every breath, filling his every need before he even knew he had one, it wouldn't have been enough. Nothing she or anyone else had to give *could* ever be enough. His was an exceptional case, the suffering he felt far greater than that of the average man, the relief he required immense.

Thank God for Alice Cherry. What a miracle it was that she'd led him to the buffer. It was as if she'd known, even before he had, exactly what was needed. Alice was gone now, off teaching somewhere in Arizona, presumably over her "academic exhaustion." Or was it Vegas? She'd sent him a postcard once. *When I look at the sky out here I think of you because it is everything and nothing all at once.* He hadn't answered. What did you say to that?

Swirls of frost coated Wilson's bedroom window. The sill was beaded with moisture. It was wintry out and not yet Halloween. He glanced at the bedside clock. 7:07—he had an hour to go before he left for work. He lay quietly on the flannel sheets. Katie had bought them as a housewarming gift. She'd chosen a hunting motif: the red of dried blood with rows of manly black bears. There was a clicking noise and the heat came on. His children's crayoned drawings fluttered on the walls.

Wilson remembered the taste of leather in his mouth. And the anticipation he could taste; the anticipation that, if truth be told, was almost better than the rush. The prick of the needle, the warmth, the magical dreamless sleep . . . But now, waking from the fairy tale, he was beginning to see that something was terribly wrong. For one, he was lying *atop* the new sheets, the matching quilt folded neatly at the foot of the bed. For another, he was freezing, despite the heat blowing across his bare chest. It was as if ice water flowed through his veins—slowly, like it hadn't quite melted. He'd never been so cold in his life.

There was the problem of his leg: he couldn't feel it; it was numb, dead weight. He checked to see if it was still there. Had he somehow, unfortunately, lost it during the night? Wilson touched his thigh. He could feel it, solid and cold beneath his palm, but *it* could not feel him. His entire body was tingling, as if something vital had failed, and was now thrumming back to life. Had his heart stopped? Had he quit breathing? A wave of nausea washed over him. Every cell in his body hurt.

He swallowed hard. On the other hand, there was something pleasant, or at least familiar about the edge, this strange sensation of having wakened not from a place of comfort and warmth, but from somewhere cold and heartless and vast. He'd left his body, floated in deep space for the night. And still you kept on. That was the miracle. You kept on, your heart pumping, blood flowing through your veins, life filling again and again the empty vessel you'd become. Had he stood with one foot in life and the other planted firmly in the grave? Had he, Wilson A. Lavender, become immortal?

The god ran to the bathroom—ran as much as one could while dragging a dead leg—and fell to his knees before the toilet. He couldn't quit shaking. Rivers of sweat ran down his face, dripped off his chin. He must have passed out, for when he came to he was on the bathroom floor, his cheek resting in a pool of vomit. The tile was ugly: single ears of muddy yellow corn on a dirty cream background. Katie would hate it. Thank God he'd moved out. Relief flooded his body. If Katie could see him now . . . Wilson shuddered. She'd have him cleaned up and committed in thirty seconds flat—after first emptying his wallet. Thank God he now had the freedom to . . . become ill . . . if needed, on his own, in private, with no hysterical repercussions. He wiped his face on a dirty T-shirt, swiped at the floor, and crawled back to bed.

There was a hardened pool of blood on his pillowcase, and several smeared drops on the new sheets. Wilson collapsed on top of them, not caring. He'd deal with the blood later, when he could think. Surely he hadn't killed anyone. If he stumbled across a body in the kitchen, then he would start to worry. It was 7:17. He had plenty of time to recover before work. Five more minutes, ten at the most.

Another wave of nausea sent him lurching to the bathroom. After a repeat of the first episode, he pulled himself up by the sink. He stared into the silver-chipped mirror. His face was pale and thin—more skeletal than usual, he thought ("Are you, like, dying?" January had asked). There was a bloody gash on his chin, starting from the corner of his mouth. He must have hit something on his way down last night, but what?

The cut was several inches long, scabbed with dark brown blood. He took a deep breath, tried to clear his head. After washing the wound, he found a tube of scar healer (excellent for tracks) and carefully rubbed the clear gel in. His hands were big and clumsy, still half-asleep. He jerked the rotting bathroom drawer, searching for the wand of cover-up he'd bought. His sisters had used something similar in high school to hide their zits. It came in handy should he ever have a mark on his arm, although he rarely did. Katie never noticed. Wilson wondered if she'd ever thought to look. It was funny how she thought she knew everything when really she knew nothing of his life away from her. Best to keep it that way. Should she ever discover the truth, she might take the kids and leave. He could lose everything.

The drone of morning traffic on Park Street rose and fell in waves. There was a skittering in the wall and then silence. In the tiny bathroom, sur-rounded by ugly tile and yellowed, peeling wallpaper, Wilson carefully blended the makeup on his chin. He brushed his teeth, found his comb, and combed his hair. He was beginning to feel almost human. The week before he'd gone to the barber and gotten it all cut off. "Your hair," Katie had cried. "All your pretty curls. It's not even you. You look like you've been skinned." Despite her reaction, or maybe because of it, he liked his new look. He felt manly. When he looked in the mirror, he saw a man who meant business. It fit his new life.

He dressed, lying down on the bed to rest after changing his underwear, and again after pulling on his pants. Socks, shoes, belt—Wilson sank to the ground, exhausted. He was an old man, an invalid, the survivor of a shipwreck, sucked in, spat out, and left to die on the rocks. It wasn't the condition he'd planned for his first day at a new job, but so be it. He had plenty of Xanax to take the edge off later, when things got rough.

In the kitchen he poured himself a cup of coffee, slowly stirring in four spoonfuls of sugar. He fought the urge to call Katie, to make sure she was up and about getting Jake ready for school. When Wilson had ruled, he'd cared for Jake in the mornings, making him sausage and eggs, giving him plenty of time to watch cartoons before they walked together to the bus. Katie, he knew, crawled out of bed at 8:00, when the bus came at 8:14. "I'm an adult," she'd said the third time he called to check up on them. "I got along fine for thirty-three years before I met you. I think I can survive now." *That's debatable*, he'd thought but kept his mouth shut.

They were friends now. They got along. Yes, he'd cleaned out the bank account a few times, and yes, she'd taken to hiding her purse and the extra checks when he was around, but other than that . . . Katie needed to understand. He had planned on buying new shoes for Jake. Shoes were important to a boy his age. And yes, he knew it had been late when he withdrew the money, but . . . "You don't empty the account at three a.m. on the north side to buy shoes," Katie had said. Well, why not? And why was he thinking about it now? He was free, alone on Park Street with nothing but time on his hands, and now, with the new job, his own source of income that he would *not* be sharing with his wife. Her grandmother had died unexpectedly and left her a nice inheritance. If he fell off the face of the earth, she and the kids would be fine. At least for a year.

Wilson's phone rang once then stopped. He *had* planned on buying new shoes. Why wouldn't she believe him? Did he care anymore? Not so much. There were the lies he told and the truth he kept to himself, and really, what did it matter? Here in the new life, the *vita nuova*, it was about him, about taking care of himself. You couldn't depend on a woman. He saw that now. It was the most painful lesson he'd learned.

He poured another cup of coffee, swept the remnants of the night before—a bottle cap, Q-tips and matches, the used rig—into the trash. The floor of the cupboard was black and rotting. His apartment was awful, everyone agreed. "What you have is mold," Katie had said. "It's all over you, on your clothes, in your hair—even in your car. You've got to kill it with bleach or call your landlord. You can't live like that. It's like death. Like the Lynyrd Skynyrd song, "That Smell." She sang a line or two in a flat tone.

"I love it when you quote the great philosophers," Wilson had said. He couldn't smell anything. He smoked too much. He'd never had much of a sense of smell. Except with Alice Cherry, when he'd caught a hint of Divinity, but that had been a lie.

7:42. Wilson set down his cup. He had a task to complete before heading off to work. The notebook was hidden beneath a pile of old women's studies handouts. *Felt like singing today!* Plus thirty-odd pages of BS. Thank God he was done. He'd planned on formally quitting the program—shaking his head no as his advisor begged him to stay—but after he failed to register for fall dissertation hours, or to meet with the women's studies director to line up classes to teach, and nobody called, he realized they didn't care. It hurt, but it was also a relief. You just didn't show. If he'd known it was so easy, he would have quit last winter.

He flipped open the notebook: pages and pages on Katie and the clown across the street, followed by a special section devoted to January, the most annoying sister-in-law on record. Wilson *had* enjoyed their last conversation, mainly because afterward, she'd disappeared from their lives.

"*How* are you a genius?" she'd asked as he smoked on the porch at Merlot Court, pre-eviction. It was late, the night before the nonsense with the "rock star." The fireflies were out, yellow light sloshing in their bellies. "Katie always says you're such a genius, but I don't get it. You're smart, I guess, but so is she. Why are you a genius and not her?"

Wilson had smiled, delighted. Not only was the conversation centered on him, it was centered on him and the fact of his genius. He explained to January that as well as being smarter in general than his wife, he was smarter about *everything*—the speed of light, the Mandelbrot set—whereas her knowledge was limited to books, movie stars, and yoga. "And then there's the torture factor," he added. "All geniuses are tortured. They can't get along in the real world because they see how ridiculous everything is, how superficial and ultimately stupid things are. Geniuses are always thinking. They're thinking of five thousand things at once, and seeing all the angles of everything, so not only does life seem futile, it's difficult and confusing, too." Wilson stepped on his cigarette, set the butt on the windowsill. He'd depressed himself. "It's a real handicap."

"Hmmm." January nodded. She stood, pulling up her baggy shorts. They were covered in hibiscus. Her legs were tan, and her blond bangs hung in her eyes. She looked like a surfer girl, Wilson thought. "I think . . ." January had hesitated. Otis's cries drifted out the bedroom window. "I think I'm going to get a Slurpee."

And then, not twenty-four hours later, she was gone. Off to New Mexico in the middle of the night, abandoning her newborn son.

In his new apartment, Wilson shoved his cigarettes into his pocket, found his cell phone and keys. He ripped a page from the notebook then tore out several more. *Kissed Alice Cherry*, he'd scrawled last winter. *What a mistake. She wouldn't stop talking. All the theories. I felt panicky. Had none of my own to contribute. When she stopped, when she climbed onto me—I was sitting in the strangest hairy chair,* horsehair *she called it, I could feel it poking me through my pants—and when she climbed onto me, I was so grateful that she'd finally stopped talking . . . Must burn this page. The guilt. And now she's looking at me. I can feel her eyes on the back of my head. Big mistake.*

His new role model was Jesus. Simplicity was his path. He needed his pants, his medication and smokes, but not much else. He'd set down his burdens: his marriage, teaching, the dissertation. Katie was the most difficult to let go. If he wanted to be obnoxious, he'd say that once they had children, their souls became inextricably bound, like the dancers on Dr. Gold's poster, but really, it was a problem of memory. Tiny moments kept bubbling to the surface. It was funny what the mind chose to keep. That morning, in the space between sleep and wakefulness, he'd thought of a spring night a couple of years ago. Katie was up late, sitting on the kitchen counter with her drawing board, working on a picture of Lovely. Wilson had glanced at it as he got a bottle of water from the fridge. The dog was sleepy and blue, curled around a pale planet in a sky flecked with stars. It was nice. "Pretty," he'd said, cracking the lid of his water.

Katie looked up. She had a smudge of blue oil pastel on her cheek. Her hair hung long and loose. She was listening to an old Journey CD, and he could see that she was still lost in the world of her picture. She looked young and peaceful, and for a brief moment, he wished he could have known her for her entire life, from the second she was born. It was the strongest urge—he felt it in his gut—and it took him by surprise. "I wish that when we were kids, we were friends," he said, touching her hair.

"Hah." Katie didn't look up.

"And then in high school, boyfriend and girlfriend. You would've eaten me alive."

"You were a crazy alcoholic." Katie looked up, smiling. "Exactly what I liked."

He'd stood in the kitchen a while longer, watching her draw, her neck bent, her hair falling across her face. The quiet was what stayed with him: the misty spring night, Jake and baby Paul asleep in the bedroom (Rose was still to come), the stillness that surrounded Katie as she worked, the cold water in his bottle, and the relief he'd felt at having found her at all. It was a tiny moment in a sea of tiny moments, all of them like bubbles, drifting randomly into the starkness of his new life.

8:01: Almost time to go. In a smaller, uglier kitchen, Wilson's new cell phone rang.

"Hey." Katie's voice was bright.

He felt the familiar leap in his chest. He wouldn't show it though. They were over. She'd kicked him out. "I can't talk. I'm late for work." He shook his leg, trying to coax some life back into it. He would be on his feet for most of the day. It was vital he have four working limbs.

"I'm so excited for you. You're going to like it, right?"

"I guess so. How hard is selling cars? It's not like you have to write a paper about it. It's not like you have to think."

"God, no." Katie laughed. "That would be funny, though. If you had to sell a car, and then think about selling the car, and then write about what you thought about selling the car."

"Ugh. You're making me sick." Wilson was starting to sweat again. He dug in his pocket for his Xanax. Why wait when you could pre-medicate? His leg hurt. What if everyone hated him?

"Otis has a cold."

"Poor bastard."

Katie giggled. "Yeah. Wheezing. I'll take him in . . ." Her voice grew dark. "No word from the mother, of course."

Wilson didn't answer. He was counting the bills in his wallet. By his calculation, he needed to sell two cars a week in order to keep himself . . . *feeling well*. He wondered how hard it would be.

"What are you doing?" she asked.

"What?"

"It sounds like you're doing something. Like you're not paying attention."

"No."

"Wilson?" Katie was quiet.

"Are you crying?" Wilson sighed. "Why are you crying?"

"I miss you. Isn't it crazy? I can't stand the thought of you going out with anyone else. Promise me you won't."

Her jealousy was pleasing. "No. I can't do that. You were the one—"

"Please," Katie cried. "Promise. I didn't know—"

Wilson tuned out. Couldn't she see he was already gone? He was a man now in a man's world, selling cars at Saturn—a completely different planet from the one she was on. He wiped sweat from his forehead, tried to collect his thoughts. His hands shook. He was sick and, if truth be told, scared of starting a new job. How easy it would be to go home, to curl into the pink shell on Merlot Court. But he wouldn't be able to . . . medicate. Returning was not an option. He shook his leg. It was on fire, the pain excruciating; he was finding it hard to stand in one place. Still, he had a task to complete. He picked up a piece of notebook paper, flicked his lighter, watched it burn. He dropped it in the sink. Katie was still going on about other girls, about how she couldn't stand the thought of somebody else touching him, kissing him, it was making her crazy, and she knew he was up to something bad now, that *he* was bad, and that only made it worse because he knew that, for her, *bad was a turn-on*. Wilson set down the phone. Standing over his stained sink, he burned the rest of his dissertation. A finger of smoke curled around his head. Sylvia Plath disappeared, taking with her the insanity he'd had the nerve to think he could ever understand.

Who was he to decipher her? Or his mother? Or Katie? No. He was done, through with the study of women. The smoke alarm went off—a high, shrill beep—but he continued, burning each page until there were none. He picked up his phone and listened. Silence. Katie must have hung up. He snapped it shut. After dousing the ashes with water from the tap, he scooped the remains into the trash bag, twisted its top, found his Saturn jacket, and was gone, off to the world of men.

# Epilogue

## Katie
1973

At the end of third grade, we had a surprise party for Miss Moss, who was going away and leaving us all alone. She didn't care about us, so who cared about her? Timmy Summers' mom was the room mother. She wore her hair in a long red ponytail, like Jeannie on *I Dream of Jeannie*. But she wasn't bubbly and fun. She was perfect and perfectly mean—and so skinny her hip bones stuck out like handles. I was scared of her and her handles. I didn't get too close.

Mrs. Summers wore a patchwork skirt and bright red lipstick, and had once made Pixie Tanner's mother cry. They were room mothers at our Christmas party. Mrs. Tanner was sad and jumpy that day, and kept missing the Dixie cups and spilling Hi-C on our desks. Mrs. Summers watched, tapped her foot. She rushed up and took the can of juice drink from Mrs. Tanner. But Mrs. Tanner held on. I watched, excited. I could see the evil Pixie in the squint of Mrs. Tanner's eyes, in the stubborn tilt of her chin.

Mrs. Summers glared. "I've *got* it, Carol." She tugged the can away, moved smoothly down the row of desks. Her voice was nice and mean at the same time. I felt the chill in my gut. Maybe Mrs. Tanner did, too, because she dropped her wad of paper towels on the floor and went outside to the playground to smoke. Mrs. Summers didn't spill a drop. I ignored my Hi-C until I couldn't stand it anymore and drank it all in one gulp.

"Hide *now*," Mrs. Summers ordered on the last day of third grade. She was the only room mother for the surprise party. Maybe she'd scared the others off. Five minutes ago, she'd crept into our room like the Grinch, right after Miss Moss had been called to the office on "false pretenses." Now Miss Moss was on her way back. We could hear her tip-tapping down the hall. When she opened the door and stepped into the room, everyone jumped up and shouted, "Surprise!" I only moved my lips. There was no *law*. Amanda B., with hair so white and thin she looked newly hatched, hit her head on her desk and cried.

"Shhh." Mrs. Summers clapped once, loudly, and took a step toward her.

We scared the crap out of Miss Moss. "Shit," she shouted, her hand flying to her mouth before she sank to her knees on the checkerboard linoleum and sobbed. Timmy Summers was sent to get her a cup of water from the drinking fountain in the hall. It was awful water—warm and it tasted like rust.

On the floor Miss Moss took a sip, made a face. She wiped her eyes, honked her nose into the handkerchief Mrs. Summers offered. After Mrs. Summers helped her stand, Miss Moss jerked down her skirt, her legs wobbly in her white patent leather heels. Her dress was short and purple with a giant white collar. It made her look like a baby. I had one just like it. Why was Miss Moss wearing little girl clothes? Didn't she care about *anything* anymore?

"Class," she said with a shaky smile. "Miss Moss is going to have a baby. I'm going to be a mom just like your moms."

*You already told us that*, I thought.

Her voice was dreamy and excited. "It's a wonderful thing, a miracle, ushering new life into our world." She hesitated, her eyes searching the ceiling tiles. "And that's why I fell down. Sometimes mommies-to-be get overwhelmed. That means too much happening at once. And sometimes," she lowered her voice, "mommies curse. But we don't mean it. We all know right from wrong. I have confidence in you children. That means that *I believe in you*." She gave a firm nod, our teacher once again. The kids in Room 3 stared, confused. What did falling down have to do with having a baby? And why wasn't her stomach big?

"Wonderful," Mrs. Summers cried, applauding Miss Moss. The kids in Room 3 turned to stare at her.

It was wrong: teachers crying, teachers falling down, Mrs. Summers with her big red mouth. Everyone got rowdy, even pale Amanda B. We drank our orange drink, and gasped when Mrs. Summers placed a full-sized Hershey bar on each of our desks to take home. I set mine in the exact center. I could hardly believe my eyes.

The bell rang and the party ended. All the kids ran to hug Miss Moss good-bye. I didn't dare. I darted out the door before anyone could stop me, and was sad when nobody did. I wanted to hug Miss Moss. I wanted to crawl into her giant yellow purse and go home with her forever. But I couldn't—couldn't hug her or say good-bye. I didn't touch anyone anymore. I wasn't sure if I ever had. When my mother hugged me, I pulled away. No hands on my body. They weren't to be trusted. Leave me alone. And who would hug a girl like me anyway? What if someone got close and sensed the badness inside? Then what? I'd be found out. They'd take me away from my mom, the one good thing.

"You know you're crazy, right?" Larry Johnson had said the week before. He frowned like he did when he wanted to look smart. It didn't work. He only looked dumber and more confused. "Do you know what happens to crazy people?" He was watching me, not the road. We passed a row of fat old oaks. Their roots knuckled the sidewalks. Their branches hung so low they swept the roof of the car. I sat pressed against the door. I held my breath, didn't listen. My body was wood—solid and still, like the trunk of a tree.

"Crazy people go to the nuthouse, otherwise known as the *bin*." Larry swung a sharp right. I held onto the door handle. "In the bin, they put you in a pit, naked and drooling with all the other loonies." He looked at me, cheerful in his silky yellow shirt, his hands fat on the wheel. He narrowed his eyes. "And then you'll never see *Mommy* again." He laughed like it was a joke, but his eyes—glassy and brown with a crescent of white beneath the irises—looked dead.

I walked the rest of the way home from the golf course. The setting sun was a bright pink Super Ball in the sky. I had to pee badly, and then a half a block later, I did. Warm pee ran down my legs and pooled in my Buster Browns. My body didn't care anymore. I didn't either . . .

*I don't care to hug Miss Moss.* I made myself believe the words as I walked home from the third-grade party. I turned cold like Mrs. Summers. *I won't be hugging you at all.* I shoved my Hershey bar into my back pocket so it would melt along the way. The cherry blossoms had blown into slushy piles on the sidewalk. I scuffed my way home, my shoes covered with squished petals.


When I was eleven, almost twelve, it stopped. Larry Johnson disappeared. Maybe he moved away. Maybe my father murdered him in the dead of night on the 9th hole. But I doubt it. By sixth grade, I was bad, the "problem child." Instead of ignoring me, my dad hated me. One afternoon, I was late for gymnastics. Dan drove—far too slowly for my liking. "Hurry up," I said, kicking the back of the seat.

Weeks earlier, I'd landed wrong in a back handspring and torn the ligaments in my elbow. It needed to be wrapped with an Ace bandage before practice. "It's too tight," I complained in the lot of the YMCA, but my dad didn't answer. He wrapped it tighter and tighter. When he was done, and had hooked the fasteners into the stretchy fabric, my fingers were turning purple. My coach had to rewrap it.

Maybe Larry Johnson disappeared because I quit caring. I met Kelly the summer after third grade, and we became best friends. Number 15 no longer scared me. It was something to bear, like church or a stomachache, before my real life, my fun life with Kelly began again. I never cried. I turned into wood and how could you hurt wood?

In the fifth grade, I cut off my long hair so no one could grab it, wrap it around their fist, and hurt me. Kelly and I got Dorothy Hamill haircuts. Mine was the color of strawberries, and hers was light brown. "You look like Keith Partridge," I said and then felt bad. Maybe she didn't want to look like a teen idol (although she did). It was the first time in a long time that I'd cared about someone else. Kelly had wise hazel eyes and was strong and athletic like me. She was loud and talked back, and when we were together *everything* was funny.

Kelly Taylor saved my life. If I walked home with her after school, Larry couldn't get me. What was he going to do, take us both? If I played at her house after school, how would he find me? And if he did, what was he going to do, take me from there? Kelly's mother was strict in her Clinique lipstick and sensible wraparound skirts. She smoked in the car, and after she smoked, she chewed cinnamon gum. She'd wither Larry Johnson with a look. I was afraid of her, but I was afraid of all grown-ups. At Kelly's house I learned about table manners, how to wash dishes, Swedish meatballs, flank steak, and braunschweiger. We fried baloney until it puffed into little flying saucers. We danced to "Rockin' Robin" and "Surfin' USA" for hours in her basement. Kelly's house was one of the fancy ones on the edge of the neighborhood. They had an intercom. Kelly's mother could order her to come clean her room, pronto, with the touch of a button. At my house we ate Hamburger Helper and yelled.

Kelly and I were ghost hunters. We spent years hunting ghosts. They were everywhere: in my bedroom and basement, in the house next door that my parents had bought to fix up and sell. We set a ghost trap of mud pies and strung-up cans around my bed. We found a haunted china doll in a deserted lot. We terrified ourselves with the Ouija board and, in the eighth grade, conjured the ghost of Sharon Tate during a séance in the girls' locker room at school.

Kelly's house was the scariest. When the Taylors moved in, Kelly said they'd discovered old abortion devices in the basement. I wasn't sure what those were, but I didn't like the sound of it. Kelly had two older sisters. When they were each thirteen, they were visited by the ghost of their dead grandfather.

On a hot night in July, we came home from roller-skating at Oaks Park. We were nine. Kelly's sister, Sammy, *age thirteen*, was in the kitchen, doubled over in her white jeans, sobbing hysterically. "It was him, it was him," she cried, collapsing into a heap every time her mother tried to pull her up. I was scared and excited. I didn't know anything about big sisters. Maybe this was how they acted. I felt bad for Sammy. Her eyes were so swollen she could barely open them, and her thick black hair, usually so neatly feathered (she kept a yellow comb like a weapon in her back pocket), stuck out all over her head.

Eventually, after much coaxing, the story came out. As we had whirled around the rink, and Mrs. Taylor nursed a cup of coffee on the bench, Sammy had relaxed at home in the basement, listening to Rush's *2112* album and thinking of her boyfriend. At the mention of "the boyfriend" Kelly's mother pressed her lips together, annoyed. "I love him," Sammy shouted, momentarily forgetting her hysteria. "I don't care what you or anyone in this house thinks."

Mrs. Taylor looked to the heavens but didn't say a word.

"He's in high school," Kelly whispered to me. "He took speed and had a seizure in the library."

I made my eyes big. I had no idea what she was talking about. I'd never heard of *speed* or *seizures* before. They sounded ominous.

"Something made me look up," Sammy continued, peering into the distance through slit eyes. Her shoulders shook beneath her oversized football jersey. "And there was Grandy, walking toward me, out of the darkened laundry room. Only he wasn't walking, he was floating . . . and he had his arm out, reaching . . ." Sammy gripped her head, started to rock back and forth. "And I'm . . . I'm in the beanbag chair, and I can't move, I'm paralyzed . . . and he's coming, closer and closer, and . . . *Oh my God, where is everybody?*—" Sammy succumbed to another round of violent sobs.

I didn't know whether to scream or laugh or cry right along with her.

"It's the ear infection," Mrs. Taylor said in her dry voice. "You have an ear infection. You're delirious." When Sammy didn't respond, Mrs. Taylor looked at us. "It's the antibiotics. They—"

"It's not the fucking antibiotics, Mom."

I couldn't believe it. Sammy Taylor had cursed at her mother. I looked at Kelly. Her eyes were bright. I could see she was trying not to laugh. I stifled a giggle. I had so many questions. If I weren't so terrified of Sammy and her awesome teenage temper (she'd once whipped Kelly off her feet by her hair), I would ask them. What did Grandy do next? And why was he called *Grandy*? Was that like a normal grandpa or something different? Was it a friendly visit? Or had he come to scare Sammy *to death*? How did she escape? Did she have to run through him? I knew that was the only way to the stairs. I shuddered. Why had I agreed to spend the night? At least Kelly's father wasn't home. I was terrified of Mr. Taylor. He was a drinker and told us long, elaborate, dirty jokes that I never understood.

"I'm gonna throw up," Sammy mumbled, her head between her knees.

"Run to the bathroom, you dork," Kelly cried.

Sammy flipped her off, started to retch.

"Girls, to bed," Mrs. Taylor snapped as she rattled in the cupboard for a mixing bowl.


Kelly had a classy bedroom, like something out of the design magazines stacked in her mother's bathroom. Twin canopy beds sat side by side. They were covered by blue-and-white spreads that made me think of sunlight on cool water. Her carpet was soft and blue, only it wasn't blue, it was "cerulean," which was even better. Her closet doors were mirrored like a movie star's, and inside one sat Sammy's old dresser, covered with Wacky Pack stickers.

I spread my sleeping bag on the bed by the window. Should Grandy visit again, I'd be farthest from the doorway. I fiddled with my bag. It was heavy and damp and smelled of mildew. Kelly had a better one: goose down, and it zipped over her head. Her father worked for G.I. Joe's. The sleeping bags at my house were embarrassing. They were red cotton with a blue batik lining, and if you drooled in your sleep—which I guess I did— you woke with blue stains on your face and neck. It was shocking, as if you'd lost circulation to your head, and the stains didn't wash off with soap and water, they had to *wear off*.

As I changed from my shorts into the oversized T-shirt I slept in, I thought again of Grandy. What if he floated up to the window and scratched on it like a vampire? What if he wanted to visit *me*? I closed my eyes, forced myself to quit thinking. And really, who cared? Kelly was in the other bed. Together we were safe.

"He got Leanne in here, when she was thirteen." Leanne was Kelly's oldest sister off at college.

"I'm never spending the night when you're thirteen," I said.

"I don't blame you. Leanne has never been the same." Kelly's voice was low and hushed. It was the one she used for ghost stories. She was the best storyteller around, able to reenact entire after-school specials during a class period. "She woke up at three a.m., and he was standing over her bed." Kelly made a zombie face, stuck out limp and trembling arms. "And guess where she was sleeping?" Her eyes were hot and green. I knew what she was going to say before she said it. *"Right where you are now."*

"Liar," I whispered, thrilled.

Kelly laughed. "OK. I'm a liar. She was sleeping where *I* am, and who cares? I *want* Grandy to visit. I liked him. He brought us salt water taffy."

I didn't say anything. I was thinking, *salt water taffy—yuck.*

"Let's sleep in the basement."

"You're crazy." I liked to scare myself, but that was too much. Kelly zipped her sleeping bag over her head. With her round face and hood of red nylon, she looked like an Eskimo. How lucky it was to have a friend who not only believed in the dark side but lived to hunt it down. When I was with Kelly, I felt normal, like any girl on the planet.

"Sammy's having sex." Kelly acted like it was no big deal.

"Really? That's *bad.*" I thought Sammy only pretended to be a juvenile delinquent.

"My mom will have a shit fit when she finds out."

I giggled. I knew about sex. I'd read *"Where Did I Come From?"* It sounded embarrassing and physically impossible. (I never associated what Larry Johnson did with sex. According to the book, sex was pleasant, like being tickled or sneezing.) Kelly and I regularly inspected Iris's copy of *The Joy of Sex.* It was funny and disgusting. The people were hairy and looked like the hippie couple down the street.

"I found rubbers and Vaseline in her room, hidden in her top drawer, wrapped up in her swimming suit," Kelly reported. "Next to all the Lip Smackers she steals from Disco Mart."

"What's a rubber? And why Vaseline?"

"Lubrication." Kelly's voice was dark. "You know, like when your mom sticks the thermometer in your butt."

"What?" I had no idea what she was talking about. I felt a sick thrill. "Why would a mom do that? It goes in your mouth."

"Uh, no it doesn't." Kelly went on to explain the mysteries of rubbers and the taking of the anal temperature. I'd never heard the word *anal.* It was all too exciting. Kelly knew *everything*, and everything she knew was shocking and dirty and wild. We lay in silence. I thought of all I'd learned since third grade. What a baby I was then.

"Do you want to spy on Sammy?" Kelly grinned.

Now, that sounded like fun.

We crept down the winding staircase. The banisters were dusted with moonlight. Oil paintings of Taylor ancestors glared at us from the walls. They made me laugh. I imagined a giant Grandma Edith watching from a wall in my house. Sock-footed and giddy, we began our search for the fearsome Sammy. Surely she wasn't so stupid as to be back in the basement? The dining room smelled of lemon Pledge and old paper. We slid silently on its slick wooden floors then crept into the kitchen. It was dark. An empty mixing bowl sat on the counter beside the sink. Kelly made retching sounds. I tried not to laugh.

We found Sammy in the den. Kelly gently tapped the door. It swung open with a creak. Sammy was eating popcorn on the foldout bed—shoving great fistfuls into her mouth—and watching TV like nothing bad had happened. I held my breath. Kelly poked me in the ribs. Almost instantly, Sammy caught a whiff of us. She quit chewing. "You sluts," she screamed. She finished the popcorn in her mouth. A paperback book came whirling through the air, catching me in the ear. I fell to the ground, my ear burning. Kelly collapsed in a fit of giggles. Mrs. Taylor got on the intercom and ordered us to bed, ASAP. This made us laugh even more.

Kelly and I talked late into the night. I fell asleep in the middle of one of her stories—the Pink Panther, a spy named Quiche Lorraine—and then it was morning, sunlight sparkling on the windowpanes, turning the cerulean carpet aquamarine. The world had flipped, and the scary thrill of the night before was gone. I didn't move. I felt peaceful, like my body wasn't yet here but somewhere else, drifting. I closed my eyes. In the distance, I heard a lawn mower humming, and questioning birds, and Mrs. Taylor rattling pans in the kitchen. Maybe she was making scones. They were lemon with tiny seeds, and you ate them with strawberry jam. I'd never heard of scones before I met Kelly. I imagined I was in a nest—a blue-feathered nest as light as Kelly's sleeping bag, drops of sunlight sparkling on the leaves around me. It wasn't much of a leap. Kelly's house was on the highest hill in Eastmoreland, and her bedroom was on the third floor, and when I opened my eyes and looked outside, I saw only miles of blue sky, and everything else—the lawn mower, the birds, and Mrs. Taylor—sounded very far away.